Nicole Varonne: She was a natural artist destined for a life of triumph and tragedy, spotlighted on the greatest stages of the world. But the designs of the flamboyant family she loved and honored would not be enough to satisfy her ambition—or her heart . . .

Vanya Borcheff: To his staid English mistress he was "Van," the impresario of a school of classical ballet. But to the wild wife who left him—and returned—he would always be Vanya, the tyrant who finally found his way to greatness by pairing his fiery ballerina daughter with her icy, technically brilliant twin . . .

Nikki Borcheff: On stage he was all cold, controlled perfection, a dancer without heart—until his uninhibited twin sister liberated the anger within . . .

Alexandra Varonne: The once-great ballerina fought for her freedom in art and love, paying an incalculable price. She walked away from her husband and son. Now her daughter would step into her shoes. Would Nicole walk the same painful, uncompromising path?

Carlo Domenici: He was the rebel of dance, born to partner the ravishing Nicole—until he left to fight for his principles and his country in a war that convulsed the world. When he dared to return, to reclaim her, he found a woman determined to drive him away for good . . .

Billy Gable: A Broadway song-and-dance man with his name in lights, he'd left behind his humble Midwestern past. He would use his wealth and disarming boyish charm to win Nicole at any price . . .

Books by Madeline Hale

Daughters of the Sun
Pirouette

Published by POCKET BOOKS

Pirouette

MADELINE HALE

POCKET BOOKS

New York   London   Toronto   Sydney   Tokyo   Singapore

To Best Friends

This book is a work of fiction. Names, characters, places and incidents are either the product of the author's imagination or are used fictitiously. Any resemblance to actual events or locales or persons, living or dead, is entirely coincidental.

An *Original* Publication of POCKET BOOKS

 POCKET BOOKS, a division of Simon & Schuster Inc. 1230 Avenue of the Americas, New York, NY 10020

ISBN: 0-671-63982-X

First Pocket Books printing September 1990

10 9 8 7 6 5 4 3 2 1

POCKET and colophon are registered trademarks of Simon & Schuster Inc.

Printed in the U.S.A.

Part I

ENGLAND

1933

~~ 1

The long moaning call of the ship's foghorn startled Nicole
from her wordless communion with the sea. For three weeks
across the Atlantic she'd had nothing to do but enjoy the
hushed swaying cradle of the water. The sharp salt tang of
the air. The stars like fistfuls of glitter strewn on indigo
velvet. Shipboard was another world. Magical. Far away
from cities and farms, rehearsals, trains, dance studios. It
was as if she'd taken a leap into the air beyond the shores of
America and stayed suspended in the heights. Like Anna
Pavlova. Or Nijinsky himself.

Now the sea was changing. Silt began drifting past in
broad brown streamers, and the simple brine scent of the air
gave way to a mixture of odors. Coal dust. Manure. Damp
autumn earth. Wet leaves. Gasoline. Very soon now Nicole
would touch earth again. Within the hour the great white
ship, forging majestically up the fogbound estuary of the
Thames, would dock. And though she had never seen
England in all her fourteen years, Nicole Varonne was
coming home.

She took in a deep breath and stared hungrily into the soft
gray pillow of damp and misty clouds which seemed to sink
into the choppy dark water below.

"I can't see a thing," she cried to her mother. "Where's

the sun? The mild breezes? Our steward said he'd never seen a better crossing for a fall voyage. Cheesecake weather, he said. And now this!"

Alexandra Varonne tore her gaze away from where the shore ought to be and arched an eyebrow at her excited daughter. Such passion for a fourteen-year-old, she marveled, and then dismissed her own astonishment. What else would one expect from the child of two temperamental artists? Such a raging fire there had always been between them.

Alexandra's thoughts drifted back to the splendid theater poster, back in 1911, when she and her husband first danced *Firebird* in the West. Had it really been more than twenty years ago? VANYA BORCHEFF AND ALEXANDRA VARONNE, it screamed in bold black letters beneath the vivid impressionist sketch. THE BALLET DUO OF THE TWENTIETH CENTURY. IMMORTAL STARS OF THE BALLET ROMANOFF. Star-crossed, Alexandra mused. That had been more like it.

"Mom," Nicole demanded. "Are you listening to me?"

The girl tossed her head impatiently, and an unruly mass of summer wheat curls escaped its snood, spilling bobby pins everywhere. With a cry of exasperation, she flung herself away from the railing. Away from the uncooperative panorama. To the small but very real problem of containing her hair.

Alexandra viewed the little scene with mixed emotions. Nicole was a dynamo. She reminded her mother of one of those sturdy little scooters so many of those American children had. Roughly built. Edges unsmoothed. But fast. A winner in any race. With time, Alexandra thought, the edges would gleam with polish. The rough build will curve and soften. And the speed . . . those damnable conductors will sweat a little to keep up with Nicole's presto allegro when she takes the stage.

Alexandra chuckled with open pride, bent down to help her daughter, and nodded reprovingly.

"Cheesecake?" she teased. "What does my baby, my little sunbeam, know of such things?"

"For heaven's sake, Mom," Nicole said, unable to conceal her blush. "Between the time we lived in Hollywood while you made that Limburger of a movie and those years on the road with the troupe . . . Well, I'd have to be deaf, dumb, and blind not to catch on to some things in this world."

Her hair as neat as possible once again, Nicole stood up. The pseudosophisticated set of her face gave way to pure joy as the English sun, bleary but determined, broke through the seemingly impenetrable wall of fog. She grabbed her mother's hand and raced for the nearest stairway. Together they descended to the lower deck where the gangplank would be placed. Together they squeezed through the excited throng of passengers and jockeyed for position along the railing. Together their eyes spanned the slowly approaching dock.

Nicole's heart threatened to burst from her body. It was going to happen, just as Mama had promised. The long years of unanswered questions, the empty feeling—as if half of her was missing—the unspeakable loneliness, were going to come to an end. For the first time she'd see him, really know what her other self was like.

She pulled a small mirror from the purse hanging at her wrist. Cupping it in the palm of her hand, she held it up before her face. Her fingers traced the rounded line of her cheek, the fierce little jut of her chin, the straight nose, the eyebrows her mother said made a statement, the coffee-colored eyes big with wonder. Were his the same? When she finally looked into her twin brother's face, would it be like looking into this mirror?

"Nikki."

She whispered the magic name and let the breeze of the Thames blow the sounds away.

"Nik-ki," she echoed more slowly. "Nikolai Ivanovich Borcheff."

It was a mouthful, and it was fantastic, almost unbelievable, to have a brother with as wonderful, as romantic, as mysterious a name as that. There were so many mysteries. Why couldn't they have grown up together? What had really caused her mother and father to split up when Nikki and she were infants? Why was her last name Varonne when her parents were still married to each other? Hadn't her father wanted her?

The mirror was surreptitiously returned to the purse as Nicole swallowed hard. She loved her father . . . as much as she knew about him from Alexandra's reminiscences. A tartar of a dancer with the mane of a lion. That's how Nicole had pictured him all through her childhood. Dressed in pirate costumes of vivid silks and satins. Thigh-high boots. Bulging muscles. His arms strong enough to swing mighty scimitars around with ease. His eyes of a startling sapphire blue that saw everything, everywhere, at once. And hair like hers but even wilder, more glorious, streaked with pure gold.

Nicole strained to see the parties of greeters, standing in small clusters along the dock. Where was her father in this hazy sea of tweedy-looking people? His arms working like machetes, he should be cutting through the crowd to get to her. Then he would sweep her off her feet and swing her around until she was dizzy, telling her how much he'd missed her. And she'd have the satisfaction of knowing his heart would break when she and Alexandra moved on . . . because Alexandra always moved on, and she always went with her. Maybe Nikki would come with them this time.

Nicole frowned and continued staring. The fog lifted completely as the ship hove to. There on shore, damp umbrellas were closing up, hats and kerchiefs removed, and mackintoshes opened. Every so often an eager hand was lifted, waving in welcome to a passenger. Smiles broke out on faces and greetings were shouted back and forth. But not for Nicole. No one seemed to know her, and she recognized no one.

Where were they, damn it? Where was her brother and where was Daddy? No, she was too grown-up to call him that. She pictured Vanya suave and sophisticated, a little world-weary. Pop. No. That was too American. He was her father. Father. There . . . that seemed right. Respectful. Adult. Proper between parent and child who really didn't know each other.

The ship had stopped now. Everyone on board and on

shore was plainly visible, and still there was no one like the father she imagined. No one who remotely resembled her. Here and there were well-to-do couples, obviously untouched by the Depression, come to greet their American counterparts. Sprinkled about were academic types, an occasional clerical collar and several small, nondescript family groups . . . like the one at the edge of the dock gates.

A typical English threesome, Nicole surmised, made up of a sturdy bird of a woman who looked like she wore an apron under her coat, a staid man whose hat covered his eyes—the only active thing about him was the smoke wafting from his pipe—and a bland, tallish young man who seemed to be singularly uncomfortable. When he wasn't fidgeting with his buttons, he was picking lint off the woman's coat. Nicole shivered. Where was her father? Her twin brother? Had no one come after all? She glanced worriedly at her mother, whose faraway gaze was impenetrable.

Alexandra scanned the crowd as her daughter had. Her deep-set, dark eyes paused questioningly and then resolutely lit on the same trio Nicole had just dismissed. For a moment she seemed to shrink inside herself. She let her eyes stare fixedly. Her mouth quavered and she shook her head in quick, tiny negation. This was Vanya? This stern, terribly English-looking man was her Vanya, her demonic tempter of a dance partner, who had teased and provoked her, unleashing her passion on stage and off?

Each time they had danced together, it was a challenge, a dare, a confrontation of wills. Each time, he melted her icy regal resolve with the heat of his charm and the brilliance of his talent. Invariably she ended up his slave, his shadow, only to pursue him with her own revealed needs. She could no more resist him than a starved lioness could deny her killer instincts.

So it had been on stage between them in every ballet mounted for them. So it was off stage as well. From the first time Vanya had partnered her in class. From the time they had decided to risk their careers, leave the Czar's own company and try their fortunes with Leonid Baschenko, the egotistical upstart of an impresario with dreams of world-wide glory. From the moment Vanya Borcheff and Alexandra Varonne made love and decided to marry. Even when the company had been marooned in South America while the Bolshevik horde overran Mother Russia and the rest of the world went to war over an anarchist's bullet.

Until Alexandra's belly was swollen with two babies and the dancing stopped. Until Vanya made it clear that there was room for one star only, that Alexandra's role was only to be "Mamushka." Through all the spats. Through the tumultuous applause their audiences continued to shower upon them. Through the staged smiles they threw to each other as waves of flowers crested at their feet. Until the curtains closed and they parted in opposite directions. Until the wars were over—the distant and the intimate ones—and they parted forever, one to England, one to America, yet each with a piece of the other in tow.

And now it was 1933, more than fourteen years later. Nicole and Nikki would observe a birthday in another few months, the first they would celebrate together since their birth. Alexandra nodded her head sharply. It was right that the children should know each other. It was her one regret . . . if she admitted such things to herself.

She turned toward Nicole and took up her daughter's hand, patting it firmly. She made herself smile broadly, believably.

"Come, darling. We have new adventure to begin."

Pray God, Alexandra added inwardly, it was not the second thing she would come to regret.

Nicole shrugged her shoulders but followed in her mother's wake. When Alexandra's voice took on that Russian intonation, Nicole thought, there was no arguing with her. There was just plowing ahead. Like a steamroller.

Down the gangplank trooped the two ladies. Dockside, Vanya Borcheff carefully examined each descending passenger. If he had any doubts as to who among the female passengers were his guests, his doubts were expunged at the sight of an outrageously dressed, stunningly attractive woman, obviously at the height of her powers. No one but Alexandra Varonne—former star of the old Romanoff and its traveling road show, prima interpreter of every form of native dance this planet had so far produced—could arrive a charity case and look for all the world like visiting royalty.

He couldn't believe it. He hadn't laid eyes on her for more than a decade, and yet she hadn't aged one whit. Her pale skin was still impossibly silken smooth, her dark chocolate hair lustrous, and her eyes snapped with arrogant command. Somehow she seemed to have grown taller, but he shook his head. She had always had that presence, the willowy self-possession that gave dancers an illusionary height.

And she had always had the ability to dominate his attention and that of every other male in the vicinity. What was it about this half-French, half-Russian, all-Gypsy woman? Her restlessness, which he had never been able to tame? Her charm, which masked an indomitable will to self-indulgence? By now, after fourteen years of peace, hadn't he finally learned his lesson about Alexandra Varonne?

Then why was he shaking inside? Why was he ignoring the smaller figure behind her, the daughter for whose sake Vanya had agreed to this reunion? Why was it this showy imperious woman, ridiculous in her cloaks and furs and feathers and fakery, who filled his eyes?

Someone was shaking his arm. Irritably, then gratefully, he looked away from the arriving mob and winked supportively at the woman by his side.

"Do you see them, Van?"

Her eyes gave a hint of anxiety but her voice was rock-steady. Trusting and dependable. That was Margaret. That's what he had always needed. She was always there for him, unselfish, unassuming. There were no surprises with Margaret. Because of her, his life had found calm.

He glanced at his son. Young Nick was a quiet, good boy because of her. In an unaccustomed, open display of affection, Vanya put his arm around Margaret and squeezed her to him. She was everything to him, and he owed her. How he owed her.

It was only three weeks since that insane letter of Alexandra's arrived out of the blue. Vanya had been stunned to read of her destitution and her announcement that she was through with America. She and Nicole were coming to stay with him until she could find work in Europe. She had written that he had responsibilities to both his children. Nicole needed his help now.

Vanya's first thoughts had been protective ones toward Margaret and his cozy den: his mistress knitting contentedly by the fireplace, listening devotedly to a Brahms symphony over the wireless, and Nick on the braided rug by her side, happily turning the pages of his stamp album. Flashes of Alexandra shattered the pretty picture. She would invade his safe world like a rocket, exploding over all their heads. Shoving the letter into the breast pocket of his jacket, he had tried to ignore the whole nasty turn of affairs. He didn't show Margaret the letter.

Vanya spent an agonizing, sleepless night. The next day had proved no better. In the midst of his work, he read the letter compulsively, looking for a way out. Everywhere he turned, whether answering a dancer's complaint, watching the company class, or at luncheon with potential patrons, he was haunted by his wife's face. It was only when watching Nick sweat with concentration in class that he knew what he must do. For in Nick, Vanya saw Nicole, his long-estranged daughter, and his emotions overcame him.

Later at home he had handed Alexandra's letter to Margaret. At first she managed to keep her face impassive, but she couldn't help blanching. As she read, the hand that held the letter had moved farther and farther away, as if blurring the words to make them less real. She turned away to face the fire and involuntarily crushed the letter into a tiny ball. Margaret's deep well of English reserve had given way only a fraction, and Vanya never admired his mistress more.

"Well, Van—" she had begun and then stopped, when her voice trembled. "That's that, then. Wife and mistress under one roof won't do, will it?"

Vanya had responded in a low rumble, his accent inevitably thickening with emotion.

"Is not matter of choice. Is duty . . . to child."

Margaret had suddenly become a bundle of energy. She gathered her skeins of yarn and jumbled them into her knitting bag. She poked at the burning logs with unusual aggression. She wouldn't let Vanya touch her.

"I'll leave then. Take a long holiday somewhere. Dad's always after me to visit him at the rectory."

It had been a miserable moment, the worst between them Vanya could ever remember.

"You must stay, Piggy. This is your home. Our home. I'll move heaven and earth to get Alexandra a tour on the continent. I'm not Director of British Court Ballet for nothing. I swear she'll be here only little while. I'll make sure she's here to visit, not to stay."

He'd actually found himself down on his knees.

"I need you, Piggy."

Margaret had acquiesced. Vanya was her whole world.

Now, determined to prevent any upheaval in that world, he smiled at her, half tentative, half encouraging, all the while aware of Alexandra's nearness. He drew deeply one last time on his pipe, knocked the contents out against the sole of his shoe, and pocketed the brierwood.

"It will be just for little while. I promise you. We'll get through this together."

She stiffened, but smiled brightly for Vanya's sake. It was only when Nick put his arm around her shoulder too that her chin quivered visibly.

"Not to worry, Peggy, old thing," the boy said, his voice breaking at nearly every other word, searching for manly depth. "Stiff upper and all that."

The three braced themselves against the imminent American onslaught.

With her feet firmly on English soil, Alexandra broke into an unladylike run. Nicole hurled herself after her mother.

"Vanushka! Vanushka, darling!"

In a moment she was embracing the husband she'd left fourteen years ago. She knocked his hat off with her swooping arms and was alternately weeping and laughing as she kissed him on both cheeks. She held him at arm's length and clucked her tongue reprovingly.

"What have these English done to you, my pet?"

She mussed his brilliantined hair with her long fingers and her eyes raked his every feature.

"Have they tamed my great jungle lion and turned him into tired old sheep dog? Next you'll tell me you've traded vodka for nightly pint of bitter," she added mockingly. "But really, darling, you look wonderful. Really distinguished . . . really . . . wonderful . . ."

Awkwardness spread through the group as Vanya worked to disengage himself from Alexandra's grasp. Determinedly oblivious, Alexandra turned her attention to the rest of the group. She moaned with the intensity of more than a decade's pent-up maternal longing at the sight of her baby son.

"Nikolai, my Nikolai," she sobbed.

Before Nikki could react, she had him crushed in her arms and was murmuring incomprehensible gibberish into his ears. Finally she lifted her head from his shoulder, wildly dabbed at her eyes, and smiled beneficently at the woman standing next to him.

"I don't know your name, my good woman, but I know you must be very kind and loving. Thank you for raising my boy. I'm sure you've been an admirable governess."

Margaret raised her eyebrows and sniffed. "Van!" she exclaimed.

Vanya stepped forward. It was time to take charge.

"Margaret, this is Alexandra Varonne, my . . . er, a great, great ballerina. Alexandra, I want you to meet Margaret Dunstable. Margaret is my . . . companion."

The smile died on Alexandra's lips. Her hand, already extended, paused and then continued forward.

"Miss Dunstable. I stand corrected."

"Welcome to England, Mrs. Borch—Mrs. Va—"

A bright smile returned to Alexandra's face as Vanya's mistress choked over her name.

"Madame Varonne will do nicely, but I insist you call me Alexandra." Syrup dripped from her voice. "And I may call you . . ."

She waited with exaggerated patience and interest while

Margaret did the right thing—the last thing the woman obviously wanted to do.

"Yes, of course. It's Margaret, though ofttimes the boys—Van and Nick, that is—call me Peggy."

Alexandra nodded, acknowledging both the name and the bit of intimacy this Peggy person threw in her face. The woman was clever. She would have had to be to keep Vanya happy all these years, Alexandra thought. But Alexandra was clever too. Destitute, with a daughter to support, she had to be. Turning toward her husband, she beamed with quiet pride.

"Vanushka, here is your daughter. Nicole?"

She beckoned to the girl, who had hung farther and farther back during the horrendous first stage of this family reunion. Nicole couldn't seem to raise her eyes from the ground. She had dreamed of this moment her whole life long. Never in a million years had she expected to feel so out of place. So excruciatingly embarrassed. She felt her mother's warm arms about her, pushing her toward these strangers.

Hard lips pressed briefly against her forehead.

"I'm pleased to see you, Nicole."

This was the welcome she had waited for? I'm pleased to see you. Period. What was that supposed to mean? Did she please him? Did he want a daughter as much as she wanted a father? With pleading eyes she glanced up at Vanya. He was staring at her. Studying her. Dissecting her. Daring to stare back, she looked for some vestige of the bold laughing pirate father she'd imagined for as long as she could remember.

"Remarkable, isn't it, Vanushka?" Alexandra prompted in a whisper. "The likeness is uncanny." She pushed Nicole toward her brother. "This is wonderful . . . really wonderful. You two children have so much to tell each other . . ."

Nikki frowned and stood his ground next to Margaret.

"Manners, my lad," Margaret said softly.

With the greatest reluctance, he shook hands with his sister. It was the most begrudging touch Nicole had ever experienced. Cold and limp. Like a dead fish. Red-faced, she withdrew her hand. She wanted to wipe it off on her coat.

Nicole was in the middle of a nightmare. Any moment now she was sure the ship's steward would knock on the cabin door and she would wake to the beguiling scent of café au lait and croissants. With another day of sparkling waves before her and her dreams of family intact.

Surely this slicked down, coldly appraising man was not her beloved tiger father. And her twin, the other half of her soul, could not be a pasty-faced unfeeling boy. These people didn't want her. They were repelled by her. She wanted to grab her mother and shake her until Alexandra confessed she'd made a mistake.

But there was Mama, dragging her and this Nick close to her delicate bosom, exclaiming and carrying on.

"Just look at our two babies, all grown up, Vanya. How they resemble you. Like two sunbeams, they are, with your coloring and your features . . ."

"They have your eyes, Shura," Vanya offered in gentle-manly fashion. "And Nick has your build . . . slender but strong."

Vanya took a tentative step toward the family tableau, drawn by the mesmerizing triple threat of blood, beauty, and born talent. He was a part of this, a part of them.

"Does she dance?" he asked hesitantly, pointing to Nicole.

"Under the proper circumstances," Alexandra offered.

"Would she dance for me?"

He was in earnest. Alexandra smiled luxuriantly. He did want Nicole.

"Under the proper circumstances," she repeated.

"I don't like it. I don't like it one bit."

Husband and wife stopped in mid-negotiation at Margaret's interruption. Their perplexed expressions were identical.

"I mean," Margaret added hastily, "I don't like the way this weather looks. It's been so changeable lately. Not good for the boy to be out in it so much. He's delicate, you know."

She bustled toward Nikki, buttoning and straightening his jacket.

"Better put up the brolly, Nick. I think it's going to pour any minute. Van?"

Vanya suddenly got very busy with the mound of baggage that had materialized nearby, limping noticeably as he lifted one heavy bag after another. The trunks, valises, boxes, and handbags, containing the sum total of Alexandra and Nicole's possessions, disappeared into two black cabs. One of them swallowed up Vanya too.

And then Nicole herself was being hustled into a much smaller cab. A narrow bench seat for two faced two knock-down perches. Sides were taken in utter silence. Nicole and Alexandra versus Margaret or Peggy and Nick or Nikki . . . whoever those people were. What was the matter with the English, Nicole mused in abject misery, that they needed two names for everything?

In a way, she was thankful for the silence. What could they have possibly talked about? Margaret had already given the weather report. Nick seemed incapable of speech. And now that her mother had listed, point by point, the physical similarities of her children, there was nothing left to discuss.

It was all so ugly. England was ugly. The London streets were as grim as the end of the sea voyage had proved to be. Sticklike leafless trees standing like sentinels over rows of gritty stone and brick buildings. A lead-colored sky. And the Thames stank. The cab stank. Nicole felt sick to her stomach. Deliberately she closed her eyes to shut out the whole stinking mess and leaned into the familiar softness of her mother.

 **2**

"Nicole, open your eyes, dear. We're home."

The girl sighed deeply and arched her back. Home with Mom could mean anything. Be anywhere. A cottage by the sea in California . . . a tepee in the Dakotas . . . a hotel suite in New York . . . a tin trailer in New Jersey . . . Nicole opened her eyes. She remembered. Home temporarily meant London. She did her utmost to curl up into a ball, hiding her head between her elbows.

Undaunted, Alexandra stepped out of the cab first and caught up with Vanya, who was struggling with the last of the trunks.

"I am so grateful to you, Vanushka," she said, gathering him in yet another embrace. "Nikki, darling," she called to the hunched figure still seated in the cab, "come help your papa."

Only Nicole saw the look of revulsion come over the boy's face.

Nick Borcheff was reeling inside. This gaudy Varonne person kept grabbing him—assaulting him, really—and no one stopped her. No one could stop her, apparently. He looked furtively up and down the street. If any of the chaps from school saw La Varonne . . . How could she possibly imagine he would do anything she asked?

Deliberately he turned his back to the woman and in an innocuous voice said, "Peggy, I'm hungry. Can we have tea?"

Nicole gasped. Rudeness aside, he sounded like a whining four-year-old.

"Of course, my boy. And you can carry the biscuits to the table. We'll have the digestive ones with a bit of jam on them."

Margaret turned to Nicole. "And you may carry the silver tray with the tin of . . ."

Nicole fled before she heard what the tin contained. Demurely she followed her mother up the stairs of a drab brick building. Rambling rose vines climbing the iron railings attempted to beautify the place. And failed.

"What a lovely quaint old house, Vanya. Just like the one we rented when we first leave Russia. We stayed here in Chelsea, for longest time. Was six months, remember, Vanushka? Could it really have been twenty years ago? I can't be that old."

Nicole turned beet red. She had escaped that frying pan of a cab only to find herself in the midst of her mother's fiery monkey business.

"But darling," Alexandra went on, entering the parlor, "this is so sweet. Such homey touches."

She fingered Margaret's antimacassars, which liberally adorned the backs and arms of overstuffed chairs and a chintz settee. She gazed above the mantel at the endless series of miniature country scenes. Shepherds and milk-maids abounded with horses and dogs. Waterwheels plashed beside vases of flowers and bowls full of fruit. In the midst of the bucolic idyll, photos of the royal family were enshrined. Calligraphied labels flourished beneath each face, dutifully honoring George V, Queen Mary, and their whole brood. There was the dashing Prince of Wales. His quiet brother, the Duke of York. The fair Princess Royal. Even the two lesser-known dukes, Gloucester and Kent.

Mother, Nicole silently and urgently telegraphed to Alexandra's back, this place is awful. It's worse than a rummage sale in Iowa.

But Alexandra was beaming.

"So perfectly English, Vanya. As you have become too, I see. Come, take out that English pipe. Don't be shy with me, old dear. Or should I call you 'Van' as little Peggy does?"

Vanya was near the breaking point, and Alexandra had only been in his house for ten minutes. What would it be like in days, weeks, from now . . . if they all survived that long? His vision of rockets exploding overhead was becoming alarmingly real, frighteningly close.

"Exasperating woman! It might as well be fifteen years ago for the lack of change in you."

Nicole's eyes grew big. No one talked to Alexandra Varonne that way and expected to breathe fresh air again. Mom could deflate the most pompous ignoramus with one razor-sharp sentence. She was flabbergasted when all her mother did was to throw back her head and laugh.

"So, the lion is merely in disguise. Borcheff can still roar when he chooses to. I'm glad, Vanya. And so, in honor of old times, I will behave. I will be pussycat for you, Nikki, and your Miss Dunstable. Yes, Vanushka?"

"Yes, Alexandra. Thank you."

Under his breath he muttered something about incorrigibility. At the same time, he couldn't keep from grinning at the pussycat.

Margaret and Nikki sailed into the room, laden with the paraphernalia of high tea. Again Nicole caught her brother's glare at Alexandra. Granted, it was embarrassing to watch a grown woman purr through her teeth at an attractive man. But for God's sake, she reasoned to herself, it was their mother and father.

"Van dear," said Margaret, pouring tea, "why don't you tell Madame Varonne about all the nice plans you've made for her."

"Right."

Vanya's whole posture changed. He became the administrative head of a prominent ballet company with the simple adjustment of his Windsor knot, a firm tug at his vest, and an impatient smoothing of his already pomaded hair. Agreeably, Alexandra sat at attention, ignoring the cup of tea and the plate Margaret had piled high with buttered crumpets, boiled eggs, and biscuits with jam.

"I've gone to great lengths for you, Alexandra. And I'm certain, even in these depressed times, the public will come out to see you dance. Your reputation is still international, despite your long sojourn in the States."

"Thank you, darling, for so much kind flattery. You've learned all the tricks from Baschenko, verbosity among them, I see. But Vanushka, you don't have to praise me to get me to dance for you. I would like nothing better than to join British Court Ballet. Now if we can agree on salary, I could promise at least one—maybe two—full seasons plus—"

Margaret banged her cup onto her saucer and began hacking away at an unyielding loaf of bread. Vanya glanced worriedly at her.

"Shura, please, say no more. You will feel foolish if you keep insisting . . . You don't understand . . . British Court is not for you . . . is not your style. We can hardly afford . . . you understand . . ."

"Vanushka," Alexandra said through gritted teeth, "I thought *you* understood. I made it perfectly clear in letter to you. I must make money. I must dance. I must feed and clothe and house my daughter. I can't do it alone anymore. I must have your help, Vanya."

At first he was embarrassed by her vulnerability, her boldness in displaying it before veritable strangers. She'd always caught him off guard this way, needing him when he least expected it, demanding when he had nothing to give. Impossible.

Margaret caught his eye, and the fixity of her smile communicated volumes about her fears. Nick had taken her hand surreptitiously and shot his father an alarmed glance. How dare Alexandra sweep into his life and bring pain to the two people Vanya loved best?

"Your letter was perfectly clear about your expectations, Alexandra. But you neglected to mention why this sudden bankruptcy. After so many years of American stardom, what happened?"

Was Mom actually turning red? Nicole couldn't believe her eyes. Vanya had her on the defensive.

"For six years I take Companie Varonne on the road. To the little people I bring the most splendid spectacles, the richest dancing, the cultures of the world. Then Depression comes. The people save their pennies for food, for things essential. In America, dance is not essential. So I say to myself, Europe will appreciate me. Here they don't keep great artists starving in tenements. Here—"

"Here ten tens make one hundred, just as they do in America. How I remember the hat bills." Vanya raised his eyes to the heavens, adding, "And shoes? Staying within a budget is something the years apparently haven't taught you."

Alexandra narrowed her dark eyes. "But at least years have taught me my art," she said, poison sweet. "They seem to have robbed you of yours. Why do you limp, Vanya?" she suddenly probed in a voice which cut like a whip.

It was his turn to redden. The leg in question hid itself behind his other one.

"It was accident," he muttered. "During a performance."

"And when was this accident?"

"Years ago."

"Fourteen years ago, perhaps?"

There was a long silence.

"You were gone, Shura, and Baschenko partnered me with everything under the sun. Other ballerinas weren't you. My concentration was gone. I said to myself, Why should I work so hard? One night there was booing when I finished."

He winced, the past vivid in his memory.

"Baschenko threatened to demote me. Everything would have been gone. So next night I tried to win audience back. I tried too hard. I felt myself falling. There was pain, like fire in my leg."

He took a long breath, smoothing his already smooth hair. "I never really healed. Baschenko let me take over paperwork that bored him. When he had his first stroke, I took his place. Six months that first time. The second stroke was fatal. And he left the Romanoff to me. So, I am the little father now. British Court Ballet, I call it. Because Britain is home."

"And for a home you would trade your soul. Yes. Was always true about you. Now you have your cozy hearth and you resent this wild Gypsy whirling on your rug. Well, relax, as the Americans say. I will be out of your neat little life again as soon as I find way to feed myself and Nicole. You help me; you are rid of us that much sooner."

Her mother sounded disdainful, but Nicole knew that the icy dismissal covered hurt. Hurt that Nicole shared.

"Shura, I would never desert you or Nicole."

The implication caught Alexandra short. She lifted her chin high and waited warily.

"You are and always have been a great dancer. But I have all the principals I can handle right now. I can't afford to bring you in as assoluta, which is what you deserve."

"So?"

"You need a showcase. Center stage to show everything you can do. British Court would limit you. We are classical; the English expect restraint from us. It is what I am good at giving them. My dancers do exactly what they are told . . . and no more."

"Then what are these great lengths you talk about, Maestro Borcheff?"

Vanya breathed again. "Interviews with only the best. Ballet de Fete is in town. Dance Festival is interested. I spoke to Dame Harriet at Swanleigh Hall just yesterday. She wants to talk to you. It will happen, Alexandra. I promise you."

"And until it does?"

"You and Nicole stay here with us. And speaking of our daughter, I have plans for her. How would a scholarship to British Court School sound? Is like our old Theatre Street— dancing and academics together. We audition her tomorrow and place her immediately."

"Vanushka, this is wonderful! Is what I hope for."

It was? If so, it was news to Nicole. The thought of dancing for this . . . this bookkeeper of a man . . . She shuddered. Only for a few weeks, a month maybe, Nicole reminded herself, reducing her pair of crumpets to shreds. Miss Dunstable wound down the tea with a dull discussion of good ocean crossings and bad weather. Finally Margaret added, "Wouldn't you like to freshen up, Madame Varonne? You've had such a hectic time of it."

Nicole followed her mother, who was still tossing out thanks and compliments like careless flowers as she climbed the stairs to the scrupulously clean, bare little room they'd been assigned. On one of the two sagging beds Nicole and Alexandra sat side by side. Their hands crept together for comfort.

"Come," said Alexandra briskly. "Is no help to sit like little orphan children. He's still your father." She patted Nicole's cheek. "Maybe we bring some life, some color, into this oh-so-proper flat, no?"

Nicole smiled obediently, but that cold-eyed man and his

clammy son were not likely to leap up and dance a jig. The only real emotion Nicole had been able to read from either of them was anger, barely contained. And she wished, as she unpacked her trunk with practiced hands, that she were a million miles away.

Nicole was awakened the next morning at sunrise by a perfumed kiss.

"I'm up with the birds, darling," came her mother's gay voice.

"Why so early?" asked Nicole muzzily.

"I'm off to find work. The sooner the better."

"No breakfast?"

Alexandra looked stunning in a black brocade suit trimmed with red fox, and a tiny black hat with half veil perched on her dark curls.

"Why should I drink that woman's tea when we all know she'd love to drown me in it? And then there's Mr. Borcheff with his charitable handful of contacts." She lifted her head proudly. "I'll make my own way. Wish me luck, darling." Alexandra raised her arms for a farewell hug.

"Wait, Mom. Please don't go yet."

The plaintive wail made Alexandra sit down on the bed and gather Nicole into her arms like a precious infant.

"I know. I know, my baby. Is hard when all our dreams come to this. But they are not bad people, sweetheart. Just different. More . . . conventional."

"Uh-huh," Nicole agreed shakily.

"So I tell you what. Imagine we're visiting a new tribe of Indians. We learn their dances, their culture. Mostly we listen. Let them teach us. Then we go on, richer for what we've learned. Yes?"

"Okay." She gave her mother a kiss goodbye and wished her *merde*.

Alone, Nicole dressed in an unobtrusive jumper, remembering her winter with the Hopi tribe. Three years ago Companie Varonne had practically moved onto the reservation to learn the Indian dances. Out of that winter *Corn*

Dreams was born, one of her mother's native masterpieces. Nicole had learned it was better, when among strangers, to remain inconspicuous.

She was conscious of her clammy palms sticking to the banister as she came down for breakfast. At least they'll be more relaxed, Nicole thought, imagining her father in a crimson dressing gown, his blue eyes softened with sleep. And Nikki, hair tousled, in a terry-cloth bathrobe, dawdling over his oatmeal.

The slight smile on Nicole's face froze when she entered the dining room. There was Margaret Dunstable, in another drab blue dress with a crisply ironed rosebud print apron. She hovered, platter in hand, over two ramrod straight figures. Vanya and Nikki Borcheff looked even more formidable this morning. Shoulders squared and faces closed. Precisely knotted ties. Vests. Hair that would never dare to tousle.

"Well, well, daughter," came Vanya's overly hearty welcome. "Come and join us. I suppose age comes to us all if even Alexandra has succumbed to sleeping late."

Nicole forced a matching jovial smile as she took a seat across from her father.

"No, actually she, er, asked me to extend her apologies for not joining you at breakfast." Getting no response, Nicole rushed on, adding, "She felt she needed an early start . . . to find a job."

The last word fell like a thud into the silence. So much for joining this tribe of Indians, Nicole thought, feeling them all staring at her.

"Well, I'm glad that you are with us, dear," said Margaret kindly. "Let me get you a glass of juice."

Nicole waited, examining with uneasy interest the formal place setting before her with its two forks and separate butter knife polished moon bright. The juice turned out to be grapefruit, and Nicole's face puckered. She reached for the sugar bowl.

"Mom and I always sweeten our grapefruit," she explained when Margaret frowned.

"We do best when we acquire a taste for the natural flavor of our food, Nicole dear. After all, not all of life is sweet, is it? A bit of a lesson in fortitude," said Margaret, patting Nicole's hand.

My God, Nicole thought as she withdrew her spoon from the sugar. Sermons at seven in the morning. She drank down the bitter juice, catching a smirk on her twin's face as she finished.

"Quite the good little girl, aren't we?" he murmured to her. "Won't you try these kippers, Nicole?" he added for Margaret's benefit.

Nikki offered her a plate of dark flat things that looked like grilled scraps of leather.

"And some scrambled eggs, of course," added Margaret, spooning cold crumblings onto Nicole's plate.

"Thanks," she muttered, gingerly taking a single kipper. "Is it like bacon?" she asked hopefully.

"They're salted like bacon," explained Vanya. "But no, kippers are herring. Smoked fish. Quite tasty."

They all watched as she took a bite. Ugh. Her mouth was filled with something burnt. Bitter. Prickling with bones. There was no way she was going to swallow. Quickly she spit into a napkin.

"I guess it takes a while to get used to them," she managed.

"Apparently so," sniffed Margaret, looking with some consternation at the napkin balled up around a half-chewed piece of fish. "Take a sip of tea, dear. We can't have sour faces at the breakfast table, can we?"

The muted conversation Nicole's entrance had disturbed started up again, with weather, haberdasheries, and the travels of old acquaintances being the principle topics. Only Margaret made a half-hearted attempt to include Nicole, who bolted down cold toast from a quaint upstanding rack and hot medicinal-tasting tea.

"So, Nicole," said her father as Margaret cleared the dishes. "You are ready for your audition?"

"Lead on, MacDuff," she answered, though a morning of

being examined by this new father of hers was about the last thing she wanted.

"Aha. You quote *Macbeth*. Your mother hasn't neglected your education completely!"

There was anger even in his jokes, Nicole thought dismally as she collected her practice clothes. Lagging a few paces behind, she followed her father to his studio.

 **3**

London remained a blur of grim stone and threatening sky which a trip on the Underground did little to enliven. And Vanya's studio, despite his evident pleasure in showing it to her, was a dank, almost windowless place. A former three-story terrace house, it had been converted into a floor of practice rooms with a pair of dressing rooms, a floor of classrooms, and offices on the ground floor. Perhaps it was the damp green walls combined with muddy-brown doors and panels that gave it such an institutional flavor. More like a clinic, Nicole thought, than a home for the dance. Even the company posters looked trapped behind their carefully dusted frames.

Vanya sent her to change into leotard and tights while he collected the staff of the British Court Ballet. At least the dressing room was welcoming, with its familiar odors of talcum powder, cologne, and sweat.

In his neat little office, Vanya draped his arm around Nicole's shoulders and said, "Gentlemen? Mademoiselle? I'd like to introduce my daughter, Nicole Varonne Borcheff."

Nicole stiffened for a second at the added last name but smiled politely at Boris Stephanovich Andreyev, an elegant graying man who topped her father's five and a half feet by only an inch or two. His bow was deep and precise.

"And this is Mr. Edmund Demsby-Worth."

As he shook her hand firmly, Nicole imagined his little round figure behind a counter at the market weighing out apples to the exact ounce.

"And our mademoiselle, Celeste Paisy."

"Welcome, welcome, ma petite," fluted the middle-aged, rounded woman. She bussed Nicole on both cheeks.

"Nicole has been studying dance in America," her father informed his staff. "As you might assume," he added proudly, "Alexandra Varonne has been her personal teacher. I'm sure she had the child dancing as soon as she could walk. With work, my friends, we'll have another Nick Borcheff on our hands!"

His arm tightened on her shoulders. He does care for me, she thought wonderingly. He wants me. Just as I always dreamed.

"You are older than Nick?" came Mademoiselle Paisy's puzzled question.

"Exactly the same age. We're twins," explained Nicole.

"Truly we are blessed, Vanya Fedorovich," Andreyev exclaimed.

On the way up to a large rehearsal room, Nicole pranced after the quartet like a pony in home pasture. In the room she waited impatiently while they pulled up table and chairs. They seated themselves in a row, expectation written all over their faces. Nicole busied herself, pointing and flexing her feet, as excited as her examiners.

"First, I expect, we'd like to hear something of your dance background," said Demsby-Worth, clearing his throat discreetly. "People you've studied with, roles you've learned, that sort of thing."

"Well, let's see. I guess my very first teacher was this hoofer named Shaleen Shea who taught me to kick my leg over my head when I was three or four. Mom was on Broadway at the time and—"

Her father's frown and a louder cough from Demsby-Worth warned her they probably wouldn't appreciate a lot of details about flashy Shaleen.

"Well, when I was seven and we were in California with Miss Naomi and her troupe, everyone was studying belly dancing with Lila of Hollywood. Mom said a steady diet of ballet might permanently calcify my torso, so she talked Lila into teaching me too. I got pretty good. Probably because a kid's spine is so flexible."

"Miss Borcheff," said Andreyev bitingly, "it might surprise you to know that our interest in your dance history is severely limited. We wish only to hear about ballet, 'calcifying' though it might be."

"Oh."

The row of stony faces said she'd really missed the boat. Her father looked the worst. Okay. Ballet it was. This tribe of Indians was very narrow-minded when it came to dance. Nicole gamely tried again.

"I think Mom taught me to point my toes before I can remember. Either that, or it just came naturally. We started when I was very young—pas de chats, pirouettes, positions of the arms—things a four-year-old would enjoy. I would try to get to the top of my jump and stop there—just like Nijinsky. I never remember ballet as work. Mom made it something joyful, natural, like greeting the morning sky."

Now what was wrong? Nicole wondered. Here she was giving them pure ballet and they still looked like they each had a mouthful of kippers.

Mademoiselle Paisy gave Nicole a tattered smile.

"Perhaps you could describe ze details, exactement what you do each morning."

"Well, it isn't exactly every morning . . ."

Four pairs of eyebrows soared.

"I mean . . . I dance every day, except when we're traveling. But not always ballet."

"Come, come," said Mr. Demsby-Worth impatiently. "This won't do at all. Demonstrate for us your barre work."

She walked over to the barre, trying desperately to remember the last one Alexandra had given her maybe two months ago. All she could remember was that they had both been very hungry. When the ham couldn't be sliced any thinner and day-old bread had become too expensive. Just before the letter to Vanya got written.

Nicole finally recalled a longer stretch of ballet work from two years back when the troupe had been stuck in snow-bound Montana for a month. With that misty memory she tried to recreate a credible set of exercises. There was absolute silence as she struggled through pliés, battements, and ronds de jambe. If only they'd given her a little advance notice, she could have brushed up.

Nicole was enough of a performer to know that her audience was not happy. She did her best. At least she was strong and could hold the positions for a long time. Where she couldn't remember the precise movements, she tried to fill in the gaps with emotion. Her mother's voice came back to her.

"When your toe strikes floor, imagine you are fiery Spanish flirt. Show Basil, that two-timer, exactly what you think of his shenanigans."

The barre began to be fun.

"Thank you, Nicole," came Demsby-Worth's dry voice. "I believe we've seen enough, have we not, mam'selle, gentlemen?"

Her father looked at the floor, his cheeks brick-red with embarrassment.

"Quite enough. Yes. Enough."

"Center work now, please," ordered Demsby-Worth.

He listed a series of leaps and turns. Nicole felt better. She knew her elevation was impressive. But no matter how wholeheartedly she threw herself into the air, the cold, closed expressions of her examiners didn't change.

As Demsby-Worth began a fifth combination, Andreyev interrupted.

"It is clear how she responds to set exercises, yes?"

There was a murmur of agreement.

"Have you learned any full pieces, young woman?"

Nicole felt better immediately. She knew she could do one of Mom's old Follies numbers. The one Alexandra had filled in for one night and then kept doing as a comic takeoff. They used to practice it together in front of the mirror, Nicole wearing the sequined cap with feathers that was her favorite when she was a little girl.

"I can do a dance that got raves on Broadway."

"A solo piece?" Andreyev asked skeptically.

"Yes," she answered happily, already hearing the brassy introduction in her mind.

"Please," Andreyev requested with an encouraging gesture.

Nicole needed no further encouragement. She launched into a five-minute hot jazz-ballet set piece complete with kicks over her head, come-hither hip gyrations, arabesques that turned into apache back bends, and hundreds of spins. For the big finish she threw herself to the floor in a full split, arms straight up, and a grin on her face to beat the band.

There were no answering grins on the grim faces in front of her. Andreyev and Demsby-Worth had a whispered conference. Celeste Paisy patted Vanya's hand. For the first time since the audition had begun, her father looked straight at Nicole.

"You will report to Beginning One," he said in a deliberately flattened voice.

Nicole's mouth fell open.

"You're kidding! I've been dancing since I was born, practically. How——"

"If I may, Maestro?" asked Demsby-Worth.

Vanya nodded. As the little Englishman spoke, Nicole's father turned his head away and his face fell into lines of weary disgust.

"We find your dancing sadly lacking in discipline, Miss Borcheff."

"Varonne," Nicole snapped.

"Varonne, then. I have eight-year-old children in my beginning class with more accurate placement than you have shown us this morning. Considering the talent you obviously were born with, I can only assume that your years in America have subverted your natural grace."

"You do have great strength, my dear," added Mademoiselle Paisy. "But it flies all over ze room. Now we must cage it, *vous comprenez?* Tame it. Polish and perfect, as our dear directeur tells us."

Nicole listened to them painting her as if she were some berserk gorilla, throwing herself from vine to vine. Did her father really see her as some kind of monster? There was pain in his averted face. And more of that anger. Nicole felt hollow inside, as if someone had scooped her out. He was ashamed of her. He agreed with them.

Her cheeks felt hot. Only by concentrating could she keep from crying. She tried to remember about the different tribe of Indians, but it was no good. Vanya Borcheff was her father and a great dancer and he thought she was crap. Without another word of protest, she let them lead her out to Beginning I.

Nicole felt like a complete idiot. She stood at the barre in a line of babies whose neat little ballet chignons reached no higher than her rib cage. Her cheeks burned with humiliation as eight and nine-year-olds collected approving smiles from Demsby-Worth while she earned only corrections. The only other adult at the barre was a berouged, overweight matron who, Nicole assumed, was the wife of some company backer.

As the exercises continued, Nicole's embarrassment turned to sadness. The children looked like rigid little puppets. All the natural grace of childhood had been replaced by a sort of grotesque copy of adult overcontrol. She could see cords of tension standing out in their soft necks and their shoulders, hard as stone.

Have they never run free? she wondered. Run barefoot through a grove of aspens? Alongside a growling sea? She'd only been four or five at the time, but Nicole never forgot the morning she and her mother had first seen the Pacific Ocean. And partnered it. They had run across the heated sand to a rearing blue-green giant and thrown themselves into dance. Sometimes Nicole was a wave, building and smashing downward. Sometimes a tossed length of seaweed. Sometimes spreading lacy skirts of foam. The pictures had flowed into her mind and she gave them back to the water with her body. She forgot that she was separate from the ocean and the sky. She just was. It was maybe the best moment of her childhood.

And these little marionettes. All that natural flow had been sucked out of them. They'd probably never know it was missing. But Nicole felt in her bones what the Borcheff form of ballet could cost. And her resistance was as automatic as breathing. What was the point of moving at all if you weren't supposed to feel? Oh, she knew exactly what Demsby-Worth wanted from her. She could even produce it without much physical effort. But then her concentration wavered. Mere physical perfection had little attraction to Nicole.

The class was finally over and the little ones tiptoed up to pay the master their reverence. Their bows, like everything else they'd done, were self-conscious and fixed. Miles away from expressing actual respect and gratitude to the teacher. It was just another step to them.

As Nicole performed her own sketchy reverence, Demsby-Worth said, "A minute, Miss Varonne, if you please."

Now what? she thought, annoyed.

"My dear," he said, "we have misjudged you, haven't we? You are quite capable of full extension and precise placement. As a matter of fact, your line is a promising one. A bit rusty in the basics. One can see that. But far too advanced for these babies. I'd like to see you instead in Intermediate Two for a few weeks. Freshen the memory. Then on to Advanced."

"Well, thank God for that, anyway. I mean, thank you, sir. This was like Gulliver with the Lilliputians."

He allowed a smothered chuckle.

"Quite. However, I can already see what mam'selle would call your 'bete noir,' " he said, pausing for effect. "Con-cen-tra-tion. Yes. Concentration. Your first developpe was lovely. Your second shaky and the third unacceptable. A ballerina can produce dozens, each as precise as the one before. Something for you to think about, my dear."

When she didn't respond with suitably cowed and grateful words, the little man frowned.

"Well, off with you, then. I'll see you again at two this afternoon."

31

Nicole managed to growl "Thanks" before she left the classroom.

Well, at least the girls and boys in Intermediate Two were full-sized, Nicole thought. Again she waited restlessly in line to make her reverence to Demsby-Worth. Otherwise, the puppet movements were identical. Just longer. More exact, if that were possible. When she rose after her bow, there was the teacher's now familiar frown of disapproval.

"Concentration, Miss Varonne. Remember."

Like an old biddy, shaking a plump finger at a misbehaving child. God, she had to get out of this place. Once she had flung herself out into the hall, her restlessness poured out of her like sand. Come on, kid, she told herself. Let's at least get out of these sweaty leotards. But she slumped against a wall, gazing aimlessly at the wood grain of the paneling.

It was the worst day Nicole could remember. Even when times had seemed the most hopeless, she had always known that excitement was just around the corner. A new backer would show up. An audience in Topeka would give them a standing ovation, and afterward, their dinner of watered-down potato soup would taste like the finest vichyssoise. Misery was temporary.

But this little whistle-stop at the Borcheffs was temporary too, Nicole reminded herself. Why all the black thoughts, then? Because, stupid, the man in charge was her father. Not some sunburned wheat farmer who drove into town to see some naked legs. And it wasn't only applause or money that kept hope alive.

Unwillingly, Nicole remembered how often she'd evoked her golden tiger father and the twin brother who'd fill the emptiness in her heart. The cold Christmas Eves in strange towns. Every front window glowing with bright gleaming trees and warm candles.

The children in hats and mittens knit by grandmothers, sitting at a dance matinee, sandwiched in cozily between father and mother while Nicole made do with the ever-changing family of Companie Varonne. Exciting, yes. And sometimes unbearably lonely. But there was always that far-off reunion with a brilliant father who would be so impressed, awed even, by his daughter's talent. He would love her so much. And with a twin brother to share her inmost secrets, she would never feel lonely again.

If you don't stop it, Nicole told herself brusquely, you're going to be blubbering like a baby. Come on. Pick up those feet. Let's get cooking. And anyway, you don't even know Nikki, really. Just that he's feeling invaded by wild Indians from America.

There was music coming from the little practice room at the front of the studio. Grateful for the diversion, Nicole walked over and peeked in. She practically had her head knocked off by Nikki, in white leotards and tights, leaping past the door.

"Oh! Excuse me," she squeaked. "Um . . . could I watch you?"

A small frown creased his pale forehead.

"Why one would ever wish to watch . . ."

Nikki's tone of irritation faded so that Nicole couldn't make out the end of the sentence. Raised in a world where everyone expressed themselves as dramatically as possible, Nicole found her twin brother's reserve a surprise.

"Well, I've never seen you dance, right? I'm curious, that's all."

Nikki waved his arm helplessly. Nicole decided to pretend it was an invitation. She sat down in a little chair near the gramophone.

"Here, I'll take care of the music for you."

She wound up the machine and set the needle to the record as Nikki watched apprehensively. When the music began, he looked so relieved that Nicole realized he had expected her to yank off the handle or, at the least, scratch the record. Stifling a sigh, she waved for him to begin.

He did. Whatever worry her presence caused was wiped off his face as he assumed the mask of bland graciousness so common in traditional ballet male roles. As she watched her twin brother move from one perfectly positioned stance to

33

another, Nicole realized that the mask of the handsome, civilized prince covered his entire body. He was graceful. Balanced.

And utterly without feeling. He concealed all effort and any sense of accomplishment. There was no strain, no pleasure, no pride. No Nikki. Nicole hadn't known that it was humanly possible to work for all the years and hours someone as technically perfect as Nikki must have worked and yet have nothing to give at the end. Without generosity, how was an artist to touch the audience?

The music stopped and so did he. Nothing in his face invited her comments, and she was glad. While she stood stock-still in shock, he walked to her side and began rewinding the gramophone. She saw his hand. It was the same shape and size as hers. But hers was tanned and his white. As though he'd never been out in the sun.

She could see tiny beads of sweat at the nape of his neck, how his blond hair soaked to the same shade that hers did. Nicole began to shake. This soulless automaton was her twin brother, the person who swam with her in Alexandra's womb. How could it be? They were supposed to be alike, yet all Nicole saw were the terrible differences between them.

Stammering out a goodbye, she ran down the hallway to the bathroom. The tears she had been holding in since the morning audition slid down her cheeks. Curling herself into a ball in the privacy of a shower stall, she wept like the child she still was. For the first time in her life a dream had been broken beyond mending. In spite of her stagey sophistication, Nicole had never known that sometimes dreams didn't come true.

Dinner has got to be an improvement over breakfast, Nicole thought as she seated herself next to Alexandra at Margaret's fanatically neat table. But Nicole's final spurt of optimism was dealt a death blow as Nikki—no, Nick—and Margaret brought out dinner. There was shepherd's pie—gray ground meat covered with runny mashed potatoes. Undercooked eggplant, which Margaret insisted on calling "aubergines," as though giving it a French name made it edible. And a mound of thickly sliced home-baked bread, gray to match the meat and completely flavorless.

When Nicole took the smallest possible helpings, Margaret gave her a commiserating smile.

"Homesick, is it, dear?" she said, patting the girl's hand. "Well, as my father would say, 'There's nothing to be seen through tears.' Chin up, child. You'll soon be used to our ways."

Is it obvious I've been crying? Nicole thought, swallowing hard. She gave her mother a quick glance and was rewarded with a warm handclasp under the tablecloth.

"I think I've got a little cold," Nicole answered. "Must be the change of weather."

"Of course," said Margaret with an approving nod. "Some more pie, Van?"

"Please. Is one of my favorites, Piggy."

Nicole knew it was just his accent, but she loved how he called this woman "Piggy." She knew from the twinkle in her mother's eye that Alexandra was tickled too.

"Is this bread a family recipe?" Alexandra asked Margaret politely.

"My father's housekeeper at the rectory taught me to bake. My mother died soon after I was born."

"Ah. I too lost my mother when I was young. Is tragedy, no?"

"I believe substitutes can do quite adequately if the child is young enough."

Alexandra's eyes narrowed and Nicole prepared to watch "Piggy" reduced to jelly. But the confrontation took an unexpected turn.

"Substitutes can do better than the blood parent," Vanya's voice boomed out.

His arms folded across his chest, he glowered like some Norse thunder god. Margaret patted Vanya's arm.

"This won't help your digestion, dear. Perhaps after dinner . . ."

"This conversation cannot be put off, Piggy," Vanya insisted.

Turning back to his wife, he began to rant.

"I auditioned our daughter today, Alexandra. Never, never have I been so outraged, so horrified. While her twin brother rehearses the *Bluebird* variation, she goes to baby class, where eight-year-olds can teach her. Is crime, absolute crime, what you have done."

"Demsby-Worth sent me to Intermediate Two," Nicole interrupted, trying to keep her voice from trembling.

"Intermed— Ah, good. Good. You are quick study," he said lamely. "Like your father."

It was as if she'd slammed the brakes of some onrushing train. But soon he began to pick up steam again.

"In the long run, Alexandra, this rushing from excitement to excitement will not serve. No. It is steadiness of purpose that will take one where one wants to go. A firm goal and methodical practice with the requisite authority. Consistency produces a child who knows itself and its capacities."

Fired up, he kept going without a pause.

"Self-indulgence, on the other hand, produces child without self-discipline or self-respect. It is great lesson the English have to teach us all. I was lucky enough to have an excellent teacher."

He threw a fond glance at Margaret, who looked down at the tablecloth with a tiny smile and straightened her knife and spoon.

A rich theatrical laugh burst from Alexandra.

"You—you find discussions of our children's well-being funny?" Vanya demanded helplessly.

"No, no, Vanushka. You. Only you. How very pompous you have become, my love. Do you remember first season of Ballet Romanoff in Paris? We were so poor we didn't have two sous to rub together. No heat in theater until opening night. Baschenko promised artists free meal to get the sets painted when none of us were eating. We didn't know if audience would even show up. And yet, I remember that winter as full of joy. Can you deny it? We were young. We could do anything. We were taking a magical leap into the unknown . . . as high and far as Milky Way itself." She brushed Vanya's arm lightly. "This consistency you speak of. To me, it is like stagnation. Nicole's consistency is her mother. We have never been apart. For the rest, she is very strong inside. And beautiful. She will be like a storm on stage. I am very proud of my daughter."

"Oh, Mom," whispered Nicole, happy tears glazing her eyes.

"And are you proud of dividing up our twin babies like baggage too heavy to carry while you 'leaped' at more stars?" Vanya sneered.

"How dare you say that? We both agreed. We'd each take a child. I have missed my Nikolai every day since that terrible moment. But was it a mistake? This I cannot tell until my son and I come to know each other again."

She turned to Nick, who had been watching the highly dramatic exchange with his mouth open.

"Come, my little mouse, who watches the angry cats squalling from the safety of his hole. What do you think of all this? How do you say . . . a pence for your thoughts."

"Penny."

Nick's voice was almost a whisper. Alexandra bent closer to him.

"What?"

"I said it's a penny for your thoughts, not a pence."

"Ah. Thank you," his mother said gravely, as to a child of five or six. "Come, Nikki. Is there nothing you wish to ask me of these long years we've been apart?"

With some difficulty Nick kept his mouth from dropping open. How exactly like the interloper to ask him such a deeply intrusively personal question. From the little he'd seen of her, it was clear she had absolutely no scruples, no limits of decency or sense. She allowed herself absolutely anything.

No! he felt like shouting at her. I don't give a bloody damn about those years. Only about . . .

His mind, sensing danger, tried to veer away. But Nick's

usual self control over "bad" or "useless" thoughts was overcome by an irresistible inner whisper. Why was it my sister you picked? Why wasn't it me?

Nick Borcheff squirmed inwardly. Don't be an idiotic baby, he told himself savagely. How utterly awful it would have been if this lunatic person had carried him off to America. Surrounded him with gangsters, with whooping red Indians. He'd've turned out as crude as this girl passing as his twin.

"Mother" was waiting patiently for his answer. He shrugged. "Do they use forks and spoons in America?"

Nicole gave her brother an incredulous look before angrily speaking. "It's a little hard to eat beans and buffalo jerky without them, but we cowpokes manage. Then we wipe our hands on our dusty chaps and roll up in an old greasy blanket with a rock for a pillow. Sure beats those dangblasted soft beds."

Alexandra chuckled. "Is all right, Nicole. Nikolai has never been to America. And truly, people are more informal there. They will introduce themselves on a train, and before you reach your destination they will tell you secrets even their families don't know. You remember the time, Nicole . . ."

She began to relate tales of her early days in America. With her flamboyance and sense of humor, Alexandra soon had the Borcheff clan enthralled. Vanya's anger was derailed for the evening. Even Nikki found himself listening intently.

A week went by, a week of inedible dinners and even less digestible family gatherings afterward in Margaret's parlor. Lucky Mom, Nicole thought, as she burrowed as deeply as she could in an armchair farthest from the Borcheffs. Alexandra's job hunt, unsuccessful as it had been, kept her out of the house most days and well into the evenings, while Nicole was stuck.

Every night it was the same routine. Everyone sitting in the same chairs. Watching the same firelight. Hypnotized by the same boring Brahms or Mendelssohn on the wireless. Piggy with her knitting. Vanya with his pipe. Nikki frowning over his stamp album, lying on his stomach on the rug like some little kid.

It usually only took five minutes before Nicole produced a yawn. Then she excused herself, though she wasn't really tired. Anything to escape the stifling coziness, especially the cheerful little smile on Peggy's face as she wagged her head to the music.

"Darlings, I'm home early for once," came the incredibly welcome voice of Alexandra.

She swooped down and engulfed Nicole in an embrace, smelling wonderfully of French perfume and the fresh scent of rain. Next she leaned down and mussed Nikki's hair.

"Sweetheart, remind me to riffle through my trunk. I have stamps for you. Especially South American, I think."

Nick scrambled up off the floor. The album slammed shut.

Gracefully Alexandra flung herself on the couch next to Vanya, letting a long sigh escape as she stretched her body sinuously.

"Has been so impossible, this searching. I begin to wonder, my dear, whether your English stage has room for real experimentation. No, no, darling. Do not put away your charming pipe. Only let me blow off steam, as the Americans say. I have been holding myself in all day."

Margaret put down her knitting. "Vanya has repeatedly offered to help you, Madame Varonne. Perhaps if you—"

"Darling Piggy, even the great Borcheff cannot convince David Wenkers that twenty flat fouettes do not become great art when the ballerina has a gilt skull tied to her shoe."

Alexandra ran her hands through her thick dark mane and shook her hair out as if shaking off the last vestige of the shallow choreographer. She fixed Vanya with her dramatic eyes.

"They are afraid of me. They fend me off with stupid excuses. Like you, darling."

As he began sputtering, Alexandra pouted becomingly. Leaping up, she strode over to the wireless.

"Come, we must have something modern for tonight. Something to blow away all the cobwebs."

She turned the knob until a brassy, mocking polka filled the room.

"Ahh," Alexandra breathed, turning back to smile at them all. "Our little Shostakovich's ballet. Wonderfully witty, is he not, Vanushka?"

He attempted a stern frown. "I will not listen to him. He is a damned Soviet."

"Darling, even the Red Army cannot destroy the Russian soul. I will not allow you to miss *The Golden Age* one more night."

She wove her way over to her husband, who looked to Nicole like a turtle retreating as deeply as possible into his shell.

Nicole hid a grin. No one could resist Mom when she was filled with the spirit. And what spirit this music had! Oom-pa-pa brilliantly laughing at itself. Energy swept into her, straightening her back, grabbing at her shoulders.

"Come," Alexandra insisted. "I show you his choreography." She advanced on her husband, her outstretched hands demanding a partner.

Nikki leaped to his feet. He was not going to watch his father turned into a marionette for the vulgar pleasure of La Varonne. He managed to duck from her bloodred kiss.

"Sleep well, my sweet dumpling," her voice sang out as he escaped up the stairs.

"I must apologize, Madame Varonne, for Nick's poor manners," Margaret said reluctantly. She winced as a particularly raucous combination of notes blared through her parlor.

For a moment hurt showed in Alexandra's dark eyes. She shrugged. "Shostakovich is not to everyone's taste," she said lightly.

"Indeed," answered Margaret pointedly. "I must excuse myself as well. There are several letters I must finish. Upstairs."

"And my headache has returned," added Vanya hastily, rising from the couch and taking Margaret's arm. Fussing, she led him out of the room.

Nicole and Alexandra looked at each other.

"Is like this every night?"

"Always. They huddle around the fire like a pack of old-age parishioners. Mom?"

Alexandra sank onto the couch with a tired sigh. "Yes, my sweet?"

"Why are you still married to him? I keep seeing the two of you together and wondering why you didn't make a clean break. I mean, my God, what a contrast! If you were divorced, he could marry his perfect Piggy and you'd be free."

Alexandra raised an eyebrow.

"Perhaps he does not wish to marry his English wren. Love can be very complicated, my little innocent. But truly, I did try to divorce him. When I first arrived in America, I sent him the papers. But he never sent them back. I think perhaps he cannot make so final a break. So I let him keep the legal fiction. As long as he no longer filled my days with commands and my nights with bitterness."

"But what if you'd met someone else?"

"Then I would have tried again. Forced him to set me free. But was never necessary." She smiled. "I think I am too independent for marriage."

"Oh no. You're perfect. You just never met a guy who could match you."

Alexandra held out her elegant arms. "Come here, my sweet rosebud."

Nicole nestled next to her on the couch and happily returned her mother's kiss.

"Of all the gifts the gods have given me," Alexandra murmured, "this love between us is my greatest treasure."

It was with great relief a week later that Alexandra heard Dame Harriet Wellington had returned to Swanleigh Hall after a fortnight of touring on the continent. A quick call and Alexandra had set an appointment for the next morning. The tiny avant-garde autocrat was one of Alexandra's best hopes, although Dame Harriet's temper tantrums were as well-known as her brilliant, innovative theater. Her reputation as a teacher was unparalleled. Some of the most impressive young choreographers in England were her former students.

Swanleigh Hall charmed Alexandra immediately. An old, converted church, it stood by itself on a grassy hill on the outskirts of London. Inside the tiny vestibule with its faint odor of incense, she passed the cardboard wicket where tickets were sold and peeked into the auditorium. It was a tiny jewel box fit for royalty, with only a hundred seats, enchanting in its miniature perfections.

"Alexandra Varonne. You have come," came a strong, hoarse voice.

Alexandra turned and encountered a small woman with a triangular face, all cheekbones, pointed chin, and enormous eyes.

"I'm honored to meet you, Dame Harriet. You are one of the true legends of dance."

The black eyes gleamed with a hint of humor. "Quite a compliment, coming from a prima ballerina assoluta."

She gestured for Alexandra to follow her down a narrow hall. Pale light slanted down from long ecclesiastical windows far above. Dame Harriet's office was damp and barely furnished, but the hot tea she offered her guest did much to dispel the room's icy cold.

"I'm sure you don't remember," said Dame Harriet offhandedly. "Why should you? But I once took company class with the Romanoff. Before the war. You, of course, were the prima."

"Did you really? There were so many. Baschenko needed the money. Ah, those were such extraordinary days . . ."

"That partnership of yours! Perhaps the most exciting pairing I've ever watched. Everyone tried to imitate you and Borcheff. But without that edge of fire and ice, no one could. Every dance was a fight to the finish. How did you two ever come to marry?"

"A very good question."

Alexandra gave the aging dancer a rueful, woman-to-woman smile. Though they had only just met, the personal question seemed natural.

42

"Forgive me, Dame Harriet, but I have a shocking impulse to call you 'Harry.'"

A bark of laughter met her confession.

"You've been in America too long, my dear. Go right ahead. I've been called far worse. But tell me about you and Vanya. If ever there was a more unlikely pair . . . You with a wild Gypsy in your soul, and he . . . Borcheff's become more English than the English. When one of his students comes to me, I have to drag emotion out of him by main force. Everything with Borcheff must be predictable. Bah!"

"He wasn't always so conservative, though he always wanted to dominate. But why did I marry Vanya Borcheff? It was the great war, you see. The Romanoff was stranded in South America for four years. And then came the terrible news. In Russia, the revolution had come. Everything was gone. My father was executed. Vanya's whole family starved. None of us could ever go home again."

Alexandra's face was pale remembering the tragedy. She took a deep breath.

"So there we were. All we had was each other. I think, for a little while, we clung to each other like two lost children. But . . ." Alexandra made a vague gesture with one tapered hand. "Is a mistake, Harry, to marry out of loneliness. This I have learned."

"Someone said that being alone is not the same thing as being lonely. I believe we both know that, my dear. Like me, you have run your own company. We know what it is to create anything we wish, to turn vision into dances. Can anything be better?"

"You are right, Harry. Is wonderful. Except for the money."

"Money! Don't say that wicked word. I spend half my waking hours thrashing about over it."

"Was why I gave up Companie Varonne. I cannot understand how people expect art to be created on a pittance. It is as important to soul as food and drink to the body."

"Exactly. And why we can't—"

A young man in sweaty leotard and tights pushed into the room.

"The bloody gas man's threatening to turn off the heat unless we— Oh, pardon me. I've interrupted you."

"Excuse me," said Dame Harriet. "Money rears its ugly head. I'll be back in a moment."

"Of course."

Alexandra sat and listened to the muffled sounds of shouting, including one good-sized shriek that made her grin. The gas fellow was probably wishing he'd never tangled with Harry.

Dame Harriet returned, her slightly mottled cheeks the only evidence of her battle.

"Let's get down to it, shall we? When can you start work with us? The pay is absurd, of course, for someone of your caliber. Ten pounds flat fee per dance choreographed. Royalty per performance two and six. Usually we perform each piece for a week, possibly two.

"I realize," Harry added shrewdly, "that as soon as you perform, the offers will come flooding in. But you need that beginning showcase. We can do that for you."

Alexandra didn't pretend otherwise, but she added, "Once I am settled financially, it will be my pleasure to choreograph for you for art's sake."

"And my very real pleasure as well. Perhaps by then you will have thought of a more decorous nickname for your employer?"

They grinned at each other.

"Perhaps."

In the early dusk Alexandra and Nicole found each other a few blocks from the Borcheff house. Hands burrowed in their coat pockets, they leaned close to each other to escape the cutting wind and the constant clamor of homebound traffic.

"I have the most wonderful news, darling," Alexandra said, kissing her daughter's cold cheek. "I search no more. Dame Harriet Wellington has invited me to join her at Swanleigh Hall. She is the most perfect tartar, screaming at her students and whacking them with great stick. She sees what fights inside of them to be free, and she cannot rest until it is out. The dancers she is making. It is a miracle. And I am going to make a dance for her. It is all agreed."

Nicole hugged her mother.

"Hallelujah! We can get our own place and I'll study with Harriet. Oh, thank God!"

"You go so fast, my little speedster. There is no money in this. After, when England sees what Varonne has learned in America, then we will have money to swim in."

"Oh."

"Come, don't hang your head like schoolgirl. Tell Mamushka."

"I hate Father's school."

It was said in a low voice, but full of conviction.

"Yes?"

"It's like being the only person who can hear in a roomful of deaf mutes. They—I—Mom, I hate to say this to you, but ballet is terrible. They want me to stop thinking. Stop feeling. Just move my legs around like some kind of machine. Do you know what Demsby-Worth told me? He said . . . he—"

Nicole burst into tears.

Alexandra put her arm around her daughter and guided her to a bench at a bus stop. When the storm subsided some, she offered her perfumed handkerchief wordlessly. Nicole heartily blew her nose.

"I'm asking a lot of you," Alexandra said. "I know this." She stroked Nicole's curls, adding, "But two weeks isn't long enough to throw ballet on the trash heap."

"It's long enough for me to know I'll never fit in there."

"Is true. Your father goes too far with control. But the discipline, it is invaluable. Ballet training turns the body into an exquisite instrument. With such mastery, all movement becomes possible."

"You already taught me ballet, Mom."

"I taught you positions. But there was never time for you to work every day, five hours a day. And this is needed to create the transcendence, the marvelous grace, the miracles."

"Sure. Maybe. But does it have to be at that place?"

"Darling, I cannot pay for lessons. Your father offers them free. And then, he is your father. He feeds us, gives us a home. Let us be kind in return. In few months it will all be different. Then you will decide where you study."

"I guess I can stand it. But hurry up and get famous here, will you?"

"I have an idea. After school you will be my assistant at Swanleigh. This much I can arrange. And so my production cannot help but take London by storm, with both Varonnes working on it. What do you say?"

Her answer was a heartfelt hug.

~~ 5

"Don't leave me," Nicole begged the sea gull that carried her swooping across the western sea through hours of dream.

But an alarm clock was ringing and the fresh bracing smell of sea salt was replaced by mildew and starch. The odor of Margaret's guest sheets. Nicole's eyes focused slowly on coy shepherdesses, gamboling lambs, tea roses, curlicues of ribbons, and practically every other fussy motif possible to print on a sheet of wallpaper. All in girlish pink on a washed-out blue background covering all four walls.

Another morning, Nicole thought, sighing deeply. If she could just pull the covers over her head and sleep through the day. But she knew she must get out of bed. In front of her hung her practice clothes, draped over a chair. They looked as limp and listless as she felt, facing another lousy day.

She was not very good at helplessness. She'd had very little practice. If a teacher wasn't to her liking, it was easy enough to find another in a troupe of dedicated dancers. If a landlady rubbed her the wrong way, it was only a few days until the troupe moved on to greener pastures.

But England was different. This landlady and these teachers belonged to her father. And he seemed to think that rules and regulations were the cat's pajamas. He probably has a rule for which nostril to pick first, Nicole thought, unable to conjure up even an inward giggle. The disappointment hurt too much.

Everything had a right way and a wrong way here. She couldn't move without being corrected. People she didn't care two cents for were running her life, and it made her sick.

It's just like a prison, she thought, jerking on her leotard and tights. She pulled a corduroy dress over her practice clothes, threw on a sweater, and grimaced at herself in the tiny mirror. I don't have to like it, she reminded her scowling image. If I can just make it through the next few weeks somehow, Mom will make some money and we're out. Home free.

She finished dressing, pulled a brush through her wiry blond mane, and slumped downstairs to eat her breakfast. For the fourteenth day in a row Margaret served a rack of toast with orange marmalade, tea with milk, eggs and those damn kippers. There they all were, ramrod-straight, ready to criticize every move she made. Something in Nicole snapped.

"Sorry I have to miss breakfast," she called. "Got an errand to run before class."

Her father was only halfway out of his chair by the time Nicole yanked open the front door and was outside. Another damp dark day wrapped its chilly arms around her and squeezed until her momentary elation slid down into the doldrums. She plodded down the same dull route to the studio, breathing the same used city air. Splashy travel posters she sometimes studied longingly only irritated her today with their relentless cheer. She bought a sweet bun from a bakery and slumped down onto a park bench. To put off the inevitable as long as possible.

But it was all there in her memory.

"Miss Varonne," drilled the patronizing voice of Demsby-Worth. "If you please, the toe must rest one-quarter inch to the front of the ankle between petits battements."

Hour after hour. Bloodless patient practice of absolutely nothing. Meaning was banished at the door of the studio. And feeling? They wouldn't know a feeling if it bit them.

She stared at the half-eaten bun in her hand and threw it to the sparrows. No breakfast was better than sugary clay. Come on, Varonne, she told herself. Up and at 'em. Just dance the way you know how and remember it's only a few weeks. She marched herself the rest of the way to the studio.

When Nicole got there, she was startled out of her grim mood by the shockingly loud sound of her father's voice. Here was the thick Russian accent, the Siberian tiger ferocity she'd only caught a glimpse of once before—the night two weeks ago when he'd torn into Alexandra. And been stopped in his tracks. Now his heavy roar boomed through the closed oak door of his office at the end of the hall as if the wood were thin as a cardboard backdrop.

"I picked you up out of the streets and just as easily I will throw you back. So you've got talent. What do you think? You know more than teachers who studied with Cechetti, with Pavlova? Fifteen years old and you're smarter than Maître Andreyev, who partnered the prima ballerina assoluta of the Russian Imperial Ballet before you were even born. You are an arrogant, ignorant whelp who badly needs whipping. Let me tell you this: Andreyev comes to me again with complaint, you are suspended."

There was an indistinct murmur from the student, whom Nicole imagined cowering in a corner, begging for forgiveness. My God, she thought, what could the kid have done to draw such fire? Miss a couple of classes? Forget to wear shoes? There was her father's voice again, battering the poor sap into a pulp.

Nicole exchanged glances with the half dozen other students lining the dimly lit corridor, listening with fascination as the exchange went on and on. Finally there was quiet that stretched into several minutes. Nicole imagined the abject apologies, sternly accepted. The fervent promises. The final warning delivered with a heavy frown.

The door opened. Vanya walked out smiling, his arm thrown around the shoulders of a lean dark young danseur with amused sable eyes. The boy moved with all the grace and assurance of a black panther prowling his own turf.

Nicole's mouth fell open. Her father's growling hadn't fazed the danseur in the slightest.

"Who is that?" Nicole asked Eunice Blodge, a skinny pasty-faced girl with a tiny blond bun.

"Carlo Domenici. I'm sure I'll never know what a hoodlum of his sort is doing at ballet school."

"But what's his dancing like? He must be something, the way he moves."

There was an audible sniff.

"Rather preposterous, actually. He does have flamboyant elevation, but when you stand him next to a classically perfect partner like your brother . . . well. There's no balance, no proportion. A ghastly sort of circus type, really."

To Nicole, any male dancer who stood in marked contrast to Nikki's bloodless poses sounded terrific. She couldn't wait to see this Carlo in action.

Her wish was answered. Vanya came up to her after Geometry. He was adding a partnering class to her schedule. Late that afternoon, when Nicole showed up outside the assigned room, she caught a glimpse of the tantalizing Italian inside. With a grin of anticipation, she entered and picked a spot at the back of the barre, at right angles to his. It was the best view in the house.

He was already working, lifting one arrow-straight leg from the floor to the side of his head with slow, exacting strength. Beads of sweat formed on his broad, swarthy forehead, though his face remained expressionless. As the other students filed in and took their places, he never showed for an instant that he was aware of anything but his own work.

He was doing an odd exercise she'd never seen before. He stood out from the barre, holding one raised leg an inch above the wooden rail and moving the leg high into the air. Then he slowly pivoted, using only his arms and the foot on the floor to turn his entire body. It was an almost impossible movement. Nicole wasn't even sure she was seeing correctly.

To top it all, when the turns were done, he lowered the leg

with incredible slowness, pausing for agonizing moments before letting it rest on the barre. Nicole found herself tensing with the drama of holding an aching leg so close to a resting place but refusing to let it drop the final inch. It seemed he was exercising his self-control as well as his muscles.

There was the sharp double tap from Maître Andreyev's cane. Class was beginning. As the rest of the students scurried to their places and obediently assumed the initial position, Carlo Domenici deliberately finished two last turns and managed to stand ready just as the last would-be ballerina found her place on the barre.

Nicole's eyes seldom left the wiry, powerful figure through the warm-up that followed. Even simple pliés and battements seemed to have meaning when Carlo applied his formidable concentration to them. She could almost feel his muscles stretching. Pulling. Trembling. His mind crying out for surcease from pain. But his will, his overpowering will, refused to rest until the goal had been met. Unconsciously Nicole worked harder herself, stimulated by his example to reach further. She was surprised when the teacher announced it was time for center work.

The students formed a line in one corner of the room, girls and then boys, for the high leaping combinations that would carry them diagonally across the room. Nicole had caught her breath from her set by the time Carlo, the last of all, came up to the front.

"Hey, Miss Archway," he called to the pianist, "faster, faster!"

When she complied with a modest smile, Carlo exploded across the floor. It was like watching a bough broken off in a storm as it hurtled through the air. He defied gravity as though on a dare. As if there were no way to contain himself. Nicole had never seen anything like it.

"My God," she gasped to the willowy girl next to her.

"One becomes so tired of the little mountebank's tricks," was the languid reply.

"Most of us left that sort of showing off back in the

nursery," added another dancer, who had had a good deal of trouble with the combination.

"You're all crazy," Nicole said. "He's the only one of us who can make you scared to look away. If that's showing off, then I'm all for it."

"Well, my dear," drawled one of the boys, "that's easily explained. After all, you're an American."

There was muffled chuckling among the dancers, which stopped instantly when Andreyev called out the next combination.

After everyone had moved across the floor again, the teacher waved his cane at a girl and then a boy, saying, "Pair yourselves up, all of you."

The dancers moved into position until all the girls had partners except Nicole. Carlo was also still alone, which didn't surprise her. Apparently his powerful style of dancing was too much for their limp little brains to take in. Andreyev gestured for Carlo to partner Nicole, and she felt a glad little leap inside.

As they watched the other couples move through a combination, Carlo turned to her and said in a mock growl, "They've probably warned you I eat baby ballerinas for breakfast."

Nicole laughed, asking, "With or without pepper?"

"With, by all means," he said with a grin.

They were next in line, and Nicole started counting out the steps, planning her placements in the musical phrases, picturing the difficult transitions in the combination. Then Carlo lifted her into the air and they were suddenly flying. He lifted her out of two dank and friendless weeks and into the region of joy.

It was extraordinary. Nicole felt as though she'd never experienced her own lightness before. Carlo showed her the world of the air as if it were his private kingdom. In a flash she understood. Whatever price a dancer must pay, in pain, in concentration, it was well worth the cost of this ticket. To fly free.

They spoke to each other so well without words, Nicole

marveled, when she could think at all. How precious that closeness was. She had been so lonely, and now his touch was like water in a desert. Warmth in the snow. Their bodies intuitively knew what the other wanted, and gave with generosity. When the music stopped, they leaned on each other, gasping for breath, grinning.

There was a stunned silence from the rest of the students, which was broken by Andreyev's pounding cane.

"No no no!" he shouted. "That is exactly the sort of tawdry exaggeration you have been warned about before. Ballet is art, not a carnival sideshow. It is not your place, young man, to pump up every step with bombastic emotionality. Let the steps speak for themselves. They have done so, quite adequately I believe, for a number of decades."

Nicole simply ignored the stupid man. But Carlo's eyes narrowed and fixed on Andreyev.

"Tell me, Maître. Did we miss any steps?"

"No," came the hesitant reply.

"Was our tempo off?"

"No."

"Line poor?"

Again Andreyev had to agree that their technical work was adequate.

"Then frankly, Maître, I'd suggest you save your personal preferences for those who agree with them."

There was a gasp from the class at Carlo's audacity, and Nicole inwardly cheered. How she had longed to give these dusty dry instructors a piece of her mind. And how neatly, how perfectly, Carlo had done it.

The teacher's pale face whitened to chalk. His mouth snapped shut. The room was so silent Nicole could hear her own blood surging in her ears. Andreyev turned to the couple after Nicole and Carlo.

"Next," he said.

Nikki and Eunice Blodge stepped forward. They moved precisely, gracefully, with polished perfect technique. And that was it, Nicole thought. As lifeless as a pair of dolls. If they found themselves in the air, it was only part of the exercise. It was not their place.

Andreyev's face was, of course, benignly smiling. The doll maker. He wound them up and they did exactly the same thing each time. Exactly what he wanted. Exactly *nothing*, Nicole thought.

In the final half hour of class Maître Andreyev deliberately kept Nicole and Carlo from dancing together. The other girls Carlo partnered looked nervous in his arms, as if they were afraid he might drop them on their heads. Nikki's partners, on the other hand, smiled confidently as he lifted and spun them. He made them look their interchangeable best. He was the perfect backdrop prince who would never miss a step or touch an audience.

Andreyev ended class and hurried out with a pointed look at Carlo. The young dancer, tugging on Nicole's ponytail, missed the warning.

"Let's get some air. All that pontificating doesn't leave much to breathe in here."

With a giggle that ended embarrassingly in a small nervous hiccup, Nicole changed in a minute flat and followed Carlo out of the stuffy building, into the damp, rain-cooled streets. She loved the way he walked, with the brisk stride of a young athlete who'd never lost a race.

"You hungry?" he asked.

"Always. It's hard to find anything worth eating in this city."

He looked at her with one sweeping black eyebrow raised. Then he took her hand.

"Come on. It's a walk, but Kali is worth it."

"You don't have to kill me off to put me out of my misery."

"Kill you . . ." He laughed, suddenly understanding. "Not Kali, goddess of death. My Kali cooks the most heavenly samosas. The best in Soho."

"Sure. Laced with the finest belladonna and a faint hint of strychnine . . ."

Gladly she let him lead her away from the ballet school, past the elegant theaters of Covent Garden, down a series of side streets.

6

They continued bantering their way to Cambridge Circus, a wide circular confluence of five streets, packed to the brim with red double-decker buses, taxis, cars, and messenger boys on bicycles. The intersection was surprisingly quiet. The English signaled each other with polite little beeps instead of the full-throated honking Nicole was used to in New York and Chicago.

Carlo pulled Nicole through the thick traffic, dodging here and there along a path apparently only he could see.

When they made it safely to the other side, Nicole asked admiringly, "You have carrier pigeon in your blood?"

"Hey there, me mucker," came a gravelly voice with the broad accents of working-class London. "You 'ear? Hards mixed it good with the Bully Boys last night. Got pinched, the lot of 'em."

"They'll be out by supper," Carlo said to a skinny unhealthy-looking kid in a black leather jacket who kept tossing a bicycle chain from hand to hand as he talked. "Unless someone's in hospital."

"Nah. Rozzers broke it up early. So who's the judy?"

Nicole tried not to flinch as the rough boy flicked his chain in her general direction.

"Nicole Varonne, meet Alfie Dumbarton, a good guy to have at your back."

The two young men gave each other a smile of complicity. Alfie's revealed badly stained teeth, one broken in half.

"A little fresh, wouldn't you say?" he muttered to Carlo, indicating Nicole with a nod.

"My friend Alfie thinks you're too posh for the likes of me," Carlo told her. "You should see her move, mate. She's a nervy one. Take my word for it."

A thrill shivered through Nicole at his compliment. Though she'd only known him a few hours, Nicole felt certain he was a person who genuinely admired very few performers. Given the unleashed power of his own dancing, his approval was well worth having. She was also relieved to see the young tough put his heavy chain in a jacket pocket and hold out a friendly hand to her.

"Wotcher, Nicole," he said. "Where'd you cadge the fancy mac?"

Nicole shook his hand, but gave his words a mystified smile.

"You've got to talk gentry to her, mate," Carlo said. "She's from America. What he means, cara," Carlo continued, "is he likes your raincoat. And 'wotcher'—that's hello in East London."

"Well, wotcher to you too, Alfie," said Nicole. "This is my mother's old cape, and she got it from a toreador years ago in Spain. He dedicated his bull to her the morning after he saw her dance."

"Cor! Musta been some fly dancer," said Alfie admiringly.

"He means clever, Nicole. More than fly, mate. The flippin' best. And the daughter's no slump herself. Listen, I'll see you down at Beggles tonight. Maybe a little trading?"

"You tellin' me to bugger off, mate?" snarled the kid.

Nicole stiffened in alarm. The tough's white-gray eyes bored into Carlo's. But Carlo just grinned.

"You got it, Alf."

The kid sniggered. "Can't say as I blames ya. I could fancy one like that meself." With that, Alfie melted into the crowd as unobtrusively as he had appeared.

"Whew!" breathed Nicole. "Where did you learn to deal with kids like that?"

Carlo took her hand in his and led her down a wide street studded with theaters. "What makes you think I'm not a kid like that?"

"Because you're on your way to the top, and Alfie isn't going anywhere," Nicole said with loyal indignation.

Carlo gave her a smile that sent warm shivers down to her toes.

"You're a fierce one, aren't you? You usually protect strays?"

"Strays?" muttered Nicole, confused by the contradiction of his intimate smile and the casual distant voice.

"Believe it or not, I was born in Castel dei Domenici, built by my ancestor Alessandro Stefano Domenici in 1726 in the far south of Italy. Near Bari. For two hundred years my family made wine that was famous. Our peasants were protected and they prospered with us. Until the fascist Black Shirt pigs chased us out four years ago, there had always been a Domenici in Bari."

His eyes dared her to doubt him, but Nicole had no doubts at all. The lone pride that bordered on arrogance, his innate confidence, these were the aristocrat in him.

"But you got away to England . . ."

"The Fascists took everything. We had nothing in our pockets when we got to London." He smiled bitterly. "We still don't. My father and mother have a restaurant in Soho the size of a piano. And I 'learned to deal' with street life, as you call it."

They had turned off the avenue and were threading their way through a maze of disreputable streets, manned by toughs and drunks and shrill-voiced blowsy women.

"Welcome to Soho," Carlo said in an ironic voice. "Home of inventive solutions for never-ending problems."

Nicole wasn't offended by his bitterness because she had the sense he was taking aim at himself. She squeezed the sinewy hand that still held hers. In answer he gave her a long examining look and then a slow approving smile very unlike his customary sardonic grin.

She blushed and looked at the ground as they walked on. For a moment his hand clung to hers as they passed a bony derelict asleep in a doorway, flies crawling up his stained pants. Then he released her and began an ironic travelogue of the slum until they reached their destination.

Carlo pointed to a sea of pushcarts and shabby wagons ahead to their right.

"Berwick Market," he said with a wave of the hand. "Everything secondhand except the vegetables."

"Even the samosas?"

"Well, I can't vouch for the other two stands," he said, steering her in the direction of a trio of rickety booths draped with faded scarves, "but Kali makes hers fresh."

Kali turned out to be a plump sweaty matron swathed in a damp sari; her gold-toothed smile welcomed them. She was even warmer when Nicole requested and devoured with every evidence of enjoyment a samosa with hot sauce.

"Ummm, wonderful," Nicole groaned between bites.

She polished off the snack in less than a minute and worked her way rapidly through a second one.

"These are as good as Fatima's back home."

Thanking the pleased vendor, who offered namaste in return, Nicole and Carlo wandered through the teeming street market.

"Fatima?" Carlo asked.

"One of the dancers in my mother's troupe back in America. Fatima was really Sally Sue Rosenberg, but of course she couldn't call herself that and do the rope dance."

"How did Alexandra Varonne get from prima ballerina to rope dancing?" Carlo asked, completely mystified.

"Well, it's a . . ."

". . . long story," he finished with her.

They smiled at each other.

"I'm all ears," he assured her.

"When my mother first came to America in the late teens, she danced ballet in vaudeville and then on Broadway for a few years. She got tired of the 'vulgar crowds,' as she called them, and found this amazing group of dancers in California who were trying all kinds of ethnic things. Like African fertility rites and American Indian tribal ceremonies and—"

"Rope dancing."

"Yeah, you got it. Fatima was with them too. She really got serious about her Indian dances. Studied the culture, the religion. Even learned how to cook. Actually a lot of the dancers were like that. It was kind of funny. Here they were doing these half-naked exotic dances, and all they talked about was how spiritual it all was."

"I'm trying to imagine prima ballerina Alexandra Varonne, the toast of three continents, performing spiritual belly dancing for a herd of cowboys . . ."

"Oh no," corrected Nicole, wide-eyed. "She studied geisha dancing and Balinese temple rituals and—"

They both burst out laughing.

"It was silly, sometimes," Nicole admitted, "especially before Mom left and started her own company."

"Who backed her?"

"No one."

Carlo's eyebrows soared.

"Oh, we did okay. Overall." Nicole smiled fondly. "Sometimes we'd heat up a can of tomato soup and add extra water, and then a patron would appear and Mom'd buy enough caviar for the whole troupe. I remember once we'd been kicked out of a theater in Des Moines because our house receipts wouldn't cover the rent. So Mom cut all the pearls off her Balinese jacket and hocked them to get us back inside."

"Wouldn't it have been simpler to get a loan on your property?"

"We didn't have 'property.' Why put all your money into a house when you're always on the road?" Nicole asked artlessly.

"If you've never had a home," he said, "I suppose you wouldn't know how important it is."

Nicole interpreted his cold tone as a mask for the loss of the ancestral Domenici castle, and adopted a deliberately cheerful voice.

"I always felt sorry for the kids I'd see in the towns, lugging their schoolbooks around the same corner every day and sitting down to pot roast on Monday night and fried fish on Fridays. Besides, I was learning to dance with serious artists. La Gallada showed me flamenco one whole season. I spent a winter with the Hopi Indians when Mom was studying native American dances for a new work. Boy, nobody moves like they do, let me tell you—"

"All right, all right. You make it sound like the perfect life. Maybe it was. I certainly can't argue with the finished product." He smoothed some runaway curls back over her forehead. "But for a gypsy, you've been pretty sheltered. Better than those baby ballerinas at school whose experience ends at the points of their little shoes, but you've got a ways to go, kiddo."

His superior tone goaded Nicole. "I suppose you're such a world-weary sophisticate, you have nothing more to learn? What are you? Eighteen?"

"Seventeen." He shrugged. "I know enough not to let fools like Andreyev control my dancing. Right now, that's enough."

"Is he the one my father was yelling at you about?" asked Nicole apprehensively, a rush of sympathy overtaking her annoyance.

"I've had the same trouble with all of them. Andreyev's just the latest. The Grand Duke Borcheff would dearly like to throw me out of his school, but he knows I dance rings around the other male dancers. . . . So far he's managed not to."

It would have sounded like boasting except that Nicole had seen Carlo dance and knew he was speaking the simple truth.

"I don't know how you stand all those blind snobs. How long've you been there?"

"Almost four years. As far as my mother is concerned, I'm still the heir to the title, and a well-bred gentleman must acquire a taste for the fine arts. A scholarship spot at the ballet school was what she could afford."

"Four years?" Nicole cried. "I don't think I'm going to last four weeks."

"Poor little gypsy," he said, his dark eyes gleaming.

They had been leaning back against a sooty limestone wall side by side. Now he turned toward her so that his face was very close to hers. Nicole swallowed. What was going to happen now?

"I may have to train you in some guerilla tactics," he said softly, his breath warming her cheek.

She knew she was blushing. She knew he was aware of her discomfort when his smile slowly widened.

"Very fresh," he murmured, "as Alfie would say."

"You know," Nicole began brightly, randomly, "in America 'fresh' means rude. What I think people mean here when they say 'cheeky.'"

Carlo chuckled, pushing away from the wall. "We'd better start for home if I'm to have you back to Chelsea before dark."

Nicole glanced up at the rosy sky and gasped. "They're going to kill me."

"Even Borcheff wouldn't kill off real talent."

"You really think I'm talented?" she asked slowly, her eyes searching his.

"We were flying together less than three hours ago. I haven't forgotten."

Nicole wasn't really surprised that Carlo had felt the same exhilaration as she, but a personal protective wall crumbled at his confession.

"Dancing with you was like being onstage," she said in a nervous generous rush. "You know, where you're so aware of every little gesture, every bit of meaning, that ten seconds stretch to ten minutes in your mind. Then you come to the end and it's all happened so fast and so completely and you come back to yourself changed."

"You like risks, don't you?"

"Why put yourself on stage otherwise?"

"A lot of people perform to perfect their masks."

'I guess I dance to uncover myself." And so do you, she thought to herself, but couldn't quite say it to him. There was an intense privacy about his dancing he had not invited her to broach. She felt herself blush again, realizing the double meaning of her words.

Glancing up at the fading sunset, she said hurriedly, "If I don't get home—"

"Come on. I know a couple of shortcuts."

They raced through the darkening streets, down cluttered, diagonal alleys and unwalled gardens. In a park not far from the Borcheff home, Carlo lifted her into a perfect arabesque without missing a step. Laughing joyously, they leaped and whirled across the grass, finding again the freedom of the air. They danced all the way to her doorstep, ignoring both encouraging nods and studied frowns from passersby.

Nicole tried to catch her breath in happy gasps.

"That was great!" she cried with a wide grin.

She was smiling at him so sweetly, with a question in those big brown eyes her mind didn't know the words for. But her body did, and so did his. He bent and gave her as gentle a kiss as he knew how. She tasted like honey and sun-sweetened hay, and it was all he could do to leave.

Nicole touched her lips wonderingly as she watched him disappear into the dusk. Her first kiss, and it was over almost before it had begun. But it was something she could treasure and hug to herself during the cold dinner about to come. Something warm to hold amid all the tattered dreams.

 7

Inside the house the air was hot and damp. Margaret must have been baking all day again, thought Nicole with a resigned sigh. All that work, and voilà. A whole week's worth of dry crusted loaves, as tasteless as the inside of an empty rosin box.

Nicole's recently revived tastebuds prompted her to remember with longing the fresh baked baguettes her mother picked up from a tiny French bakery in New York City whenever the company was in the chips. Crust that gave the teeth a real challenge. The snowy interior . . . fluffy as clouds with a delightful sour tang. And instead of Margaret's snip of a satisfied face, there would be the continental kiss on the hand from the dapper baker.

There was nothing satisfied about Margaret's face at the moment, however, Nicole thought with alarm, as the older woman bore down on her like a gardener on the prowl for cabbage snails.

"Nicole, where have you been? Your father and I have

been worrying for quite two hours now. This sort of lateness simply won't do."

On cue, the man himself in his very English tweeds appeared in the entry. His eyes looked flat as ice.

"Your mother, I assume, lets you run around like wild Indian, but that will not do here. Punctuality is important part of self-discipline. Something you would do well to learn. In future, if you find yourself unavoidably detained, please send word so others are not inconvenienced."

Whenever he started one of his lectures, he was the biggest boor Nicole had ever come across. Why didn't he just roar at her and get it over with? All this tsk-tsking . . . It was like being scolded by a pair of Alice's White Rabbits.

"Sorry I'm late. Looks like I beat Mom home anyway."

"We haven't heard a word from her either," said Margaret with a sniff.

Her face spoke volumes about inconsiderate guests and irresponsible parents who set poor examples for their children. At least she wouldn't have to hear about it, Nicole thought. That was one good thing about all this British reserve nonsense. But she had reckoned without the special resourcefulness of a rector's daughter.

"I'm afraid we'll have to go to table without her," said Margaret with unmistakable satisfaction. "I've reheated supper twice, and it will lose its flavor if I have to return it to the oven again."

"Perhaps a meal of bread and water will teach the woman a well-needed lesson," Vanya seconded.

"I'm sure she'll be home any second. Look," Nicole reminded, shooting her father an appealing look, "it was her first day of rehearsals, and you know how that is."

"Rehearsals at my studio begin and end on schedule. We don't encourage self-indulgence."

"Right. I've noticed that."

"We'll leave a plate at table for your mother just in case," Margaret said cheerily.

"Darling, your Sally is utterly perfect," Alexandra said, hugging Jillian Edgemont, the muscular athletic young woman dancing the lead in *Hands Across the Waves*. "I give you single suggestion. After you leap up to catch baseball, move both your hands back to show force of the ball hitting."

The huge damp studio where Alexandra had been choreographing her new dance was lit only by a pair of sconce lamps. Long shadows cast by the dancers leaped up the walls. Two stories above they melted into the night dark that smudged the studio ceiling.

"And I'll jerk my head in unison," suggested Tony, the slender man whose elegant style had made him perfect for the role of the English suitor.

"Exactly! Be sure to make grimace. She's being so indecorous."

"Jolly good."

It was sheer heaven, Alexandra thought, making dances with this company. They were trained, talented, and openminded, a breathtaking combination. For nine hours they had leaped and climbed up on each other's ideas, sweating to make them work. Shaping, fine-tuning, discarding, recasting. And creativity was still pouring from them all.

"Make your throw back to the catcher very athletic, Jillian. Remember, you are all-American kid sister of famous baseball player and you know how to throw a ball."

"But actually I'm British and I haven't the foggiest notion of how to do it," said the big girl in a sweat-stained leotard, smiling.

Alexandra imitated a pitcher leaning and squinting at his target, going into a windup and delivering the ball. The company broke into good-natured laughter.

"You're mad, every one of you," came the husky voice of Dame Harriet.

Her tiny body effortlessly dominated the room.

"It's the middle of the night and you're recklessly spending both my electricity and the patience of your families."

She walked up to Alexandra, making shooing motions with her hands.

"Go home, go home. Tomorrow is another—"

Alexandra interrupted her mentor by throwing her arms

around the graying woman and giving her an exuberant bear hug.

"You have given me everything I ever dreamed of. Thank you, darling Harry."

Dame Harriet stepped back and patted the cheek of the Russian who towered over her. "Only you, Shura, will ever call me that! Now send these fading dancers home before they drop. And you too."

Alexandra floated home on clouds of purest wish fulfillment. Details of exquisite choreography mingled in her mind with future fame and personal accomplishments. On the top step outside her husband's home, she let her cape swirl out around her as she pirouetted and blew a kiss to the full moon. She entered the dining room, and her luminous smile felt like cool fresh water to poor parched Nicole, who was trying unsuccessfully to make an inroad in a withered baked apple.

"Mom!" she cried, leaping up. "How did it go?"

"Better than I ever dreamed! Harriet is marvelous, the dancers are so exciting they take my breath away, and we are going to make a masterpiece."

Alexandra swooped down next to her highly annoyed husband and put a confiding hand on his sleeve.

"You remember *Les Sauvages*, Vanushka? That wonderful piece Baschenko was always threatening to make whenever you and I started fighting? Of course, he was going to use French woman and Russian man, for us."

Despite himself, Vanya smiled, remembering the vivid flavor of their old bouts offstage and on.

"Since he never made it, since larceny is sincerest form of flattery, I'm going to do it with English lord and American heiress. And," she added mischievously, sending Vanya a slanted provocative glance, "the conflict mostly comes from two families instead of two lovers, since apache dancing is not going to work on British stage."

He laughed out loud, a booming Russian laugh that startled Nick and Margaret and drew a grin from Nicole.

"Apache. Yes. That was us, Shura. And they loved it, didn't they?"

"I'm sure they did," cut in Margaret. "My parents' generation considered the Ballet Romanoff the peak of the season." Into the silence she added, "I really must ask you to return home by six o'clock, Madame Varonne, if you wish to join us for dinner. Van and I believe that an orderly home produces secure children. I'm sure you will agree."

Nothing could quell Alexandra's ebullience for long. From her peak of joy she could even feel a flash of sympathy for the dowdy woman whose whole life was bound up in a man still married to another.

"Darling Peggy, I am truly sorry for upsetting your routine. We artists get so carried away sometimes. I will go into kitchen and make omelet aux herbes fines. In five minutes I will be back, all the work done and order restored."

Nicole followed her mother like a child chases a beam of sunshine after a rainy day.

"You'd better take off that cape," she suggested. "This kitchen's so small, you'll knock over Margaret's teacups the first time you turn around."

"We can't have that, can we?" her mother said, draping her cloak over the edge of an open cupboard door. "The least we can leave her is her teacups."

Mother and daughter then fell into the old, familiar routine of cooking a simple delicious dinner, perfected over many happy years on the road.

~~~ 8

When Alexandra and Nicole woke the next morning, the sky was the same dull gray it had been since they'd arrived in London. But Alexandra exclaimed about the delicate pearl light a winter morning casts, and Nicole chimed in about the soft delights of living in a cloud. It was almost like being back in America, Nicole thought. Where it had always seemed natural to give thanks for every morning.

While they dressed, Alexandra warbled about plans for her rehearsal, but Nicole hugged her good news to herself. For the first time she could remember, she didn't want to confide in her mother. Carlo Domenici was too private an excitement. Too fragile and wonderful a possibility to tell anyone else about.

How he danced. Like he owned the whole earth. Like nothing could frighten him. Nothing could stop him. And yet he was gentle too. When he had kissed her . . . She shivered, the memory so vivid she could feel the feather brush of his warm lips. He had kissed her as though she were the princess in *The Nutcracker*. Half child, half woman. Lost in dreams.

"You are praying, my sunbeam?" came Alexandra's a-mused question.

Nicole found herself standing half dressed at the window, her hands clasped at her breast.

"Just daydreaming, Mom. We better get cracking, huh?"

"Don't leave your dreams too quickly, darling. They'll make wonderful dances someday."

Nicole put her arms around her mother. "I love you, Mom."

"Sweet rosebud."

When she got to the school, Carlo was nowhere to be found. Not in the halls. Not in or out of the men's dressing room, though Nicole managed to hang around the door for several minutes. She even peeked into her father's office, but it was empty. The happy nervous tumult in her stomach subsided as she sauntered over to the barre for her morning class with Demsby-Worth. Maybe Carlo was already there. For the first time she was looking forward to a class at the British Court Ballet.

Her mind drifted to the two dancers she respected. Mom had promised her that practice did lead to that unique transcendance. And Carlo had demonstrated it, filling British Court's stodgy ballet with emotion and life. Perhaps there was room for her in this dance form after all, Nicole thought. She lifted her leg into a developpe, imagining a slow wind lifting a wave. Her arm swayed gently and accentuated the circling of her leg.

"Arm steady, please, Miss Varonne," corrected the teacher.

"I'm moving my arm so it will dramatize the developpe," she explained.

"Drama is the antithesis of classical grace. Purity of line is the focus here."

It was about time someone challenged this crap, Nicole thought.

"You know, even the Greeks had passion. Carloads of it, as a matter of fact. Where does it say in the ballet manual that you can't have feeling when you dance?"

There was a stifled gasp from the rest of the class. Demsby-Worth gave Nicole an infuriatingly patronizing smile.

"You really are an absurd little twit, aren't you? At fourteen you have decided that four hundred years of tradition can fly out the window if it doesn't strike your fancy. Where would we be if everyone decided to do just as they pleased, with no regard for our responsibility to the past? Imagine that, if you will. It would be chaos, utter chaos. Well. Enough said on that score, yes?"

There was no point arguing with him, Nicole realized. He thought that self-expression would make the sky cave in. I'll put him in a dance someday, she promised herself, and the world will see just how stupid he is. She continued her personal exploration of ballet gesture and ignored the teacher's comments. Carlo's voice was all she heard inside of her.

The rest of the day went by. And the next one after that. Carlo never appeared. Worry, continual anticipation, and excitement swept over Nicole in waves. She was grateful when Wednesday came. He'd have to be in partnering class.

Finally she could stop rehearsing her greeting and imagining his answer. Finally they would fly together again.

When she entered the room, a quick glance told her that again he was missing. She wanted to shriek with frustration. Instead she turned to Nikki.

"Do you know where Carlo Domenici is?"

"I dare say he's throwing himself about in an alley somewhere."

"What?!"

"Suspended. He's gone and gotten himself suspended for the week."

There was a smug edge to Nick's casual explanation, which made Nicole want to slug him, but she was too worried to get into a fight.

"But . . . but why? How?"

"Insubordination. Talking back to the teachers and all. They can't have it, really. So he's out for a bit. Cool his temper. Examine his behavior. Waste of time as far as I can see. But there it is. Not the first time."

"And . . . and the alley. What did you mean by that?"

"Well, a week without practice dulls the technique. And you know Domenici. An extremist of the worst sort. It's gotten about that when he's suspended, he still dances. Alleys, vacant lots, whatever. Amusing, really."

Nicole repressed a shudder. "Thanks," she said absently.

She could feel gloom closing in on her like fog shrouding the Thames. She moved through the set of barre exercises automatically, arms and legs going through their paces like little tin soldiers moved around by someone else. She only noticed one thing about the boy she was paired with for partnering. He wasn't Carlo. Lifelessly, she allowed him to pick her up and put her down as they copied the combinations done by the couple in front of them. Her senses had retreated deep inside where nothing else could hurt her. Life was gray.

Maître Andreyev favored her with an approving smile.

"You are coming along famously, Miss Varonne. Today for the first time I could see the accomplished ballerina that waits inside of you. Let us see more of her in the days to come."

Amazing, Nicole thought, giving the teacher an unbelieving frown. Maybe if I get suicidal, he'll make me a star.

Although next Monday's arrival didn't seem possible, Nicole knew the day of her reunion with Carlo would dawn. Partnering class didn't meet until two in the afternoon. She was on pins and needles by lunch, peeking around every corner, hoping that Carlo's lean intense face would appear and break into a grin at the sight of her. Or maybe he wouldn't even remember her. "Nancy, was it? Or Nanette? The little American, right?" No. No. He had to remember. As Nicole had remembered and relived every glance, every word of that short afternoon. Oh, where was he?

Her heart pounding, Nicole finally entered the classroom and spotted him instantly. God. He was just as gorgeous and dangerous and exciting as she remembered. More. This time he was doing soubresauts, leaps straight up from standing in fifth position. One of the hardest jumps to get any elevation on, but his were as high as most men's grand jetés. He stared into some middle distance, ignoring the sweat zigzagging down the sides of his face. And he kept leaping, fifteen, twenty, twenty-five times. Unbelievable. How could he keep it up? The class filed in, arranged itself along the barres, and still he jumped.

Was he going to miss the first plié? Would Andreyev throw him out again before class even started? Carlo finished number twenty-eight, shot Nicole a cheerful smile that sent a dart of excitement all the way through her, and wiped his brow. Andreyev tapped his stick for attention and the warm-up began.

Thank God the barre work was short. When the maître called the class to the center of the room, Nicole made a beeline for Carlo. Andreyev's voice halted her.

"Miss Varonne. I'd like to see you with Mr. Wilson this afternoon. Mr. Domenici, with Miss Avon."

Carlo met Nicole's indignant look with a light shrug. Well,

she told herself, there's nothing they can do to stop us after class.

In spite of her impatience to shed Wilson, who partnered her as if she had large rocks in her tights, Nicole was caught up in the adagio work. It had long slow gestures that Carlo made so sinuous and sexy, he made her feel all melted inside. Even from halfway across the room. She pretended she was inside his skin, moving as he moved. How beautiful he was. Every step he took came from deep within him. She left her arm out in the air that extra half second and added a stretch outward just as he did. Perfect.

She was so caught up in dancing her homage to him that the end of class caught her by surprise. She wandered out of the room in a gentle dazzle that stopped when she realized he wasn't with her. Damn. He was back in class, talking with Andreyev. Impatience suddenly filled her like a spout of carbonated bubbles. She danced from one foot to the other.

And there he was, his sable eyes on hers with a kind of warm gladness that made everything else disappear.

"Change, cara."

His voice was as thrilling as she remembered.

"I'll meet you at the door."

It was the fastest peel Nicole had ever done. They went out together into the frost-hardened streets, Nicole following Carlo without any thought of where she was going. All she knew was that he held her hand inside his coat pocket.

She kept thinking of opening lines and discarding them. Everything was too ordinary or too honest or too something. He must think I'm some kind of idiot, she thought, and shivered.

"You're cold."

"No . . . yeah, I guess I am. Must be below freezing out here."

Great, she thought. The first thing I say, and it's about the stupid weather.

His voice was a soft growl in her ear.

"I know a private place where we can get warm."

"You do? I mean sure."

She swallowed. What was she agreeing to? He looked very dangerous, dark and purposeful, with the glint of a private smile on his face. Was she going to end up in a sleazy hotel room? A back bedroom? A white slaver's den?

Probably not. He was taking her up the Strand to Fleet Street, up to a line of ancient-looking buildings. In the middle of London's bustle they were in a secluded square, surrounded by classical brick walls trimmed with ivory stone. It was very quiet.

"What is this?" she whispered.

"The Temple."

"A temple to what?"

"It's where barristers are trained. But it used to belong to the Knights Templars, seven or eight hundred years ago. The knights of God. They took oaths to defend the helpless and save the Holy Land. Powerful guys."

"You mean monks with swords? Isn't that kind of a contradiction?"

"Is it better to let savages overrun everything that's precious to you? If I'd been around in 1100, I might have joined up." His eyes danced. "Well, except for giving up women."

He brushed a damp tendril of golden hair out of her eyes. She shivered again.

"Let's go inside. The church is usually empty."

It was. Carlo led her to a pew and sat next to her, his arm around her shoulders. Hesitantly, Nicole leaned back against his chest, feeling as if she was sinking into something she'd never come out of again.

"They're all around us," she murmured shakily.

His heart beat against her shoulder blades and she breathed in his clean musk scent.

"I guess you don't have a row of sepulchers in American churches, hmm? Don't worry. They've seen just about everything in eight hundred years."

"E-Everything?"

"Well, you know I'm about to kiss you. I thought you might be nervous with all those stone faces watching."

"Don't . . . don't laugh at me," she said into his amused face. "It's just that . . ."

"You've never been kissed before, except once, a week ago, very lightly."

His finger traced little curlicues on her flushed cheek. Her lips tingled with anticipation.

"How did you know that?"

"Because you invite me closer and then turn away. Either you're a tease or an innocent. And you're much too straightforward to be a tease. I don't think there's a devious bone in your sweet little body."

"Carlo?"

"What?"

"Kiss me."

"Ahhh."

He smiled. Then he lowered his head to hers.

 **9**

They were soft kisses. Like a bee sipping honey from a flower. And they filled Nicole with warmth, down to the tips of her toes. His mouth lingered on hers, pressing deeper. Without thinking, Nicole wound her arms around Carlo's neck. Her fingers threaded through the black waves of his hair, finding the tender skin at the nape of his neck.

"Cara," he whispered.

Then they were winding against each other sinuous as snakes, mouth on mouth, straining closer and closer, as if to get inside each other's skins. Suddenly Nicole was dizzy. Shaking.

Carlo released her mouth, held her out from him to look into her glazed brown eyes, then tucked her against his chest like a child, one hand cupping her head. She could feel his heart pounding frantically. It slowed in tempo with her own breathing. Until she could think again.

"That was . . . dynamite. Are all kisses like that?"

"Not usually. Not quite so combustible."

"You've kissed a lot of girls?"

"I've had my share. Usually on forced vacations, like this last one."

"Do you really dance in alleys?"

"You've been listening to gossip."

"I missed you. I needed to know where you were."

He stretched his whole body, his dark-lidded eyes half closed.

"I was collecting my contribution to the restaurant. My mother gives away too much spaghetti," he explained, and laughed without humor. "They can tear Lady Bountiful out of her castle but they can't stop her from feeding every half-starved kid she sees. So the money runs out. Alfie and I do a little work on the black market, fence a few tiaras or signet rings, and Mama can make more pasta."

"You . . . steal things?"

"I probably would make a good cat burglar." He grinned. "Let's put it this way. Stolen goods pass through a chain. By the time I get my hands on something, it's probably been months since it was lifted in some other town. I buy it or trade for it, and when I sell it to the next guy, the profit is mine."

"But isn't that dangerous?"

"Living is dangerous. I like a little edge to my excitement. It's good for the dancing."

She couldn't tell from his face if he was kidding. It was true that he took risks when he danced. Even today with the adagio. He had made it so sensuous, so personal.

"Well, it didn't hurt your dancing any, that's for sure. Talk about combustible. I couldn't take my eyes off you today."

He frowned. "That was obvious. You were dancing like a sleepwalker. You're a fool to copy anyone else, Nicole."

She felt like he had slapped her.

"I just admired what you were doing," she said in a low voice. "Is that a crime?"

"It's worse than criminal to be someone else's mirror. Only an idiot ignores what's inside them," he answered in that cutting voice she was coming to dread.

"Well, excuse me for being bowled over by your work. Maybe I should concentrate on how 'vulgar' it is."

His face hardened. He took his arm away from her shoulders. "Seeing through Andreyev's eyes makes as little sense as seeing through mine. Maybe, if you're lucky, you'll grow up someday and see through your own."

She jumped to her feet. "You think you're the only person who knows anything, don't you? You're so arrogant it's unbelievable. Well, go judge someone else. I've had just about enough."

She marched out of the temple as decisively as she could. Pride kept her walking sturdily down the icy streets, but hurt blinded her to everything she passed. What a ridiculous boy, she thought, the lump in her throat swelling. And I thought we really had something. I thought we were so much alike. And then he just shoved me away. What a stinker. A real blue-ribbon stinker.

Nicole joined the Carlo watchers. She added nasty little jibes about his crude melodramatic dancing to the usual class comments that greeted his stupendous leaps and incomparable endurance. But there was no joy and little satisfaction in attaching herself to the crowd. Her only pleasure in the following weeks came at Swanleigh Hall.

Dame Harriet had welcomed Alexandra's daughter as a choreographic assistant. At first Nicole could see that Harry was amused watching a fourteen-year-old order around dancers twice her age. But the director's fun gave way to careful observation when several of Nicole's suggestions found their way into the dance.

One late afternoon Nicole created a short dream sequence on the dark side of the stage that paralleled the lead male and female's sprightly proposal and acceptance. The movements suggested the inevitable and perhaps even dangerous attraction of opposites that lay at the heart of their relationship. Dame Harriet intercepted Alexandra and Nicole as they were about to leave the studio.

"I envy you your daughter, Shura," said the older woman, taking Nicole's chin in her hand and studying the girl's face intently. "The talent runs true, doesn't it?"

"For generations, my dear. My mother danced cancan in Paris until she found she was carrying me."

"I haven't seen this one dance, but I'll wager that choreography will be at the center of her art. At fourteen she shows more psychological insight than most dancers ever attain. And a very real flair for the dramatic."

She patted Nicole's cheek with her heavily ringed hand.

"You're in for a good deal of suffering, my child. And exaltation. I envy you."

"Harry," interrupted Alexandra, shaking her head. "Put crystal ball back in the closet. This is an uncomplicated American innocent, very direct, very simple. In the new world they don't have to pay for insight with pain."

"The mother's the last to know, isn't she? Very well. But you're always welcome at my door, Nicole, with problems, digestible or not. At worst, I'll commiserate."

Nicole kissed Dame Harriet's wrinkled cheek.

"Thanks. This is the only good thing that's happened to me since I got to London. Maybe I'll camp out here if my father gets any more impossible."

The two older women exchanged little smiles. Impossible was only one of the adjectives they could have used about Vanya Borcheff if his daughter hadn't been standing beside them.

Maître Andreyev surveyed his partnering class.

"Miss Varonne with Mr. Domenici."

Nicole was startled. For two weeks the frosty Russian had carefully avoided pairing her with Carlo. Well, she told herself, he's not blind. Carlo and she hadn't been exactly falling over each other after class. In fact, she had deliberately left each session with other dancers. And Carlo hadn't given any sign that he cared one way or the other.

Good riddance, she thought. She needed Mr. Know-It-All like a hole in the head. But when Carlo's lean arms circled her waist for the first combination, Nicole felt herself tremble.

Okay, Varonne. He's just another boy. And an obnoxious one at that. Let's not get hot under the collar.

It worked for about three leaps. Three soaring, yearning leaps. On the fourth, she had to go with him.

I belong in these arms, Nicole told herself with amazement, giving herself over to the magic they seemed to create between them. The communication flowed, wordless and perfect, as if they had never been apart. His lines extended and finished hers. Her weightlessness underscored his. They spoke in unison . . . of freedom.

Andreyev's irritation passed over them unnoticed. Even when he made the unprecedented move of changing the partnerships in the middle of class, it made no difference. Soon enough the class was finished and Nicole walked out with Carlo into the weak winter sunlight. They clasped hands tightly in the patched pocket of his greatcoat.

"Dancing with you was even better than I remembered," he said, his voice husky.

"It's like we've known each other since birth or something."

She looked up at him as if for the first time as he studied her wondering face.

"I won't let you get away so easily the next time."

"You're already planning our next fight?"

Carlo laughed, saying, "I don't imagine that'll be our last one. Do you?"

She remembered how much he had hurt her.

"You know, a little tact would really make it easier to listen to your, uh . . . advice."

"Tact's a waste of time. If something is true, why hide it in evasion?"

"Because people don't listen to you if they're insulted."

"Then they're not worth bothering with."

"Yup. That sure isn't going to be our last fight."

"We'll fight, cara, and we'll make up. You have my word on it."

He brushed her lips with his. She had to try the words twice before her mouth would obey her.

"I . . . I was wondering. Would you like to see Mom's dance? We open this Saturday night, and I can get you a ticket."

"We?"

"I'm her assistant."

"I'd come for that alone. God. A chance to see a legend. And you collaborated. Of course I'll come. Thanks for asking me."

"You know where it is?"

"The dance world's a small place, cara. The buzzing's been going on for weeks. Camargo will be there in force, and Ballet Russe, and whoever else they can fit in that tiny place. Madame Alexandra's going to have quite an audience."

"They're going to have quite a night. Just you wait and see what we wild Americans have cooked up for you."

The icy rain, threatening to turn to sleet, could not dampen the electric excitement of the crowd that milled in Dame Harriet's tiny theater foyer. They filed into their seats until every mauve velvet chair was claimed, and still more choreographers, dancers, patrons, and aficionados filled any available spot at the back and in the aisles of the room.

The cream of the dance world had come to see Alexandra Varonne's creation. She had been the ballerina everyone aspired to become or create for. Could she choreograph? Even more interestingly, what would she choreograph? There had been rumors of near-naked savagery, of archaic idealized poses with veils and bells, of almost everything. But no one outside of Swanleigh Hall knew, and Dame Harriet had done a thorough job of sealing lips.

"Darling, is that a seat I see before me?" came a theatrical voice, high and sweet.

Vanya stood and bowed over the hand of Alcina Martinova, the doll-like prima ballerina who had starred in every major ballet company in England, including British Court, and the continent.

"Please, be my guest," he offered. "Margaret is suffering from a migraine and had to bow out."

"I'm so sorry to have missed her," Martinova fluted, seating herself next to Nikki. "But how delightful to share this evening with both Borcheff men. Do my eyes deceive me or is that the young tiger Domenici I've heard so much about?"

Carlo stopped running his finger around the tight collar of his old and only dress shirt and gave the tiny graceful hand of the ballerina a single shake.

"I'm here compliments of the assistant choreographer."

At Martinova's puzzled frown, Vanya explained, "My daughter Nicole has been working with Alexandra on the piece. She's backstage with her mother."

"Rather young for collaboration, wouldn't you say?"

"The custom in America, or so Alexandra tried to tell me."

"Yes, we're all so very eager to see the 'Americanization' of Alexandra, darling."

She had a laugh like tiny bells.

Carlo leaned over and gave Nikki's shoulder a light punch. "Wake up, chum. Didn't know your mum was so famous, did you?"

Nikki's dazed eyes swept over the glittering assemblage. "I never did," he murmured.

Nikki had been to plenty of opening nights. But none with the anticipation he felt in this inadequate little theater. The crowd was indecently eager for the spectacle his mother had made for them. Unwillingly, he felt the hunger stir in himself. It disgusted him, making him feel like any common laborer excited by a traveling carnival.

Dance should never lower itself to the level of the masses; that's what he'd been taught and truly believed. Dance was elevating. It separated one from crude emotions, from animal instincts, from vulgarity. From the selfishness that allowed a mother to desert her own child. How could an exquisite dancer like Alcina Martinova admire such coarseness? He watched the prima, kissing her fingertips to the stage.

"Fifteen years ago," said Martinova, "your mother deigned to compliment me on the lightness of my piques, and I lived in a dream world for months. She was incomparable . . . But look, the lights are dimming. I believe we are about to begin."

Nicole's stomach filled with vibrating wings. How could Mom stay so calm? The curtain was going up and there was the applause and she had never felt so nervous in her life. It seemed as if all the famous dance names she'd ever heard had suddenly acquired bodies. And particularly eyes. Judging, discriminating, knowing eyes.

Had Mom and she gone too far? Using two sides of the stage for two different dances. One side motionless in the shadows while the other moved in the light. Making fun of both Americans and Englishmen. Was the satire too biting? Would it offend these proper British?

The story was certainly loving. A young Englishman on vacation in New York falls hard for an American girl. He courts and wins her. Each family adjusts to the news. Everyone meets in London for the wedding.

Nicole believed that the fun Alexandra poked at the excesses of both cultures was loving too. Yes, the audience had started to laugh now. Of course. It was the girl's come-hither dance. Brash. Flirtation laid on with a trowel. What about the boy's namby-pamby response? If they went for that, maybe Nicole could let go of the edges of the stool she was gripping back in the wings.

There he was, not knowing what to do with this attractive young thing, fending her off oh-so-reluctantly, and the audience was laughing again. Thank God. It was going to be okay. Now she could concentrate on the dancing.

Vanya was entranced. Like everyone in the audience, he was amused by the shrewd cultural contrasts and moved by the sheer beauty of the evocative pas de deux. But this piece of wonderful theater was created by his own wife, and it seemed to say much to him about their effervescent, early life together. Young love. Flying in the face of all caution, all reason. The magnetic attraction sweeping all else before it, inventing itself moment after moment, irresistible.

So good it had been with her. So alive. She made him win her every time they came together, and it kept him alert as a stalking tiger. Every sense alive. As the hunt hones the predator, Alexandra made colors bright for him, made every taste vivid. And he had lost her. Lost her forever. Had there ever been a time, a way back . . . No. There it was on the stage. The man proposing properly in the light. And in the shadow, the danger of their differences. The very differences that attracted them to each other. The dance a warning.

There was scattered applause from the people around him at this sensitive undershadowing. Vanya could not join them. Though the artist in him appreciated the choreographic insight, the husband in him winced at its accuracy.

Shura, my Shura. Will you never stop pulling at me with your double-edged promises? So beautiful is this dance. And you. You.

He gave himself over to his wife's vision, agonized with the lovers, worried with the parents, and finally celebrated the making of the marriage, the union of hands across the waves. As the curtain closed, Vanya was the first member of the audience to leap up and applaud wildly. His lame leg throbbed. It was as though he had been dancing with Alexandra for the entire performance.

With all his heart he cried, "Bravo!"

The stars of the dance world echoed him. *Hands Across the Waves* was a brilliant success. It was several curtain calls before the choreographer herself with Nicole at her side bowed to the audience. The beaming girl gave her mother an exuberant hug which met with a swell of chuckles. It was what they all wanted to do, Vanya most of all.

Carlo leaned toward him. "How in hell could you have let a talent like that get away from you?" he hissed.

Vanya jerked upright. "What would a seventeen-year-old boy know about it?" he snarled.

Carlo snorted and turned away.

I never let her get away, Vanya realized smugly. I never divorced her. Now it was clear why he'd neglected to sign the papers she'd sent him. Thank God, in her careless way she'd let him hold on to at least their legal connection. So that he still had a hold on her. A hold it was time to exploit.

Backstage, all was happy pandemonium. Vanya, with Nikki behind him, worked his way past all the congratulations, the choruses of amazement, the welcomes and the toasts. Finally he found Alexandra, in the formidable embrace of Dame Harriet.

"Shura," he cried, grabbing her away and into a bear hug. "Is wonderful. Spectacular. You take away my breath."

She freed herself except for her hands. Her husband held those so tightly her fingers were turning numb.

"Finally you admit. I learn something in America. All this 'undisciplined' wandering adds up to something, yes?"

"Yes! I give you a thousand yesses to put in your pocket, if only you come make dances for British Court. Work with me again."

Nikki gasped. Had Pater gone mad? Allow this . . . painted, tasteless clown onto the classical ballet stage of British Court? Dear God, he'd have to see her day and night. She'd make a mockery of everything he loved. Chaos. She'd make chaos.

His mother finally reclaimed her hands.

"I have had three other offers, and is only halfway through evening," she teased, her dark eyes laughing at him. "What will you give me?"

"Anything," he pleaded. "Complete artistic freedom, big percentage of the gate . . . You know my dancers are best trained in London."

"And least imaginative, so I've heard."

"So they need you. I need you. Shura, come back to me."

"Pater," Nikki barked. "It's—it's very late, and Peggy . . . Peggy will be wondering where—"

"Hush, Nikki. Is your future I arrange too."

But his son's words brought Peggy's horrified face to Vanya's mind. How in God's name was he going to break the news to her that Alexandra was joining British Court? Because Alexandra was going to do it. Her dazzling smile told him that.

"Is great irony, no?" she said. "Fifteen years ago, if you could have let me do this, we would still be together. And now, my darling, is much too late for any of that. But still we can have something. We will make art together. Okay, as the Americans say. I am yours."

She kissed him on both cheeks, whirled, and disappeared back into the sea of celebration.

In the cab going home, Nikki shivered. His father threw an arm around him and drew him close. It was an unusual gesture, startling and disturbing the boy.

"Pater?" he ventured.

"We'll be home in minutes. A cuppa will warm you up."

"It's difficult to imagine, uh . . . Mother working with us."

It was the first time he'd called her that, but how else could he name her to his father, her husband?

Vanya shot his son a shrewd glance.

"She is a bit overwhelming, yes?"

"Overwhelming?" Nikki's words tumbled out like rocks from a smashed retaining wall. "She's impossible. The most arrogant, pushy, vulgar—"

"My son," said Vanya, "you disappoint me."

Nikki gulped back the rest of his complaints. "Sorry," he muttered.

"I had hoped Piggy and I had taught you better. Where is your Christian charity, your tolerance and forbearance for others?"

"Well I . . . yes, of course, Pater. But—"

Vanya's rich voice rolled on, stifling his son's emotions with the ease of long practice.

"Civilized man may choose his neighbors carefully, but that is not to say he can dictate where they must live. You understand, Nikolai?"

Nikki hung his head while Vanya pressed on.

"She'll be good for the company. You can trust my instincts on this."

"If you say so, Pater."

~~ 10

Vanya was grateful that Margaret was all tucked up in bed, fast asleep, when he and Nikki returned. Maybe by morning an explanation as irresistible as Alexandra's smile would occur to him. He slid under the quilt as imperceptibly as he could. Piggy would agree that he had no choice because . . . because . . .

"Van?"

He started guiltily. "I woke you. I'm sorry."

"No. I'm sorry." Her voice was fuzzy with sleep. "I was waiting up for you and I must've dozed off." She reached over and turned on the light. "Sorry," she repeated more firmly. "I know how important this performance was to you."

He cleared his throat. "Yes. Was very important."

"Well?"

"Hmm?"

"Tell me about it. Was it . . . acceptable?"

"Was brilliant. Was very good. In fact—"

"I'm so glad, my dear. Glad for all of us."

Margaret looked as animated as he ever remembered seeing her.

"We'll help her find a flat. I spoke to my friend Gwennie just the other day, just on the chance, you know, that all this might work out. Pimlico's a good bet. Such a nice working-class neighborhood. Or maybe the South Bank, where it's cheaper. Or—"

"This is all premature, Margaret," he began . . . because he had no other choice. "Shura has no money yet. For tonight she gets four or five pounds. No more."

"But surely she'll have offers now. That's the point, isn't it?"

"One dance probably won't be enough," he lied. "I've decided to showcase her at British Court."

Vanya watched his mistress out of the corner of his eye. Her face paled to the color of the sheets. He plunged on.

"On the same basis, of course. A flat fee. If she has another success, maybe someone will hire her as a company choreographer. That will be decent money. If she's good enough, who knows? I might hire her myself."

The laugh with which he intended to ridicule the idea sounded hollow. She was staring at him as if she'd never seen him before.

"Piggy, please understand. You can't want me to throw my daughter out on the streets before her mother has enough money to take care of her."

"Your daughter," Margaret began in a low voice. "You certainly managed to forget about her for fourteen years, didn't you?"

"Is not true. I didn't speak of her because . . . it hurts me. Inside, is like torture, knowing there is this part of me so far away, and I can't see her, can't touch her. And now, Piggy, for first time, I have chance to be father to my daughter. Now I can make a difference in her life. And she in mine."

"It's deep fatherly affection, is it? Fourteen years ago you turned your back on her, and now she's only here because her mother dragged her along." Margaret's lips thinned as she fixed him with a cool stare. "You've never lied very well, Van. You hired Alexandra because you're falling back in love with her."

His mouth fell open. The silence stretched on too long.

"Piggy, Piggy, how can you tell me this thing? How can you think . . . after all our years together . . . Is not so. No. I love only you, and she is . . . she . . ."

His face twisted in anguish. How could he still love Shura, after all their terrible battles? It was Piggy he loved. Piggy only. Wasn't it? He covered his face with his hands, trying to hide from the vision of glorious, triumphant Alexandra that night. Bowing to the audience. Throwing her admirers kisses from cupped elegant palms. That red-lipped smile he longed to have pressed to his mouth.

Vanya moaned aloud. Tears welled from his eyes.

"Help me, my dear one. You are right. Always right. She is like siren, calling to me. Even when we hated each other, when we parted, I was never sure . . . It was torture being alone, not knowing if I had done right, and then I found you. So steady, so clear, so rational. You were a cool stream, breath of air for me. You healed me, my darling. You gave me everything I dreamed of. A home. A family. With you, I found what I was after." Tears streamed down his face. "Help me now, Piggy my love. She is danger for me. She could take away everything, everything I love."

"Oh, Van, Van," Margaret cried, taking him in her strong pale arms. "Of course I'll help. My poor poor dear. You know how much I love you. My darling."

She rocked him and dried his tears, her own eyes wet. It was a long time before they slept.

"Tut, tut," expostulated Nicole, climbing up the pedestal and squeezing herself between a pair of statues that were exchanging a stony kiss. "In England such a brazen display of affection simply will not do."

She pretended to push them apart. Below, on the winter-browned grass, Carlo laughed.

"Even in privacy, one must maintain decorum, yes?"

"God," Nicole said, jumping down next to him, "don't they even have passion in their houses? I mean, just think of my father and Margaret."

She sat down on the park bench and Carlo joined her.

"I'd rather not."

"No, I mean, really. She's so cold and proper and picky about everything. I can't even imagine them kissing, let alone . . ."

"Well, there's no real proof of it. No children. Maybe they read Dickens to each other in bed. There's a lot of Dickens."

"Don't I know it! That novel they assigned us must be

nine hundred pages long. How do they expect us to dance and read encyclopedias at the same time?"

"You didn't do much reading on the road?"

"Well, at least I didn't have to sit in a classroom between rehearsals and memorize the names of popes and kings."

"What did you do between belly dances?"

Nicole gave him a friendly poke. "Oh, you know. Tutors. Mom kept hiring them, and they'd last for a season or two. I guess we traveled too much for them. So I ended up with a stack of textbooks . . ."

"That you never opened . . ."

"Actually, I ended up reading them on trains. And when we'd pass some famous site, Mom'd stop the troupe and we'd all learn some history or geology or whatever."

"So that's why Ancient History One at British Court bores you. No trains."

"Bingo."

She fell into a mock-tragic pose, the back of one hand pressed to her forehead. "Without those clacking wheels, my mind turns to oatmeal."

"Crazy kid," Carlo said, pulling her to rest against his arm on the back of the bench. "Why do I spend so much time with you?"

She rubbed her head against his neck happily. "I dunno, but don't stop."

He kissed her ear. "I wasn't planning to."

"Now Mom and my father, they're easy to imagine making children. Especially the way he was before."

"What?" His breath was warm on her ear. "Oh, I see. I kiss you and we're back to sex among the English."

"Well, can't you just see them? Wild artistes. Creativity oozing from their fingertips. The perfect match onstage and off. Wow!"

"Vanya Borcheff the wild genius? Now that's hard to imagine."

"He was a holy terror. That's what Mom says. A perfectionist with tantrums you wouldn't believe. You know. An artist."

"My father is domineering too, but always with charm. And the best of intentions. After all, il padrone only has the best interests of his people at heart."

"You make him sound like a king or something."

"Our family owned the same estate for ten generations. Stefano Domenici knew every one of his peasants intimately. Births, weddings, funerals—he was there. Half the time he paid for the party. They came to him when the grapes wouldn't ripen or the daughters ripened too fast. A little kingdom, far from the cities, but we were happy there."

His voice had gotten very low, his black eyes misted. Nicole felt his homesickness take hold of him.

"Tell me about your mom," she demanded quickly. "Does she let your dad run her too?"

He chuckled. "Sure. But he can't do without her. She's the one who brings grace to his court. My mother was born a great lady. To see her brought to the level of a café hostess . . ."

He was shaking his head as if at an errant child. Amazing, thought Nicole, how cooly he described his own parents.

"The way you sum them up, it's as if you're the parent and they're the children. Domenici, has anyone ever accused you of being a little arrogant?"

"You think I'm arrogant now? You should have seen me . . . There's a family story my parents love to tell about four-year-old 'Prince' Carlo Raimondo. It seems my father's overseer, Fabiano, was having a big argument with him over some new strain of grapes. I wandered past the salon and overheard what must have been the height of the battle. Clearly it offended my aristocratic sensibilities, because I stormed in and demanded that Fabiano not simply apologize, but get on his knees before my father to show his loyal subservience. The fellow was so startled that he actually removed his sweaty cap and bowed his head before my father stopped him."

"Me too. Me too," Nicole chimed in. "Mom called me 'Tiny Highness' when I was a kid. I used to order her dancers around something fierce."

He chuckled again. "Two bullies who found each other. One good thing about trying to run the world—you get what you want more than most people."

"And they don't even mind. Most of the time," she added, cuddling closer. "Most people want to be directed. Now the question is, who is going to rule this roost, you or me?"

He sat up and offered his hand. "Arm wrestle you for the title?"

"Oh, pooh. Mere brute strength doesn't prove anything. Now if you could catch me . . ."

She leaped to her feet and began racing across the park, throwing arch looks back at her companion. He was faster than she was, but she had a good head start. The crisp tawny grass hissed under her boots, and gulps of icy air invigorated her. Very soon she led him back to the statue. They circled it only twice before she found her legs surprisingly weak. Carlo was coming closer and she didn't speed up. He caught her in his arms and held on tight, laughing.

"Since I won, you have to obey me. Anything I want. Isn't that right?"

Her heart was beating much faster than she would have expected from such a short run.

"Um, right," she hazarded.

"Then kiss me, woman, and don't stop."

She shivered and raised her mouth to his. He swooped down on it like a hawk claiming its prey, and Nicole forgot to think for a long time. When she could think again, all that she found in her mind was desire for another kiss. Carlo was glad to oblige.

"Non, non, mes enfants," Alexandra called to the pair of British Court dancers she was rehearsing for her first piece with Vanya's company. "Is not what I want. Enid, you must move like snake down Avery's body."

How many times had they done the lift? Fourteen? Twenty? Each time, timing perfect. Placement perfect. Feeling, nyet. Blank. Had neither of these little chicks ever made love? Alexandra asked herself despairingly. Felt hunger?

PIROUETTE

Seen Valentino or Theda Bara? What must I do to awaken them?

Coming out of his office, Vanya heard his wife's frustrated voice and decided to make another short visit to her rehearsal.

"Vanushka, darling," she exclaimed. "You've come at just the moment when I need you. We've been working for hours and it's no better. You will know what I want. Come. We show them."

She took him by the hand and led him to the center of the room. As she spoke, she demonstrated the movements.

"So. A young man and woman. Very interested in each other. But so different. She is like ice goddess, and he must conquer. He is like lion, all passion and fire. He has pursued her and caught her. He lifts this icicle into the air. She is rigid. Pillar of no feeling. But then, his heat reaches her. She begins to melt. Onto him. Down his body. Undulating like snake, like swan. He has won."

A raft of warning bells went off in Vanya's head, but before he could find a reasonable excuse to leave, Alexandra was dragging him to her, setting herself to leap into his arms, and his body automatically moved into partnering position.

"Regardez, mes enfants," she ordered Enid and Avery. "This is what I want."

She threw herself into Vanya's waiting arms. She was still so soft and strong. And resistant. The musk of her sweat-warmed body maddened him. He wanted to bury his face between her naked breasts, but she would not let him near her heart. He would make her yield to him everything he wanted. He poured his want and his power over her and felt the triumphant moment when she wavered. Yes. Yes. She was melting to him, giving herself completely, and he gloried in his victory.

He caught the eyes of the dancers. They were staring at him in utter shock. A sick wave of embarrassment washed over him, as if he'd been stripped naked before them. Sweet Christ. What had happened to him? History had taken over his body, and even more terribly, his soul. He shook with his

89

arousal and fear, looking into their young faces. Anywhere
but at Alexandra. Enid's face was pink. Avery's mouth open.
They must be as horrified as he . . .

A silken hand stroked his cheek.

"You see, my Vanushka? Some things never die."

He gasped, unable to offer any retort. But Alexandra had
already turned back to the issue at hand.

"Now, *mes enfants,* let me see your lift."

Of course, this time the young pair was far better.

"Merci, mon vieux," murmured Alexandra with a dazzling smile. "There is nothing like inspiration, yes?"

Vanya fled. Piggy, Piggy, he cried inwardly. Where are
you?

~~ 11

The one problem with the dress Nicole had picked for her
first official date with Carlo Domenici was its color. Vieux
Rose, it was called. Actually, she loved the dark misted pink
and it looked great on her. But nowhere in the entire
contents of Alexandra's trunk or her own was there anything
for her hair that would match. And her head looked like a
tumbleweed, compliments of the perpetual fog. Carlo would
be arriving any second. Maybe Nikki had something. He
was always wearing those little scarves around his neck. She
scurried down the hall.

His door was closed. No answer when she knocked. She
pushed the door open and dashed inside, stopping short.
Her twin's bedroom was a place unlike any she had ever
seen.

Every single object was lined up straight as a ruler. Little
stoppered jars of marbles, each jar filled with a different
color. Six cans of pomade. Tin soldiers, in pairs. All across
one shelf, starting with Greeks, then Romans, knights in
armor, and all the way up to modern doughboys from the

Great War. A box neatly labeled BUS SCHEDULES was filled with schedules, of course.

Everything was labeled. There were two whole bookshelves of butterflies, pinned carefully behind sheets of glass. It was hard to imagine the bright things ever flying across a summer sky, so neatly and exactly were they arranged. School books were stacked from largest to smallest on his desk, with one closed notebook and a sharp pencil lined up next to it.

Unbelievable. Her brother was a very weird guy. She shook her head.

The door bell rang downstairs. Oh no. Nicole yanked open drawer after little drawer in Nikki's dresser. Where were the damn kerchiefs?

Here. Stacked so neatly on top of each other she could only tell the color of the first one. Nicole riffled through the pile. She held a mauve and black paisley up to her dress and shook her head despairingly. The scarf landed on one corner of Nikki's bed. Another one, in shades of purple, joined it.

"Finally!" she cried out loud, hurriedly tying a length of gray and dark pink around her head, looping the bow by one ear.

Leaving the dresser drawer open, she rushed to her own room to grab purse and coat, and scampered down the stairs.

"Nicole, your young man has arrived."

Margaret, apron for once removed, had ushered Carlo in. He leaned nonchalantly by the front door. It was the first time she'd seen Carlo in this tidy, highly conventional setting, and he stood out like a rich oil painting in a pile of watercolors. So real he took her breath away.

"My, my, you look pretty as a picture, Nicole dear," Margaret murmured. "Just a tug or two on the skirt," she continued, matching action to words, "and let's button that collar, shall we?"

Nicole shot Carlo an exasperated look and he smirked.

"Bring your young man in the parlor, won't you?" the well-meaning woman continued.

The last thing Nicole wanted to do was to subject Carlo and herself to endless minutes of Margaret's chitchat about the weather. Maybe they could say they were rushed for the movie, or—

There was a heart-rending shriek from upstairs. It sounded like the death bellow of a rhinoceros . . . or something worse. Nikki, his face a white and black mask of tragedy, raced down the stairs and stopped short at the sight of his ascot in Nicole's hair.

Features twisted in pain, he whispered, "You. You went in my room. You took—"

His voice broke as tears rolled down his cheeks. His pale fist pounded the railing.

Nicole put out an imploring hand and dropped it. God. The poor kid. She was dismayed by what she'd done. But who'd have ever imagined . . . She whipped the scarf out of her hair and held it out to him.

"Here. Here, Nikki."

He cupped the wrinkled square of silk in his hands as if it were a wounded bird.

"Look what you've done," he wailed. "We were happy here before you—"

"Nick," said Margaret sharply, "we'll have none of that. No matter how we feel inside, we must never make a guest feel unwelcome. Control yourself, lad."

"I . . . I . . ."

He took great gulps of air, looking down at his precious scarf. Nicole gave Carlo a let's-get-out-of-here look, and he smoothly extracted them from the Borcheff ménage.

"I'll have her back after tea," he assured Margaret.

Nicole could hear Nikki racing up the stairs as she and Carlo left.

"A boy of many faces, your brother," Carlo said.

"God," Nicole breathed. "I had no idea. . . . He seemed so controlled all the time. And you should see that room of his."

She described the obsessive neatness, the collections, the labels.

"I guess, to him, pulling a couple of scarves out of order

92

was like breaking and entering," Nicole concluded. "But I swear to God, Carlo, I never meant—"

"Hey," he said, pulling her to him, "it's all right, cara. You don't have a mean bone in your body. I know that. He's a bit nuts. Borcheff'd do that to anyone."

She swallowed hard. He shook her lightly.

"It's not your fault. Listen to me."

"But what's going to happen when I get home? What will I say to him? What about at school?" she wailed.

"Tomorrow Nick Borcheff will be just as distant and Olympian as ever. He'll never even mention it. Trust me."

"You mean . . ."

"He cracked. For a minute you saw what he doesn't want anyone to know about. Including little Nick. Believe me. Unless you go home and mix up his marbles, he'll be back to normal."

"If you think I'll ever go into that bedroom again without permission in writing, you're the one who's nuts."

"Then you have nothing to worry about."

Nicole was grateful for the dark in the movie house. It gave her time to think through her own actions and Nikki's. She realized that she sometimes pushed her way into situations that needed more delicate handling. And that her brother was a very delicate creature. Not insensitive at all. Withdrawn, yes. But not cold. Nikki was full of emotion.

She wished she knew more about how he felt. He was an odd one, all right. Secretive like a snail, curled up and happy in his own little room, his little world of straight and perfect lines. Of leaps that went nowhere but up and down, and turns that never spun off center. And when he partnered, he shadowed the girl so exactly he almost disappeared. Her secret twin. He fascinated her now. But she had no idea of how to get closer to him.

The next day Nicole found that Carlo had been right. Nikki didn't say another word to her. He was back to normal. She watched his quiet, orderly ways with relief and an odd sort of protectiveness. She found herself glad when he answered Alexandra's pokes and prods with unrevealing monosyllables. Not everyone had to be dramatic, she realized. Quiet could be restful. Even dignified.

In the weeks that followed, Nicole's adjustment to her father's house was greatly aided by Maître Andreyev. The aristocratic Russian instructor had bowed to the inevitable and paired her with Carlo in partnering class. Nicole filled her mother's ears with details about lifts and arabesques and wonderful tension when she and Alexandra walked home together from British Court, as they often did now that Alexandra was there too.

Nicole and Carlo's dates were like a continuation of their unfolding dance partnership. Unpredictable. Tender. Angry. Exhilarating.

One soft evening in early spring, Carlo accompanied both Nicole and her mother home from British Court.

"So, Signore Domenici," Alexandra began, "what do you think of my ballet, *Labyrinth of the Heart*?"

"I think you're a dangerous woman, Madame Varonne. Bravo!"

Alexandra laughed her throaty laugh, snatching her windswept muffler and wrapping it around her white neck again. "Such a wild boy you are. My daughter has good taste."

He sketched a bow. "She owes it all to her mother."

"All right, you two lovebirds," Nicole interrupted with a laugh. "Carlo, you're going to have to choose which Varonne you really want."

"But why, when both have such grace? In fact, I have an invitation for the two of you. My mother and father would love you to come to dinner at Trattoria Bari."

"That's their restaurant?" asked Nicole. "The one you showed me in Soho?"

"Yes, although I think they plan to take you upstairs and feed you some special Domenici cuisine. How about tomorrow night? Will you come?"

"Well . . ." Alexandra paused, pretended to consider. "I don't know, Nicole. Didn't Margaret plan on making Toad-in-the-Hole tomorrow night?"

Nicole shuddered. "We'd love to come, Carlo."

"Ah, but I wouldn't dream of making you miss a unique meal by Miss Dunstable," he retorted with eyes twinkling.

"Darling," breathed Alexandra, "we make the sacrifice."

They all started chuckling at the same moment, as the sky warmed to sunset peach before them.

Both Nicole and Alexandra dressed with real care for their dinner with the Domenicis.

"Not too expensive-looking, Mom," Nicole warned nervously.

She outlined the sad story of the family's fall. Alexandra obligingly removed half her costume jewelry and exchanged her fur for a warm wool coat.

"Not all nobles in reduced circumstances, as we say, feel jealous, sweetheart," Alexandra said, "but it is kind of you to think of it. My mother could never bear to see violets in winter after her duke left her. His special gift, you see."

They walked down the dusk-hung streets to the Underground and stepped onto the train to Soho.

"You were so young when she died," Nicole puzzled. "I can't imagine how you could remember Paris at all."

"Ah," breathed her mother, "for all those years when my father kept me secret in Leningrad, I held those memories of my mother to my breast like warmth against Russian coldness."

"Didn't you hate him?"

"He had his family to protect. Even when I was six years old I understood I was a love child. But I wanted my own life, and dance was the way out of the prison he made for me."

She laughed merrily. "You know, when I graduated from Imperial School, and this handsome older aristocrat gave me jewels, a villa, anything my heart desired, everyone thought I was his mistress. How jealous the girls were. But no. Was just my father. Finally he could help me publicly. In those days many noblemen patronized ballerinas."

Nicole had to interrupt. "Mom, this is our stop. It's only a couple of blocks from here."

They walked quickly through the sour-smelling streets.

"Is not a place to walk alone at night," Alexandra murmured.

"Not unless you're Carlo Raimondo Domenici," Nicole proudly answered.

~~~ **12**

Trattoria Bari was very small. The green-and-red-striped awning barely sheltered both their heads. Nicole's hands shook with more than cold as she tried to peer inside the steamy window. There were people eating, but that was all she could make out. With a deep breath she pulled open the door.

Warm, moist air, fragrant with tomato and basil, swirled around them. The five tables, with their red-and-white-checked tablecloths and fat Chianti bottles sporting candles, were all full. The waiter bending attentively over a family of four was Carlo. He finished ladling spaghetti onto thick plates and twisted between the tables to his own two guests.

"You look lovely, ladies," he said to Nicole and Alexandra. "If you'll wait one minute, I'll get—"

A short, muscular, older man complete with sauce-stained apron tied over his big belly emerged from a door at the back of the room and Carlo motioned him over. The heavy man was surprisingly nimble. He reminded Nicole of a bull, moving proud and sure on his own land.

"Nicole and Madame Varonne, may I introduce my father, Stefano Domenici? Papa, Madame Alexandra Varonne and her daughter Nicole."

His little eyes under smooth thick brows were inviting. "Such an honor you do our house, signora, signorina."

He really means it, Nicole thought, and her nervousness started to melt away.

"You are most welcome to our little bit of Bari." He

waved his broad arm to indicate the chatter-filled room. "Please," he continued, "if you would be so kind as to come with me. My wife wants so much to meet you."

His voice was like rich, hypnotic music, Nicole thought happily. Like waves, building one on top of the other. Every sentence was a dance.

She followed him through the back door and into the kitchen, where battered pots of every size bubbled and steamed on two ancient stoves. A tiny woman wove between them. She stirred one pot, then dropped a handful of vegetables into another while adjusting the heat under a third. When she saw her visitors, she broke into a smile that made them feel the sun had come out.

"Ah, the ladies have arrived." She came toward them, wiping elegant hands on a towel at her waist. "It is so good of you to come," she said, taking first Alexandra's hands and then Nicole's, pressing them warmly. "Carlo has told me so much about the beautiful ballerina and her talented daughter. I am Francesca Domenici."

"Signora Domenici," breathed Alexandra, falling in easily with the rhythm of old-world graciousness. "The honor is very much ours. How we have looked forward to meeting parents of your remarkable Carlo."

"He is a special one, our impetuous boy," Signora Domenici agreed with a rueful, loving glance at him, smoothing his thick curls back over his forehead. "Carlo, take our guests upstairs and make them comfortable. Papa and I will be with you as soon as Guido comes in for tonight."

The flight of stairs next to the kitchen creaked under their weight. As they climbed, light from the restaurant faded until they were moving in darkness. Carlo opened what Nicole guessed was a door, and faint lamplight shone from inside.

"Welcome to our humble abode," said Carlo. "For once, a polite cliché is accurate."

He was certainly right, Nicole thought. The few pieces of furniture were so old it was hard to tell what color they had once been. The walls were completely bare except for an antique jeweled rosary that hung above a small shrine.

But who cares? Nicole asked herself fiercely, feeling very protective of the gracious couple she had just met. They might not have a nickel, but this place was just as clean as Margaret's stuffy parlor. Even cleaner.

She seated herself on a sofa whose legs, though scrubbed bare of lacquer, were carved into regal lion's paws. What was it Carlo had said? You can take the duke out of his castle, but . . . Nicole patted the worn brocade cushion like an old friend.

"That is a beautiful rosary," Alexandra said. "Very old. Maybe fourteenth, fifteenth century?"

Carlo looked startled. "You've got quite an eye, Madame Varonne."

"Please," Alexandra protested. "Madame Varonne sounds like eighty-year-old dance teacher, retired to a room of old photographs. I am Alexandra, yes?"

"Alexandra it is."

"And I know antiques because I am Gypsy. Like my daughter, my head is filled with so many scraps of knowledge from here and there—"

"Mostly from trains, from what I hear."

His eye caught Nicole's and she couldn't suppress a grin back.

"See," she said. "I'm not the only one with a weird education."

"But your mother first had a classical education at Theatre Street, right?"

It was Alexandra's turn to look startled. "And where did you learn about my childhood, Signore Domenici?"

"Oh, I have my sources," he said airily. "There's very little you can't learn if you—"

". . . know everything and everyone, as my son does," finished Signora Domenici, entering the room with a stack of dishes and silverware. Her husband followed holding a platter of delectable-looking antipasto.

"I hope he has also been making you comfortable."

"Eh, brigante," said Carlo's father, "commandeer for us the bureau from the bedroom."

"Si, Papa."

Carlo returned with a low chest of drawers and placed it in the center of the room.

The plates were distributed along with forks and napkins, and five hungry people made short work of their appetizers.

"Mrs. Domenici," exclaimed Nicole, "you are one terrific cook. What is this dish called?" she asked, pointing to a rolled-up item.

"I am so pleased that you enjoy the food, my dear. Actually that dish is not an Italian appetizer. But Stefano loves it. It was taught to me by a Rumanian cook in my father's house."

Alexandra took a bite. "Is fish! Delicious. What kind do you use?"

"A herring, smoked for the dark color and the flavor. I wrap the fillet around a sweet . . . I do not know the word in English . . ."

"Gherkin," supplied Alexandra.

"Gherkin," the signora repeated, nodding her head in thanks. "Si, and leave them together for two or three hours. The sweet takes away the bitterness that can sometimes stay in smoked herring. Really very simple."

Hard to believe, Nicole thought, that these were made from the same fish as Margaret's kippers.

"And you take all the bones out," she added gratefully.

"Of course. If we leave the bones in, it is like eating a comb."

Her smile was warm and puzzled. She glanced at her husband for support.

"You must be thinking of the English way with herring," said Stefano Domenici. He lifted his eyes to the ceiling and shook his head. "We are very grateful to the English for their hospitality to this family, but their cooking . . ." He raised his hands and shrugged. "I think maybe we opened the restaurant to protect ourselves, si?"

Everyone laughed. Nicole felt a tightness inside her

loosening. How long had it been since she had laughed freely with a group of people? Eating and joking and feeling free. It felt so good.

"How lucky we have been," Francesca murmured. "Even in England now there is so much hunger."

Alexandra shook her head. "In America the Depression has hurt everyone. Very democratic. But here, only the workers seem to suffer. Did you see those pitiful Welsh miners marching last week?"

Stefano patted his wife's hand. "She gave away my spare boots to one of them. Ah, poor man. His feet were bleeding. And the pots of pasta she has served . . ."

"To me they are like starving children coming to my door," Francesca pleaded. "What else can I do?"

"No, no," cried Stefano. "How could I want you to do anything differently?"

His loving smile embraced his wife, and Nicole reveled in their sunny generosity like a cat basking in the warmth of summer.

"Mama, more people should be like you," Carlo added fiercely. "These English can be so cold."

Nicole dared to say, "Actually, I haven't found anything I like about them either."

Signore and Signora Domenici turned to her, their olive faces soft with sympathy.

"Poor little girl," murmured Francesca. "The English, they are like oysters, you know? It takes a lot of work to get inside. And then you must get used to the taste. But when you do this, such rewards! They are the most honest people in the world. And very gentle souls. You can see this in their dance."

Nicole and Carlo exchanged a look of disbelief.

"Pardon me, Mama," said Carlo, "but we've seen nothing in their dance. They work very hard to keep emotion out."

Francesca turned to Alexandra. "Madame, you must know what I mean."

"Please, call me Shura. And yes, I know. The English have gentle dreams of gossamer and clouds and meadows in spring. Such yearning there can be in their dances."

She reached across the bureau-cum-table and patted Nicole's cheek. "Don't judge all England by Borcheff, my children. There is much more."

"Well, I can't wait to see it," exclaimed Nicole, her eyes glowing from the pictures Alexandra's words conjured up.

"You will. You will," Stefano Domenici assured her. "Shura, I must compliment you on this beautiful daughter of yours. She is as fresh and as open as our wild pink roses that fill the fields of Bari with their perfume." He kissed his fingertips in tribute.

"Like a young Hebe, bearing wine for the gods," agreed Francesca, turning her admiring dark eyes to Nicole. "So full of the most wonderful promise."

"And who but an artist of exquisite sensibilities would have allowed such a flower to form?" asked Stefano, bowing his head to Alexandra.

Her mother looked as delighted as Nicole felt inside. She wasn't sure if she should thank them, or what she should do. If only she could stop blushing.

"You give me too much praise for this precious blossom," protested Alexandra, not missing a beat. "She is as God made her, and if any credit must go to me, is only that I do not try to make beetle out of butterfly."

The three adults laughed the fond knowing laugh of parents. Nicole looked at them with a kind of wonder. This is what she had imagined Europe would be like from all her mother's stories back in America. Sophisticated. Gracious. What Mom had called Old World charm. The Domenicis had it coming out of their ears. They were great.

Francesca shook her finger at Carlo with mock severity.

"This budding beauty you have found. Do not let me hear that you have knocked the dew from the rose."

Carlo looked down, his fingers tugging at his tie. It was the first time Nicole had ever seen Carlo embarrassed.

"No, Mama."

"Ah, the young," exclaimed Stefano with a great sigh. "They bring such memories back to all of us." He gave Francesca a fond look before picking up the empty tray and stacking the dishes on top of it. "I return in only a moment with our veal marsala and eggplant parmesan."

"It sounds delicious," pronounced Alexandra.

She was right. The meat was tender as butter, with a simple wine sauce perfectly seasoned. And the vegetables were fresh, lightly cooked, and dusted with crumbled spicy cheese. Nicole was in heaven, and no one spoke while there was still food on their plates.

Dessert was zabaglione. Nicole savored every rich creamy spoonful. Afterward they piled the dishes on the bureau and leaned back in their seats, sated.

For a long while the Domenicis plied Alexandra with questions about her life in dance. Nicole floated along, thinking she'd probably be hearing these same stories when she was old and gray. And still love them just as much. She watched Carlo drink in her mother's stories, wide-eyed as a child. It felt as if he was becoming part of her family. What could be better than that?

"But come," said Alexandra. "We have been speaking all night of my adventures. Now you must tell me of yours. Carlo says your family was in Bari by the early 1700s."

"Yes," said Francesca. "Stefano's great-great, I don't know how many—"

"Ten," supplied her husband gravely.

". . . very great-grandfather was a wealthy merchant, and he spent his money on land. The south of Italy is mostly very dry, but near Bari the land is perfect for grapes."

"Giustino Stefano," her husband continued, "had one powerful advantage over the other landowners. Since he was not noble, he did not have to spend his days at court, kissing the backsides of the powerful. He managed his own vineyards until Domenici wine from Bari was recognized in every part of Italy."

"And his sons and their sons have done the same," added Francesca. "Lived like feudal lords with their hundreds of peasants to till the soil."

"But what does a Domenici do when it is time to marry?" asked Alexandra.

"Ah," breathed Stefano, his eyes twinkling, "there are visits to the capital."

"And visits from the capital," said Francesca. "My father had exiled me to our estates near Bari because he disapproved of a frivolous boy I thought I loved. It was like being sent to the back of the moon. And then I met Stefano."

She shrugged a slow Italian shrug, her graceful hands waving in the air. "The moon became paradise to me. I even learned to dine with the mafioso, though they frightened me at first."

"Part of the family," explained Stefano. "We help them, they help us. It is the way of life in southern Italy. And we all give thanks to God that the mafia loves Domenici Chianti."

He laughed his rich chuckling laugh, and Nicole saw him clearly. Il padrone. The master of land and family, as Carlo had described to her. Sure. Why not? His family'd been at it for two hundred years. It seemed impossible they could have left it.

"But then what happened?" Nicole demanded.

"Why didn't our mafioso protect their good friends?" he asked, and shrugged massively. "For five years Mussolini left us alone. Even he had no wish to tangle with the Brotherhood. But if he wanted to rule the whole of Italy, he had no choice. At last the war for the south began. He moved in his troops, and there we were. Caught in the crossfire."

"They were killing our peasants," said Francesca with a catch in her voice. "Setting fire to the vines. Our foreman was murdered in front of us."

"Then we knew we could not protect anything we loved," said Stefano. "I knew we would be next, that we endangered our people by resisting. We had to flee, with nothing in our pockets. All we had was in the land, in the cellars. Francesca's rosary is all of our history we took with us."

"So you are homeless," said Alexandra, shaking her head, "and your poor peasants are without mother and father. Is terrible tragedy."

"I pray for them every night," said Francesca fervently.

"It is the fortunes of war," said Stefano. "No one, whether he lives in the city or deep in the country, escapes it forever. We are lucky to be alive, to be eating well, to be safe."

"While Mussolini's pigs swill our hundred-year-old wines," said Carlo in a strangled voice, "and brutalize all of Italy."

Stefano gripped his son's shoulder reassuringly. "Governments, nations, empires rise and fall. Some are better than others, and everyone regrets their loss. But no power lasts forever."

"I can't be philosophic like you, Papa. If I ever get the chance to fight that Fascist tyrant, I'll take it, no matter what it costs." His dark eyes glowed with dedication and his whole face thinned, making him look like an ancient bowman who'd spotted his target. "A chance to fight for freedom," Carlo cried. "And for Domenici revenge."

How fiery and alive he is, Nicole marveled, looking at his clenched fists. He means every word.

Stefano shook his head fondly. "Such a hothead, my son. Francesca and I have decided he must be a throwback to Massimo Domenici, the family pirate."

Carlo grinned, adding, "Don't you think I'd look good with a cutlass between my teeth?"

Nicole was startled at the rightness of the image. "Except you wouldn't kill people just to get their money. Not with that code of honor you've got stuck in your head."

"Ah, signorina," said Stefano, pleased, "you have learned much about our boy. He has always been the lone wolf. He makes his own rules, no matter how heavy the stick that is used to beat them out of him."

"Si," agreed Francesca. "I have always thought my Carlo would either rule the world or become very skilled at breaking out of jail."

She laughed, but there was worry in her face, a misgiving of many years.

"Come, Mama," Carlo soothed. "I'm a dancer, not a pirate. The worst that I could do is steal someone's leotards, right?"

"Stealing . . . this reminds me." She glanced at her watch and then turned to her guests. "At nine o'clock the London Symphony will be playing Rossini's *La Gazza Ladra* on the radio."

To Nicole's puzzled face, Francesca translated, *"The Thieving Magpie,* dear. Would you like to listen to it?"

When Alexandra and Nicole agreed, Stefano turned on the program and the sonorous tones of the BBC announcer filled the air. The overture began. Stefano stood and held out his arms to Alexandra.

"How sweet of you. Yes, I would love to," she murmured, allowing him to lead her in a stately minuet.

Carlo bowed an invitation to his mother, who accepted gracefully, smiling back at Nicole as her son guided her chivalrously around the room.

It was all so wonderful, Nicole thought, moving her shoulders to the sprightly music. She loved how Carlo treated his mother. So respectful. So reverent. And Stefano was whispering something in Mom's ear that made her giggle like a kid.

The first theme ended. Stefano bowed low to Alexandra and returned her to the couch.

"Come, my boy. You must ask your little rosebud for the next dance."

"Yes," agreed Francesca, sitting down. "Show us, children, what they are teaching you at school."

The next theme was quicker, suggesting a fandango. Carlo swept Nicole onto the floor and she willingly gave herself to him, to the speed and spirit of the music. Their dance turned into a duel of sorts with Carlo's magnificent swooping turns, and Nicole, light as a feather, darting behind him, beneath him, over him. The parents breathed a sigh of pleasure as Carlo caught her and spun her extended body in perfect time to the commanding music.

Then, in perfect unspoken communication, the pair began clowning, their duel forgotten. Together they created an airy circus. And just as suddenly, as the music changed again, the playfulness was gone. They were pure romance. Charged. Intense. Unforgettable. The last lift, Nicole suspended seemingly forever, was breathtaking. She arched, circled her arms, her back, her neck to the clear glad flow of sound. Once again Carlo had given her the freedom of the air.

There was a choked "Oh!" from Francesca and she dabbed at her wet eyes.

"Such fire," murmured Stefano, enthralled.

The three parents looked at each other. Alexandra spoke for them all.

"Is what we have worked for. What we dreamed."

The two mothers clasped hands fervently as their children danced the music to its glistening end.

 **13**

The next morning Nicole was awakened by the soft brush of a kiss on her forehead. She opened her eyes and saw Alexandra's tender smile.

"You must awake, darling. Is school day."

"You're skipping 'Piggy kippers' again?" Nicole asked.

"I must take you to little sweet shop I found near British Court. Much preferable to Chez Dunstable."

"It's a date," said Nicole fervently. She watched her mother glide toward the door. "Hey, your ankle's all better."

On the way back from Trattoria Bari, Alexandra's leg had suddenly given way, almost spilling her on the train platform. She had limped badly the rest of the way home, and Nicole had insisted on heat and a massage before she allowed her mother to go to sleep.

"Your hands have magic in them, darling."

Throwing her daughter a gay smile, she closed the door behind her.

Not that magical, Nicole thought with a frown. But the little mystery was chased from her mind by delicious memories of her evening with Carlo's family. Stefano and

Francesca Domenici had taken her to their hearts, she thought, as she put on a navy-blue sweater and skirt.

She combed her hair, seeing the wiry waves as a sunburst or a mass of daisy petals, instead of an unruly mess. No one except her mother had ever made her feel so good. So appreciated. The Domenicis' poetic compliments, like colorful bouquets of flowers, drifted through her mind and made her smile at her reflection in the mirror.

Mom had been right after all. There was plenty of warmth in Europe. People didn't spend all their time worrying about folding washcloths correctly and being on time for dinner. Poor Nikki. He had the bad luck to grow up in this household. With a better roll of the dice, he could have had Alexandra's mothering or parents like Carlo's.

She pictured the little boy he must have been. Trying so hard to be good. Ashamed when he felt angry. Alone with his fears, because feelings in this house were something that you couldn't let out. Nicole felt a lump in her throat.

She wanted to make it better for her brother. To be his friend. She went to her trunk and searched through it until she found something she sensed he would really like.

This time at his door she tapped lightly and waited.

"Hi," she said cautiously, unsure of her welcome. "Um . . . could I come in for a second?"

Wary, he hesitated. What could she possibly want now?

"I guess so." Then he caught himself, with automatic politeness adding, "Please do." He motioned her to the chair at his desk.

"I wanted to apologize for the other night. I was in a terrible hurry. . . . I should have asked. . . . Well, anyway, this is for you."

He took the oriental carved box with a quizzical look on his face. So his sister had some manners after all.

"That's very kind, I'm sure. You didn't have to."

"I know," she said softly. "But I wanted to. Here, look. I'll show you what it does."

She demonstrated how the panels slid open, in one particular order, until the secret compartment at the center of the puzzle box was revealed.

A fascinating contraption, Nikki decided. He amazed himself with his next thought. This sister of mine has good taste.

"You can keep something inside it," she explained. "I used to keep the key to my diary in there when I was a kid."

"Here now," he said, "let me see if I can do it."

Nicole warmed to the faint edge of excitement in his voice. Hidden under all his reserve, she sensed a little boy with a new toy. She closed up the panels and handed it to him, watching his sensitive hands find their way.

"You did it in one try," she exclaimed. "You're good at this stuff."

His cheeks reddened slightly. "Thanks," he murmured.

He looked down at the box, his fingers unconsciously caressing the glossy surface.

"I got it from a contortionist named Le Chinois who was with our company for a couple of years. He told me there was a legend that went with it."

Nicole paused, unsure if Nikki wanted to hear any more. He was so quiet.

"Anything to do with this dragon on the back?" he ventured.

"Right," she agreed happily. "That's supposed to mean it belonged to someone in the royal family. Le Chinois said a princess kept a tiny bottle of deadly poison in the secret compartment. She had sworn never to marry because the man she loved died protecting her. So when her father made a political marriage for her, she carried the box with her in the huge sleeves of her wedding kimono. And during the ceremony, pffft."

"It could be a ballet," he said, his eyes soft with imagining.

"Wow, you're right," she said eagerly. "Can't you just see that wedding dance?"

For a moment, as the twins pictured the dance possibilities, they looked very much alike. Then Nicole sighed.

"We'd better get downstairs for breakfast."

"Right you are. Wouldn't want to start off Peggy's day with a problem, would we?"

He carefully placed Nicole's gift in the center of his bureau, aligning it perpendicularly to his comb and brush, and the pair went downstairs together.

There was a surprise for Nicole that night when she came upstairs. On the top of her dresser was a small collector's box with a single butterfly neatly pinned inside. It was a lovely creature, almost as big as her hand, with spangled wings of iridescent blue, their edges lustrous black with glowing crimson dots. But the best part of all was its name: Morpho Peleides Nikkoli.

Two weeks later Alexandra's first dance for British Court Ballet was about to have its dress rehearsal. Like the savvy businessman he was, Vanya had invited all the company patrons to see the spectacular work their money had purchased. Joining them in the audience were the rest of the company's choreographers, staff, and dancers.

At a signal from his wife, Vanya stood, smoothed his hair, and nodded to the gathering.

"I welcome you all to what I am sure is going to be a brilliant and evocative dance event. Alexandra Varonne, not content with becoming the greatest ballerina of her generation, has created for herself a new, even more spectacular career as choreographer."

Vanya noted with relief the sage nods, the encouraging smiles of the patrons. They had no idea he was nervous. Inside the dark tailored suit, his clammy shirt clung to his skin. It was the first time he would see more than random bits and pieces of Alexandra's work. So much was at stake. He grabbed mentally at the next sentences of the prepared speech.

"She has traveled the world in search of a more supple, more personal vocabulary of movement. Today you will see the richness she has gathered. We expect vision today, ladies and gentlemen. We expect greatness."

There was the polite patter of applause he expected.

"Thank you for joining us. Without your support, none of our humble art could reach the world."

Another bow, another bit of applause, and Vanya returned to his seat. Alexandra appeared alone on the stage.

"My friends," came her rich, dramatic voice, "the dance I give you now comes from my heart, my very core, as all good dances must." She pressed both hands against her heart. "Is true I have found new ways of moving, as my husband tells you. But any movement, old or new, must uncover something important about who we are inside. Is what I have done here, in *Labyrinth of the Heart.*"

She paused artfully, and Vanya smiled with appreciation at the applause. How his Shura could hold an audience. Yes. He needed her success badly, for Margaret's peace and for his own. But deep beneath all of that, Vanushka was on pins and needles for his wife's work. May it go well, my darling. May it be all you hope and more.

"Is customary," she continued, "for the artist to explain intentions, to tell the story before it comes before your eyes. But I will not do this. Instead, I will allow the dance to speak to you for itself. For I believe the body has a voice more eloquent than any words I could make. Ladies and gentlemen, I give you *Labyrinth of the Heart.*"

She came down from the stage and the curtain opened. A single girl in a pale tiny skirt, white leotard and tights, moved through a precise, icy set of arabesques. She covered the stage, as though setting up a maze of icicles. Thin beams of silver light appeared in each spot she danced. Only a flute accompanied her, lonely and echoing itself.

To the rich clamor of horns, a man leaped out behind her. He wore the puffed and jeweled satin doublet of a Renaissance prince, and his golden tights matched his jacket. In a series of high dazzling turns he covered the entire stage, splintering the icicle maze, the interweaving lights, without even seeing them.

Is the way I used to take the stage, Vanya remembered. He watched with great interest as the man discovered the girl, who was still perfecting her cold arabesques, and put out a lordly hand to get hold of her balance. At first she ignored him. Vanya tensed at the rebuffs. But the man had no concept of what it was to be ignored. He shouldered himself behind her in a single catlike twist and put his hands high on her rib cage, lifting her out of her static perfection.

When he allowed her down out of the air, he pressed her rigid body against his golden one. Vanya grinned. And though she did everything she could to escape him, the leonine male forced her to become his partner, to give herself completely. Mesmerized, Vanya watched encounters that were partly rape, partly seduction, sometimes fragile agreements. But each time the two separated, the woman returned to ice and had to be remelted.

A dramatic flow of violins heralded a change in the woman's dancing. Now when she was released, she danced full-bodied. Her arabesques were warm embraces of the air. She turned and spun as athletically as her partner. When he pulled her to him, she did not resist. But neither did she melt. Baffled, he released her.

Vanya frowned. Where was the excitement? The fire? The soul-stirring partnership was falling apart. Could he do nothing to reach her again?

Ah. She was reaching out to him. But like a lioness. When he leaped into the air, spinning like a dervish, she joined him there, matching power with power, mastering him as he mastered her.

Vanya clenched his teeth. Wrong. It was all wrong. Suddenly he saw what his wife was up to. It was the two of them up there on the stage, Vanya and Alexandra themselves, stripped of all privacy, all dignity. She was blaming him for their split. Look at the woman, offering to partner him just as he partnered her. What kind of unnatural bond would that be? A terrible renunciation of everything important between man and woman.

Vanya gasped. The woman leaped off the stage as the man had leaped on. And he, all alone, began the arabesques of ice. No! No! No! How could she tell all these people these lies about her husband? He looked furtively around him. They were all staring, mouths open. It seemed as though everyone believed her. They thought he was cruel, blind, a tyrant, and Alexandra was the lily-white victim who outgrew her chains.

He wanted to kill her. But the music had come to a stop. Alexandra was up on stage hugging the pair of dancers, congratulating them on their intensity. Her bouncing voice rang through the silence of the audience. Vanya stood up abruptly and faced the onlookers.

"I must apologize to you all for this unseemly spectacle. I'm as shocked as you are. Let me assure you that no one else will see this . . . this bastardized . . ."

His voice failed him. He had to clear his throat twice.

"Thank you for attending today. I will personally speak to each one of you, my valued colleagues, by the end of week."

He forced himself to wait until the last patron had filed out the door. Then his hand found Alexandra's arm and he dragged her into his office, slamming the door behind them. He threw her into a chair.

"You make me look like cossack!" he roared. "How dare you make dance about us in *my* company?"

"You act like cossack! Is good dance. Is true dance." She glared at him. "I give them the heart of me, and you stamp on it like stupid peasant. This is artistic freedom you promised me?"

"I give you freedom. I do not give you permission to lie."

"Lie? Where was the lie? You wanted to make me feel, to force me to express myself. You never think how this is for me. I am only Vanya's woman. Never Alexandra. Never until I leave you."

It was what she had said to him the morning they parted. Vanya did not think it was possible to hurt so much again until this moment.

"You were stupid shallow girl when I found you," he gritted, each word a bullet. "I made you a star. I gave you everything a woman could want. Even babies. But you were never real woman. No real woman could choose between her two children. No real woman would abandon her son."

Alexandra whitened.

"We made decision together," she said in a low voice. "You left Nicole. I left Nikolai. Whatever guilt there must be is for both of us."

His face suffused with blood.

"I've suffered my share, but at least Nikki is a good boy. Look what you've done to my daughter. She is barbarian. She is not fit to sit at my table, let alone dance in my company. You destroyed—"

He stopped abruptly as Alexandra swayed. She looked as though he'd shot her through the heart. Without another word she crumpled to the floor. Vanya was beside her in an instant.

Shura, my Shura. What have I done? he cried to himself.

Margaret's hiss woke Alexandra.

"It's simply impossible, Van. We will never be rid of her."

"Piggy, my wife may be many things, but she is always direct. She does not play tricks. It must be she is ill."

"Forgive me, dear, but you truly can be blind at times. It's a well-known part of the female arsenal. When an argument goes against her, she simply faints and effectively wins the point."

Little Piggy, you are wrong, thought Alexandra. She pulled the blanket on the guest bed up to her chin for comfort. Tomorrow she would see the second doctor again and everything would be better. He would give her medicine, and all this fainting and falling would stop.

She was almost asleep when Nicole tiptoed into the room.

"Mom? Mom? How're you feeling?"

"Better, darling."

"I need your permission to kill that man."

"No, no, darling. Was just a misunderstanding."

"Misunderstanding? I hear he's canceled your dance."

"A few details to work out, is all," Alexandra whispered.

"God, I'm sorry, Mom. Those kids'll say anything. You sleep now."

Nicole leaned down and kissed her mother's pale cheek.

Sir Arthur Pennington closed the buff folder containing a sheaf of laboratory reports and fixed his detached medical gaze on the famous woman seated gracefully across his desk.

"Madame Varonne, you're an intelligent woman," he began. "You know something is wrong with you. I'm truly sorry to have to confirm that the news is not good."

Alexandra's breath remained as even as it would have if she had faced the death squads in St. Petersburg. Whatever came, she would meet it with her own brand of courage. *Is not important what he tells me,* she told herself fiercely, as the doctor visibly hesitated. *Only how I match it.*

But what about Nicole? came the anguished thought. *No. I cannot think this way now. Whatever is my fate, I will spare her all I can.*

She braced herself, dark eyes watching the doctor's face.

"Your symptoms are unmistakeably those of amyotrophic lateral sclerosis, ALS. It is a progressive degenerative neuromuscular disease that usually begins, as yours has, with sudden weakness in the hands and feet."

"And after?"

"The weakness spreads. Within a year the legs and arms are involved. Then the rest of the body follows. There can be cramps, spasticity. There is physical therapy for some of the symptoms, but we have no cure. Some people have lived with the disease for as much as seven years."

The bullets had entered her body, hitting each vital organ. Only her pride was intact.

"How long will I walk?"

"Another eighteen months, perhaps, judging from the progress of the disease."

She nodded once, decisively. There was nothing more to say.

"You will need help," he said gently. "A renowned dancer such as yourself must have thousands of admirers. But do you have someone at home? You see, within two years at the most, you will be bedridden."

She held her head imperiously high.

"I will manage. I have always managed."

Alexandra stood and thanked the doctor for his time. With a regal nod of her head, she left his office.

Her pride enabled her to find her way back to the nearest

bus stop, pay the ticket taker, and find a seat in the reary of the upper level of the double-decker bus. But once she was seated and the surging sounds of the wheels dimmed the chatter around her, a shaking seized her body and didn't let go for several miles.

Like strokes of a heavy gong, black thoughts struck and struck again. She'd never dance again. It was impossible. It could not be that audiences would never applaud for her again. Love her again. She'd be pitied. Reduced to a limp heap of bones. Helpless.

Alexandra stifled a scream as the terrible image assaulted her. Her mind still alive, still feeling and wanting so much, trapped inside a bag of paralyzed flesh. Not even a finger to be moved. No words. No breath.

Alexandra forced the onslaught of panic to stop. The inner discipline that had been a part of her for as long as she could remember built a wall against the darkness, a wall she would reinforce with all the strength at her command.

I am a nobleman's daughter. I am a daughter of Mother Russia. I am a great star. These assertions calmed her. The darkness comes to everyone, she reminded herself. I will stand against it. I will win every moment of time I can.

And Nicole? One cry escaped the great dancer as she stared unseeing at the city rushing by. My sweet innocent rosebud? How can she possibly endure this? So young. So full of hope. No. I will not allow it. I cannot allow it. I will spare her this terrible debasement. Somehow.

Her decisions made, Alexandra saw the landscape beyond the walls of the bus for the first time. She was somewhere on the outskirts of London. It was time to turn back.

~~~ **14**

It's like a skittering of raindrops, Nicole marveled, as she counted out the combination to the dance accompanist's Chopin waltz. Waiting her turn in partnering class, Nicole threw Carlo a giddy glance. He reached over and mussed her hair.

"Sometimes I wonder how old you really are."

"This music makes me feel about four," she murmured back.

When they started dancing, her light twinkling reaction sparked an answer in him. Together they looked as if they were dancing on air, moving through the untouched pleasures of childhood. Andreyev's stick came down and the music cut off abruptly.

"Begin again," he ordered. "And this time watch the angle of your extension when you hold your arabesque, Miss Varonne."

"Bah, humbug," muttered Nicole.

Ignoring him, the two dancers returned to the sunlit world of childhood they had envisioned. Again the stick came down.

"The angle was no better, Miss Varonne."

After the third time Nicole ignored his correction, Andreyev sighed with exaggerated patience. He gestured for Carlo to step aside and sent Nicole into the final arabesque. Standing behind her as if he were her partner, the teacher grasped her ankle and moved the leg into the correct position.

"You see?"

He gestured with his stick to show the perfect line.

"That's fine if I'm moving slowly," Nicole explained. "But this music just cries for lightness, a kind of quick pointed step. I can't extend out that far and still have the feeling I want."

"Young woman," Andreyev began with a sardonic curl on his lips, "I suggest you purchase a recording of Chopin and take it home. There you can prance before your mirror all you wish. But here, I will not tolerate such indulgence."

"There was nothing self-indulgent about her dancing," interrupted Carlo. "Nicole is an artist. I've seen her choreography. What possible good will you do by trying to cage the wind?"

Nicole came out of her arabesque with a big grin. What a compliment! The maître's face had returned to that blue-white pallor only Carlo's challenges seemed to bring up.

"Whatever you might believe, Signore Domenici," the teacher bit out, "arrogance is not a virtue. You seem to have made a religion of it."

The other students were still as statues.

Carlo shrugged, stating, "If something is true, it's true. That's all I care about." He drove his fingers through his thick dark curls, tossing his head like a restless horse. "That's always been my problem with the teachers at British Court," he added. "This business of hiding emotion—it's a waste of time."

The stick in Andreyev's hand trembled as if he were forcing himself to refrain from bringing it down on Carlo's head. Through stiff lips the older man said, "Get out of my class. Both of you."

"Wait a minute," Nicole protested.

"The director will handle this."

"Come on, cara," Carlo coaxed. "It's his class."

"And it's my father," Nicole said, seething, as they walked down the hall. "I think it's about time I told him what I think of his school."

"After lunch," agreed Carlo. "Andreyev's got to have his tantrum first."

By the time she walked into her father's office, Nicole was ready for a knockdown drag-out fight. She didn't wait for Vanya to begin his lecture. As soon as Carlo and she were seated across from her father's desk, she delivered her first punch.

"Father, I've been wanting to tell you this since the first class I took here. I want out of this place. It's impossible for me to get any real work done. There is absolutely no creative freedom. Every time I get anything started, one of your teachers comes up with some dumb correction and my concentration goes, just like that."

She snapped her fingers, wondering why he wasn't protesting. Why he just sat there watching her like she was eighth on the bill at the Follies.

"The stuff you teach is dead. And the teachers are dead. I've had just about as much as I'm going to take."

"Until you are twenty-one years old, you will do as your parents tell you," her father said without visible emotion. "Your childish protests show only that you need guidance. You will learn self-control at British Court. Is something you have none of, obviously."

He turned to Carlo. "As for you, your influence on my daughter has come to end. From now on, you will have opposite schedules. No classes together. No performances in same ballet. You will stop this destructive friendship and put away any thoughts of partnership. Should I hear you've disobeyed in smallest way, you are out of British Court. Permanently."

He sat back in his chair and folded his arms, looking down at them.

Carlo narrowed his dark eyes and in a dangerously quiet voice asked, "Have you ever wondered why Nicole's freedom of expression makes you angry? Why you are threatened by the honest voice of a fifteen-year-old?"

There was no answer. In the silence, Carlo took aim with an accuracy fueled by fury.

"You're nothing more than a petty, aging dictator who betrayed his own talent long ago."

Nicole sucked in her breath, staring from one to the other. Carlo put his hand on her shoulder.

"This girl breathes creativity. Intensity and imagination pour out of her. And you want her shackled."

Carlo got up and leaned over the desk, staring into blue eyes clogged with fury. But the tight mouth didn't say a word.

"You're envious, Borcheff. That's it. And since you run this moth-eaten kingdom, you think you can pull any strings you want." Carlo straightened, looking to Nicole like a princely hero, facing the dragon that must be faced. "You may have left the Czar, but the Czar hasn't left you."

If I kill him, I lose my best dancer, Vanya told himself, clenching his teeth until some semblance of self-control returned. Impossible insolence in this boy. And lies. Lies. But the accusations made him tremble inside with more than anger.

The former dancer felt the dizzying lurch of long unacknowledged truth. Had Shura stolen his artist's soul from him when they parted? Like a Gypsy disappearing in the night with a precious child bundled under one arm. Crazy thoughts. Crazy. He felt physically sick. This was going to stop.

Taking refuge behind a shield of patronizing calm, Vanya said cautiously, "Don't be a fool, Domenici. You are jeopardizing your whole career with such hotheaded behavior."

Nicole's agonized, pleading glance caught Carlo before he delivered his final riposte. Don't get yourself kicked out because of me, she begged inwardly. Nicole felt raw with fear and fury. No one had ever ordered her to dance in her entire life, and she wanted to slug Vanya Fedorovich Borcheff right in his pasty face.

"How dare you tell me who my friends are going to be?" she demanded. "Who the hell do you think you are, deciding where I dance and who I dance with? Carlo's the only real performer in your whole stinking company, and you say I can't dance with him?"

His silence rubbed salt into the wounds. He sat back in his chair like some flabby pasha and gave her nothing but the ice of his eyes.

"Answer me, damn it!" she shrieked.

"I do not talk with children having tantrum," he said calmly, taking bleak satisfaction in her frustration.

The maddening willful mother might be beyond his control, but the daughter he would master.

"Well, I don't talk with dictators," she cried, and stormed out of her father's office.

Mom, you've got to be home, you've got to be, Nicole thought as she raced through the stony streets. The wind dashed the tears from her cheeks but more kept slipping from her eyes. He couldn't get away with this. Just wait till Mom heard what he did. She'd stop him dead in his tracks.

She'll take me out of that school so fast he won't know what hit him. And maybe, finally, we'll get our own place, and some decent meals and . . . She was home. In the middle of the afternoon the flat seemed eerily quiet. No one downstairs.

She stiffened as a tiny shriek sounded from the direction of the bedrooms. Nicole took the stairs two at a time and found her mother seated on the edge of her bed. A broken coffee cup lay in a pool of brown on the carpet. Alexandra was staring with horror at the stain spreading across her dressing gown.

"Mom? Are you all right? Hey, it's okay. We'll get it later. You've got to listen to me."

But her mother was holding up her two hands and eyeing them as if they didn't belong to her. Nicole grabbed her hands.

"Listen. Borcheff's gone off the deep end this time. You've got to get me out of there."

The strong small hands that had soothed and led and fixed everything for Nicole as far back as she could remember were trembling. Her mother's mouth opened but no words came out.

"Mom? What's wrong?"

Alexandra burst into tears.

"Mom. Oh God. Mom."

Nicole threw her arms around her mother, disquiet like ice sharp in her stomach.

"It's all right. It's okay," she kept repeating.

But it wasn't. What could have happened? Mom had never cried like this. Like she was defeated. Helpless. Never. It was a terrible realization. Alexandra wasn't all-powerful. Her mother was mortal. Like everyone else.

Alexandra wept until it seemed as if there were no more tears in her body, until she was so worn out that Nicole urged her to lie down and rest.

"I'll take care of the cup," Nicole assured her.

"Don't worry about this, darling," came her mother's roughened voice from the pillow.

She was clearly struggling to reassure Nicole.

"You're all worn out." Nicole kissed her cheek. "Just get some sleep."

"Yes," came the whisper. "We will talk . . . in morning."

Broken pieces of crockery in her hands, Nicole gazed at her mother's swollen, sleeping face from the doorway. Everything was going wrong. Everything.

When the throw rug's stains were soaked out and Nicole had closed the bedroom door, she knew she had to talk to someone or burst. Was Carlo still at school? She'd left him in the hall, throwing a sentence over her shoulder about how her mother would fix everything. Nicole found herself striding toward British Court. Toward Carlo's arms and Carlo's certainty.

But when the sickly hospital-green walls surrounded her, she felt like ducking around every corner. The last thing she needed was to run into her father now. Even if she could find Carlo, and then Vanya saw them . . . Nicole swallowed hard. As much as she needed to see Carlo, it was too dangerous. She wanted to scream with frustration. Beat back the heavy walls that marched to enclose her.

A practice room door was ajar. She pushed inside and confronted herself in the mirror. She looked brooding as thunder. Jagged as lightning. She threw an arm diagonally into the air in a jerky, angular set of motions. She slammed a foot onto the floor, then whipped herself around and landed in the angry stance of a wrestler, fingers clawed like talons.

Giving herself a tense nod of permission in the mirror, Nicole began pouring out her fury at Vanya, her fear for Alexandra, and her frustration about Carlo into a set of movements about tortured search. A search for the way out of the punishing trap England had become.

Images of wings filled her mind. White swan wings, pounding at iron bars, bruising themselves. Feathers bro-

ken. Stained rust-brown. Hammering. Striking the barricades. Unyielding.

"I say, didn't you notice the sign-up sheet on the door?"

Nikki stood in the doorway in his white practice clothes, a
record under his arm. Nicole needed to dance too badly to
stop.

"One signs up in advance if one wants the room, you see,
and I . . ."

Nikki's protest died as the helpless agony and raw power
of Nicole's dancing reached him. An expression of pity
appeared on his usually bland face.

"You're . . . you're really quite talented, you know."

She spun wildly, each turn plunging her closer to the floor.
Her fingertips clawed vainly at imagined barricades.

"If you harnessed that energy, my word, you'd be an
impressive dancer."

"H-Harness?" she muttered, thrusting her arm out jag-
gedly.

"Just so. May I demonstrate?"

He took up a position behind her, as if he were her
shadow. When she opened from a hunched position into a
splayed leap, he brought a circle of his arms down to his
stomach, and then opened them up as he did an exquisite
jeté en avant. Each angry thrust of energy from Nicole he
turned into a powerful dance phrase.

"Hey!" she cried. "That's good. That's really beautiful."

Hesitantly Nicole tried his version, copying him carefully.
Moving in Nikki's world for the first time, she saw clearly
why his dancing was so controlled. He had learned how to
survive in the Borcheff family. You didn't express feelings
around Czar Vanya. So you channeled them into formal
dance. Siphon 'em off and they won't be around to trip you
up.

The twins were dancing together now, and Nicole took to
it hungrily. Nikki was showing her something she realized
she had to learn. Protective coloration. Emotional camou-
flage. When the bullets are flying all around you and you
can't make a sound. So you do this disappearing act. And
have it all. Because only you know what you're pouring into

this fancy-looking dance. Where all the fear and pain and need are going.

She caught her breath as she glimpsed the twin forms in the mirror. How perfectly they fit together. It looked like the dream she used to have back in America. Her secret twin. The other half of herself.

～～ 15

The afternoon was as dark as an empty stage. Cross-legged on her bed, Nicole stared down at the sequined cap with its broken green feather she'd foraged out of Alexandra's trunk. Mom's old Follies hat. Nicole smiled sadly, remembering the chubby little girl with her waving plume, posing with her mother in the mirror. The two of them doing buck and wings. Arms outstretched. Palms up and moving in circles.

In the last few weeks their closeness had evaporated. No more intimate chats about the day's events. No more consoling advice. In fact, what was Mom doing? She always seemed to be out looking for work, but she never found anything.

Okay. So Czar Borcheff had nixed *Labyrinth*. That had to explain the big cry and the broken coffee cup. But he wasn't the only guy in town. It just didn't make sense. And all these twisted ankles. It seemed like every other night there was Alexandra with her foot in a basin.

Carlo agreed that there had to be something going on. The few times they'd been able to steal some time alone, they talked about Alexandra. But first they'd fought. Carlo resented sneaking around. He wanted to be open about their friendship and the hell with the consequences.

Nicole was not going to be responsible for getting him kicked out of British Court. What were the chances he could get another scholarship? He was a brilliant dancer, but his folks had no money. She wasn't going to let friendship with her turn him into just another street kid.

After practically tearing her limb from limb, he'd finally agreed, adding with that self-mocking look of his that he was glad one of them had more sense than pride. She never knew what to expect with him.

Nikki was another story. She was finally getting to know him. It was just like Francesca Domenici had said: prying open an oyster. And worth it. He listened to her stories about America like a little boy hearing fairy tales; as if he couldn't imagine anyone really living that way. In return he showed her the ropes. The little considerations that made Margaret overlook the mistakes. The usefulness of knowing exactly where your body was in space every minute of your dance. Control. She was finally starting to understand it. Thanks to Nikki.

In fact, if it weren't for her twin, she'd be absolutely miserable. No Carlo at school. And it seemed like less and less Mom at home. Nicole upended the broken half of the green feather and let it fall again.

"Darling, I'm so glad you're here."

Nicole sat bolt upright as her mother swung into the room and sat down next to her. Alexandra looked almost like her old self, assured and full of energy. Wonderfully different from the tired, worried woman of the last four weeks.

"Is time for heart-to-heart talk, my little sunbeam."

Hope surged through Nicole. Of course there was a simple explanation for all of it. Then they'd be back to normal. At last.

"Dame Harriet has made me a proposition I cannot refuse. She offers me half of studio. We work together and live together. Money, of course, will be very little." Alexandra shrugged dramatically. "But the opportunity for art . . . is very exciting."

"We don't need much money, Mom," Nicole reminded her joyfully. "God knows we've had practice living on a shoestring."

"Sweetheart, dearest . . . I cannot take you with me. There is no room. And it would be tragedy to separate you and Nikki now. After all the years, my twin children begin to

124

love each other. No. No. You must stay here. I will visit you. My little room is too small for visitors."

Nicole stared at her mother, mouth open. This was worse than anything she could have imagined. Alexandra was walking out of her life, announcing it like it was nothing at all. Nicole fought back the tears that threatened to overtake her.

"Just like that? No discussion? Don't I get to say a single word before you desert me?"

"I don't desert you, darling. You are almost grown. You have good home with your father." She patted her daughter's cheek gently. "I will see you."

Her mother's touch had changed, Nicole thought with growing panic. The sureness was gone. Mom touched like an old woman.

"But this is crazy. We never make changes this way," Nicole wailed, "without planning together. What's happened to you?" Her frantic hands crushed the green feather that drooped forlornly between them. "Why are you acting like this?"

"Is simply adventure of my own. You are moving into your own life now, darling. You don't need to be dragged through my hard times."

Nicole looked her mother straight in the eye. "Something's happened."

For a moment Alexandra's eyes faltered and her bright confidence seemed paper thin. Then she tossed her head and became again the woman nothing could daunt.

"My sunbeam's always had such imagination. Is sudden, this parting. And I am sorry for that. But could I say to Harry, 'Wait, please, I must ask my daughter's permission'?"

Her smile was teasing, beguiling. Nicole did not smile back.

"I thought we were a team. Good times and bad. Now you're shutting me out."

Alexandra looked down at her hands. "Nothing is forever, child," she said in a voice that withdrew further with every word. "Everything changes. The snake sheds old skin and grows new one. When you are older, you will understand."

"Sure, Mom," Nicole said in a strangled voice. "Sure."

She looked away so that the sudden stranger on her bed wouldn't see her tears.

"I think you pick my reserved times on purpose," said Nikki, pretending to pout as Nicole showed up at the door of the practice room at British Court.

"Let's not talk right now, okay, Nikki? Just dance."

He gave her a sweeping ballet bow and held out his arms. She moved into them like a tragic waif, leading her twin into a set of long and longing postures that ended in hesitations and regret.

As he opened her arms up from around her head, Nikki murmured, "Sad as Giselle, sadder than Odette."

She didn't answer. Just kept dancing. He cleared his throat. Blinked his eyes.

"It's easier sometimes, talking about it," he ventured.

Nicole began an elegiac turn on one toe, Nikki leading her around. Both his hands held hers in wordless sympathy.

"I don't know if I can," she whispered, but the tears started pouring down her cheeks. "Mom's going away. Moving out and leaving me."

She leaned to rest her cheek on the back of his clenched fist for a moment. Slowly his hands tightened. When she looked up, he shook his head as if clearing it. Then he loosened his almost hurtful grip.

Steady on, he told himself, as completely unexpected pain cut through him. After all, La Varonne's sudden exits were nothing new. But for his sweet bouncy little twin . . . Sympathy welled up in him.

"She doesn't even care how I feel," Nicole said. "Didn't even ask. There must be something wrong. Maybe I did something."

He lifted her high as if to remove her from fear. "That can't be it, I'm sure," he insisted. "Mother is . . . flighty. Now that you're home, I daresay she feels free to follow her fancy." He brought her down facing him. "But it's rather hard on you, isn't it, depending on her whims."

"I just wish she'd been open about it, that's all."

She sniffed. He offered her his towel to wipe her face.

"There," he said. "Better?"

She nodded and led him back into their dance. Abandonment. Aloneness. With Nikki showing her how to shape the powerful impulses and Nicole showing him how to underline feeling with drama. The beauty of their sharing had almost brought a smile to her face when Vanya walked into the room.

"Don't stop," he commanded as they wavered. "Show me what you have been doing."

Self-consciously the pair returned to their dance of sorrow. Vanya watched intently. When they broke off, embarrassed at his scrutiny, he crossed the room and put an arm around each of them.

"You have found your partner, my son. The woman who will be your other half. Who will make you explore your own depths and bring them to the stage. Finally it has happened."

Both of his children seemed to shrink under his arms.

"Oh, surely not, Pater," Nikki demurred. "I'm . . . She's . . ."

"We're different as night and day," Nicole explained. "Sure, we can teach each other things. But partners? I can't even imagine it."

"Leave imagining to me," Vanya boomed. "I know things you can't possibly see at your age. Is contrast that makes partnership exciting. Conflict."

He turned them to face each other and gave Nicole's reluctant hand to Nikki.

"We begin."

This partnership had to be the strangest thing ever imagined, Nicole thought as she tied on her toe shoes. Vanya'd been coaching them for a month, and still she and Nikki looked like marionettes operated by a rank beginner.

Outside the dressing room, Saturday morning was dripping away, just like Friday morning and Thursday and Wednesday. Nicole sighed. April in England.

At least Mom was coming today. At the twins' joint sixteenth birthday party last week, she'd had to leave right after the cake. Some rehearsal scheduled at what must have been dawn. But before she disappeared, Nicole had extracted the promise of a visit.

I hope she's getting enough rest, Nicole thought as she warmed up at the barre. She had seemed totally exhausted after only an hour or so of the party. Nicole's face lit up as Alexandra peeked in the door.

"You look beautiful," Nicole exclaimed as her mother kissed both her cheeks.

Alexandra was wearing a softly cut suit in a buoyant shade of lemon. "Is delicious color, no?"

Vanya and Nikki entered the practice room.

"So you have come to see my discovery," said Vanya, a tight smile on his face.

"Is intriguing idea, darling. Baschenko would congratulate you."

She sat down slowly on a hard wooden chair. He chuckled, his smile growing warmer.

"Twins as partners. Can't you see the posters? Lines at box office?" He turned to his son and daughter. "But first we have work to do. Much work. Come."

Alexandra watched as her children danced. There was no question. Nikki was a technical genius. Unfeeling. Withdrawn. But perfection itself. And Nicole was beginning to truly express herself through ballet, and that was joy to watch. Even in this most disciplined of traditions, Nicole's power shone clear.

Alexandra frowned. Nikki was getting in her way. There. Again. As Nicole opened up the turn, Nikki cut her off. Alexandra shook her head. They were working against each other. Nicole pushed at the edges of every movement with her great strength, her individuality. And Nikki was forcing her to stop. Yes. There again. He wouldn't let her finish the lift in her way.

Alexandra shuddered. This was wrong. Unhealthy. It was not the awkwardness of new partnerships, she thought as she watched the rest of the session. Something intense, subterranean, was working in her children. Something best left alone.

When the practice was over and the twins had gone to change, she went to her husband.

"Such potential, no?" he exclaimed. "We created something more than we knew, Shura."

Alexandra made herself look directly into his glittering blue eyes.

"Darling, you want this partnership. But I watched them. Is not right. You will make them hate each other, our children. And why?" She swallowed, stopping herself. Better not to make accusations. "Let our Nikki and Nicole become friends. Offstage. Onstage they will never find each other."

His blue eyes seemed to spin with fury. Her ankles felt wobbly as she braced herself.

"You are doing it again," he bellowed. "In every partnership you see man and woman hating each other. You tore us apart. You made a dance that shamed me before my whole company. And now . . . now when I find something rare, something pure, this you want to destroy too."

She flinched before his tirade. If only she felt stronger. If only she weren't so tired.

"No. No, you have it all wrong."

"Get your hands off my work. Get out of my studio."

Her purse dropped from nerveless fingers. Contemptuously he handed it back to her.

"Go make your castrating dances with that other man-hater Harriet and leave partnerships to those with the courage for them."

Her eyes fell. Without another word she limped away, looking as though his words had physically beaten her. Vanya stared after her, suddenly uneasy. This was not the Alexandra he knew. She was supposed to accuse him of trying to repeat their history. She was supposed to match him glare for glare, blow for blow. It was always this way between them.

He rejected his own disquiet, reminding himself that she had finally taken herself out of his life. The last thing he wanted to do was invite her, with all her storms and troubles, back in.

~~ **16**

Thank you, Mom. Thank you, Nicole sang inwardly as she climbed down from the cherry-red double-decker bus at the train station. By agreeing to the story that her daughter was spending the day and night with her, Alexandra had made Nicole's escape possible. It was one phone call to Mom that had worked out perfectly.

It was perfect weather too, Nicole thought, taking an appreciative breath of soft springtime air. The perfumed sunshine billowed about her, making her think of maypole dances and daisy wreaths.

And there he was.

"Carlo!" Nicole cried and began running to him. "This is really going to happen. I can't believe it!"

He smiled only slightly, but she knew he was excited from the bright dance in his eyes.

"You're sure Miss Dunstable's not following in a taxi?"

"What an amazing feeling to walk out of that house without hearing a single word about macs, brollies, or dinnertime. I feel like I could hop on that cloud up there and sail out of the city."

With a grin he circled her waist with his hands, as if to lift her into a leap. The touch of his hands sent warmth snaking up and down her torso, and she pivoted to face him.

"We can dance all day if we want," she exclaimed.

"Not all day," was all he answered.

She shivered. Kisses, she thought. Under the wide sky. Under the stars.

"Not all day," she agreed.

They were silent, feeling anticipation pulse between them.

130

"What is Stonehenge, anyway?" she asked offhandedly as they walked to the platform.

"Just a pile of rocks," he teased. When she gave a puzzled frown, he added, "A very old pile."

"Boy, you're a great help. Did you ever think about being a tour guide?"

"Maybe a tour caterer. But just for small intimate groups."

He took her hand. It was hot to the touch. Nicole leaned her head on his shoulder. Her eye caught the packed rucksack hanging on his back.

"I see what you mean. I think you forgot the watermelon, though."

"If you're thirsty, there's wine."

He gestured at the leather wineskin hanging at his belt.

"What else did you bring?"

They both examined the contents. Salami. Crusty bread. Olives. Oranges. Chocolate. Nicole sighed happily.

Twenty-four hours of freedom. With Carlo. What could be better? The train puffed up to them and they boarded, luckily finding two seats together in a car full of Sunday day trippers. Nicole unrolled the two thin blankets she'd liberated from Margaret's linen closet and put them behind her head and Carlo's.

"You planning to sleep?"

She laced her fingers through Carlo's before answering.

"Nope. But they're better there than tied to my back."

The train started up, chugging its way out of the station and out of London.

He turned their hands over and uncovered her palm.

"Let us see, my child," he began in his best Rumanian accent, "what the gods of destiny have drawn on your palm."

Nicole giggled.

"Journeys. I see lots of journeys. And fame."

He looked up at her owlishly, his face puckered like an old woman's.

"You are on the stage, perhaps?"

"No, no. I'm a . . . a plumber."

"Zo perhaps you will unztop the toilet of the king." He made an airy gesture. "Zomething like that. You will be renowned, the pair of you."

"Two plumbers?" she asked, giggling again.

"Zis I do not know. What I see is ze partnership. It burns across ze whole lifeline." He drew a finger down her palm, causing a shiver throughout her body. "Do you not see it?"

"Uh, yes. I do see it. Thank you very much, Madame Zarathustra." She retrieved her hand.

"Speaking of partnerships," said Carlo casually, "how's little Nick working out?"

His nonchalance didn't fool her. She knew he must hate the idea of her brother taking his place.

She answered carefully, "I'd much rather dance with you. He's got about as much fire as a kettle of water."

"Bizarre combination, you two."

She shrugged and said, "My father likes the contrast."

"What could he possibly expect to come from it?"

"You've got me. At least Nikki is a help. He's taught me a lot. He's really a good egg, Carlo."

He snorted. "I'll take your word for it, cara. Just do me a favor and finish up your training so they'll kick you up to performing. The giraffe they've got me paired with onstage can hardly get off the ground."

"Sara's not that bad."

"She's not you, cara."

He took her chin in his hand and tilted up her face. "As long as Nick doesn't do this," he muttered, and fitted his mouth to hers.

A sweet ache shot through Nicole, leaving a long tingling wake behind. Separate again, they stared at each other. Nicole found it hard to catch her breath. There was a melody under all their words, the promise of coming intimacy. The music of the night before them. Nicole snuggled closer to him and put her head on his shoulder.

"Nikki better not," she said. "He's my brother."

The train was rushing past villages now, and spring had painted a luscious rural backdrop in a hundred shades of green. They climbed the undulating hills to a wide flat plain, stretching limitless as the sea in every direction. The plain dipped down into a peaceful valley and the cathedral town of Salisbury appeared, its slender spire climbing the blue sky seemingly forever.

What a bustling little town, Nicole thought as she followed Carlo out of the train station and down the street to the bus terminal. The air was soft, tinted a pale blue from the wood smoke of a thousand hearths. People moved briskly, stopping their errands to visit with neighbors who looked as sturdy and timeless as the gray stone buildings. She was almost sorry when the bus for Amesbury arrived. But she loved listening to the local gossip that filled the bus, even if the thick accents made it hard to follow.

The bus pulled to a stop at a small village. As Nicole and Carlo stepped down, fresh wind poured over them. Nicole took in breath after deep breath like a thirsty desert traveler at an oasis. Could anything be more delicious?

She examined with delight the cobbled streets and ancient shops. Amesbury was a village filled with thatched-roof cottages and burly red-faced Wiltshire farmers. The girl they rented the bikes from had chestnut braids wrapped around her head, and she actually bobbed a curtsy when Carlo thanked her for directions.

They began pedaling the two miles to Stonehenge. The path ran in long loops across pale golden rocky ground, dotted with lush tussocks of grass. Larks flew up as they approached, sending spirals of flute-clear notes back down the heady air.

They sang "Santa Lucia" and "Smoke Gets in Your Eyes" and were just beginning "Forty-Second Street" when, over a gentle rise in the golden land, the ancient circle appeared. A shiver ran across Nicole's skin that had nothing to do with the breeze.

There were no more songs in her mind. Only an awe with equal parts of wonder and dread. They pedaled silently, reverently, the rest of the distance to the mysterious temple. Then they parked their bikes and stood in line to pay their half-shillings.

"Want a booklet?" Carlo asked.

"Later, maybe," she murmured. "This is a place to learn through your skin."

He cocked his head, smiling. "Maybe there's Druid in your blood."

"Feels earlier than that. Stone Age," she said as they walked across a bank of earth.

She felt as if she'd left the real world behind, a sense that grew more intense when they entered the second banked circle and leaped a ditch that surrounded the giant stones. They crossed over a raised mound and passed into the heart of the monument.

Nicole felt very small amid the iron-gray monoliths rearing above her. The rocks seemed alive, as if their positions were only a pause in a giant dance. Slow. Stately. Eternal. Like the wheeling of the stars above them. There was something about this place . . . so open . . . so clear . . . as though the earth had thrown open her arms and bared her breast to the sky.

"Nicole, take a look at this."

Carlo was on the other side of the great arch, pointing outward into the open field.

Nicole followed but paused at the opening between two stones.

"I can't . . ."

She had to walk around the arches to join him.

"They won't fall on you, cara," he joked.

"It's not that. They're kind of like doorways. I don't know. A door in this place—who knows what might be on the other side." She smirked as if mocking herself. "Pretty dopey, right?"

He shrugged, squinting at the upright stone far out in the field.

"There're places like this in Italy, old ruined Etruscan temples, that have the same eerie feel. Who knows? Maybe if people worship someplace long enough, it seeps into the . . . what . . . the ground? The air? Hell, I don't know."

"Look, Carlo!" Nicole said excitedly. "That stone out there lines up exactly with the horizon."

"And with this long flat stone in the center of the circle."

They looked at each other, faces full of speculation.

"Time for a booklet," said Carlo at the same time Nicole said, "Booklet time."

They spent the rest of the afternoon tracing out the structures of the temple and imagining the uses of the heel stone, the altar stone, and the aubrey holes, many of which had human ashes buried inside them. It was dusk before hunger called a halt to their explorations.

"You want to stay here tonight?" Carlo whispered in her ear.

Nicole shuddered and a smile of anticipation appeared on her face.

"Not inside the circle, but close. Yes!" she murmured back.

"It'll take a little trickery," he warned with that pirate grin she loved.

"I'm game."

"We get our bikes and leave. Far enough away so the guards don't see us. They think we've gone back to Amesbury."

"That's easy."

"When they leave, we sneak back. Simple."

"Wait a minute. How do we know when they're gone? How do we even know they don't stay here?"

"I've got an instinct about these things. Must be my bandit ancestry."

She gave him a long assessing look and said, "All right, Signore Brigante. Let's see if the family blood runs true."

Carlo's instincts were on target. They hid near the road, and soon the thick country voices of the guards rang out.

"In a hurry, are you, Timothy?"

"Aye, man. Me missus 'as the bubble'n squeak tonight."

The warm circle of light from their kerosene lantern bobbed past the hidden couple and was lost over the next rise. Carlo and Nicole, crouched beside their bikes, turned and smiled at each other. Nicole silently offered him a handshake of congratulations. The wind had risen when the sun went down, making whispered conversation impossible. Carlo signaled to her to follow him. Quickly they pedaled back toward the monument and searched for a place to stop.

"Look for a hollow," Carlo shouted over the wind.

"How about this?" she yelled back.

They sat down in a gentle dip in the land and pulled the blankets over their shoulders. They were only a hundred yards from one side of the stone circle, out near the heel stone. Nicole could see the monoliths looming like gray-blue ghosts against the darkening sky.

"I don't think food has ever tasted so good," she groaned as the spice of Francesca's homemade salami hit her tongue.

"We got carried away," Carlo said around a hunk of flaky bread.

He unhooked the wineskin from his belt. Tilting back his head, he squirted a long crimson stream into his mouth.

"You're easy to get carried away with," he added with a smile, offering her the wineskin.

"I'm probably going to get this all over me."

Using the light of the moon, she trained the tip of the skin at her mouth and prayed. All of the wine landed within an inch of her mouth, and most she managed to swallow. Laughing, she handed the wineskin back.

"There's an old Italian custom," Carlo said, staring at her wine-spattered skin. "We help the novice clean up." He pulled her closer to him. "I'll show you."

He began half kissing, half licking the sensitive area around her mouth. First above the two peaks of her upper lip. Then one corner. Nicole turned to offer him the other side, her fingers pressing into his chest like a purring cat. His tongue licked slowly underneath the curve of her lower lip. She sighed, sliding her hands up over his shoulders.

"The wine tastes better on you," he growled.

His eyes were darker than the new-minted night sky.

"Oh Carlo," she groaned. "Kiss me forever."

Murmuring something in Italian she didn't understand, he lowered himself on her so that she could feel the whole length of his body against hers. Yes. Yes. This is what she wanted. This is what she'd been waiting for.

Their whole bodies kissed each other. Rubbed and undulated and pressed. From mouths to chests to thighs. Then he was touching her, sweeping his hand over every part of her. She felt like she was melting from head to toe.

"Nicole, I'm going to take your clothes off," he said in a voice thick with desire.

He told her instead of asking because he was Carlo. But she could feel his hesitation. His need for her encouragement. He fumbled with the buttons on her blouse.

"Here," she whispered. "I'll help you."

But her fingers were just as clumsy as his. She giggled nervously.

"You'd think I never undressed myself before."

"Damned buttons," he said, finally pulling her blouse open. He took a deep breath. "Oh cara, cara," he groaned, burying his face between her naked breasts.

She held onto him in the dizzy spiraling darkness, his warm breath on her skin the only anchor. He raised his head and looked at her, taking her breasts in his hands.

"You're beautiful, Nicole."

"I . . . I'm so small."

He shook his head. "Perfect. Exquisite."

He bent his head and kissed her nipples, actually sucking on them. Between her legs a pulse began, pounding, contracting, even when he stopped.

"Oh, Carlo, why did we wait so long?" she cried.

She pulled at her waistband, ripping down the rest of her clothes. He grinned, somehow holding onto her while he shed his shirt and trousers and underwear.

"I don't know," he said breathlessly, and then they were together, with nothing in the way at all.

Rapture. A hundred sensations all at once, and she let them overtake her, pouring over her in a magical cascade. The hair on his chest tickling her nipples. The soft slide of his belly. And his hardness that she'd felt pressing against her through his pants. What was it really like?

"Carlo," she murmured. "Your . . . could I touch your . . ."

"In English it's called a penis," he teased.

She could barely see his grin in the starlight.

"And in Italian?" she retorted.

"Il pene," he muttered. "Cara, you can touch and taste any part of me you want."

But still she hesitated. "Has . . . has anyone else ever . . . touched you there?"

"Si! One other woman."

Nicole stiffened.

"But not for many years. I started washing myself when I was less than three."

She laughed with relief and excitement and let her hand grope downward until she touched a length of velvety skin. So soft, she marveled, running her fingers up and down the shaft.

Carlo emitted a long "Ahhhh."

And it was hard too. Right inside the velvet covering. Experimentally she squeezed a little and was rewarded with his groan of pleasure.

"Wait, wait," he gasped. "You will make it over too fast."

She let go of him as fast as she could.

"Sorry!"

"It's all right," he laughed, still breathing hard. "It wouldn't be a tragedy. But I wanted . . . you too."

It was Carlo's turn to explore her most private places, and Nicole's turn for helpless, pleasure-ridden groans. She was spiraling down into that black and crimson place again, her body bucking like a wild thing.

"Do something!" she cried. "Please, Carlo, darling, something . . ."

He threw himself on top of her, his face twisted with passion and anguish.

"I'm afraid I'll hurt you," he groaned. "The first time, it's supposed to hurt the woman."

"You won't. I don't care. I want . . ."

He gritted his teeth and plunged inside her. It did hurt. He was right. Despite her best efforts, tears leaked out of her eyes. He cradled her face in his hands.

"Cara? Cara, are you all right? I'm sorry."

He covered her face with tiny kisses until she opened her eyes.

"It's okay. It feels better already." She grinned. "God! We did it!"

He raised one black eyebrow. "No. Now we do it."

He began a gentle moving in and out that had her wincing at first but soon was so electric that all she could think of was more. She moved on her own. Matching his rhythm. Urging him with her body to go deeper, harder.

"Don't stop. More, Carlo. More."

"I don't want to hurt you," he muttered into her hair.

"Oh God, you won't. Please."

He tried one experimental deeper plunge and was rewarded by her pleasured groan. She felt the moment when he stopped protecting both of them and gave himself to need.

"Yes. Yes," she sobbed, matching thrust for thrust, shudder for shudder.

Whatever barriers of skin or history had been between them, all of it was erased. They were one generous yearning creature, seeking the stars, the deepest culmination of the earth. And together they found it.

Nicole opened her eyes to a sky lustrous with stars. Carlo had thrown a blanket over their sweating bodies and they drowsed together soft as horses. She turned to look at his face, his dark, drowned, unbearably dear face.

"I love you, Carlo Domenici," she whispered. "I love you forever."

His night-dark eyes slowly opened. *"Mia bella, tesoro mio. You are the woman in my heart."*

They clung together, both with tears in their eyes. Heat seemed to spiral up between them like summer sun. Suddenly Nicole's eyes opened very wide.

There, around them on the ground, the grass sparkled as if it had been dipped in starlight. She followed the path of light with her startled eyes. It led straight up to the stone circle on one side and back to the heel stone on the other. Carlo had seen it too, for she felt him start and mutter something in

Italian. With one impulse they rolled off the mysterious line of light.

It was suddenly very cold. They huddled together under the blanket, warming each other, until exploring hands and tender mouths began again the primitive, eternal dance of love. Slower, richer, they found the oneness again and slept in each other's arms.

The quick jubilant songs of grassland birds awoke them. Warm and replete under their blanket, they watched the sun rise over the heel stone of Stonehenge. Slanting rays of misty gold lighted up the circle of stones. Nicole felt joy welling up in her, as if a fountain had been freed to pour through her whole body.

"I feel so new," she whispered to Carlo. "Like I was just born this morning."

He looked so young, so open, as he smiled up at her.

"And you too," she added.

"It is a magic place, cara. A place to be reborn."

They both looked across the grass where the stone giants had seemed to dance, now standing up to their knees in sunlight. Did I really see that silver path last night? Nicole wondered. She didn't want to put it into words somehow. But she felt in her bones that the magic, the stirring of mystical forces they had found on the Salisbury Plain, would illuminate their dancing together in deep and wonderful ways. Theirs would be a partnership made in heaven.

~~ 17

Summer followed lushly after spring, and fall burned and cooled into winter. By the beginning of the new year Nicole and Carlo's precious if infrequent trysts had become the focus of both their lives. They were lovers when a vacant room or a hidden spot in the vernal woods presented itself. Even better, they became each other's best friend.

It was a fiercely intense relationship, marked by strenuous

fights and tempestuous reconciliations. Carlo taught her the city of London, from the British Museum to the unpredictable fare at Speaker's Corner in Hyde Park.

Nicole's need for Carlo's complete if sometimes sardonic attention became all the more intense as Alexandra withdrew further and further. Nicole almost came to expect her mother's excuses, though they stung each time she heard them.

Alexandra's condition steadily worsened. There were less good days when she could allow Nicole to see her. There were mornings when rising from bed was a monumental task. But she had determined to treasure the moments of mobility left to her. She would walk as long as her will and her wasting muscles held out.

Margaret rejoiced as her household returned to normal. The impossible rival gone, Margaret could return her undivided attention to her boys and give poor homeless Nicole some steady mothering. Something every child needed, no matter how independent he or she appeared.

Vanya appreciated the calm. Completely immersed in creating the dancing duo of his dreams, he was hardly bothered by Alexandra's disappearance. A younger, far more malleable Shura was in his hands, and this time the partnership would go exactly as he wished.

For Nicole, the extra practice sessions every morning before class and all morning on weekends were a royal pain in the neck. She was eating, drinking, and breathing ballet, and it was giving her a case of creative indigestion. Damn, she thought as Vanya corrected the angle of her wrist again and again. How could she remember when it made no sense to her?

But when Nikki hissed "wrist" just before she was about to intensify the gesture yet again, she stopped. Obediently her hand stayed in static place.

"Bravo, child," said Vanya. "Your body is beginning to listen."

He smiled down at her, warming her with his blue eyes. There was a cold dank space inside her where her mother's love used to be. For a little while, when her father approved of her, the cold receded.

"Nick, I'd like to see you put her through the opening of the first pas de deux in *Giselle,* Act Two."

There was a sigh from her twin. "Actually, Pater, we've only gotten through the first thirty bars or so . . ."

The two men exchanged what Nicole thought of as the Borcheff look. Judgmental. Determined. Cold as a fish on ice.

"There's quite a lot to undo," Vanya said in clipped tones. "It will come easier when the technique is there."

"Right."

Her brother knelt at an imaginary gravesite, counting to Nicole. She started on cue, trying for the weightlessness of a Wili, the ghost of a girl dead of unrequited love. She crossed to the right while Nick—as Albrecht, the prince who'd rejected Giselle—crossed to the left.

"A good beginning," her father murmured. "Exact and light. Foot placements are perfect."

She dared to take a breath.

Nicole and Nikki met center stage. Behind her, he placed his hands about her waist. Slowly, she cautioned herself. This whole sequence is a dream in slow motion. But rising en pointe in slow motion needed a lot of support. And raising one leg to the knee and then out to the front needed even more. Damn. She was wobbling. She toppled over.

"You've got to give me more support, Nikki. Look. Let me show you. Move both hands forward. Rest them on—"

"I'm afraid not. Can't be adding to the choreography."

"The ballerina's dependence on her partner must be very light one," Vanya began, frowning. "He is there as counterpoint, not as barre. You must find your own center of balance."

"But I'll never be able to go as slow as I'm supposed to. I've got to have time to make the leg look like it belongs to a ghost."

Vanya snorted. "And what is conductor supposed to do while you slow everything down?" He gestured impatiently. "The lightness is built into choreography, Nicole. Do steps perfectly and you will look like a ghost."

"So what you're saying is there's no room for interpretation in ballet?"

Her father's eyes narrowed and his voice became sternly calm. "When you are prima ballerina, when public comes expressly to see you, you will do as you like. While you are my student, you will do as I tell you."

His dominance, his absolute sureness, were almost visible. Like a current of air around him. Hell, maybe he was right. About ballet, anyway. Maybe a ballerina was supposed to be a paper doll and have dances stuck on her with little tabs. She couldn't stand her father looking at her with disgust anymore. Not anymore.

"How do I find this balance?" she asked quietly, her head down.

"It's the arms," said Nikki eagerly. "They're above your head in fifth position, and you pull up with the torso. Nothing the audience can see, of course, but all the difference to you."

The balance was better. Count on Nikki to know all the tricks. And her father really liked how she let her twin turn her around.

"Yes. Yes. Let him do as he will. Only your arms move."

Vanya and Nikki exchanged a faint smile.

She was on her own for a moment. The big jump. Grand jeté en tournant.

"One day you will be known for your leaps, daughter," said Vanya, nodding approval. "Still ragged, of course. But I can see shape beginning to emerge."

He had her repeat the move six, seven, eight times. She was gasping for breath.

"Take break, children. Nicole is losing focus. Ten minutes."

Losing focus, was she? How in hell was she supposed to contain all the freedom and purpose and escape inherent in a leap in a single, narrow jeté? She walked to the one window in the rehearsal room, a towel slung around her neck. Blotting her face, Nicole stared at the passersby, baring their heads to the weak winter sun. Pockets of fresh snow filled every nook and cranny of the trees.

She could be with Carlo right now. Taking in a Saturday concert. Poking through fake antiques in a street market. Just walking side by side, watching the smoke of their breath curl and mingle as they talked about everything under the sun.

Instead she was letting herself be turned into a ballerina like some flower being forced to bloom in the back room of a florist's shop.

Oh, it was a great compliment. No question. Vanya Borcheff coaching her personally. Seeing great promise in her. Pairing her with one of his up and coming stars. And she wanted to please him, to live up to his high expectations for her.

But it felt so wrong sometimes. Like a jacket too tight in the arms. Stretched to tearing across her back. Had Mom ever faced this problem? Felt too big for ballet? She must have. Look how she'd changed once she got to America.

Filled with a need to know, Nicole called Swanleigh Hall on her father's office phone after making sure to close the door. There was other news to report as well. A letter from Alexandra's American agent had arrived that morning.

"Yes?" a voice answered.

"Mom, it's me. You got a minute?"

"Actually, darling, is very busy here."

Nicole frowned. Her mother sounded so draggy. Like she had to push the words out of her mouth.

"Well, maybe I could drop by, take you to tea. I've got a letter from Manny for you. Who knows? Maybe he's found you a real plum."

"A letter?" Alexandra said faintly.

Of all times for her agent to have come through, Alexandra thought bitterly, now that the body would hardly obey her. It had been an especially difficult week, and this morning . . . she didn't want to think about the morning. Whatever it had cost, she was sitting at her desk and earning her pay. But her sunbeam must be put off. One look at Mamushka and Nicole would know. It could not happen.

"Darling," she said, trying for a jaunty voice, "read me this prodigy of a letter."

"Over the phone?" said Nicole in a low pained voice.

No. She could not allow herself to feel her daughter's pain. How much worse the child would feel if she gave in. Let Nicole see her mother hunched over like an old arthritic babushka? See the struggle to force her fingers around a pencil? No.

"I haven't much time, Nicole. The letter, please."

The cool voice bit like a lash. Mom. Mama. Where are you? Why are you doing this to me? Lifelessly, swallowing the lump in her throat, Nicole read Manny Schumann's four-exclamation point message. He had an offer. A Broadway show about ballet. Modern ballet! Right up Alexandra's alley!

"No, isn't quite right," Alexandra said dismissingly. "But is nice to know he still thinks of me. Thank you, darling. Now I must go."

Alexandra hung up quickly so her voice wouldn't quaver, wouldn't betray her. Thank God Nicole couldn't see her cry.

There were tears in Nicole's eyes as she replaced the phone on its hook and made her way back to the practice room. Nikki intercepted her on the way in.

"What's the matter?" he asked diffidently, peering at her face. "There is something, isn't there?"

It all burbled out. The frustration. The hurt. The anxiety. The uncontainable confusion.

"I haven't heard a word from her in over two weeks, and she brushed me off like I was a Britannica salesman."

Tears were sliding down her face. He took her up in his arms and hugged her delicately.

Over her head he murmured, "It just proves what I've always thought. She's undependable. Don't waste your tears."

There was a cutting edge in his voice she hadn't heard in a long time.

"A year ago I would have fought you tooth and nail about that, but now . . . I just don't know. You never knew her like I do . . . did. I just don't understand."

"Perhaps she never dazzled me, blinded me, as she did you. Alexandra Varonne deserted me early, you see."

He bit his lip. The words were out. It was Nicole's turn to hug her brother.

"She told me about you all the time, Nikki. You were on her mind so much. I know that doesn't fix it, but . . ."

He forced back the tears threatening to appear on his face and pulled himself out of her embrace, backing away. "Please. I know you mean well."

There was her twin's powerful reserve, shutting her out again. She'd learned to respect it. But damn it. It was crazy. He kept all his hurt bottled up inside like some evil genie he didn't dare let out. What would happen to him if someday all that black pain exploded? Poor, sweet Nikki. Didn't he realize that some things shouldn't, couldn't, be controlled?

"Well," he said, clearing his throat, "I know one thing. We've a rehearsal to finish. Up to it?"

"Sure. Let's show the old man a thing or two."

Maybe if she really opened up to her father's instruction, she could give him what he wanted. With all the attention he was paying her, it was the least she could do.

The work went much better after the break. And her father's compliments, his sincere pleasure in her accomplishments, were all the motivation she needed. By the end of the rehearsal Vanya's blue eyes shone with pleasure.

"Your sister is partner made in heaven for you, son. I see emotion in your dance. Feeling added to your technical perfection. You two will be stars."

He hugged both of them and they both hugged back. Nikki was changing, Nicole thought, happy at least to have found her twin. There had been some real tension in the lifts. Maybe it was going to work. Maybe they really could dance together.

~~~ **18**

The next year passed quickly. Nicole's proficiency as a ballerina grew by leaps and bounds, fueled by her mother's continued fading from the girl's life. Vanya's praise became all important. Suppressing her own doubts about his instruction came to be automatic.

She only saw her mother twice during the entire period. At the twins' seventeenth birthday party and at an opening night of the British Court season. Both times Alexandra had complained of some awful influenza that kept her from staying more than a few minutes.

More than ever, Carlo became Nicole's mainstay. Every moment she could steal from her busy schedule, she spent with him. And she was especially proud of how she'd wrangled this Saturday morning.

She'd overheard one of the other students complaining about the hours it took before a seamstress fitted a dress correctly. Nicole had pretended exasperation to her father. Would her own frock ever come right at the dress shop? And he, with an indulgent smile, had rescheduled rehearsal for late afternoon. The ridiculous things people believed!

Nicole grinned as she boarded the Underground for Soho. She settled back in her seat, thinking of Carlo and picturing his handsome face alight with laughter when she told him about the excuse she'd cooked up. And Francesca protesting that sometimes it did take a dress many hours to fit. And Stefano agreeing, with some charming compliment about beauty being worth waiting for. Reaching her destination, she tore up the road to the trattoria. But the story died on her lips as she encountered the pale troubled face of Francesca at the door to Trattoria Bari.

After a kiss on each cheek, Signora Domenici said soberly, "We wait upstairs, Nicoletta. Come."

Nicole followed her, wondering what was wrong.

"Ah, Nicoletta, you are a wonderful sight for these sore eyes," came Stefano's rich, sonorous voice.

He stood and took both of her hands in his. He too looked haggard. Carlo looked as if he wanted to tear something apart with his bare hands.

"Good to see you too," Nicole hurriedly answered. "But what's wrong? It looks like thunderclouds in here."

Carlo shot her a glowering look. "You don't listen to the wireless?"

Nicole was used to Carlo's barbs, but her cheeks reddened at the idea of his parents hearing it.

"None of it is her fault, my son," remonstrated Stefano. He turned to Nicole, explaining, "Il Duce has sent tanks into Ethiopia. They fight there with bows and arrows, the proud tribesmen of the desert. Their blood pours like water over the sand. He is evil, this Fascist. He is inhuman."

Carlo turned his bitter face to her. "As we sit here stuffing our faces on provolone, they are falling by the thousands. Innocents. With nothing but fists and rocks to stop the machine guns."

"God," Nicole breathed. "Can't somebody do something to help them?"

Carlo snorted. "Is that what happens in America? Send in the cavalry?"

"Carlo, you will not talk to our guest like this," Francesca said in an unusually sharp voice. "This is your sweetheart. She does not deserve your anger."

He looked up and apologized.

"It's all right." Nicole said. "This is an awful day."

"Yes," agreed Stefano. "I had never dreamed I would feel shame for my own country. It is Italy who is doing these terrible things. Men turned into ravening wolves. My own countrymen."

He buried his head in his big gnarled hands. Francesca went to him and murmured something in Italian in his ear.

"Yes, yes," he agreed. "You are right. We are out of it now."

Quiet despair filled the room. It was time for the older Domenicis to go downstairs and open the restaurant for lunch. Nicole and Carlo were left alone on the sofa.

"I've never seen them so upset," Nicole said. "Even when that slimy landlord of yours doubled the rent last summer."

"That was only money. This is honor. You've been with us

long enough to know what's most important to a Domenici."

"Is everyone in Italy as concerned about honor as your family?"

Carlo was cynical about most people's sense of right and wrong. If she could remind him of that, she thought, maybe he'd snap out of his helpless anger. But there was no hard grin on his face, no judgmental narrowing of those dark eyes.

"Many are, yes. But what can they do? Mussolini's goons pour into town like rats with machine guns. The only way now is underground." He ground his teeth in helpless fury. *"Gesù Cristo e sua Madre dolce!* If only I was old enough to fight. To tear into those pigs."

Alarm iced Nicole's heart. "But you're just a kid," she cried. "And a dancer. You could die . . ."

She grabbed him, held him as if to shield his precious flesh from bullets and trunchions and all the other senseless machinery of war. "Hold me, darling," she murmured brokenly. "Please. We've had so little time."

He kissed her, but his heart was clearly not in it. When she twined herself around him, tugging him down on top of her, he unhooked her arms from around his neck and stood up.

"Sex doesn't cure everything."

"You never know unless you try."

She came up behind him and leaned her cheek against his tense back.

"Damn it, Nicole. Get your hands off me. Use your brain for once."

She sank back on the couch. "All right. I'm sorry," she said, trying to keep the hurt from her voice. "But sometimes when you're in a black mood, it helps—"

"I don't need a lecture about sunshine right now. Do you understand?"

"Then what the hell do you need? You want me to just leave?"

"Fine," he growled, his face averted from her.

With a sob, Nicole grabbed her bag and raced down the

stairs. Back to the Tube. Why couldn't she learn not to let him hurt her? she asked herself. She knew his moods. By now it was clear as day that his brooding and his angry lashings out at the world had nothing to do with her. But logic had little to do with it. When he hurt, she hurt. Maybe if she didn't love him so much. Sure, she told herself. Maybe if I stopped breathing.

How could she sit by and just watch him die inside? When he cared so much. So passionately. It was what she loved most about him. When that passion was focused on her, when he gave everything of himself to her and demanded everything in return . . . Nicole trembled, remembering encounters with Carlo. Bodies naked. Needs unmasked . . . She groaned.

"You all right, dearie?" asked a grandmotherly woman who was sitting next to her on the train.

"Yes. Sorry. Indigestion, you know," said Nicole hastily, patting her stomach.

When Nicole reached British Court, her father met her at the door with a surprised smile.

"Fitting went better than you expected, I take it."

"Quicker, anyway," she muttered. "Is Nikki here? Might as well make use of the time."

"Excellent," Vanya called to her retreating back. "Change and we'll meet you upstairs."

Nikki was in black practice clothes, Nicole noticed with a frown. Pretty common for him these days. It seemed to match a new somberness. His detachment was no longer cool, and Nicole found herself wary of some new person emerging out of the shy sweet twin she'd grown fond of.

"Come," said Vanya, clapping his hands sharply. "Today we will see what you children can do with fish dive."

"Not *poisson* something?" Nicole asked. "Funny name for—"

"Would you mind allowing Pater to explain the position?" Nikki cut in.

"Sorry. Go ahead."

"We begin with arabesque en pointe in third, Nick in modified fourth."

They quickly assumed the position, one that was familiar to them both.

"Nicole, move into a single pirouette. Nick will support your turn with one hand at the waist."

It was a combination they'd done a hundred times, she thought as she began her spin, aided subtly by his light push.

"Hey," she protested.

Nikki's hand had brought the pirouette to a halt with a grab that hurt.

"You're not precise enough," he explained coldly. "If you can't find the spot yourself, I'll do it for you."

"Then how am I supposed to learn?"

"That's not my concern."

"Not your—" began Nicole, astonished.

"Nick's been patient enough," said her father. "This is an old lesson."

He was right, Nicole thought. Precision was the hardest part of ballet for her. She resolved to practice the stop on her own until it was right.

"You're in a rare mood," she murmured to Nikki as they resumed the position.

He didn't answer.

"Now for dive itself," began Vanya. "Nick's right arm comes firmly around your waist, Nicole, as you move into arabesque en pointe in second. Right in front of him."

Nikki, whose touch used to be feather-light, felt uncomfortably tight. Maybe it was just the position, Nicole thought. Maybe.

"Good. Now get firm hold of her raised thigh from underside."

Whew. She felt surrounded.

"Ready? With a swooping movement, Nick, you bow forward, sending Nicole's pointed leg back into the air and her head down toward the ground."

It was like vertigo, the way he made her dive. It didn't have to be like that. What the hell was eating him?

"Good position, Nick. Nicole, your leading arm bends forward across your chest and your head arches up, to line up with the toe in the air."

"Okay. Got it, I think," she said. "You can let me down now, Nikki."

He did. Gracelessly for him. As they practiced the new lift the several million times any new ballet move seemed to require, she could feel the tension in him. Almost an anger.

"You leave the arm *here!*" he grated, grabbing her hand and putting it where he wanted it.

"Nikki, just give me a second."

"Ah. Yes, I have been waiting for this," came their father's voice. "The tension between you is starting to develop. A good partnership must have it."

It got no better that night. When she asked Nikki to pass her the boiled potatoes, he ignored her.

"Come, come," admonished Margaret. "Mustn't indulge our little fits of temper at table, Nick."

In answer, he shoved back his chair and marched away from dinner. They could hear him tearing up the stairs. His door slammed. And locked, Nicole thought. Undoubtedly.

"Van, I've never seen him like this. What's gotten into the boy?"

"Is art, Piggy," he said expansively, a satisfied smile on his face. "Our Nick is finding his soul."

Nick stared out of his window at the blank night sky. It was dark out there, but nothing as black as these moods that had started to overtake him. Thick and oily as treacle. Oozing through him until he was trapped so thoroughly it was all he could do to continue breathing. And he would not succumb. He could not succumb. Pater was counting on him. The company needed him. Everyone expected good old Nick to carry on. Of course. Hadn't he always gritted his teeth and held his tongue and treated physical pain like an old friend? But this pain was different. It seemed to start in his throat, like a great lump of tar, spreading to every muscle of his body. And he would find himself feeling as if he could not raise a fork to his mouth or point his toes one more time.

There was only one way he'd found to mobilize himself. Getting angry. Angry at the pain. At the people who caused him pain. And the more he called on his feelings, the more his anger seemed to grow. Until it was a constant companion at his side—an ice-white sword to slash the darkness.

Nick shuddered. Sometimes he felt as if he wielded one of those legendary Norse weapons with a curse on it, that had to drink blood before it could be sheathed again. Was it really him humiliating Nicole, snapping at her like some mad dog? There were times when he actively hated himself. But what else could he do when the black descended? And she seemed to bring it on faster than anyone else.

Nicole left the table as soon as she could. Was she the only reasonable person left in London? How could the turmoil seething just below Nikki's surface be something to crow about? Okay. Yes. He was a repressed person. A repressed dancer. Vanya, for once, was right on target. And Nikki'd be healthier if he could release more. And a better dancer. But this stuff that was leaking out . . .

Nicole shuddered. As far as she could tell, it was aimed at her. Dislike. No. She had to be honest with herself. It was hatred. Her brother hated her. What had she ever done to earn that? Nothing. Nothing at all. Oh, steal a scarf once, a hundred years ago. But then they got to be friends.

She couldn't believe their closeness was all gone. Just like that. If only she could talk to him. Well, why not? He'd had some time to calm down. Maybe they could have it out and be friends again.

She took the stairs two at a time and beat a cheerful tattoo on his door. The thunderous expression on his face when he saw who it was did nothing to encourage her. Nicole brazened it out.

"Could I talk with you, Nikki? I'd really like to."

"I'm very busy," he answered curtly.

"Just for a minute."

She saw him wanting to slam the door in her face. Then he tamped down the impulse and motioned her inside with an annoyed jerk of the head.

Deliberately, she seated herself in the chair he used to offer her. Turning his back on her, he looked out of the window.

"Nikki, what is it? You've been acting like I was Typhoid Mary. Have I done something to hurt you?"

He colored, stealing a peek at her. Then he returned his gaze to the window.

He didn't want to hurt Nicole. He wished he had her honesty, her openness. But when he was with her these days, those very qualities grated on him. He didn't understand it. But he knew he was going to explode at her if she didn't leave off.

"You've done nothing. Nothing at all."

"Well then, what's eating you?"

He folded his arms across his chest. "If this is what you came to talk about, you can leave right now."

"And you'll go right on snapping at me and throwing me around like a sack of potatoes. Forget it. I'm staying here until we get to the bottom of this."

He gritted his teeth. "I'm asking you as politely as possible to leave my room."

"Nikki, come on. What can it be? You tired of partnering me? Can't say I blame you. Ballet isn't exactly my natural stomping ground. You're not jealous of Father paying so much attention to me?"

He snorted derisively.

"If it's not me and it's not Father, there aren't too many possibilities left. I'll bet it's Mom. She swoops into your life after fourteen years of zero contact and then, poof, she disappears again. You can't scream at her, so you take it out on the nearest facsimile. Me."

She peered at his rigid back. He was trembling.

"Nikki? Am I right? Am I wrong? She's made me pretty mad too. But at least I talk about it. And I cry. Oh, Nikki, if you could cry about it, maybe you wouldn't feel so . . . so . . ."

She knew she was breaking all the rules she had learned to follow with her brother. She was invading his precious privacy. Damn. But his silence was maddening.

Now he looked at her. And his face was white.

"You are undoubtedly the rudest, most ill-mannered girl

it's ever been my misfortune to know. You storm in here with your foul accusations and expect me to smile and agree with you?"

Nicole's mouth dropped open. He was actually shouting at her.

"Why in bloody hell should I care what Alexandra Varonne does? She's not my mother. She never gave me a moment of her time. She can rot in hell, for all I care. Now get out. Out! Before I throw you out."

Nicole got out. She huddled in her room and waited until she stopped shaking. Until she could think. Until she realized that she'd hit the jackpot. Unfortunately she'd hit it with a sledgehammer.

Now she knew what was eating Nikki. And there wasn't a damn thing she could do about it. Maybe Mom could . . . if she knew how Nikki felt . . .

"Mom?"

Alexandra's indistinguishable garble shocked Nicole.

"Mom, did I call at a bad time?"

Alexandra cleared her throat repeatedly. "So sorry, darling," she finally said. "I was . . . sleeping."

"You have a hard day?"

"Yes. And another tomorrow. Dress rehearsals this week."

"That sounds exciting. Everything going okay?"

"Wonderful. But I must get beauty rest. You understand?"

"Sure. I just wanted to tell you about Nikki. And Carlo too . . ."

"I kiss my sunbeam between her wonderful eyes. Good night, darling."

Alexandra managed to guide the mouthpiece back onto its stand. Then her legs wavered and she fell to the floor. She stifled the moan so Harry wouldn't hear and come running. That had happened last week. So unbearably humiliating. Sometimes now, without warning, the feeling would be gone from her legs or her arms. She was learning to stay close to walls or furniture, in case she needed sudden support.

Ah. She could stand again. She inspected her legs, her torso. Only bruised. No blood. Nothing she would need to bandage in secret.

Alexandra limped back to her tiny bedroom under the eaves of the roof. Painfully, she lowered herself onto the sagging bed with its nest of twisted sheets. She took another pain pill from the rickety table near the bed and swallowed it with water from a glass thick with days of lipstick smudges.

She looked around at the heaps of clothes, the brush and comb clotted with dust and hair, the mirror with its dried streaks of makeup, all a mute testimony to her unsteady hands. In this room she didn't need to pretend. Outside that door she performed a dance more brilliantly than any she had ever done before. The dance of Alexandra Varonne, invincible prima ballerina assoluta.

Sleep had come hard for Nicole. Worries had chased each other around her tired brain like a litter of puppy dogs scampering after each other's tails. But finally she drifted off, only to be awakened by a gust of night wind.

Her window was open. Wide open. A piece of paper was on her nightstand. She reached over and opened the note.

Cara,
  I was a real son of a bitch this afternoon. You didn't deserve it. Forgive me? If you do, or if you want to tell me to my face what an insensitive rat I am, I'll be waiting near Kali's stand tomorrow at three.
  I love you so much.

                                                    Carlo

Laughing, she kissed the dashing, thick black scrawl that was his signature. It was all right. Everything would be all right. He was crazy and wonderful and impossible. And she was hopelessly in love with him. Three o'clock. How was she ever going to be able to wait till then?

Nicole's palms felt as damp as the dark autumn fog outside the theater. Fifteen minutes until Vanya Borcheff's brainchild met the English public. Fifteen minutes before the most unlikely duo she could imagine—Nick Borcheff and Nicole Varonne—displayed their immense differences to a sophisticated audience.

She took a peek at the crowd from a far corner of the curtain. Damn. Father was right. The house was packed. This idea of twins partnering each other was hot box office. Was this glittering know-it-all audience about to see an eighteen-year-old fall on her face? Most ballerinas started training at seven or eight. Ten years of practice before their debut. She'd had three.

Instinctively she began to warm up, letting her thoughts wander over those past three years. They seemed more like twenty, particularly when she thought of the endless hours of practice.

Then there was the loneliness at night. For a year now Nikki hadn't said a word to her outside the rehearsal hall. And there was no one else in the house for her to talk to, and no point in calling Mom. There'd been a blunt suggestion from Alexandra last spring. Don't call us. We'll call you. Usually Alexandra didn't.

"Five minutes," came the traditional warning.

Nicole moved to the wings along with the rest of the company. Carlo tugged discreetly at the skirt of her pink tutu.

"Merde."

He was gone by the time she looked up, on his way backstage with the rest of the dancers whose performances were already finished. He'd danced with his giraffe again, as he had the whole of last season. The critics loved him and were polite about her. She would do, but she wasn't the right girl for Domenici.

Not now, she told herself, as Nick glided up to lead her onto the stage. It was most certainly not time to think about dancing with Carlo.

"Remember, two beats before the glissade," he hissed.

"Jesus, Nikki, I know. I know."

"You had it wrong just yesterday."

He looked like some glowering storm prince, his doublet of indigo slashed in the sleeves to show the white underneath, and his tights white to match. Vanya'd ordered his pet choreographer to create a dance fantasy for their debut. Nick as roving rake, coming to a masquerade ball to snare a woman. And Nicole a sweet innocent, hungry for experience, who resists, falls in love, and succumbs.

Nick's black domino mask would remain on his face through the whole dance. Nicole's was handheld. She would keep it on as she struggled not to fall under his spell. When she failed, the mask would fall too.

Their music began and Nicole took a deep breath, straightening her pale pink bodice and covering her eyes with the mask of rose petals. Nikki took her hand and bowed over it as if they'd just been introduced. The curtain opened.

The house was stone silent as they began with a little dance almost minuetlike in its dainty impersonality. It stressed how incredibly alike they looked. They posed in the same positions, then made turns that were mirror images of each other. Then Nick insinuated one arm around her waist and attempted to draw Nicole into a bolder pas de deux.

She didn't have to act much to show the maiden's shudder. Anger coiled in Nick like some unpredictable snake. There was something so icy about her twin now. Ice with a cruel cutting edge. Exact. A whiplash of angles and lines.

Far more acting was called on when Nicole simulated the maiden's capitulation. The natural generosity of her dancing was challenged at every turn by her partner's perfectionism. His dancing sought to limit hers. To cut off her giving warmth. To deny her completion. It was a fight, dramatizing the innocent's yielding to her own sensuous nature awakened by a cold, excitingly demanding man. Nicole's dancing became all fire, passion unfurling within the lyrical mode of ballet.

It was a fight to the finish. The audience went wild. Every lift won applause. Nikki's bravura set of leaps in all its cold angry splendor earned cheers. Nicole's erotic adagio drew gasps. By the time the pair moved into the last fish dive, the audience belonged to them, breathed with them. There were five curtain calls before the young pair was allowed to return backstage.

Behind the curtain was chaos. Patrons, critics, anyone important enough to join the crowd was hugging, shaking hands, laughing joyfully, exchanging superlatives. Vanya bore down on the twins, chest puffed with pride, shoulders erect as a Russian prince. It was his night and he was completely aware of it. Every eye was on him as he grabbed Nick's shoulders and pulled the slender exhausted young man to him.

"You were everything I knew you could be, my son. *Pozdravlenya*. I am so proud."

He moved to Nicole, taking her perspiring face in his hands tenderly and kissing both her cheeks. "Brava, my little girl. You have become ballerina. I am very proud."

He stood between them to receive the homage of passionate admirers. Nicole smiled and nodded and accepted compliments until she thought her cheeks would crack. "Creative tension!" "Artistic meld of innocence and decadence!" "Fearless exploration of the faces of love!" The admiring cries sounded like newspaper headlines. And her father, beaming at her side, drank down the tributes like fine champagne. All Nicole wanted to do was to wipe off her neck and her forehead.

Her eye caught Carlo, towel over one shoulder, brooding, watching the hubbub from a shadowy corner. His disapproval wasn't much different from her own. Because it hadn't been all sweetness and light and lovely young talent up in front of that audience. More like guerilla warfare. A couple of times she'd actually been frightened. . . . She didn't want to think about it. Looking away from Carlo, Nicole concentrated on returning smiles and practicing nods of gracious acceptance.

Alexandra sat in the emptying theater trying to steel herself to go backstage. But she felt as if she'd been hit in the stomach. This travesty . . . this cruel mockery of romantic ballet . . . This was Vanya's answer to *Labyrinth of the Heart,* her aborted dance about their love. This savaging of innocent Nicole . . . her sweet sunbeam fighting for her life at the hands of her twin brother. The budding affection between brother and sister would not survive. Vanya had destroyed their tenderness. And for what? Applause. Revenge. Yes, always he had to win.

Alexandra shook her head. Backstage the press would be hungry as tigers. She would have to face them and the fawning crowd and lie through her teeth. How she admired her husband. How proud she was of the children. Once she could have done this. But not anymore.

Painfully, with the aid of her cane, Alexandra pulled herself up. The children would have to understand, she thought as she slowly made her way out of the theater. No one recognized her. She had been worried about it, planning for days her excuses. None had been necessary. And somehow that hurt most of all.

When Nicole was finally allowed back to her dressing room, she found the tiny cubicle lit up by an explosion of crimson roses. Two, no, three dozen! Their long stems set in an exquisitely cut crystal vase on her dressing table.

The card read:

Tonight I pass the baton to you, my beloved child. Always there will be a Varonne onstage, dazzling as a star, courageous as a lion.

With all my love,
Mamushka

"Oh, Mom," Nicole murmured out loud. "Oh, Mom."

Bittersweet tears starred her lashes. She was sure Nikki had gotten the same wonderful gift. Here was something they could share.

Pausing only to mop her dripping neck, Nicole rushed over to his dressing room, forced herself to knock, and went in crying, "Can you believe what Mom—"

She stopped short at the sight of three dozen rose stems up in the trash can. Nikki was standing impassively before Margaret, letting her straighten his tie. In his white-knuckled fist was the crumpled card.

"The great ballerina couldn't be bothered to attend our debut."

His voice cut like ice. Nicole went to him, sympathy for his hurt welling up in her.

"Oh Nikki, sweetheart, I'm sure she—"

He grabbed her wrists in a punishing grip. Twisted. His face contorted. Nicole let out an involuntary moan. She stared at him, at her imprisoned wrists.

"Nick," Margaret protested, aghast. "What's gotten into you?"

She freed Nicole's hands from her brother's grasp. Carefully Margaret turned the reddening wrists.

"I'll get you some ice, dear. You'll soon be right as rain."

"No. I'm fine. Really."

Damned, intrusive little bitch, Nikki thought as he thrust his hands deep into his pockets. She was so much like his mother, it made him sick. All lurid emotion, oozing from every pore. And not an ounce of real feeling when it counted. It was hellish for him to partner La Varonne's daughter. But he knew what he owed British Court, what he owed his father. Nick Borcheff gave what was required. All little Nicole did was complain and shrink away from him. Her mother had trained her well. Duty was as foreign to her as self-control.

Peggy couldn't understand, of course. He looked at her averted face as she held out his coat to him. He'd make it up to her. Another predicament he owed to Nicole. Another one he'd owe her back.

He's staring at me like I'm poison, Nicole thought, rubbing her swelling wrists. This was a nightmare. With a shudder, she rushed away to the safety of her own dressing room.

She threw herself onto the stool and avoided looking at her face in the mirror. Her shoulders felt hard as concrete. Wincing, she pulled down the straps of her costume and massaged slowly, fingers circling and pressing the tense cords of her neck and upper back. A ragged sigh escaped her. Nicole reached back to undo the hooks and eyes of her bodice.

"I'll do that," said Carlo, emerging from the shadows at the back of the room.

Her start of surprise melted into pleasure. Gratefully she gave herself into his hands. Let him unpin, unhook, unlatch her out of the elaborate costume and coiffure. Massaging as he went. Warming her goosebumped flesh. It felt so good. What would she do without him?

"You worked very hard to earn this night, cara," came his deep voice out of the silence. "You danced beautifully."

Their eyes met in the mirror. She saw genuine respect in his. A slow smile slid across her face.

"Why is it that two sentences from you are worth more to me than hours of everyone else's jabber?"

His somber eyes softened. "Because I have high standards. And I know you."

His caressing hands stopped. They both looked at what he had uncovered. Matching bruises on her upper arms. More circling her waist. She closed her eyes for a second. Then opened them to meet his challenging stare.

"Another trolley fall?" he asked.

Nicole swallowed hard. There it was. Physical evidence of how much Nikki hated her. Her own brother. Her twin.

She burst into tears, weeping in outrage and sorrow. The tempest finally poured forth. Carlo held her shoulders in his strong hands, pulled her back against him and let her cry.

"It's not really me he hates," she sobbed, "but that makes

it worse. My father and that woman he lives with—they've never let him feel anything. Anything. He's all boxed up inside."

She clutched his hand on her shoulder. Clung to it.

"Then Mom and I showed up, and then she left. All his life he's been angry, I think. Angry because his mother didn't choose him. And his father, who can do no wrong in his eyes, insists he dance with me, the one she chose."

A new rush of tears overwhelmed Nicole. *"Me.* The one Mom didn't desert. The one who feels everything he's afraid to know about." She buried her face in her hands. "I really think when he's dancing with me, it's Mom he's hurting. And he knows I know. Oh God, Carlo. What can I do?"

She rushed on before he could answer.

"I could stand the pain. Pulled muscles hurt more than a few bruises. And he's only done it twice before. But to face that hate night after night with everybody watching . . ."

Carlo turned her stool around to face him and knelt so that they were eye to eye.

"Get the hell out, cara. You're star quality. After tonight, everyone knows that. You can write your own ticket, and Nick Borcheff doesn't have to be on it."

She looked at him with red-rimmed eyes, hearing what he was really offering her. A dance partnership between the two of them. He wouldn't say it openly, risking her refusal. Maybe even risking their love.

Conscious of treading on thin ice, Nicole said, "How can I walk out on three years of my father's work? He's given me so much. And now, when it's just going to pay off . . ."

Carlo stood up abruptly and looked down at her.

"He's not the one who faces Nick the Ripper across a stage. You tell him about that. Tell him what he's raised. See what he has to say about a partner who turns his ballerina black and blue."

"Oh, Carlo, I can't do that."

He grabbed her by the arms and pulled her to standing. "Sure you can do it. But maybe you don't want to."

He tossed her arms back to her, anger crackling in the air between them.

"What is it, Nicole? The applause? Daddy too strong for you? Hell, where's your self-respect? You going to sell yourself to get a smile out of that petty tyrant?"

"God damn it, Carlo, that's not it and you know it," she cried. "You know I want to dance with you."

"Then tell him. What are you waiting for?"

Yes. Why was she hiding the truth from Vanya? This partnership was his creation. Let him see what he'd made.

"All right. I'll tell him tonight. Kiss me. Kiss me for courage."

He pulled her into his arms and growled against her lips, "I'd kiss you for any reason at all."

~~ **20**

Dressed again in street clothes, her dander up, Nicole found her way to the obligatory party one of the patrons of British Court was having for the company. Carlo had bundled her into a cab and taken off.

"I'll read what the critics think in the morning," he'd said. "I don't need caviar and champagne."

And petit fours, oysters, and something tomatoish in aspic, and tarts of every fruit known to the civilized world, she thought after giving her jacket to a houseman and moving toward the sumptuous spread and its elegant devourers.

Lord Henry Jocelyn's home in exclusive Hampton Court was quite a pile. But Nicole was in no mood to be impressed. She accepted the absolute minimum amount of compliments before making a beeline for her father. It wasn't hard to spot him. He was the man with the invisible crown and scepter, holding court under a blazing chandelier.

"Ah. My beautiful daughter. At last."

He beamed at her, snaking an arm around her waist and pulling her close. Nick was poised at his other side.

"So, what do you think?" he asked the crowd of admirers surrounding them. "My matched set, no?"

A wave of well-bred laughter met his smug joke.

Beneath the barrage of witty rejoinders, Nicole whispered, "Father, I need to talk with you." To his involuntary frown of protest, she hissed, "Alone. Now."

"My friends," he boomed, "you must excuse me for a moment." His eyes twinkled as he added, "A question of art, you understand."

"And exquisite art it is," said a nobleman with a bow.

Nicole smiled tightly as Vanya led her away.

"I think the library will be private," he said as they moved past guests raising brimming glasses to them and dancers stuffing themselves with more food than their thin bodies seemed capable of holding.

Private it was, as well as opulently lined with gold-embossed matched book sets and hunting prints on the oak walls. Vanya seated himself on the buttery leather sofa and patted the cushion next to him invitingly. An instinct for distance, for separation, prompted Nicole to pick a tweed club chair across from him instead.

She cleared her throat several times as he looked at her with warm indulgence.

"What is it, my sweet?" he asked finally.

Oh God. How was she going to tell him? That his son, his perfect Nick, was a brute, a crazy man. Vanya'd never believe her. And then when she showed him . . . She couldn't imagine what would happen next. It was impossible.

"Father, I . . ." She licked her dry lips. "Nikki . . . he . . ."

"You don't have to say a word to me, darling. I have eyes. I can see struggling between you."

Nicole's mouth fell open.

"Your mother and I, we too began with this fighting, this war on the stage."

"How could that be?" she protested. "You were in love."

He shrugged dramatically, his hands rising with his shoulders.

"Love. Hate. One is twin of the other, child. You are coming to an age to understand that. Later our battles were only stage drama, but at beginning were very real. The ice goddess no man could conquer, and the hero, warrior of the sun, wielding a weapon no man could defeat."

Nicole, child of two performers, was enthralled. "You must have knocked 'em dead."

He grinned, nodding at the memories.

"At beginning Baschenko could get no cooperation from us. He gave us ultimatum. We would find way to work together or kaput. One would be fired."

It brought Nicole back to her own anxiety. "What did you do?" she pleaded.

"We had no choice. We had to let the other in. And when this happened, combustion!"

He raised his arms in a gesture like leaping flames.

"But . . . but Nikki and I. What about us? How will we ever . . ."

She trailed off despairingly.

His smile was understanding. "I will try to explain to you. You see, is rare process. Like magic." He leaned toward her and spread his two hands far apart. "Two halves, far apart, yearning to become one. Fighting. Afraid. Of what? To give up independence? To lose aloneness, even if it is painful? To trust so much? Yes. I think all those things."

He inched closer to her as she frowned at his mystic gobbledegook. She wasn't yearning to become one with Nick Borcheff. Was she?

"Was wrong, what your mother and I did. There is a deep bond between twins. You should never have been apart. Didn't you dream of Nikki when you were little girl? And think about him all the time?"

"Yes," she cried. "How did you know that?"

Vanya sat back, satisfied. "He too, though he was such a quiet boy, he never said it in so many words." He gave her a sad smile. "I must apologize, daughter, for the years Shura and I stole from you and your brother. We built this wall between you, and now you must fight to tear it down."

There were tears in Nicole's eyes. "Oh, Father," she whispered.

He followed up quickly on his advantage. "Now, finally, there is something I can do to make this up to you. This partnership will make you one again." He waved away Nicole's weak protest. "Yes, yes, in this moment it seems all fighting. This is part of grand process. But I promise you, just as it worked for your mother and me, so it will for you."

He gave her his sympathetic smile again.

"Imagine, all those lost years, all the closeness you missed. To be partners. To dance with hearts and minds and bodies as one. Is the most beautiful thing in whole world."

"Father, if only I could believe you," Nicole said in a choked voice.

He reached across the space between them and took her hand.

"Has not been easy for you. Your mother leaving you alone. I know. I've watched you suffer. How hard it must be to trust anyone now. But I am here, Nicole. I want to make up these lost years to you. Can you let me do this?"

She held on tightly to his warm hand, searching his soft blue eyes. The lonely little girl dreaming of her twin reared up deep inside her, demanding fulfillment. Nicole found herself sitting on her father's knees, her head pressed against his wide chest.

"Yes," she whispered.

Over her head he smiled, satisfied at a job well done.

Back among the vivaciously chattering guests, Nicole caught Nikki's eye. Nikki. The other half of her soul. She sent him a sweet and soaring smile. His glance ricocheted off her face. He pivoted sharply, turning his back to her.

Nicole looked at Vanya, standing at her side. He took her face in his hands and kissed her forehead.

"Be brave, little bird," he murmured.

In class the next day Nicole found her status had changed. She was a member of the company now, not just a student. The snubs were still there, but tinged with respect, as if she were a rival rather than a charity case. Even the teacher's corrections were a shade less arrogant.

She concentrated on this amusing switch instead of meeting Carlo's interrogating eyes. When class was over, she hurried toward the girls' dressing room and slipped inside before he could ask her anything. She fussed with her hair as long as she could, mentally practicing her excuse for needing to rush away. But it was no use.

As soon as she appeared outside the dressing room door, he growled, "Come with me."

What could she do? He was Carlo. He practically force-marched her to the nearest park bench, sat her down, and gave her his dangerously undivided attention.

"What happened last night?"

"Oh, Vanya just blathered on about ancient history. Mom and him in Russia. You know."

After an uncomfortable silence with Nicole staring down at her mittened hands, he said, "And?"

"Well, that was about it."

She looked up to check his face, saw implacability, and looked down quickly again.

"What did he say when you showed him the bruises?"

"Well, I . . . I didn't, as it turned out."

"But you told him about them."

"Damn it, Carlo, I'm dancing with Nikki for now," she exploded. "And that's that."

His eyes narrowed. "It's hard to believe even Borcheff would let you get physically abused in a partnership. So you didn't tell him, did you?"

"You just don't understand," she cried. "We . . . we are halves of a whole, and halves war with each other before . . ."

God, it sounded even sillier this morning.

"Horseshit," Carlo said. "You're acting like a brainless puppet, Nicole. Borcheff pulls a string and you jump. He told you some idiotic pap about creative conflict and you swallowed it whole."

How he could hurt her. His scorn was like the stab of a knife.

"Think what you want. It's up to me to decide who I dance with, and I've decided."

She folded her arms across her chest and took a deep dismissing breath. There was a long silence.

"Then I will tell you what I have decided," he said in a low voice. "Our love is finished. I can't love a woman I don't respect. Without esteem, what is there between a man and a woman? Lust? That's something you can buy on street corners. No," he pontificated with all the idealistic fervor of youth. "I will not accept such diminishing of our love. Better we part now. Better we—"

Nicole burst into tears, stunned by his conclusion. His arms went around her.

"Cara, cara, don't cry." His lips sought her wet cheeks, her trembling mouth. "*Mi bellisima. Mi inamorata,* please. Don't cry."

There were tears in his eyes too. She held onto him, squeezing him with all her might. "I didn't mean it."

He held her anguished face in his hands. "I love you. You know that."

"Don't ever try that again," she stormed. "If I lost you, if I ever lost you—"

A new bout of weeping overcame her. He held her against him tightly, stroking her tumbled hair over and over.

"You make me crazy sometimes. That's all it was. I would never leave you."

She looked up at him, and her whole soul was in her eyes.

"I need you so much it scares me. No one's ever been so deep inside me. I feel like we're one person. If I lost you, I think I would never be whole again."

They clung to each other for a long time, oblivious to passersby. The winter wind. Time itself.

~~ **21**

Two years later London continued to pay homage to the second coming of a Borcheff and Varonne duo. Vanya, smug in his role as sly impresario, was never more gracious—or effusive—with the press.

"I knew from first moment extraordinary partnership was possible," he spouted.

"Was that first moment when the twins were reunited, Maestro?" asked a reporter. "Or later, when they were paired in class?"

Was nothing sacred? Vanya sighed to himself. Ever since his children had made their debut, little in their lives had remained private. Vanya attempted to steer a smooth course, making himself available but keeping his dancing darlings away from professional snoopers. So far his methods were right on the mark. Between his carefully planned press releases and the silly gossip that inevitably surfaced, the public yearned, begged, demanded more performances by Nikki and Nicole. British Court Ballet had reached its zenith.

As a result, Vanya stifled a glower of annoyance and flashed his blue eyes at the inquiring reporter.

"My dear St. James, whether you call it professional eye of father or paternal eye of artist, I knew destiny from moment of their birth!"

The reporter furiously wrote down Vanya's every word.

"And their mother? Did the lustrous ballerina, Alexandra Varonne, agree? Or was that what your separation was all about?"

Vanya's eyes narrowed at this display of impudence.

"Is old hat. History no longer interesting to public. Is sufficient for me to say we each love our children. If you have questions of Madame Varonne, let her answer them herself."

"But, Maestro, she won't respond to any of our requests for interviews. She won't even take our telephone calls."

For once the infernal woman was using her head, Vanya thought. And her silence, her absence from the scene, suited him immensely.

He shrugged sympathetically and said, "My wife was never predictable. One moment center of attention. Next, demanding seclusion. Who can understand women?" he asked conspiratorially, winking at the reporter and, at the same time, shooing him from his office.

"You will excuse me, dear boy, but is time for rehearsal. New work for Borcheff and Varonne. Come back next week. Maybe I give you little preview."

He stomped down the hall importantly, only pausing for a moment at the door of the twins' rehearsal room to listen to the music within. It was daringly modern, full of bright blaring horns and pseudosophisticated counterpoint, a change of direction for the company, but a necessary one. There were only so many classics, and public demand had to be met. They'd seen Nikki and Nicole in all the old warhorses. Now was the time to dazzle them with something more, something new, something unexpected.

Love and Duty would certainly fill the bill. What a scene he'd had with Piggy when he told her he was recasting Edward VIII's abdication into balletic form. She denounced the idea as thoroughly unsuitable, and worse—un-English. She'd left a trail of tears all over the house, only drying them when Vanya promised not to mention the actual names in the program notes of the prince led astray and his American hussy.

Vanya's musings went on. Actually, he wouldn't even need to hint at the unfortunate Windsors. London was already hysterical, swooning and clamoring for their favorite duo. Nikki and Nicole were besieged by storms of flowers showering the stage as they made their bows to full houses. Every night fans lined up six deep at the stage door in hope of catching a glimpse of the twins. And it would only get bigger and better, as the children claimed their title as king and queen of the dance world.

Life was good, Vanya thought, puffing out his chest. Nikki had burst to life as a dancer, a magnificent dancer. Nicole, it had turned out, was tractable after all. One simply had to hold the leash tightly, correcting constantly to remove the impulse to deviate. It was hard work, but gratifying all the same. His children were doing just what he wanted them to do.

He entered the room, smiling broadly.

"How goes it, children?"

Nicole was elevated in a grand, open arabesque, held in a steely grip by her brother. He was attempting to spin around and still maintain her position overhead. Both were lathered in sweat and breathing hard.

"Hold the position, damn it," he said through gritted teeth.

"I can't breathe," she wailed.

In a second she curled up and tumbled out of his hands. She lay on the grimy floor, clutching her sides, panting. Nikki and Vanya stared at her. No one lifted a hand to help her up.

"Nicole," chided Vanya. "This is hardly difficult sequence. Is simply matter of physics. Nikki puts you up. You stay up. Nikki brings you down. Then and only then, you come down."

Slowly, she pulled herself to her knees. Massaged the burning ache in her ribs.

"I know the step, Father. If he . . ." She couldn't even bear to say her brother's name anymore.

"If he could hold me here," she said, pointing to her hips.

"You think I don't know where your center is?" Nikki challenged her. "I've been dancing with you every day for years, and I don't know how to hold you? That's a rich one."

Nicole looked from Nikki to Vanya. One closed face after another. They didn't want to listen to her. They never considered what she had to say. Even about her own body. What was the use? Around them, it wasn't her body. It was theirs to do with as they pleased. Pulled in one direction. Pushed in another. Tugged off balance. Shifted from toe to toe. Now she was in the air. Then she was on the ground.

Wait a minute, she wanted to cry. Just one bloody minute. But nobody gave the time of day to a wooden doll. A puppet. That's all she had become. She didn't dance. Didn't flow to the music. She was placed. She was squired. Vanya told Nikki which of her strings to pull, and he did. Obediently she flopped forward or hung limply or went rigid. Whichever hurt the least.

Abruptly she got to her feet. If she just gave herself up to them, it would be over soon. Bear the pain. Do the step. Hold on as she had learned to. Don't argue. Never argue. Grit her teeth and bear up. The English way. How very English she had become.

"I can do it, Father. Let's go, Nikki," she snapped.

"That's my girl," said Vanya approvingly. "Time's wasting, Nikki."

Nikki gave his sister a vicious look and swung her up before she'd taken her preparatory steps. Her eyes glazed over. The music beat in her ears, ticking the time away until she could get out of this hell.

"Beautiful!" she dimly heard her father cry. "Is rapturous. Is perfect, my little Gemini."

An hour later the ordeal came to an end.

"Same time tomorrow, Pater?" Nikki asked.

"Perhaps half hour earlier. Nicole needs extra work on her pas seul. I want you there, Nikki, for criticism. On time tomorrow, Nicole. Yes?"

"Yes, Father," she replied, bland as butter.

Then her hand was on the doorknob and she was out. Free for the rest of the morning. Free until afternoon class. Free to fly to Carlo. Her feet took wing. In a matter of minutes she showered, dressed, and was on the street, headed for the Underground and Soho. She knocked at the back door in the alley, knowing Stefano and Francesca would be at the markets or entrenched in the kitchen, concentrating only on their cooking.

She fell into Carlo's arms, letting him kiss the tension out of her body, feeling him hold her in his arms. At once he was strong, supportive, yet tender.

"Did you dance well today?" he asked soberly as he kneaded the taut knots from her neck and shoulders.

"I tried, Carlo. I really tried. I must've done something right. The great Vanya called us his 'Gemini.'"

"An interesting comparison. Castor and Pollux, as I recall, were supposed to be inseparable. One of them died of grief after the other was killed in battle."

"I'd like to kill Nikki," Nicole grunted under Carlo's digging fingers.

"Sorry," he said airily. "You'll have to get in line behind me."

She sat up and twisted around, throwing her arms around his neck. "I love you, Carlo. You're the only light in my life. If I didn't have you . . ."

He held her tenderly, whispering in her ear, "But you do, cara."

She looked up at him, her eyes glistening with unshed tears. "How did I get myself in this mess? I hate it. Every last second of it. I feel so lost, except when I'm with you. Then I know who I am. But when we're not together . . . I'm a ghost. Half alive. Mostly dead." A lump rose and stuck in her throat. "And I miss Mom. I still don't understand, Carlo."

"I never understood how she could have left you to the wolves. And here you are, stuck with Nefarious Nick, darling of the S and M set. I never wanted you to dance with anybody but me."

"Forget the M. He's all S," Nicole snorted.

Carlo planted kisses along her bruised ribs.

"Would you chuck it all, right now? Go to Vanya and tell him you've given him three years of partnering with Nick and enough's enough?"

Nicole looked away, frowning. She felt tears trickle down her face. Carlo always asked hard questions. Impossible ones.

"I know," he said, cradling her again. "It's in your blood to dance. Even when it hurts. When you think it's killing you. Maybe it is and maybe it isn't. But you'll keep on dancing, and damn Vanya and Nikki and the whole lot of them, because you're good and you must. Because it keeps you alive like nothing else. How do you think I manage, dancing without you? One day you'll have had enough. And I'll be waiting."

She couldn't imagine that the day would ever come. The rut she was in sank deeper and deeper. Day by day. She had no other choices. Not as long as her father and brother were in charge. For once Carlo was wrong. She danced because she had no other alternative. What could she do? Run away? And subsist on what? Broken dreams and charitable handouts? The only person she knew on her side was Carlo, and he couldn't do a damn thing to change her life. The best she could do, the only thing for her to do, was hang on. For now she clung to Carlo, seeking the vast comfort of his arms.

 22

One day was like another to Nicole. In some respects the monotony made life easier for her. Having learned what was expected of her, she gave exactly that much and not one whit more.

It was simpler not to argue with Vanya. That way, she reduced the number of regurgitated references about her faults. The endless monologues about the sloppiness she had obviously inherited from Alexandra. Always Mom's name had to be mentioned. And Vanya's own rendition of his glory days as premier danseur.

Simpler not to compete with Nikki. Their partnership seethed with emotion. Primeval. Animalistic. Like the earth at its dawning, in a state of upheaval where the only constant was that there were none. Like prehuman creatures who signaled to each other by means of indistinguishable grunts and who survived by the grit of muscle and a furious need to conquer.

Nicole was in the rehearsal room. Again. This time alone with Vanya, who was putting her through her paces. There was blood again seeping along the pink satin of her toe shoes. She ignored it. She had to. There was only one task to perform, and that was making her feet keep to the tempo. Vanya beat his cane against the floor, pounding out the timing. Her toes, dulled to a numb whine, obediently hit their marks.

The pounding stopped, followed by an unusual silence. Nicole stopped, mid-jeté, and looked at Vanya. She followed his glance, more a glare, to the door of the room. It opened, injecting Dame Harriet Wellington into its tense sweaty midst.

"I know I'm interrupting," she began, "and if you did the same to me during a rehearsal of mine, I'd probably have you thrown out. So don't glare at me, Vanya Fedorovich. I'm only here out of necessity."

"You could make appointment," he said caustically, "like a normal person."

"And well I might," replied Dame Harriet, undaunted by the Russian bear. "But this isn't a normal situation." She marched across the room and shook hands with Nicole, saying in an uncharacteristic, soft voice, "How are you, my dear? A bit frayed about the edges, but that's to be expected under this dictator," she added for Vanya's benefit.

"All right, Harriet. What do you want?" Vanya asked in a voice half weary, half irritated.

"It's about Alexandra—"

"Mom? I thought she wasn't working with you anymore," cried Nicole excitedly. "You've talked to her? You've seen her?"

"Guilty as charged, child. More so than you know. And now it's gone too far. I should never have agreed—"

She stopped, at a loss for words. Snatching out a large, gentleman's handkerchief from her sleeve, Dame Harriet blew her nose and stuffed the used linen square back into a pocket.

"Look here, Borcheff. I took on a responsibility that, by rights, ought to have been yours. I did it for an old friend and a colleague. You should know how hard it is to say no to her. There's no one quite like Alexandra Varonne."

"Then you know I have no rights when it comes to her."

"Dash it all, man, you're still her husband. Though why the two of you didn't make a clean break of it, I'll never understand."

Vanya raised an eyebrow and, without shifting his gaze from the older woman, said to his daughter, "Is better you leave us, Nicole. Go now."

"No," insisted Dame Harriet. "This involves Nicole as much as you."

Something was wrong. Terribly wrong. Nicole knew it. And it had to do with her mother.

"What's happened?" she whispered.

"Three, almost four years ago, Alexandra confided in me about her calamity."

"You mean her inability to get work," offered Nicole.

"No, darling, I mean her health. She swore me to secrecy. In the beginning I thought she had made the right choice, sparing you the shock and the sadness. The long road downward."

"What is this rigmarole, Harriet?" shouted Vanya, suddenly angry and worried at the same time.

"I was wrong. I should never have agreed. But there it is. I did. Now it's gone too far. Even she can't pretend anymore."

The whirlpool was sucking him in, back into its depths, from which there was no escape. Something had happened to Alexandra. She'd gone off on her own and gotten her life into another muddle. And he'd have to fix it. She'd be back in his world again. Making trouble. Making him confused and excited. Alexandra's favorite ploy. How well he knew it. Hated it. Still, after all this time, he found himself unwillingly welcoming it.

Nicole was clutching Dame Harriet's jacket, staring into her face for a glimmer of truth. She held onto the woman as though she were an anchor in an ocean turned upside down. Nicole was unable to mouth the words. Or ask the fatal questions. What was wrong? How horrible could it be?

Dame Harriet's face fell into a piteous frown.

"She's sick. Very, very sick. She can't manage herself at all anymore. I could've just arranged for the hospital to take her, but I felt the family had a right to know. She doesn't know I'm here, telling you. She didn't want you to know . . . about the illness . . . the failure."

Nicole glanced at her father. Be strong for me, she prayed. At once she realized he wouldn't be. She'd never seen him so gray, cowed, a look of fear etched on his face. Helpless, he looked to her. It was up to Nicole to dig deeper. Was she up to it? She had no choice, for her mother's sake.

"What does Mom have?"

"You'll have to ask her yourself. I've presumed as much as I possibly can. All I can say is that she's lost the use of her limbs almost completely. She's quite weak. Too difficult to eat, she says. She's wasting away. All skin and bones. Now her voice has started to go."

Out came the handkerchief again and another hearty blow. Dame Harriet couldn't continue.

With each stinging phrase, Vanya and Nicole moved closer to one another, until they were holding onto each other. Each symptom was like a blow to their own bodies.

"Can't be, can't be," Vanya moaned over and over.

"Sorry I had to be the bearer of such sad tidings," Dame Harriet said stiffly, fighting her own emotions. "Sorry I waited so long to come. Now it's up to you. Something must be done for her immediately."

"Before it's too late," said Nicole, finishing the cliché.

"Now listen to me, both of you," the older woman said sternly. "It is too late. Alexandra's been to the best physicians on Harley Street. They've all told her the same thing. There is no hope. No cure. You must make the end easy for her. Do you understand?"

"Where is she?" Nicole asked, barely able to stay on her feet with her father hanging on her like a dead weight.

"Above my studio. In the garret."

Nicole's mouth flew open and Vanya rose up, consumed by a fearsome anger.

"You knew," he growled. "You had her all this time and you didn't do anything about it."

"My hands were tied, Vanya."

"You're traitor to all of us!" he roared. "Come, daughter,"

he said, pushing his way past Dame Harriet. "We've got to take Shura home . . . where she belongs."

They ran out of the building, hand in hand. Vanya flagged down a cab, barked out the address of Swanleigh Hall, and handed his jacket to Nicole so she could cover her practice clothes with something a little more presentable.

"Hurry, man," he yelled to the driver.

Vanya sat at the edge of his seat, tapping his foot in an agony of impatience. Nicole sat wedged into the corner, holding her legs, resting her head on her knees. It wasn't possible. It was just another nightmare. A cruel joke. They'd get to the studio and find Alexandra laughing, flashing her teeth, her mischievous eyes. Just a joke to get them to come and see her masterpieces. It was her work that had kept her so busy. Too busy to be a part of their lives. They'd be angry, her father and she, but they'd laugh too, admiring the wonderful dances her mother had created. Making it all worthwhile. Making it all understandable.

Vanya paid the cabbie. He and Nicole went into the hall, hustled up the crooked old stairs to the garret. Vanya knocked at the door, rattling the doorknob. No answer came. Father and daughter exchanged glances, then jointly rammed their bodies against the door. It gave way, bursting on a scene that took their breath away.

Here was the nightmare. A small, dark room with a few sad pieces of furniture and clutter everywhere. Clothes discarded and dropped by hands too feeble to hold them, much less hang them on the cheap pegs that stuck out from one wall. Empty vials of medicine. Evidence of spilled doses spotting the threadbare carpet. Scraps of paper. Two tiny windows veiled in smoky grime. Too dirty to see out of. Too dirty to let in the light.

And the smell. Nauseating. Food gone moldy. Urine. Disinfectant. Mildew and the damp mustiness of worn, unwashed clothes.

Vanya and Nicole stood in the doorway, aghast at the squalid jungle, searching for Alexandra. They saw her. She lay inert on a thin mattress, its ticking leaked onto the floor. She hardly made a dent in the bed.

"M-M-Mom?" whispered Nicole, taking a step forward and then another.

It couldn't be. Not this dried-up stick of a woman. Not this limp rag doll. Where was the beautiful shapely body? The long legs. The artful arms always animated. The shining dark mane. The vibrant skin.

"Mama?"

It was Alexandra. Those were her eyes. Still flashing. Full of life. Communicating everything she felt. Surprise. Anguish. Regret. Love. Death.

Her lips moved. No sound. Deliberately forcing the words out.

"Ni-cole. Little sun-beam."

Nicole rushed to the edge of the bed and fell on her knees. She kissed her mother's face, wanting to wrap her arms around the wasted body, but dared not. She had never seen such fragility.

"Mom, how did this happen? Why didn't you tell me?"

"I never wanted you to see me like this," came the words in prolonged, rasped agony.

"I would have taken care of you," Nicole cried brokenly. "I could have. Better than this."

"Not what your life was meant for," Alexandra murmured, ineffectively slurring the words. "Dancing. Not nursing."

"That was my decision to make, Mom. Now I will take care of you. And Father will too."

Vanya, who'd hung back all this time, finally came forward. Tears plunged down his cheeks, leaving wet smudges on his shirt.

"Shura, my silly fool, my beautiful angel, we'll get more doctors, best medicine. We'll find cure. You'll dance again and tear my heart out for years to come."

"Vanushka." She managed the ghost of a smile and whispered, "Is disease with only one end."

She tried to raise herself, to lean on an arm, but couldn't.

"You see how I am. Slowly I've lost control. Nerves. Muscles. Is no good for dancer. Body stops working. Breaks down completely."

She had a spasm of coughing which wrenched her whole body. There was no fighting back. She had nothing to fight with. Nicole had to wait, helpless, with a glass of water in hand, till the attack subsided. It took a quarter of an hour to get Alexandra in a comfortable position and the water in her to ease her parched, raw throat. When she could speak again, she was barely audible.

"I'm almost paralyzed now," came the hoarse, slow ghostly rattle. "I have trouble swallowing. Soon I won't talk. Then, all that's left is muscles for breathing. When they're gone, I'll die."

"No, no, never!" Vanya cried, and fell to his knees beside his daughter.

Completely drained by the effort it had taken to explain, she closed her eyes, willing her arms, one arm, either arm, to work. With her last ounce of energy she was able to caress her husband and her daughter. All that was left were tears running inconsolably down three faces.

 **23**

Margaret was dusting in the parlor, humming along with the radio, when she heard a great commotion at her front door. Loud, frenzied knocking followed by fierce pounding caused her to scramble to the window and then to the entryway. The door had already flown open.

"Piggy," Vanya shouted, his arms loaded with what looked like a pile of old quilts. "Out of the way. No. Stay here and help Nicole. She can't haul trunk upstairs by herself. Move, Piggy."

She had just enough time to press herself against a wall to let Vanya pass. As he did, she gasped. There, among the nest of blankets and shawls, lay a poor sad creature, perilously thin, a strange translucent sheen to the skin on its one exposed hand and its face.

That face! Even ravaged and worn by illness, it was

strikingly beautiful. Margaret couldn't help staring until the light of recognition hit her. She gasped again and raised a hand to her breast. It was Alexandra.

Margaret forgot about Vanya's orders. She didn't even see Nicole struggling with her mother's paraphernalia. Mesmerized, she followed Vanya up the stairs, hearing him murmur the craziest things to Alexandra.

"It will be fine, darling. Don't worry about a thing. We'll make it work, like in beginning, long time ago."

Margaret followed him into their bedroom, watching him tenderly tuck his wife into his and Margaret's bed. Incredulous, she listened to him make the most unimaginable promises to the first woman in his life.

"I'll take care of you. Whatever time is left . . . you'll want for nothing. Is better now, yes? You are comfortable? Feel better? Just a little bit better?"

The wraith could only extend a few fingers from the edge of the bed. But the warmth exuding from those eyes, so alive, so melting with feeling, made Margaret look away as though she had barged into something quite private, quite special. With Vanya still bent over the bed, Margaret slipped from the room, only to run into Nicole, who had finally pulled Alexandra's trunk to the top of the stairs.

"I'll do that, dear," Peggy said, forcing the spriteliness into her voice.

"I can do it," Nicole insisted.

"Of course you can. I just thought you'd rather be with your mother."

Nicole hesitated, but only for a moment.

"Th-Thank you, Peggy," came the unfamiliar words.

Margaret made quick, efficient work of the bags, cases, and trunk, quietly maneuvering them into a corner of the bedroom, stacking them neatly, leaving Vanya and Nicole to hover at the bedside. It became apparent to Margaret that the situation was serious. Alexandra was as helpless as a fledgling fallen out of its nest. The woman couldn't move under her own power. There simply wasn't any power left. She could barely sip a spoonful of medicine. And her speech was terribly slurred, barely understandable. The more she tried, the worse it became.

Margaret stole up behind Vanya and rested her hand on his shoulder.

"One minute, Van. Please," she said softly.

He nodded. But it took several minutes to extract his hand from his wife's, to smooth the covers for her, to give Nicole unnecessary orders, to walk away from the bed. Finally he closed the door behind him, giving himself once again to his mistress. He tried to look at her with the British aplomb she'd taught him, but he failed. Instead he pulled her to him and clung to her.

"I never thought it could come to this," he cried.

She held him gently, patting and petting him, and when he was calmer, she said, "I need to know, Van. Is there no hope for her?"

"She might have months . . . or only weeks."

She hugged Vanya fiercely, territorially.

"We'll do our best for her then, dearest. You and I and Nikki and Nicole. We'll make her last moments happy ones."

"Oh God, Piggy," he cried, burying his face into her hair. "How will I ever live through this?"

"You will, Van darling. We'll get through it together. And after—"

He shook his head violently, not wanting to hear the words, not wanting to acknowledge the inevitable. Margaret pulled his head away from her and forced him to look at her.

"Yes, Van. Listen to me. After it's over, I'll make it very easy for you. We'll go away for a little holiday or we'll send the children on tour . . . just a short one. And it will be just the two of us. As it was always meant to be."

He nodded miserably.

"Now you go back and hold her hand. Tell her one of your wonderful stories. And send Nicole down to the kitchen to make a pot of tea. Alexandra will feel so much better after a cuppa. You mark my words. Now I think I'd better go to Nick and break the news to him."

Vanya kissed Peggy gratefully. "Would you do that for me, darling?"

"Of course, Van. You know I'd do anything for you. Now off you go."

She watched him dash toward the bedroom. Undisturbed, she turned and proceeded down the hallway to Nikki's room. She rapped sharply on his door.

"Nick dear, may I come in?" she inquired, waiting for him to undo his locks.

He opened the door for her and returned to his labors.

"My, my!" Margaret exclaimed, sitting down next to him. "I've never seen your soldiers shine so brightly."

"It's been awfully loud in this house," he said sulkily. "Impossible to drown out the noise."

"I've never seen anyone with your power of concentration, dear," she said, petting a hank of hair away from his brow. "And you're quite right as usual. All this hurrah had been awfully upsetting. For every one of us."

She looked hopefully at him. He didn't seem to take the bait. If anything, Nikki seemed to become more engrossed in his task, flecking minute dust motes from each tin soldier, buffing them till his knuckles went white.

"Yes, Nick," she went on artfully. "I never doubt your mental powers. Such a careful, orderly little boy you've always been. Now you're all grown-up, almost all grown-up. Ready to take on the problems of a man."

Mechanically he mumbled something about his upper lip being stiff.

"That's it exactly! That's how we all must be. Carry on as we always have. Show the mettle we're made of."

She took his hand away from the toy and held it, finally succeeding in getting his attention. Irritated, Nikki frowned and pursed his lips.

"We'll get through this situation together, you, your father, and I."

"Peggy," he said in exasperated tones, "give me my soldier back. He's the last one, and I want to have the set finished before tonight."

PIROUETTE

"I don't think you'll be going to the ballet tonight, dear."

"Why not?" he whined.

"Nicole will probably be staying home."

Nikki couldn't hide his smirk, saying, "Pater's not going to like that."

"Well, dear, you see, Van won't be going tonight either, I shouldn't think."

Now she really had him. He put down his polishing cloth and let his hands fall limply into his lap.

"Is everyone sick?"

"Not your father, dear boy. Nor your sister. It's . . . well, it's your mother. This is going to be a shock, Nick, so I want you to squeeze my hand just like you used to when you'd cut yourself and I'd have to put a plaster on it."

Obediently, the twenty-year-old squeezed her hand.

"Good boy," she said, nodding her approval. "Well, there's no easy way to tell it, so here it is in a nutshell. Your father has brought Alexandra back. She's very ill. In fact, Van says she has only a short time left. So we're going to be very, very kind and—"

Dropping her hand as though it were burning him, Nikki jumped to his feet. His face turned livid and then white. His breath came fast. He began to shake from head to toe.

Margaret jumped up, suddenly scared for him.

"Dearest Nick, what can I do to help? What can I say?"

"Shut up!" he screamed, the words seemingly torn from his throat.

"What?" Margaret said, tottering slightly.

"I said *shut up!* I don't want to hear about her. Nothing. Not a word. I don't care if she lives or dies."

"Nick Borcheff, where are your manners?"

They had exploded, along with the fragile cord that tied together Margaret's well-behaved little boy and the young man who lashed out at his mother through his dancing.

"Damn her! Damn her!" he shouted.

He took a wild step toward Margaret, froze, and turned away. Eyes wide as saucers, Margaret stood rooted, hand covering her mouth in disbelief as his arms flailed out like

185

blind scythes, sweeping, smashing, mowing down his precious collections from their shelves. Glass bounded and shattered. Wood snapped and splintered. Metal dented and gouged. His world, so carefully designed, lovingly gathered, faithfully maintained, was falling to pieces about his head.

Meanwhile, Vanya had shooed Nicole away.

"But I don't want to leave her," Nicole cried. "I just got her back."

"No argument, daughter. You must do this for me," Vanya persisted. "Give me little time alone with your mother. Is all I ask. Is not asking that much."

Nicole felt an iron glove descend and grip her shoulder. She couldn't say no, not to this man. Her taskmaster. Her mentor. Her tormentor. A wave of jealousy gripped her stomach, churning and fomenting concealed emotions. Don't let him see, she warned herself. Don't let him know how much it matters.

"Shura needs many things. Woman things," Vanya went on. "New bedgowns, clean and fresh. We will throw out old ones. And flowers. We must fill room with magnificent, beautiful bouquets. And perfume to scent her handkerchiefs. You know what she likes, Nicole. Here is money."

He took out a wad of notes from his pocket, began to count it out, and then handed Nicole the whole amount.

"Spend whatever you need to. Spend it all."

She stared at him, seeing how much he cared. She saw how great was his pain. As great as her own. The jealousy vanished, replaced by a seed of sympathy. Of empathy. Of understanding.

Blinded by a cascade of tears, Nicole crushed the money in her fist, gave her father a glancing hug, blew a kiss to her mother and rushed from the room. She would get the very best for Alexandra and bring her plenty of surprises. She would charm and cajole her mother, joke with her, make her well. It wasn't too late, she told herself. It couldn't be too late.

* * *

Instinctively, automatically, despite her intended destination, her feet carried her to Soho.

"My God, Nicole, are you sure?" Carlo asked soberly. "She's that far gone? The doctors can do nothing?"

She lay in his arms, miserably nodding her head against his chest. He caressed her mass of wheaten hair, murmuring sympathetically at the sad tale.

"The worst of it is, she's given up. She had such pride in her body and her appearance. Now it's all gone. I could see it in her eyes. If she's given up, then there is no hope."

Nicole lapsed into another tide of tears. All Carlo could do was hold her, giving her the release she needed, now more desperately than ever.

"What a tragedy, cara mia. Terrible."

"It didn't have to be this way," Nicole sobbed. "Why didn't she tell me from the very start? Christ," she said, rage fueling her pain, "I don't even know when she first got sick. And then to walk away from me . . ." she sputtered, defiance building in her. "Why didn't she turn to me? Why didn't she let me be with her? Go to the doctors with her? Take care of her?"

"You really don't see it, do you?"

Nicole's head shot up and she stared at him, amazed. "And you do?!"

"Look at it this way, cara. Alexandra's been strong all your life. She's been your tower of strength because she had to. There was no one else for you or her to lean on. Think back to the hard times."

Nicole frowned, pictures of her childhood crowding her mind. "There were no hard times."

"Sure there were, Nicole. A dancer on perpetual tour hasn't exactly chosen the easy life."

"Mom always made it fun," Nicole said, lost in a dream of the old days.

"Sure she did. Because she didn't want you to see the hard side of life. But it was there. Jesus, Nicole, it was so hard she finally had to give up and come crawling back to Vanya. Don't tell me you haven't realized that yet?"

Nicole gulped, swallowing the bitter pill of truth. Maybe she'd always known. Maybe she'd refused to admit it.

"You're so much like your mother. Strong and stubborn as a mule."

He went to kiss her. To nuzzle the soft spot at the base of her earlobes.

"No, Dr. Freud. You finish your little analysis."

"Well," he said, leaning his head on an arm, "it's simple. Your mother's gone right on protecting you. She was going to save you from the agony, the degeneration, the death. How could she share the worst with you after building this fairy-tale life you all believed in?"

"She was wrong," Nicole said, shaking her head. "You can't protect anyone from death."

"I think she loved you so much, she was willing to sacrifice everything for you."

"But look what it cost us, Carlo. Three years together. Her last three."

This time when he kissed her, she accepted it. Needed it.

"You've got time now, cara. Make it count."

"I will," she assured him. "But how will I possibly bear it when she's gone?" she cried, unable to stem the flow of insistent tears.

There were tears in his own eyes. He wrapped his arms around her trembling body and held her. Just held her.

 **24**

Life was no longer empty. It was an abyss filled with pain. With dread. Mounting anxiety. Constant sorrow. It was having to watch Alexandra lose a little bit more of herself, of her dignity, day by miserable day. The disease barreled over her helpless body, crushing any resistance in its path and reducing bravery to a mockery. An insult.

It was watching Vanya fight for control over his emotions,

which inexorably seeped and spread. From the sanctity of the sickroom. Through Margaret's house. To the halls of the British Court Ballet.

It was watching Nikki lock himself further away from feeling the impending, final loss. Negation was his answer. If there were no communication, no bond, then there was no hurt. No need to feel anything. No need to share feelings that didn't exist.

But they did, and Nicole knew them intimately. She felt them each time he took charge of her in the practice room. In rehearsal. On stage. For as much as life hurt, the dance had to go on. Vanya insisted. Nikki insisted. Carlo insisted. And so she hurled herself daily from her mother's bedside to Nikki's mad, cold grip. Back and forth. Forth and back. Until she was sick with need for release—release only Carlo could give her.

Every moment with him was a reminder of what life should be. He was her spark. Her flint. She needed to brush against him. Rub against his hair. His skin. His clothes. Any part of him ignited her. She had never felt more passionate. More in need of his passion. Grabbing for him was like grabbing for the very force of life. Life was so precious, Nicole realized. So fragile. It was death that was strong and immutable and had to be fought against. What better way to fight than with passion?

She made love to Carlo whenever and wherever she could. The more perilous the place and time, the better. Then, triumphant, she felt as though she was cheating death. Proving life and love the constant winner.

One morning in the midst of company class, the need struck again. Impulsively she snubbed her brother and flung herself into Carlo's arms. They danced a couple of combinations together. Nikki, with cold fire smoldering in his eyes, stalked out of the classroom, to the amazement of the ballet master.

Nicole danced with Carlo for the rest of the class, ignoring the whispers that spun about her. After the reverence, after the dancers had filed out of the room and only the two of them were left, she kissed him, placing her hands all over him and wanting to climb onto him, into him.

"Here. Right here, right now," she proposed.

Carlo was tickled by her suggestion but protested, half joking, half serious, "I don't know, cara. The next class will be here in ten minutes. We could give them one hell of a demonstration, but old Demsby-Worth would claim it wasn't ballet."

"Shut up and kiss me."

For a moment he obliged her. Then he pushed her away. Nicole frowned.

"There's always the costume room," he said offhandedly.

The smile returned to Nicole's face. "Yeah. Just you and me on yards and yards of velvet and tulle, chiffon and—"

". . . smelly cotton jersey. Mildewed dancers' belts and—"

"C'mon," she said urgently, pulling him out the door, down the hall, and into the stuffy room filled with tutus, tights, and tunics.

Locking the door from the inside, she turned to face him. "Now love me," she demanded.

She pulled her leotard down off her breasts and pressed against him. Pushing at him. Entangling her legs around him. Making him forget everything but her. They fell in a heap on the floor, amid the disarray of old pillows and discarded garments, scraps of fabric and yardage bolts. Carlo maneuvered Nicole beneath him and she stretched out. Sinuous as a cat. Eyes half closed.

"Yes, yes," she purred, oblivious to everything but his lips, his touch.

A key was inserted precisely into the lock. The doorknob turned with one flick of a wrist. Nikki walked in, his face first registering shock and then a sneering smugness.

"Red-handed. I've caught you red-handed."

In one swift, smooth movement, Carlo threw a square of silk over Nicole's nakedness and rose up, protecting her from Nikki's raking eyes. Utterly cool, the Italian stared straight at his rival.

"Just turn around, walk out, and close the door behind

you, Nick. Forget what you saw—what you think you saw—just go. Now."

Nikki blinked as though he were suddenly unsure. He even started to take one step backward, until his sister scrambled to her feet, clutching the silk to her exposed flesh.

"You won't tell, will you, Nikki?"

Her voice gave too much away, and her awkward attempt to cover up the situation as well as herself broke Carlo's spell. Nikki stood his ground, curling his lips with disdain in the best of cardboard princely fashion as she scrambled to dress herself.

"Rutting like pigs in the muck. Spilling your filth all over the costumes."

Carlo laughed at him. "What's eating your craw more, Nikki boy? That you've never taken a girl in here yourself or that Nicole and I are lovers?"

"Shut your mouth, you son of a bitch. That's my sister you've dishonored. You've brought shame to the name of Borcheff."

"Forgive me," Carlo said in exaggerated deference. "I thought her name was Varonne."

"Don't play with me, Domenici. I'm talking about family honor, something a lowlife wop would know nothing about."

For the briefest moment Carlo's eyes narrowed. Nicole could see the panther in him readying to attack. Then the menacing stance and the clenched muscles evaporated. Carlo threw back his head and laughed.

"You pretentious little puppy. Go run along, back to Daddy. You're as bloodless as your dancing."

"Bloodless, am I? Pretentious?" he bleated, his pale face turning lobster red. "Don't you know, Domenici? You're the company joke. The monkey on a string my father brings out to entertain the cheap seats."

The room heated up, and Nicole jumped between the two men before the verbal jabs turned physical.

"Stop it, the two of you. You can trade insults all you want some other time. Right now, Nikki, I want to know if you're going to keep this to yourself." Suddenly she was pleading with her twin, tugging at his shirt, twisting it in her fists. "You don't know what's at stake . . . all the ramifications . . ."

"Don't I?" he retorted, the smugness returning to his face.

He flicked open the door. Staring at Nicole and Carlo, he yelled into the hallway, and a small boy in school togs stuck his head in.

"What's your name, boy?" Nikki demanded.

"Clark, sir," the boy responded, eyes big as saucers.

"Aptly named. Now do as I say, Clark. Go to the director's office and tell him to come here immediately. Tell him Nick says it's important."

"Maestro Borcheff? Himself?"

"Himself. Now run, boy." Nicole stood sheltered within Carlo's arms. She looked at her brother, whom she didn't know at all.

"Why, Nikki? Why?"

There was scorn in his eyes, veiled by a distant pity. "To protect you, of course."

She shook her head. He was incomprehensible. A complete enigma. But there was no time to figure him out or convince him to change his mind, because Vanya walked in. Nicole giggled nervously, mesmerized by her father's eyebrows, which seemed to want to rise all the way into his hairline.

"What the hell's going on?" he asked. "Nikki, you explain."

"I've kept my eyes on them, Pater. This time I followed them. They didn't even know, they were so busy. . . . Not five minutes ago, I found her," he said, pointing at Nicole with a damning finger, "being poked about by that bloody wog."

"You saw them?"

"I caught them . . . in the act!"

Nicole expected her father to rise up and smite both Carlo and her with a full-blown storm of Russian outrage. Instead he sagged, seeming to shrink inside himself. If Nikki's tattling had any effect, it was a diminishing one. For just a second she felt ashamed. Her father already had so much to contend with.

Vanya glanced from Nikki to Nicole to Carlo, back to Nicole, and finally to his son.

"Leave us, Nikolai. I will speak to you later."

Nikki nodded. He started to go, hesitated, then stopped. He gestured toward Nicole, offering her his hand. An invitation to go with him. An opportunity to make a statement. To make the choice for him. She stared at her brother's outstretched hand and shook her head slowly, deliberately, wrapping both arms about her lover. Nikki turned away and left the costume room.

"Would have been better for you to have gone with him," said Vanya in a steely quiet voice.

"Smarter maybe," she responded, "but not better."

"Then you will hear what I have to say to this . . . traitor," he said, finally turning his attention to Carlo. "I gave you every opportunity. More than most would have given. I will not bother you with tiresome reproach. I will only say this: get out of my sight, my company, my life. Don't ever come near me or the school or the theater again. And don't ever let me catch you near my daughter. You may not see her. You may not correspond with her. You may not come anywhere near her. You're out. Permanently. Forever."

Vanya set his hands firmly on Nicole's shoulders and yanked her from Carlo's embrace. Held her and wouldn't let her go.

"This is clear to you, Nicole, yes?"

No, it was not clear. Her father couldn't do this to her. She would be with whomever she pleased. Whomever she chose. And she wanted Carlo.

"You'll have to put me in chains. Tie me down," she cried. "I need him, Father. You don't understand. You don't understand."

"No, cara, no," implored Carlo. "It's all right."

"All right? It's not all right. It's all wrong. Let go of me, Father."

But Vanya didn't release her. He stood there, motionless and blind as granite.

"Let her go, Borcheff," Carlo finally demanded. "You've got nothing to worry about. I was planning to leave anyway."

One pair of blue eyes and another of brown popped wide open.

"I'm sorry, cara. I wish I could've told you some other way."

Calmly, he walked past Vanya and Nicole and went out the door. Nicole managed to break away from Vanya. She ran after Carlo, ignoring her father's orders to come back.

"What do you mean? Damn it, Carlo, stand still and tell me what you're talking about."

She chased after him, following him into the men's dressing room, blessedly empty of other dancers. He cleaned out his locker and stuffed his gear, all of it, into a duffle bag.

"It's my homeland. Mussolini alone was bad enough. But Mussolini allied with Hitler . . . War is right around the corner, Nicole. Chamberlain thinks he's made peace with the Munich Agreement, but he's wrong. Hitler won't be content with Czechoslovakia. And Mussolini wants to be in on the next kill."

Nicole looked at Carlo as though he were speaking a foreign language. "I don't understand . . ."

"I know, cara. You're not political and I am."

"Dancers are citizens of the whole world, Carlo."

"That's very cute and very naive. You haven't lived with the threat of persecution like I have. My family has."

Nicole couldn't help but think of her current situation. She did know what persecution was. She'd had firsthand knowledge of it for the past several years.

"Look, cara. Some of us emigrés have promised to help the British government any way we can. Let me just say that secret mobilization against the Axis powers has begun, and don't ask me any more."

"But you haven't told me anything."

"Christ, Nicole, I've volunteered to head an undercover intelligence unit in Italy."

"Italy?"

She thought he was leaving British Court. Going to another company in London. At worst, another company outside London. But Italy . . . He might as well have said Siberia or Greenland or the moon. That far away from her.

"I've got to go, cara. For me there is no choice."

A lump stuck in her throat. She felt like gagging, choking, crying, screaming. But the words were stuck there in her throat with the lump.

"But my mother is dying," she managed to say. "How can you leave now?"

Spine stiff, he turned away from her, slammed his locker shut and hoisted the bag over one shoulder.

"I have to."

And then he was gone. Leaving her to stand alone. To stand shattered.

~~ **25**

In the next few weeks Nicole clung to each member of her family like a child drowning. Suddenly Vanya's opinion was important to her again. Margaret's efforts to cook enticing concoctions for Alexandra were endearing. Never mind that the food was still inedible. Even Nikki's aggravated aggressions were acceptable. Because, if nothing else, they were the norm. Change of any sort was the enemy to be feared.

Nicole had come face to face with the enemy. Carlo had made sure of that, wrenching her only security from her tenuous grasp, leaving nothing but fury to take its place. And the fury was useless. Directionless. Railing at Carlo was as effective as ramming a stone wall with a feather. He was unbending, leaving her with only one recourse. To be as rigid as he. To be unforgiving. To reject. No matter what the cost.

Now only one person mattered. Nicole spent every free moment with her mother. Her lips ached with the forced smile she plastered on her face for Alexandra's sake. No need to let Mom know her heart had been broken. No need to let Mom see the distress that permanently dogged her spirit. In the sickroom only gaiety and light were allowed. The silliest of popular songs. The sweetest of scents. The most delicate savories. The funniest reminiscences.

Nicole's acting ability was sorely tested. She passed, but the price was obvious. Especially to the senior Domenicis, who came to call on the Varonnes one wintry day. They chose their time carefully, arriving during a weekend matinee when Vanya and Nikki were not at home. Margaret, busy in the kitchen baking a rice pudding with stewed prunes for Alexandra's teatime, called out to Nicole to answer the door.

There on the doorstep were Stefano and Francesca, snug in their old winter coats, hats, and scarves. Father and Mother Christmas incarnate . . . Italian style.

"Piccola!" cried Carlo's mother, smothering Nicole in a warm embrace. "So thin and tired you look. Who's taking care of you?"

No one, she wanted to say. Instead she hugged Francesca, instantly aware of the difference between this healthy woman's body and Alexandra's. Tears sprang to her eyes. She felt like a never-ending fountain of woe.

"There, there, poor chicken. How hard this has been on you."

Then Stefano took over, bustling his wife and Nicole into the warm house. He juggled boxes, coats, and women, making them chuckle.

"For you, Nicoletta, and for your mother. We bring the finest zuppa, the flakiest of pasticcerias, and a torte di riso the angels above would fight over."

"The secret is the rice. You must use Arborio rice, an Italian specialty," confided Francesca.

"Bah," Stefano retorted. "The secret is the amaretto."

He kissed the tips of his fingers and rolled his eyes suggestively, making them all laugh again.

"I've missed you both so much."

The words tumbled out of Nicole's mouth. She blushed.

Their absence from her life was her own doing. Carlo's doing. She was so confused. She only knew she was losing everyone she had ever loved.

"And we've missed you."

In a moment Francesca had pulled out an oblong of linen and was dabbing at her eyes.

"These are horrible times. First we hear about your sainted mother, struck down by this diabolico disease. Then Carlo, may God watch over him, decides to take on Il Duce singlehandedly."

"Francesca, the boy has the government of England behind him. He'll be fine."

"What do fathers know?" Francesca chided. "We women are the ones who'll suffer, who'll wait at home and worry. Nicoletta agrees with me. Just look at her face. She misses Carlo already, don't you, carina? See, Stefano? She cries for him already."

Somehow it was true, and it felt good to cry with his mother. But she stifled the hearty sobs when Margaret approached, hastily wiping glutenous chunks of boiled rice from her hands onto her apron.

"Guests, Nicole? You should have come and gotten me, dear. Bring them into the parlor."

"They're friends of mine . . . and Mom's. Carlo's parents. Stefano and Francesca Domenici, meet Margaret Dunstable, my father's . . . companion."

"The Domenicis," she said, nodding her head slowly, swallowing the information. "What a pity," she added brightly, "that Van isn't here."

"We came to pay our respects to Nicoletta's mother," Stefano stated, the emphasis unmistakably tying respect to Alexandra and no one else.

"Well, isn't that dear of you. But I can't think she'd be able to receive you. Perhaps you could leave your little gifts with Nicole. She can spend all of teatime reporting to poor Alexandra just what you said and did——"

"Oh, I think Mom would love to see the Domenicis," Nicole interrupted. "I think it would give her a real boost."

"Of course, you know best, Nicole," Margaret said,

smiling in the direction of the visitors. "Perhaps the visit oughtn't to be too long, though. The boys will be home by five. Van and Nick do love to have their cuppa in front of a lovely fire."

Everyone smiled politely, understanding the implicit message.

"Let's go up and surprise Mom," Nicole interjected.

The group broke up. Margaret retreated to her kitchen, and Nicole and the Domenicis went up the stairs. Nicole knocked at her mother's door, opened it, and ushered in the visitors.

For a moment all was hushed. The room had an air of sanctity about it. Lush tribute to the invalid lined practically every square inch of space. Amidst a bower of radiantly blooming flowers, gift boxes of every size and shape, topped with abundant bows, were scattered. And at the heart of the array was the sick bed, piled with satin-covered pillows and plump downy quilts. A dainty Wedgewood bell, water in a lead crystal carafe, and a cedar box of French lace handkerchiefs lay ready for use on the bedstand.

But the richness of the room only served to underscore the severity of Alexandra's condition. She was propped up against the bulwark of pillows, wrapped in a luxurious jacket of Chinese silk. The beauty of the disguise couldn't hide the emaciation. The waste. The agony she had undergone and was undergoing. Her head leaned limply to one side. Eyes closed. Breathing slow. Tortured. The dark, once flamboyant hair was caught in a single braid that hung lifelessly over one or two of the pillows, as though it had been tossed there by an uncaring hand. As though it were somehow disconnected.

Nicole tiptoed over to the bed and whispered to her mother, "Special visitors, Mom. The Domenicis have come to see you."

A gurgle, almost disembodied, emanated from Alexandra's throat. The eyes opened with painful effort. Blinked. Finally focused. A muscle twitched at the side of her mouth, the extent of a smile left to the proud woman.

Two more sounds in marchlike cadence came from her mouth.

"She can still say my name," Nicole explained to Stefano and Francesco.

The Domenicis exchanged a private glance and instinctively clasped each other's hand, squeezing hard when they watched Nicole lift her mother, as though she weighed no more than the feather pillows that supported her, and rearrange her tenderly so that she could see the couple more easily.

"What, Mom?" Nicole was asking.

The Domenicis couldn't make out a sound, couldn't see that any form of communication had taken place. But Nicole, aware of every nuance, every shading of body language, had seen the subtle shift of her mother's hand. The minute, upward jerk of a knuckle on one thin finger.

"She wants you to come closer," Nicole told the couple.

Complying with her request, Stefano and Francesca took seats by the bed. Stefano leaned forward, picked up the limp arm and kissed Alexandra's fingertips. Francesca brushed her lips past the pale cheek.

"I pray for you every night, my dear," she murmured as she drew back to sit beside her husband.

A twitch of the muscle near Alexandra's lips threatened to quaver.

"I understand," Francesca said. "No need to exert yourself, Shura. We are of the same mind, you and I. We know what is in the heart without having to say it."

Stefano suddenly became busy. He opened the boxes they had brought from the trattoria, held each of the containers close to Alexandra so that she could breathe in the appetizing aromas.

"Puts these flowers to shame, eh? Come on, Nicoletta. Help me convince your mother. Take a sniff, deep into your lungs. Ahhh. I'm right, eh? Now take a taste. Tell me if I'm wrong. If Solomon himself were here to judge, he would throw up his hands. No contest, he would say. Here is nectar and ambrosia, fit for the gods. Here, Francesca. A little for you . . . a little more for Nicoletta. What do you say, Signorina Ballerina? How can you resist?"

Nicole swore Alexandra arched an eyebrow and fluttered her eyelashes. At least gave the impression. Nicole clapped her hands in delight. From some deep reserve, Alexandra managed to move her head toward Stefano and open her mouth. Just slightly.

Nicole was able to give her mother a few teaspoonsful of the sparkling broth, a crumb of the Italian pastry, and a bite or two of the torte di riso. A satisfied sigh escaped from the woman's lips.

"I knew it," boasted Stefano. "A little Bari cooking and she'll come round. We'll just put the rest in the kitchen for later . . ."

Nicole gulped. She didn't want to consider what could occur if the Domenicis and Margaret mixed it up in the kitchen. The onset of World War II was not out of the question. Margaret would see that Mom had actually eaten, something they all had thought was now impossible.

Worse, there would be the comparisons, the snipes, the hurt feelings. Margaret slaving away, preparing dish after dish. Even now she was down there whipping up a ghoulish, lumpy version of rice pudding. Of course, Mom wouldn't be able to swallow it, much less look at it. But if Margaret found out about the Domenici's torte di riso . . . saw it . . . tasted it . . . If it sat there in its crowning glory next to her own lump of lead . . .

"I don't know what's come over me," cried Nicole, heading straight for the soup, the pastry, the pudding. "I've never felt so hungry. I tell you what. Let's make a party. Here and now. Celebrate the good food and the good company. I'll turn on the radio and find some music."

The Domenicis watched with great pleasure as Nicole knocked off their delicacies, offering tiny morsels to Alexandra, who occasionally accepted one or two.

"If you came to the ristorante like you used to," Francesca chided Nicole, "there'd be some meat on those skin and bones in no time. Why aren't you coming, Nicoletta?"

Nicole looked steadfastly at the diminishing food, mumbling, "You'll have to ask Carlo."

"Alexandra," Francesca said, including the sick woman as her ally, "the children have quarreled. We must get them back together."

Alexandra's eyes traveled, settling on her daughter. Nicole could feel her mother's glance without looking up.

"It's not my fault," she choked out, feeling like a child caught, found out in an act of mischief. "I didn't tell him to go away."

"Nobody tells Carlo anything, my child," said Stefano. "He was born with his eyes open and his hands in little fists. When he sees his duty, he does it."

"But it's wrong. And stupid."

"Who, among us, decides what each of us must do? Who, alone, must judge?"

The weight of Alexandra's gaze was more than Nicole could bear. What is this all about? she telegraphed silently.

"Carlo's going off to save Italy," Nicole scoffed, finally meeting her mother's eyes.

Alexandra did arch an eyebrow. Nicole couldn't mistake it this time.

"I don't care what he does," she insisted. "I have no hold on him."

"Yes, you do," Francesca said softly. "I've never seen my son in such a state. You know the last time I saw him cry? He was just a bambino and his favorite toy broke. You remember, Stefano, how he loved that little stuffed dog? It had been darned so many times, I'm surprised it lasted as long as it did. When I told him it couldn't be fixed, he became so serious. So quiet. As though he had suffered a little death along with his little doggy. He never cried again. Not even when we were forced from our home. Not even when we saw our beloved Italia for the last time."

Francesca paused for a moment, searching Nicole's eyes for some sign of understanding, for some crack in her emotional armor.

"He cries now, Nicoletta. He cries for you. Please see him

one last time. Before he leaves all of us. Let him leave with his heart intact."

Nicole couldn't look at Francesca. She sought Alexandra for solace, for guidance, as in the old days.

"He said he loved me, Mom. But he's leaving me when he's all I've got left."

There it was. Raw and ugly and selfish and hurting and true. Who would be there for Nicole?

Alexandra's eyes, filled with exhaustion, mirrored the aching heart of the mother. Of the loved one. Mirrored the unspoken fear . . . What if you never see him again? Is this the end you want to remember? Is this the end you won't be able to forget? Go to him, Nicole. Then the eyes closed.

Nicole's resistance crumbled. "When does he leave?" she whispered.

"Tomorrow night," Stefano rumbled.

"I'll come tomorrow morning."

"Grazie, Nicoletta," cried Francesca. "We'll make sure Carlo is home. Alone. And now we must let your dear mother rest. *Molti benediziones,* Shura."

The Domenicis found their own way out, leaving Nicole with Alexandra. Like the little girl she'd once been, the little girl she felt like again, Nicole climbed onto the bed and lay next to her mother. Seeking the haven. Holding on while she could. While there was still time.

 **26**

What was Nikki's secret? Nicole had spent the entire night tossing, turning. Not sleeping. Mind churning. How did he do it? How did her twin store it up . . . the anger and the spite and the malice and the hate . . . and only let it out in his dancing?

Nicole yearned for such control. If she could only bottle the hurt and the fear, putting all emotion away until she'd conquered it. She'd be content to be numb. To be contained.

To be like Nikki. Letting it leak out here and there. No one suspecting she wasn't in control. No one guessing how much the emotions controlled her.

That wasn't what she wanted at all. She wanted to be free. To feel the glory of every emotion. To know love conquered all. That it could cure Alexandra. That it could make Vanya and Nikki accept her for herself. That it would keep Carlo from being swept into the senseless winds of war.

If she loved him . . . if she showed him how deeply he was rooted in her . . . maybe he'd stay. Maybe she could get him to give up this lunacy. He had no obligations to a country. A piece of unforgiving rock and soil. The land didn't care about him. Need him as she did. Anyone could till the earth. Only Carlo could tend to Nicole.

She would go to him. Tell him. Show him. Love him. Finally she slept for an hour or two, until the first dreary rays of dawn woke her. Flushed with hope and determination, she arrived at his door. Knocking bravely, she suddenly felt shy. What if her plan didn't work? She banished the thought. It had to work.

Carlo opened the door. The strain of worry and misery was etched on his face. Nicole's only thought was to erase it. To wash it away with her kiss and her caress. She was in his arms in an instant. He was burying his face in her hair. His hands were like chains, binding her to him. Tighter, tighter she wanted to demand. Never let me go.

"Cara . . ."

She put a finger to his lips, shushing him.

"Not a word. We don't need words," she murmured. "Just love me and let me love you."

They made tender, passionate, desperate love to each other. In Nicole's mind there was only one thought. One goal. To be his instrument. His plaything. His anchor. His echo. To be perfect for him, satisfying everything he wanted in her. Then be able to offer him more.

Excite him. Tantalize him. Give him the challenge so that the question couldn't be raised. Give him the storm, banishing the doubt forever. Give him the ultimate surcease. So that he would stay with her.

Then, only then, when they lay collapsed in each other's arms and Carlo was utterly sated, did Nicole feel safe. Then she was sure he couldn't leave her. Then she asked him. Just to hear him say yes, it was true.

"I can't, cara."

She clung to him all the harder. Desperately kissing the lips that had betrayed. He couldn't have understood her. It was her fault. She didn't ask the question properly. There was no other excuse. He didn't mean it. He couldn't mean it.

"Cara. Stop. Stop it, Nicole." Gently, firmly, he pushed her away. "I must go."

She was shaking her head. Her face was falling into a frown. Her breathing came hard. Quick deep pants turning into sobs. She covered her cheeks with her hands, holding herself together.

"I'm so scared, Carlo. Do you know what my life will be like without you? It's all I've thought of since you told me you were going away. My mother will be dead. Nikki and Father will put me over the edge. I'll go crazy; I know it. I'll have no one to turn to. No one to remind me of who I am. My God, Carlo, what will become of Nicole? There's so little of her . . . me . . . left."

"You're stronger than you know, cara. You're not going to crumble. I believe in Nicole Varonne." He cradled her in his arms. "But if I stay," he posited, "I won't be able to live with myself. It's a debt of honor. I know you've never understood what that means to me."

"How can it mean more to you than life?" Nicole asked brokenly. "More than love? More than us?"

"You are a gift to me, tesoro mio. Your love is the greatest gift a man can receive. But this other . . . it's obligation. It's duty. Before all else, I owe this to my family, to Italy—the land of my youth—and to England—the country that gave me a home."

"God damn it, Carlo, that's just rhetoric. Fancy words to ease your guilt. But none of it's your fault. You didn't ask to be born a Domenici. You didn't put Mussolini in power. You can't knock him off yourself."

"Try to understand, cara. Please."

"Why?" she cried, moving out of his arms. "You're leaving me when I need you. When I love you more than anything or anyone. You're jeopardizing our future. And for what? A chance to be blown to hell. A chance for one moment of stupid masculine glory."

He was silent, staring beyond her. Already he was distancing himself from her. Already she had lost him.

"You'll never come back. We'll never dance together. Never make love again."

He crushed her in his arms and she couldn't help but cling to him.

"Don't send me off like this, cara. I'd die if I lost you. You're my life. Say you love me. Tell me you'll love me your whole life long."

He wanted undying declarations when he wouldn't give her an inch. He couldn't have it both ways. Not when she got nothing. She pulled away from him, stepping back.

"How long will yours last, Carlo? Three months? Maybe four?"

Without a last glance, without one lingering gaze to memorize his face, she turned and ran from him. It was over. She had lost. She had no one.

It took her hours to arrive home. She had wandered the streets, letting her feet make their own path. If Alexandra weren't there, she might have kept on walking. She slumped into the house and checked quickly to find her mother asleep. Short rasps of breath were torn from the useless vocal cords. Nicole closed the door and went back downstairs. Not to the dining room or the kitchen—she couldn't handle Margaret at this point—but to the parlor. She'd sit quietly by the roaring fire and stare into the flames, getting lost inside them.

But Vanya was there, hunched over in his favorite chair with his head in hands, sobbing. Her heart sank. She didn't think she could take any more bad news. But her legs carried her mechanically forward. Her hand went to his ragged head.

"What is it, Father?"

To her shock, he wrapped his arms around her, burying his head against her waist.

"The doctor just left, Nicole. He says soon, any time."

Nicole swayed, her legs disobeying, threatening to buckle. She found herself holding onto her father for support.

"No," she mumbled. "Not yet."

"Piggy says we must be brave."

Peggy. What the hell did she know? Cool, impersonal, dunderingly efficient. When had she lost something, someone, so precious? When had she felt the agony, the utter helplessness?

"I . . . I've got to go to Mom," Nicole said.

She tried to disentangle herself from her father and failed. He was surprisingly strong, and she couldn't budge from his grip.

"Better to stay a minute, daughter. I've made some decisions that will affect all of us."

She struggled even more. More decisions being made for her. About her. Damn it, when was it going to stop?

"I don't care what you've decided," she practically screamed. "Do whatever the hell you want. Just let go of me. I've got to be with my mother."

Instantly he released her. His face went grim with tension.

"Don't you understand, Nicole? We all must be with Shura. You, Nikki, and me. No more separation. I was wrong to insist we take care of her one at a time."

The pain on his face seemed to stretch his muscles and his skin tight. He looked completely exhausted, completely beaten.

"I was doing it to save myself," he said, barely audible, as though he were talking, confessing, to himself. "I couldn't stand idea of having to feel your pain as well as your mother's. I couldn't stand to have anyone, not even my children, see how much I suffer . . . how much I feel . . . how I bleed each time I'm in that room with her."

The taskmaster felt the cruel flick of the whip too. It was a revelation. And it opened the door between father and daughter.

"Being alone with the pain is the burden," Nicole whispered. "Sharing it . . . having someone to share it with . . . makes it bearable."

"Such wisdom," he said, bringing her close enough to hug. "Who taught you so much?"

Nicole's eyes traveled in the direction of the sick room. Vanya nodded in acknowledgment.

"Let's go up together."

It was a plea as much as a command. A tiny smile glimmered across Nicole's face. They went upstairs to Alexandra, arms about each other's waist.

The surprise didn't end there. Nikki, who hadn't set foot in the room since the day his mother returned, sat quietly at her side reading aloud Shakespearean sonnets. Alexandra's eyes were open and glistening with tears. When he finished, Nicole softly applauded. Nikki colored and shut the book.

"Didn't know you were about."

"You read beautifully, Nikki," his sister offered.

"I shouldn't've come in," he mumbled.

"Is high time, my son. Is high time you became member of this family."

Nikki glanced warily at his father.

"Piggy understands."

"I know, Pater. She's the one who convinced me."

His eyes were cast low. Unable or refusing to look at them? Nicole wondered. Being here was probably the greatest challenge her brother had ever faced.

"You won't be sorry, my son. Is lesson for all of us to learn now."

Then the dark eyes, usually hooded, looked up clearly. "I don't mind, Pater. I think she likes to hear me read," he said, glancing at his mother. "Peggy's always said my voice was smooth as treacle. Peggy says that's what's needed now."

"Piggy's not only one who knows things," huffed Vanya. "For you, Shura, I do the impossible, the unheard of. Company and performance schedule be hanged, the children and I will be here day and night. Too much time has been wasted. We have been stupid . . ." He raised both hands in a grand gesture of self-abnegation. "I have been stupid. For all our sakes, I get smart. Is not too late, eh, Shura?"

He presented her with a united front. Nicole and Nikki on either side of him. Shy tenuous smiles on three faces. From the bed came a rattle of a gasp. Air escaping from lips. Trying so hard to say something to her loved ones. Nicole broke away from Vanya and Nikki and rushed to her mother.

"It's okay, Mom. We know."

She took up the withered hand, skin etched deeply by bone, and put it to her lips.

"You did it, Mom," she whispered. "You gave me my family."

It was the wrong time to tell her about Carlo.

There never was a right time. The next few weeks, as Alexandra's condition spiraled downward, Vanya and Nicole ministered to her as though she was a fragile, newborn baby. Nikki, at first having given in to duty because of Margaret's influence, was drawn more and more into the family circle. Nicole could see him watching. Hovering. Attracted by the ephemeral delicacy. How they treated Alexandra. How she seemed to be poised on the thinnest of dividing lines between life and death. How each moment held unimaginable significance. Capturing qualities, essences of time and feeling, so delicate, so short-lived. Like the glassed butterflies he had collected. Only this time he could get close. Inside the glass cage.

Yet Nicole found him outside the bedroom door one afternoon. He was tearing the book of Shakespeare apart. Page by systematic page. Then ripping haphazardly whatever would yield to the anger in his hands. She raced to him, taking what was left of the book away.

"Stop it! Stop it!" she cried. "Nikki, what's the matter with you?"

"I'm losing her," he said, seething like a hot caldron. "And I never had her to begin with."

She flung her arms around her brother, rocking him back

and forth. "She always loved you, Nikki. Ever since I can remember."

"But I didn't know," he sobbed. "And then I didn't care."

"You do now, Nikki. I know it and Mom knows it. Go in and tell her, Nikki. While you still have time."

Caution . . . uncertainty . . . gratitude blazed across his face. He went back into the room and stood at the side of the bed. Nicole followed, silent, choking back glad tears when he leaned over the spare figure and lightly kissed his mother on both cheeks.

For those few weeks the abundance of freely flowing emotion among the family members held Alexandra within a gentle embrace. Yet each day she grew less able to respond. The eyes so alive began to dim. To look inward. To look beyond the realm of flesh so cruelly constrained.

As the body declined, her spirit seemed to swell with a spark of its own, igniting the room with an otherworldly strength and surrounding those she loved. She was cherished by them as the woman they had known slipped away.

The morning came when the last bonds were broken. When Vanya brushed his lips against his wife's cool mouth. When Nicole lovingly folded her mother's withered arms into graceful repose. Alexandra was finally free from the pain and the useless body. Free to rise unencumbered from her earthly prison and dance among the immortals.

Tears streaming down his face, Vanya held out his arms to his children. Nicole slipped into his embrace, weeping with him. Nikki stood rooted to the floor, staring at his mother . . . what had been his mother.

"Nikolai . . ." Vanya said, calling to him.

Nikki shook his head violently, bolted from the chamber of death and shut himself up in his own room. He hugged himself. He paced the length and breadth of his room, clenching his jaw till it hurt and fighting the swell of shudders that swept through his body. He surveyed his room helplessly. The remnants of his broken collections roosted sadly on mostly empty shelves. He couldn't look at them.

He hunched down to the floor next to his bed and sent an arm searching between mattresses. His hand clutched and withdrew a packet of letters tied together with a piece of rough string. He sat there on the floor, his back against the bed, and stared at the packet, turning it over and over in his hands.

Finally he pulled off the string and opened the envelope on top. He inhaled deeply, putting the fine paper near his nose. It was her scent. Mamushka's. The one who had sent him all those dense, puzzling letters before he could even read. And when he had learned to read and he read them, he hadn't understood a single word. Now . . . now if he looked at them, would they make any sense?

> *My darling,*
> *By now you have forgotten my face, but my breasts ache for you . . .*

He closed up the letter and put it aside. The next and the next and the one after that, all of them, were more of the same. He stared at each one, seeing the words fall from his mother's pen, one by one, onto the page, impregnable. They would not penetrate. He could not let them.

Neatly, he repackaged the whole lot, even retying the string. Then he got up, picked up a shallow copper bowl, and walked over to his desk. First he extracted the flowers from the bowl and threw them in his wastebasket. He emptied the water into the basket too. He took a handkerchief from his pocket and carefully wiped the bowl dry.

Opening a desk drawer, he removed a box of wooden matches. He lit one and stared at it for a while. Before it burned down completely, before it could touch his fingers and burn him, he set the letters into the bowl and dropped the match on top of them. He lit another and another.

He lit all the matches until the bowl was ablaze with charring paper and scorching sticks of wood. He stood and watched until the whole thing was reduced to a pile of ashes. When it was cold, he dumped the remains into his wastebasket, along with the flowers and the water and the empty match box, and took it down to Margaret.

27

As usual, Alexandra kept everyone busy. Arrangements for cremation. Arrangements for the memorial service. The reading of the will. All the rites that were designed to remind the family of the rich life she had had and to forget the horrible end.

The first few days passed by in a comforting veil of tears. Vanya, in his many-faceted roles as bereaved husband, saddened professional associate, responsible executor of Alexandra's last wishes, took great sympathy from the whole world.

Nicole found solace with her father. In the beginning he kept her at his side like a little lap dog. Patting and petting her. Showing her off as though she were his greatest prize. Hungrily, she groveled in his attention.

But by the end of the following week it was clear to Nicole her place in her father's life was precarious. Margaret began making subtle comments about getting things back to normal. Then she began taking blatant steps.

Without a by-your-leave, as Peggy herself would say, Alexandra's effects were packed up and moved out of the sick room. Overnight, the room that Nicole cherished as a shrine, where she still believed her mother's spirit prevailed, was unceremoniously restored to its former function. Vanya and Margaret emerged from their bedroom the next morning self-consciously holding hands. With his patient, faithful companion by his side, he slipped . . . skipped back into the comfortable fit of his British facade.

And when Vanya returned in widower's weeds to British Court, it was Nikki who accompanied him. Sat closeted with him in his office. Escorted his father from class to class, business appointment to business lunch, performance to performance. Nicole was left to mourn on her own.

Apparently, life was going to drag on. Despite the loss of Alexandra. Despite the departure of Carlo. Despite the lack of interest by Vanya. No one seemed to care that Nicole was left alone. And with no one to care for, Nicole lost her last anchor. There was little reason to get up in the morning. Little reason to eat.

"Little reason not to," Margaret cajoled.

But the house seemed empty and, all at once, too big. Before, when Alexandra was alive but had exiled herself, it was easy for Nicole to keep up the pretense. Mom was just away for a bit. She had so much to do. There was always the hope Alexandra would come back and reclaim her. Even when her mother lay wasting away in Vanya's bedroom, the house had seemed full of her. Overflowing with bouquets sent in homage. Awash with her indomitable courage.

Now the residue of the last days, horrible and familiar both, had drifted away. Nicole came to feel as though she had unluckily survived a devastating flood. Had been carried away to the ends of the earth. Left in uncharted waters with no signposts to tell her where she had come from, where she was, or where she was going. All she knew was that she had arrived on this distant, foreign shore where she was likely to stay for the rest of her life.

Her father knocked on her bedroom door one evening. "Nicole, is time to talk."

"I'm tired," she called out through the closed door.

"Is enough, Nicole," he said gruffly. "I'm tired of seeing you like this."

She turned over in bed and pulled the blankets over her head. She didn't think he'd seen her at all lately.

He charged in and jerked her covers off, demanding, "Is this how you honor your mother's memory? Feeling sorry for yourself? Playing the orphan child? Is enough," he repeated. "And is wrong. I will not allow it while you're in my house."

The unfeeling bastard! The gall! Blood began to course through her veins. Her pulse quickened. The blush of life colored her cheek.

"How dare you?" she cried. "Mom's been dead only one month. What do you expect me to do? Put on my toe shoes and dance my troubles away?"

"Yes, Nicole. That's precisely what I want you to do."

"Well, I won't. I may never dance again."

"I may never dance again," he imitated, languidly raising a limp hand to his forehead and falling gracefully into a mock swoon. "Don't be a silly goose. Is dancing that gives us life. Alexandra, may she rest in peace, taught you that. I'd stake my life on it."

Nicole shook her head, refusing to listen. He could say anything. Inveigh her mother's name. But it wouldn't work. Nothing would work.

"Look, Nicole. Look at what newspapers say."

He grabbed her chin and made her see the headlines. LEGACY OF VARONNE LIVES ON IN TWINS. He made her read the eulogies, praising the old partnership and the new.

"Is truth and you know it. You and Nikki are the future. The present. Is your time now, more than ever, to grab brass ring. Use the dance, daughter, as Nikki has. Play out your emotions. Let the dance inspire you, heal you, give you back your soul. I can't ask you to dance for me. I'm not that selfish. I can't ask you to dance for Alexandra either. But I will beg you to dance for yourself."

Oh, he was a clever one, that father of hers. He was one hell of a con artist. A prize manipulator. Pulling out all the stops, and not ashamed to do it. She wanted to stare him down. Call his bluff. Tell him to leave her alone. She wasn't ready. She might never be ready. But there was that one ounce of truth that managed to bore into her. Nag at her. Shake up her self-pity. Make her wonder.

"Have you asked Nikki?"

"He's champing at the bit. He would have come to you himself, but I insisted is director's job," puffed Vanya, winking at her.

Damn it. He knew he'd won. She'd lost another battle.

"I'm rusty."

"That's what practice room and rehearsals are for."

"I feel shaky."

"Is natural. Everything will come back to you once you are in Nikki's arms again."

Nicole didn't find the notion reassuring. What was Nikki like these days? Since the morning their mother had died, he had withdrawn into himself again. It was as bad as when she had first come to London, invading his home and his family.

"You're sure Nikki wants this? Wants me?"

"Nicole," Vanya said impatiently, "stop with the questions. Tomorrow morning you come to British Court and see for yourself."

She went, surprised to find her way so easily and surprised to see the outside world hadn't changed. She was greeted warmly at the school. The teachers gravely shook her hand, and Mademoiselle Paisy kissed her. Members of the company hugged her. It was as if she had come back from the dead.

She made her way to Vanya's office, consulted the schedule, and went to the practice room assigned to her and Nikki. He was already there, finishing his warm-up.

"Fifteen minutes. You'd better be ready."

Nicole shivered. At least he was talking to her. At least he'd given her time to stretch her muscles. But his tone. It was like steel. Rigid and razor-sharp.

She set to her barre, concentrating on the turn out. On the arch of her foot. On the straightness of her spine and the thrust of her torso. She curved her arms just enough. Turned her head the precise number of degrees. Held her developpe and arabesque. Pivoted and pirouetted. Bourréed across the room so that tiny pains, well remembered, shot through her toes.

Before she knew it, Nikki was at her side. Twirling and twisting her. Tossing her high overhead. Catching her at the ultimate thrilling moment. He was taking chances with her, leaving her no time to react.

She was scared. This violence went beyond anything she had experienced before. He didn't just want to leave bruises, reminders of his power over her. He seemed to want to be rid of her. Yet each time he held on. Not quite letting her go. Holding on to keep her dizzy. Holding on to hear her gasp.

Holding on to make her suffer. To feel the knuckles wrench and the bones snap. To make her angry. As angry as he. He was pushing her to respond. To get back at him. He wanted war.

"Bravo! Bravissimo!" Vanya shouted from just inside the door. "I build whole next season around two of you, and then we conquer Europe. Too bad we must skip Germany, and Italy too, but rest of continent will lie at your feet. If God is on our side and we don't go to war . . ."

He clapped his hands, lost in dreams of grand triumphs.

"What your mother would have given to see this. The perfect partnership reborn again like phoenix. Is good idea for ballet, no? I go find choreographer and start on idea. Yes, phoenix rising from its own ashes. A double phoenix . . . hmmm."

Vanya turned back from the open door to say, "Keep it up, children. Another hour at least."

For an hour Nicole fought off Nikki's unrelenting attack. With each passing minute the fog that had paralyzed her, that had put her in emotional limbo, slowly began to dissipate. It was Alexandra's life that was over. Not hers. Her life was only beginning. In her mind's eye it stretched out like a vast plain waiting to be explored. Waiting to be peopled and traveled and experienced and danced.

Yes, she wanted to dance. But not with Nikki. Not with this twin who was crippled by his emotions. Who wanted to stifle the very life out of her dancing.

At that moment she began to fight back. At first she merely dodged his brutal hands, making him swipe at her and miss as she shrank from his grasp. Then, more bravely, she kept him at arm's length, half a step ahead of him. Finally she faced him. She turned on him, outguessing his moves. Squelching them with the wedge of her shoulder, a thrust of her foot, the speed of her turns, her sudden self-assurance.

He was reduced to a spectator. A harmless gawker who whirled about, slightly off balance, in an attempt to keep up. With a roar of frustration he launched himself at her and brought her crashing down to the floor.

Nicole wasn't hurt. In a funny way, she had almost expected this reaction from him. For a moment she lay still, feeling him pant and sag over her. Feeling the fury and frustration expelled in short, hot gusts.

"Satisfied, Nick? Do you finally have me where you want me?"

"It's your fault," he sobbed. "You're disgusting and I hate you."

"I see," she said calmly. "Then you won't mind letting go of me and letting me leave."

"You can't leave."

"Wanna make a bet on that, brother dear?" She pulled herself out of his grip, slithering from under Nikki's sweaty body. She stood over him, pitying him. "It never had to be like this."

He looked up at her with tears spilling down his face. "What am I supposed to say to Pater?"

"Tell 'Pater' the truth, Nikki. If you dare." She swept past him and headed out the door, adding, "I'm going home now. Goodbye, Nikki."

There was only one thing to do, Nicole realized, heading back to Chelsea. Make good her words. With her mother and lover gone, nothing was keeping her here. Surely London would never be a home to her. And the people she lived with, her excuse for a family, would do quite nicely without her, probably not even noticing she was gone. If they did, they'd breathe a sigh of relief. The wild Indian loping off into the sunset. Good riddance.

Back again in her shabby little bedroom, she plunked herself down in the middle of the floor. Where could she go? What could she do? Frowning, she reached out a hand and rubbed the battered old leather of Alexandra's trunk. What would Mom have done? Nicole wondered.

She unlocked the trunk and opened it, taking out the mementos of Alexandra Varonne's life and career. The answer was here. Somewhere. She knew it.

On top was a brightly painted wooden bird from Peru. At least as old as she was, if not older. Beneath it, Nicole saw a challis shawl scented with Alexandra's favorite perfume.

She closed her eyes and rubbed her face in the shawl. She smiled and put it around her own shoulders.

Next she unwrapped a delicate teacup and saucer from Vienna. It had been a gift from the old king after Alexandra and Vanya's first triumph outside Russia.

Then, a faded theater poster of the dramatic couple themselves. Brilliant and mysterious. The bird of fire and the sorcerer prince. How magnificent they must have been. If she had only seen them then . . .

There were playbills by the dozens, covering the last thirty years. Among them was Alexandra's last. The amusing pen and ink drawing on the cover of *Hands Across the Waves*. Dame Harriet herself had sketched the squiggles that suggested both stiff British standards and brash American leanings. Such hope they'd had.

And then Nicole saw it. Her heart did a flip-flop. The answer was there. The letter from Manny Schumann, her mother's New York agent. Nicole remembered him. A funny, stubby man with a charm you could choke on. Part-time producer. Full-time meddler. He had adored Alexandra. Maybe he would adore her too?

She tore open the envelope, scanning the page, grinning.

Come on home, gorgeous. Broadway misses its favorite star.

P.S. How's the half-pint? You still spoiling her rotten? I love her like she was my own. When that kid grows up, look out! What a talent! What a future!

Nicole could already smell his fat cigar. See the smoke wreathed about his bald head. She remembered, as a young girl, thinking of him as Humpty Dumpty with legs, of once climbing under his desk in search of his legs . . .

She jumped up and ran to Alexandra's old velvet pouch where the money was always kept. Money for a rainy day. Mad money. All the money Nicole possessed. The seasons of meager salary Vanya had grudgingly paid her. The fat wad of bills Alexandra had somehow managed to put away, year after year, and hadn't touched to take care of herself. She had kept it for her daughter's inheritance. Alexandra's will had read: If I can give you nothing else . . .

"You have, Mom," Nicole said softly. "You've given me my freedom."

There was enough money to buy a ticket for one of those new transcontinental flights. She didn't care how many out-of-the-way stops the plane made. Just as long as it got her out of England and back home to the States. Resolutely, she began to pack her suitcase. It was the right thing to do, she told herself. The only thing to do. Abruptly, she stopped, pulled a sheet of old stationery from Alexandra's trunk and started to write.

> *Dear Father,*
> *Please understand. I've got to go back to America.*
> *Don't worry about me. There's a job waiting for me on*
> *Broadway.*
>
> *Nicole*

It was only a little lie. A temporary lie, and soon—Nicole was hopeful, certain—it would be the truth. She folded the note, wrote Vanya's name on it, and put it on her pillow.

She finished packing and closed her bag. She counted the money one last time and tucked Manny's letter into her purse. Taking a last look around the room, filled with nothing but unhappy memories, she stared long, hard, at her mother's old trunk. She couldn't leave it behind. She just couldn't.

Hoisting her bag and purse on one shoulder, she lugged the trunk down the stairs, one stair at a time in slow motion, praying Margaret wouldn't hear the muffled thunks. At the bottom of the stairs she paused to take a deep breath of caution . . .

She was safe. With a rush of adrenaline, she swung the front door open and pushed her belongings outside. She'd done it. She had struck the first blow for liberty. With all the conceit of a transplanted New Yorker, she whistled for a cab and allowed herself to be swallowed up by the first one to come along. Nicole was on her way.

"Piggy," Vanya shrieked. "Nick. Come here!"

Margaret, finely dusted with flour, and Nikki with Chinese puzzle box in hand, came running. They found him in Nicole's room, holding a single sheet of paper in one hand and gesturing to them with the other.

"She can't do this to me," he sputtered.

Nikki grabbed the note from his father. His eyes traveled line by line, once, twice, three times over the page.

"She can't go. She's my partner. What am I supposed to do without her?"

He dropped Nicole's farewell letter and the puzzle box she'd given him to the floor. Margaret knelt to retrieve them, read the letter, put them both into her apron pocket.

"I'm glad for her," she said.

Both men's mouths gaped open.

"Where is your head, Piggy? She's walking away from stardom, from a life of security, to do what? Some ridiculous vaudeville act, thousands of miles from home."

Deflated, Vanya collapsed onto the bed, looking to his son and mistress. "She's cut me to the quick."

Tight-lipped, Nikki sneered, "Like mother, like daughter."

"We'll have none of that, Nick," Margaret snapped. "This must've been a difficult decision for Nicole. Poor thing probably tried to sort it all out by herself."

"Has the world gone mad?" Vanya demanded. "Why are you taking her side? What about me? I've just lost my daughter. And a very salable commodity to boot. How will British Court survive without her? Without a Borcheff-Varonne combination, Nick's back where he started."

Nikki's glare bounced off his father's lowered head.

"I told her not to go," he grated. "She wouldn't listen to me."

"Dear boys," Margaret began, extending both hands toward Vanya and Nikki, "I know you're hurt. Both of you, in your own ways. But when you've time to think about it, you'll see how unhappy Nicole must've been to willingly throw away her future with you. It would only have ended in greater misery for all of us."

"She wouldn't listen. She never listened. Neither one of them," Nikki mumbled.

Shaking his head, he stumbled from the room. Vanya and Margaret could hear him go into his room and shut the door. They heard each one of his locks snap shut.

Margaret sat down next to Vanya and snaked her fingers through his hair. She put an arm around him, letting him sag into her.

"I'll talk to Nick later. He'll come round."

"He'll be lost without her. Like he was when he was only a baby and his mother first left."

"Pshaw, Van. He's done fine all these years without Varonne women. Just like you." She kissed him and then added, "Surely you know they never belonged here. Alexandra knew it. And try as we did, Nicole never really felt at home. She's better off finding her own way."

Vanya put his arm around his helpmate. "I never knew her, did I, Piggy?"

"You did your best, old dear. No one can fault you."

Part II

~~~

AMERICA

1939

~~ 28

It was corny. The act of a real hayseed. The kind of thing Nicole laughed at when she watched a similar scene play out on the silver screen. But she found herself trembling uncontrollably, her knees threatening to desert her. As her feet touched American soil—so what if it was only the oily tarmac of New York's North Beach Airport—she sank down and kissed home ground. It was gritty against her lips and rancid to the nose. Not quite the rose-petal, apple-blossom, ticker-tape-bestrewn pathway to home awaiting soldiers of war and fortune.

She breathed in deeply and exhaled in pure joy. The odor of the Thames was gone. There wasn't even a hint of fish and chips. Getting up off her knees, she inhaled again and a smile broke out across her face. She swore she could catch a whiff of a hot dog . . . or was it corned beef on rye? Or was it only the wind of the East River playing tricks with her empty stomach? Whatever it was, she was home. Alone. Totally on her own.

"Get a move on, doll. You're holdin' up the woiks."

A rough masculine voice barely preceded the elbow she felt jab against her shoulder blade.

"You on vacation or somethin'?"

That was one way to look at her time in England, she

supposed. A long, dreary, nightmarish vacation. Well, she had finally awakened. She was done with that hatefully quaint old place forever. If only her mother were here too. But she wasn't. There was no one to give a damn about her, Nicole thought.

She'd just have to get on with it. Get down to business. Nodding fiercely, she silently repeated the pep talk she'd given herself all across the Atlantic, pounding her fist against Alexandra's carpet bag for emphasis. Stronger than strong . . . shrewder than shrewd . . . bull-headed . . . pig-headed . . .

Nicole used the words, even the intonation, of her mother. Somehow, on the plane, it had made her feel better, safer, as though Alexandra herself were guarding her, guiding her home to America. She cajoled herself, exaggerated, goaded herself into taking charge of her life. She'd sounded terribly convincing ten thousand feet high in the air. Westward from Ireland over the Atlantic to the northernmost tip of Canada. Long wearying hours, sitting rigidly in her seat, repeating, repeating . . . Her chant worked well enough to give her the courage to curl up and doze off during the last leg of her journey from Montreal to New York City.

Now, with her feet on the ground, Nicole felt anything but sure of herself. Forget about the bull and the pig. She had all the confidence of a weak-kneed Wili—one of those infuriating, bloodless sylphs who were perpetually losing their men in one ballet after another. A quick jab to her shrinking spine made her forget herself.

"Bloody cheek!" she cried out, and turned to face her assailant.

She faced a mob. In the time it took to lose her nerve and find it again, the airport terminal had come to life. People poured in and out of every doorway. Red-capped luggage handlers. Brown-toned shoe-shine operators. Gloved and hatted, silver fox-trimmed matrons. The jaunty cock of a white sailor's cap. Here and there the shiny buttons and crisp black uniform of New York's finest. One such burly policeman emerged from the crowd and came toward her.

"Are you lost, ma'am? New to these parts, are you?"

Nicole gazed up at this mountain of community protection. For the briefest moment she wanted to swaddle her coat about her and bawl like a baby. But she hiked up the straps of Alexandra's carpet bag high on her shoulder. She shook her head.

"Lived here all my life," she said glibly, and melted into the crowd.

Along with everyone else, she bustled to the baggage area, fought to remove her suitcases, and found herself facing a bank of yellow and checkered cabs.

"Lady, you're next. Where to?"

Nicole shook her head and edged out of line. She hadn't anywhere to go. Not until she made that phone call. Her nerves started in again. Sweaty palms. Quickened pulse. She wanted to run in the opposite direction. There was no opposite direction, she realized. You're here. On your own. You're here because you want to be here. Because this is where you belong.

She found the nearest phone booth and dialed. "I'd like to speak to Manny Schumann, please."

"Can't hear you, miss. Speak up or I'll have to disconnect."

Nicole cleared her throat several times. "I say, it's imperative that I talk to Manny Schumann. Tell him Miss Nicole Varonne is on the line—Alexandra Varonne's daughter."

"One moment."

Nicole tapped her fingers against the glass of the booth. So far this conversation had as much punch to it as a rehashed vaudeville routine. Flashes of a doctor-and-nurse skit from her mother's last Follies show flitted through her mind. Mother and daughter, watching from backstage . . . until Alexandra's turn. A star turn. Her hair braided with a rainbow of ribbons. She'd worn a brilliant red tutu with netting of royal blue. Matching red toe shoes with ribbons of blue that sliced the air into fine precise segments. Nicole recalled a tambourine. A dazzling smile. She never got tired of watching Alexandra dance . . .

"Hey, who's this? Is that really you, kid?"

"Mr. Schumann—"

"Hey, to you, kid, it's Manny. Just like when you were a little girl. Remember when you used to sit on my knee? You and your mama would come into the office—Hey, I'm sorry about your mom, kid. Alexandra Varonne. I can still see her name in lights over Ziggy's. Now that was a class act. Did you get my wreath, kid? Pretty tough gettin' anything sent over to the old country these days."

"Mr. Schumann!" implored Nicole into the phone.

"Yeah, kid, I'm listening. And remember, it's Manny. Once you're in Manny's stable . . . well, you're part of the family. Hey, can you hear me all right, kid? We got a bad connection or something? You aren't calling me from limey land, are you? Am I talkin' across the ocean?"

"Manny!" Nicole blared. "I've left England for good. I'm here in New York. You remember that offer you sent my mother?"

As she paused for breath, he cut her off again.

"Damn shame about that show. Your mother coulda saved it. Did I mention what a class act she was? But what are you doing here, kid? Don't tell me you brought the kid brother to the land of opportunity? You two need representation, or did your old man set up a tour? Is Borcheff here too?"

Nicole leaned into the glass wall of the booth. She could practically hear the man panting on the other end of the line. Manny Schumann had all the finesse of a jackhammer. Any moment she expected to see cigar smoke emanating through the receiver.

"Manny, I've just spent thirty-four straight hours in the air. I'm standing in a phone booth at North Beach Airport all alone and I think I'm going to faint."

"Hey, kid—" Schumann said urgently.

"Listen to me, Manny. I'm getting into a cab now and I'm giving the driver your address."

"That's right, kid. Manny'll take care of the whole kit and caboodle. We'll talk shop. I'll have some deli brought in."

She hung up the phone without answering. With her bags huddled about her feet, she whistled for the next taxi. In a minute she was beating a path to Manhattan and the Broadway district.

Her face was beaded in a fine sweat that only August heat in the city could generate. She flung off her coat and scarf, shaking out her mop of damp curls from its confining hat. She probably looked like a banshee from the darkest corner of Hell, but no matter. Manny Schumann was going to give her a job. She was going to dance, and find a place to live. On her terms. Her mother had done it a million times, and now it was her turn. She was just following the family tradition. She jammed her fists at her eyes to darken the suddenly vivid tableau of the family left behind, reading her note of farewell.

"I'm sorry," she whispered, and felt sick. "No I'm not. I'm not sorry," she said, raising her voice.

"You say somethin', lady?" the hack asked.

"Yeah. Can't you drive faster?"

Manny Schumann came out of his inner sanctum to greet Nicole. The motley assortment of singers, dancers, and would-be actors waiting in the reception area were stunned to silence. Manny never showed his face to any but the biggest stars, and this girl—this bedraggled waif with dark circles seemingly ingrained under her eyes, coming through the door—looked like an orphan from Hackensack or Peoria.

"Kid," he boomed with open arms, "you look . . . well, words fail me. You weren't kidding on the phone, no siree."

To his credit, he hugged her in spite of her appearance, then led her into his office. Autographed photos hanging from cheaply veneered paneling, green imitation-leather chairs, a desk long and wide enough for someone of Manny's broad physique to sleep on—they were all there just as Nicole remembered. And Schumann was a trouper. There was a spread of food on a side table that made her mouth water.

While Nicole stared at the food, Manny gave her another once-over.

"Now Nicole, you'll wash up; you'll eat; we'll talk. Maybe you'll eat first, eh?"

Nicole demolished the mounds of cold meats and salads in short order, and Manny's fully equipped bathroom was an unexpected blessing. When she was done, Manny beamed at her from his chair behind the desk while sucking on a fat cigar. Nicole felt woefully young.

"Now," he said, "now that you don't look like something the cat dragged in and rejected . . . Now spill."

She knew what he expected. That she'd start weeping. That she'd confess she'd run away from home. That she'd beg him for any old job, for her mother's sake. That she'd do anything he said. Manny Schumann didn't know anything if that's what he thought.

"Mr. Schumann," she began, "I'm making the United States my professional home. I've finished with ballet. Don't believe the English press. My partnership with my brother and my association with my father's company are over. I'll never go back."

"So," Manny said, nodding his head. "Burned all your bridges, have you. I can see the headline in *Variety*. 'Upstart Yank Starts Second Revolution.' Now, now, don't start with the fire-breathing dragon bit. I'm taking you seriously, kid. But I know what you're up against. You're one of a thousand fresh-faced kids with stars in their eyes. Yeah, so you have a helluva pedigree. Yeah, so you've skyrocketed to the top in a foreign country. You're nothin' here, kid. 'Specially if you turn your back on the hand that feeds you. What do you think you can do if you don't dance? Make pretty pottery? Sell ladies' lingerie? Run for office?"

"I'm one in a million, Mr. Schumann," pronounced Nicole in a voice of steel. "I was born to dance. It's in my blood. And I made it in London because I worked like hell. I earned my place in the limelight. I'll earn it here."

"Without Daddy?"

"Without my father or my twin . . . or my mother."

"You'll dance anything? Anywhere?"

"No, I won't. I'll choose what's right for me."

"Even if it's a small part? Without program listing?"

"If it's right . . . and it pays . . ."

Manny got out of his chair, came around his desk and planted a wet kiss on Nicole's forehead. He could be a shit, but at least he was a lovable one.

"Kid, I think I have something right up your alley! It's just a spot in the chorus, but they're desperate for someone with experience. Anyway, the producer owes me a favor. Let me just make a call . . ."

Nicole closed her eyes and breathed deeply. She'd been put through the wringer but she'd passed the test. Alexandra had always said if Manny will take you, there'll be bread on the table.

Manny slammed the phone down with his usual intensity and grinned. "You're in, kid."

It took every bit of control for Nicole to keep from leaping into his arms and hugging him to death. She was going to make it. She had a job, and tomorrow she was going to find a place to live.

In the next ten minutes Manny gave her the name and address of the theater she was to report to and directions to the nearest YWCA. He even helped carry her bags back down to the sidewalk and hailed a cab for her. Within the hour she was installed in a tiny room, and fell asleep the moment her head hit the pillow.

~~ 29

Nicole slept for fifteen hours. When she awoke, she was a bundle of raw energy. She sat bolt upright in bed. Today was the day she would do battle with the subway system and the rental ads. She kicked the blanket off. Tonight she would sleep in her own bed in her own home. Even if it were only a mattress or on the bare floor itself. Tonight she would be truly home.

After a dormitory-style shower and breakfast, she re-packed her suitcases and left them with the desk manager in the lobby.

"I'll be back for my things this afternoon," she called out as she sailed into the streets of New York.

Clutching her purse, a newspaper, and a couple of maps, Nicole descended into the maze of underground trains. It was dirtier than the London Tube and the lines seemed far more complicated. But she found her way to the Seventh Avenue Local, boarded, and, like a million other natives, studied her newspaper to the exclusion of all else. She exited at Christopher Street. She'd arrived in Greenwich Village.

As she walked, shuffling her maps and her paper, Nicole mentally ticked off her own requirements for a place to live: at least four walls, a ceiling with no leaks, maybe a window or two, and a door to lock. It would be nice to have running water and electricity and a bathroom she needn't share with too many other people. Then her mind went hazy. Every-thing else—a kitchen, a closet, a few sticks of furniture—all seemed like luxuries. But wood floors. Really good wood floors were a necessity. How could she possibly dance or do a barre on carpet or linoleum?

She came to the first building on her list and stared at it from street level to the roof. It was a three-story red brick, with blotches of water and coal stains along one side. Perched on the windowsills of the ground floor were wooden flower boxes, alternately filled with thin strands of petunias, an occasional geranium stalk, and a brave daisy or two. A vision of Peggy's perfectly proper, perfectly blooming En-glish garden intruded on her mind. She willed it away. Either New York air was unhealthy for plants or the landlady had a black thumb. There was only one way to find out.

Modestly pulling down on her skirt and flattening her frazzle of blond curls, Nicole strode up the steps to the front door and rang the buzzer. In a moment she had her answer.

"Black thumb," she whispered to herself.

"Whaddya want?" demanded a woman dressed in a short-sleeved housecoat that had seen better days. "Nah," she went on, "lemme guess. Gypsy, right?"

Nicole couldn't keep from staring. All those words emerged from the woman's mouth but her lips never moved. They were clamped shut on a lit cigarette. And her outfit. Above the housecoat, which resembled a resort awning, was a helmet of pincurls. Rust had begun to form on some of them. Nicole's eyes darted downward. There were more amazing sights to behold below the befringed housecoat. The woman wore a pair of heeled slippers. The highest Nicole had ever seen. They were adorned—maybe festooned was the right word—with pristine, candy-red pompoms.

"Am I right, kid?"

If anyone looked like a gypsy, it was this woman, Nicole thought. She shook her head.

"I was born in South America—Rio, actually. But I'm French and Russian. Does that make a difference? You see, I've been living in England—"

"What're you talkin' about, kid? I don't care if you're black or green. I just thought you was a dancer. I can spot 'em a mile off," she said with a hint of pride, swinging the hem of her dress. "I used to be in the chorus line myself a few years back."

Nicole caught on and grinned, saying, "Can't fool you. I'm a gypsy all right. A gypsy in need of a room."

The woman's whole carriage changed before Nicole's eyes. Her eyes narrowed and the cigarette was worked furiously.

"I'm very strict about who I take. No funny business goes on in my building. Mr. Fudderman—that's my husband—and I don't like trouble."

"Oh, I wouldn't be any trouble, Mrs. Fudderman. I'd be quiet as a mouse."

"Mice? We got no mice and no rats. I keep a clean building. None of those nasty roaches neither. Don't pay no attention to what the other tenants tell you. Come along, dearie. I'll show you the room. It's a flat really. And so lovely."

The vacancy was on the top floor, and with each step up the staircase, seemed to increase in features and desirability. Nicole was afraid to ask the price. When Mrs. Fudderman finally opened the door to the suite of small rooms, Nicole breathed a sigh of relief.

It was no palace, but it was light, airy, and the flooring was wood. The front room was long and narrow. More like a hallway than a living room or a parlor. Nicole fought the urge to leap into a series of tour jetés. One wall begged to be mirrored. Its opposite had a bank of windows. At the far end were a built-in set of cabinets, a small round table, and two cane-backed chairs in one corner. A tiny back room served as the bedroom, dictated as such by a vintage army cot.

"And now, the piece of resistance!" declared the landlady.

She swept aside a curtain and revealed a pocket-sized kitchen, complete with sink, countertop, hot plate, and bottle opener.

"The real attraction of this apartment is the facilities, if you know what I mean. Privacy is so important, I always say. Take a peek, dearie. It's just down the hall, across and two doors down."

Nicole peeked and came back quickly. "How much?"

"Two months in advance plus cleaning fee. Sixty bucks."

That would leave her with ten dollars until payday . . . whenever that was for Broadway gypsies. And it was only the first apartment she'd looked at. She'd marked another half-dozen ads in the newspaper, some cheaper. But this flat seemed decent enough. What if she let this one go, and none of the others were as good, and she came back to find it rented? Nicole made her decision. She fished around in her purse and handed the exact amount to her new landlady.

"I'll take it!"

Nicole strolled through the Village. It was the most glorious summer morning she could remember in a long time. Here she was with a job and a home. And she'd achieved it all on her own. She was glad to be alive. Glad to look up through the web of green treetops at the limitless blue beyond. Glad to feel the heat of the sun surge through her bones. She felt she would burst with all these feelings.

She walked past the arch in Washington Square and sat down on a park bench. She'd have lean days, but she was prepared. She'd had the best teacher. She remembered . . . Alexandra making tomato soup from a can of juice and a roux concoction. Alexandra stretching a loaf of bread over weeks with the most surprising array of finger sandwiches. Alexandra washing the laundry and herself in the bathwater. Alexandra darning and redarning the most exquisite pattern of stitches over fraying costumes and everyday clothes. Her mother had invented game after game . . . at least so it had seemed to a young and susceptible daughter. Nicole had believed and trusted and shared and learned.

Tears blotted out the sunny view. She lowered her head into her hands and wept. Mom, I miss you. All she could picture was Alexandra at the end. The great melancholy eyes. The graceful arms limp. The elegant arched lips thinned and flat. The pain was as immense and as real as the first time she realized she would lose her mother. Then it had paralyzed her, freezing her in a time and place she hated. This time it propelled her to action. I promise, Mom, she vowed silently. You'll be proud of me.

Later that afternoon, after retrieving her belongings and hurriedly stashing them in her flat, she took her fourth subway ride of the day and dashed to the stage door of the Imperial Theater. It was dark inside, but she followed the sound of voices to the stage. Two men and a woman were laughing and talking. They seemed to be old friends. Nicole stood timidly in the wings. She felt awkward, as though she didn't belong to this branch of the dancing world. Then she was noticed.

"Thank God you're here!" exclaimed a slim man—more of a boy, Nicole saw, as he came closer. "Babette would positively die on the vine if she had to dance one more night in this tragedy."

"Oh, Jonathan," Nicole heard the other man say, "don't scare the girl off. She doesn't know you well enough to ignore everything you say."

Nicole couldn't suppress a giggle. Was there anyone in New York, she wondered, who wasn't some kind of character? Then Jonathan was pulling her forward, down to center stage.

"Now here's the story, honey. You're American some of the time and Russian some of the time. God knows why, but this is a political musical comedy, something to do with foreign embassies or other. You'll figure it all out from the sets and the costumes. We've got some really hokey routines, but at least they're easy to learn. Show her, kids."

Babette and the young man launched themselves into a series of steps. Nicole watched intently and then allowed herself to relax. It was music-hall stuff, easy combinations, completely unoriginal. The kind of thing you could do in your sleep. Babette was living proof.

"Got it, honey?"

Nicole nodded swiftly.

"Great. Now show her the hard part."

Nicole figured he meant the Russianized steps. It was mostly hoopla and a few standardized folk dances.

"Okay, Buzz. Give her a whirl."

Babette gratefully slunk off and leaned against Jonathan. Buzz stood at attention, clicked his heels together and offered his arm. Nicole moved into position as she'd seen Babette do.

As Jonathan set the beat, Buzz whispered, "Don't worry. You can fake the steps if you have to. We'll be in the back row and nobody will be counting feet."

She didn't have to fudge on a single step. When she finished, Buzz and Jonathan applauded and Babette even looked alert.

"Say, what's your name, girl? You're really good! Where'd you say you worked last?"

Nicole blushed. She mumbled something about London. When she saw the raised eyebrows, she quickly added, "I watched my mom a lot. She was in the Follies once."

Jonathan clapped her on the back and said, "Forget about experience. It's all in the blood, and yours, kid, is dancing blue. So humor me, princess royale. Let's run through the whole thing, okay?"

This time Babette and Jonathan danced alongside Nicole and Buzz. It was a snap. It was fun. America was going to be easy, Nicole thought. Maybe it would be possible to forget about England and dancing with Nikki. The back row in a silly musical seemed like the answer to her prayers . . . until three nights later, when she took over for Babette officially.

On the way to the theater, walking into the dressing room, she knew she was going to throw up. Not delicately, as she'd seen a couple of dewy-eyed corps members do before a performance in London when they stuck an ever so tapering finger or two down their throats. Not apologetically, like a sick child caught in the throes of a bullying virus. But full force, projectile punishment for believing, even hoping, her life was on the mend.

She felt as though she hadn't danced in months, in years. Her legs felt as thick as her tongue did. She could hardly swallow. Music whirled madly about in her head. God, no, she prayed. The heavily crashing chords of Nikki's and her last insulting pas de deux refused to dissipate. Concentrate, she demanded of herself. You're a frothy Washington wife tapping away at the White House. You're a minx from Minsk who kicks her fur boots as high as the next good Communist. She shut her eyes tight and hummed the opening bars of *Mr. Ambassador* until everything about her quieted. Stomach . . . legs . . . head . . . room.

She opened her eyes to a deadly silent dressing room. Nine pairs of eyes were trained on her.

"Feelin' all right, toots?"

"It's just a case of the jitters."

"Here, finish this cuppa coffee of mine. It'll hit the spot."

Nicole looked gratefully in the direction of the kind

words, but the notion of coffee—much less the permanently stained cup—were impossible to accept. She offered a weak smile.

"Whaddya say your name was?"

"Aw, can the crap, Pearl. You know who she is. We all know who she is." This upstart, who could only be from Brooklyn, switched to indulgently dramatic tones, uttering, "Ni-cole Va-ronne . . . star of the classical stage . . . A ballerina, no less!"

"Leave 'er alone, for Chrissakes."

"It's all right," Nicole murmured, used to the presence of the green-eyed monster. Backstage jealousies were as common as a dancer's bloody toes.

Brooklyn was still not content. "A little far from home, aren't we, mamzelle?"

"I live here now."

"My, aren't we the international star, or is it just that we're slumming now?"

Nicole stared straight ahead into a mirror, applying her makeup with a tense hand.

"I don't call making an honest living 'slumming.' "

"Ooh, pardon me, Your Highness. I didn't mean to offend you. It just seems to me—don't you agree, goils?—that somethin' smells fishy here. You know? I mean a star of the ballet hoofin' it in the back row of a show bound for the Borscht Belt. It don't add up."

Nicole turned to the brash girl and smiled sweetly. "Perhaps you can add this. Mind your own frigging business!"

"Careful, Irma," Pearl simpered. "This one has teeth."

The other girls laughed, breaking the tension. They turned back to their own toilettes. Pearl helped Nicole snap up the back of the dress she was to wear in the first act.

"So tell me, Nicole," she said chummily. "Betcha left a few broken hearts back there in England, huh? You got one special feller?"

Nicole had long forgotten how brassy she'd seemed to the people in Vanya's school and company. She'd gotten used to the shell of privacy the English drew around themselves.

Now she depended on it. The wall she'd put around Carlo and herself extended itself further.

"You Americans are so nosy!" she said testily.

Pearl retreated, raising her hands in submission. "Hey! Just tryin' to be friendly."

Nicole wasn't ready for friends. She had too many ghosts to dispel first. But there wasn't time for apologies or explanations. The call for the chorus to take their places on stage came, and she was aquiver again.

There was always tension when she went on stage. Tension between Nikki and her, wondering when he would strike. Between her and Vanya, pressing her to match Nikki's splendid fury. Between her and the audience, which took such delight in the macabre confrontation of siblings. She'd always felt their expectations, compiled on her own. At each performance there was the unending grind of demands. No matter how she danced, no matter how much of herself she gave, more was always wanted.

Nicole's eyes glassed over as the overture was played. Next to her, Buzz was whispering something about her leg.

"What?" she asked fuzzily.

"Break a leg, Nicole. Hey, relax. You'll enjoy this."

Soon she was dancing. One of those lighthearted, meaningless routines that filled the stage with the sound of tapping feet and mindless joy. When it was over, the audience roared its appreciation. The comedy proceeded smoothly; the songs were warbled; again the dancers frolicked. Act I became Act II. Nicole's nervousness was gone. By the time she'd changed costume for the Russian part, she had the rhythm of a Broadway gypsy down pat. Best of all, she was just one of the crowd. The nearest thing to a star turn was a precision lift and pirouette in the air each of the boy-girl duos had to perform at the conclusion of the act.

Nicole had hardly been aware of the combination during rehearsal. Here on stage she was instantly aware of Buzz's hands hugging her waist. She winced, anticipating Nikki's squeezing grip, his dig and ultimate pinch. But she was in the air, spinning, and brought down gently, feather-light. She hadn't even had time to tighten her muscles against the blow to come—it was over that fast. It was a moment of exultation. She wanted to turn to Buzz and thank him. She wanted to stop the orchestra and ask the conductor to repeat the music.

The show went on. Act III, pure corn pone, was a romp for her. She danced fiercely, enjoying every hackneyed step, every predictable spin, free of the fear of Nikki's haunting touch.

~~ **30**

Over the course of the next six months, Nicole established a regular routine. By night she performed on Broadway. When *Mr. Ambassador* closed, she found a spot in the chorus of *Football Frenzy*, a rah-rah college musical. It paid her rent, her sundries, and her way into the daytime necessity of taking class.

She tried a number of different studios. Each one was an eye opener. Unlike her experience in London—where, according to Vanya, there was one right way to dance—New York threw away the rule book. There was no one God of dance; there were dozens. Each studio seemed to embrace its own set of deities, its own set of truths.

Dutifully, Nicole enrolled in an advanced ballet course. She hated it. She hated herself. Throughout the barre she was intensely aware of how rigidly she held her body. In center work she felt increasingly awkward, as if she couldn't quite find her center of gravity. She found herself returning with greater frequency to the studios exploring the world of modern dance.

She began to play hookey from her morning ballet class. Ballet was England and pain and endlessly stultifying structure. Modern dance seemed to hold a promise. She caught glimpses of its kaleidoscopic realm of possibilities. Movements with fluid angularity and angular fluidity. Movements without definition. Movements that freed the body from convention and tradition. It made her dizzy, as though the very air she breathed was too fresh, too rich.

She dropped ballet altogether. Soon she was taking three or four classes daily from her favorite teachers. Monday nights, when Broadway was dark, and weekend afternoons when she was not in the matinee, she'd take in a performance by one of her teachers or a new choreographer. It was almost as exciting to watch the dimensions of dance stretch and grow as it was to do it herself. No longer did she have to confine her arms or her head to a prescribed set of placements. Her legs were free to turn outward, inward, and a little of both, because the music or the feeling called for it, not because—as she saw it—the choreographer was blindly following an arbitrary number of commandments.

The world of dance she was discovering in New York possessed spirit, joy, imagination, freedom. And it was hard work. As much as she wanted to dance instantaneously like her fellow classmates, she had to undo years of rigorous training. She had to learn new disciplines, new patterns. She had to let go of the mountainous muscular tension she'd built up while succumbing to Nikki's savage partnering.

Nicole set to work, asking for no special favors. She downplayed her previous professional experience. A few of her instructors, who had fledgling dance troupes of their own, took her under their wings. It was strictly a matter of talent, they told her. She had the makings. She was an asset.

That summer of 1940, she knew she had arrived. Mathilda Wiggins asked Nicole to perform with her dance troupe. Wiggins was the best there was, the most innovative and the most respected of any dancer/choreographer to come out of the Denishawn era.

"Mattie, are you sure?" Nicole asked.

"I doan say these t'ings for my pleasure," the rawboned Jamaican woman retorted in her singsong voice. "This new piece of mine, it needs a dancer like you. Small. Compact. But very explosive. Now we rehearse every day next week, all week, even the weekend. You must cancel everything. My dance is all there is. It is all there can be. This performance is very important. The critics have promised to come."

"Next week?" Nicole repeated. "All day, every day?"

"And into the night," Mathilda cackled, rubbing her hands together. "We have much work to do."

"I can't," Nicole said in a whisper. "You don't know . . . yes, you do know how much I want to do it. Such an honor . . . I've worked for just this moment. But my show, Mattie," she wailed, "I can't take another night off. I'll get fired. I've already missed four performances this month."

"Well, girl," Mathilda said, resigned, "you must make a decision. Do you want to dance or do you want to dance?"

Her emphasis and her meaning were unmistakable. Was Nicole going to make a living at dance or was she going to make dance her life? There was no decision to make. She had only to figure out how to manage it.

She made another appointment with Manny Schumann. He greeted her with a sloppy kiss.

"What is it with you, kid? You only come to see me when it's sizzling outside?" he asked, mopping his considerable forehead with a damp handkerchief.

"It's good for the extension," she teased, and neatly lifted her leg parallel to the wall where her mother's picture hung.

"Show-off," he snapped back. "Now sit. Have a bottle of pop. I hear you're doin' aces . . . though some little bird with a big beak's been whispering in my ear. You're missin' shows, kid. Not good. You tryin' to louse up Manny's reputation?"

"Manny," she deadpanned in her best Brooklynese, "you're a regular saint! Really, I'm grateful for everything you've done . . ."

"Uh-oh. I can smell it coming. You got a better offer."

"Yes and no," Nicole replied. "That is, I know what I really want to do now. I'm going into modern dance, Manny. Hook, line, and sinker."

Manny tapped his fingers on his desk. He pursed his lips. The laugh lines disappeared. Nicole had never seen him look so serious.

"So, kid. How you gonna put bread on the table? You got a rich uncle I don't know about?"

"Oh, for heaven's sake, Manny, don't be ridiculous. I'm

not about to starve. Mathilda Wiggins asked me to be in her company," Nicole said proudly.

"Who? Never heard of her. How much she pay? She offer you more than what you're gettin' on Broadway?"

Nicole was silent.

"Well, would you be makin' the same dough?"

"It's the honor, you see," she said softly. "It's a way to establish my name. . . . I'm learning so much . . ."

"Nicole, I'm gonna talk to you like I'd talk to my own daughter," he said, and paused, taking a deep breath and then lighting a cigar. "You're nuts. You're throwing away a nice little career. You were the toast of the town in London and you threw that away. You won't let me move you up on Broadway, though it's killing me . . . You could make us both a tidy sum of money. Now you're gonna hook up with the artsy-fartsy set. You dancin' on your brains or something?"

"I appreciate everything you've done for me, but I told you last year, when I first came to you, I'll take the jobs that are right for me. This is right, Manny."

"This ain't a job, Nicole; it's charity. There's no money in it."

"It's what I'm going to do. Will you help me get out of the show? I really need your help, Manny."

He sighed and rolled his eyes upward. "Some people wear mules on their feet . . . I got mules for clients. Okay, kid. Don't say I never did nothing for you. If you ever change your mind, the door's open. I don't say that to too many ex-clients, you know. But Alexandra and you bamboozled me years ago when I was young and foolish. . . . Well, now I'm old and foolish."

Nicole hugged him fiercely. "Come see me dance, Manny. I just might make a convert of you."

The want ads came to Nicole's rescue again. A small, uptown, private school, the Chester Academy for Girls, was advertising for a part-time physical education teacher. The position would be available after the Labor Day holiday. When the two tiny headmistresses interviewed Nicole, they told her what they really wanted was dignified exercise for their girls. She was hired on the spot after demonstrating a form of Swedish rhythmics, taught to her by Kirsten Lundberg, another of Alexandra's exotic finds during their touring days. The pay was minuscule, but she had more time to devote to her dancing.

Here again, Nicole was struck by the difference between English and American loyalties. In London a dancer chose a company, seemingly for life. It made Nicole think of the Indian caste system. One could dance for Vanya Borcheff at the British Court or Dame Harriet at Swanleigh Hall or Dance Festival. Only one. And if one had the audacity to switch . . . well, it was most undignified, quite un-English, embarrassing, and not to be spoken about.

In New York a dancer was loyal to dance. Modern dance companies and troupes, no matter how diverse, existed for the pursuit of art. There were no boundary lines drawn. Dancers weren't the property of a choreographer or a company director. It was important who one danced for, but it was more important to dance often and to explore the whole range of the modern movement. The goal was growth, not preservation of a static ideal. Nicole saw it as the epitome of America. Freedom and open spaces.

She took advantage of every opportunity. With Mathilda Wiggins, Nicole captured the undulating pulse of animal sensuality. With Ernest Land, she caught the tribal beat of urban turmoil. From Gar Fortune, she learned to move to silence, in the process discovering her own internal rhythms. From Olive McKinnah, Nicole acquired an eye for staging. Light and shadow, color and space—the use of pivotal props were as integral to the dance as the music and movements themselves.

Personality was no longer an issue. Nicole and the people she danced with threw themselves into the created art form. It was just what Nicole needed. No personal relationships. No inevitable conflicts. No intimate exposures. The dance was all. It was the dance that had character, brought to life by the ardent struggles of sacrificing faceless dancers. True, some of the troupes Nicole participated in took their cause less seriously than others.

Gar Fortune's group balanced their hushed mood in the studio with total pandemonium in the dressing room. Nothing seemed more important on stage than sanctifying the verities of Gar's vision. In fact, offstage, nothing was more important than ridiculing his private life. If it wasn't his torrid love affairs—Gar didn't seem to care if the object of his lust was male, female, vegetable, or mineral—it was the revelation of his name change. Gar confessed it to the biggest gossips in the company. He could only have done it on purpose, Nicole assumed, knowing his penchant for notoriety. Within hours "Gus Fagenbaum" was public knowledge. God, Gar, or Gus only knew what was coming next.

"I guess it sells tickets," Nicole said to Mattie Wiggins and shrugged her shoulders.

"It doesn't make his work any better," sniffed Mattie.

"Why, Mathilda Wiggins, do I detect just a whiff of envy?" Nicole teased.

"Doan be silly, girl. It's my professional opinion. Now let's get back to work."

Mattie was mounting a new work on Nicole. It began in adagio, suspensefully escalating the pace until it erupted into a jungle frenzy. In the section being rehearsed, Mattie had constructed an intricate duet between Nicole and another dancer, an elongated version of Nicole, lankier, taller. First they danced alongside one another. Then each took turns, falling behind the other. As the tempo picked up, they were to face each other, mirroring their steps. Finally they were to burst outward, back to back, attempting to wrench apart but unable to.

Nicole concentrated with all the power she could muster. She could feel the taut contractions of her own body but none generated by her partner.

"Come on, Lenore," she urged. "Put some muscle into it. I don't even know you're there."

Mattie put down the drum she used to keep time.

"Lenore's fine. You're working too hard at it, Nicole. It should come easy. Natural. Look."

The big-boned woman with the grace of a languid cat demonstrated what she wanted, creating a mood of appetite with the simple pattern of her steps. Mattie was not a fleshy woman, but she projected a voluptuousness that could not be denied.

"You see, Nicole? This dance is about the soul. How it is the same but different. When you and Lenore 'split' into two halves, you're celebrating the inevitable wholeness of the soul. The energy is about symbiosis."

"No. I just don't see it that way. I think Alan should dance Lenore's part. There's a whole male/female urgency to the piece."

From the rear of the studio Nicole dragged forward a man from the cluster of dancers watching the proceedings.

"Just let me show you, Mattie . . . Start here, Alan. Now separate. Come back . . . and now lift me. Higher. Higher. Now down and race along just a step behind . . ."

Nicole was sweating from her exertions, exhilarated by the picture she'd created. The choreographer applauded.

"You see what I mean, Mattie? Now there's thrust. And purpose. It was pretty your way, Mattie. Kind of soft but sly."

"Like it got under your skin and wouldn't let go?" Mattie asked quietly.

"Yes. Exactly. But—"

"That's what I want. That is my **style**. You're full of ideas, girl. Good ideas," Mattie emphasized, and put an arm around the smaller woman. "Valid. But they're yours. This is my dance."

Nicole felt ridiculously small and thoroughly chastised. What a way to repay the woman's kindnesses to her.

"You hear what I'm saying, girl? You go home and make your own dance. And when it's good enough, you show it to me," Mattie added.

"You're giving me the chance to choreograph?" Nicole asked.

"You think I'm doing you a favor?" retorted Mattie. "You

don't know the demons that will drive you mad if you're meant to make dances."

Nicole threw her arms around her mentor's neck in gratitude.

"Now, can I get some dancing out of you, girl? My way?"

Nicole nodded and gave herself over to Lenore and the lazy heat of Mattie's music. But her mind was already conjuring up different, private images.

The first thing Nicole did when she got home that night was to count her savings. The long wall of the front room was about to get what it deserved . . . if she could afford it. Pulling Alexandra's old velvet evening bag from the depths of her trunk, now functioning as her coffee table, she extracted a wad of bills. Ten. Twenty. Thirty. Forty. Fifty. Sixty. Nicole put two of the ten-dollar bills back for a rainy day. There were so many rainy days . . .

"Forty bucks to mirror the whole damn wall. So be it," she declared.

For the wall had to be mirrored. How else could she know what she was creating, much less how good it might be?

With a cold, clinical eye, she studied her apartment. Until now she had viewed it as living space. It was comfortable enough. A sofa rescued from the junk man. Spread over it was Alexandra's large, square challis scarf. The big black trunk. A small bookcase which housed a used phonograph, a few books, programs from shows and performances she'd been in since coming to New York, and a vase of flowers. At the end of the room was the spindly table and chairs that came with the flat. The built-in cabinet was chock full of mementos from Alexandra's career. The little bedroom still held the cot with no space to spare, except for the walls, which were littered with dance pictures.

Yes, Nicole confirmed, good enough for a dancer to live in. All wrong for a choreographer to create in. She spent the rest of the night rearranging her few belongings, measuring out her new studio space, and dreaming . . . of the dances she'd mount . . . danced by her choice of dancers . . . and someday a company of her own. . . .

Nicole celebrated the advent of 1941 with the premiere of her first work. Mathilda Wiggins, true to her promise, not only encouraged her protégé, but had given her, free of charge, the use of her large studio where *Skirmishes* was to be unveiled . . . also free of charge to the public. Those of Mattie's dancers who were not performing in the dance attended, as well as Nicole's other teachers and the dancers she had come to know through classes. As she peeked through the curtain at the assembling crowd, she was amazed to see a few erstwhile Broadway acquaintances straggle in. Manny Schumann appeared and took a seat in the back row. And horror of horrors, sitting on either side of Mattie, front row center, there were two newspaper critics.

It's just another opening night, Nicole told herself.

But it wasn't. All of Alexandra's one-night stands in tents, in school auditoriums, and in the open air, plus Nicole's own formal ballet seasons and her experience on Broadway, did not prepare her for the sheer weight of paralysis that now took hold of her limbs. She knew she couldn't move. The curtain would open and she'd be standing there. Her dancers were limbering up . . . they'd be on their spots, ready to go . . . and she'd be stuck at center stage with a mouthful of apologies. Her career as a choreographer would be over before it was born. Nicole Varonne, her reviews would read the next morning, R.I.P.

"For Chrissakes, Nicole, get back here," the stage manager hissed. "The lights are jammed and your tape's come unreeled."

Reality drove Nicole back to action. When the production problems were solved, she had just enough time to get into costume and makeup before the music began and the curtain rose.

PIROUETTE

The stage was bare, and bathed in rose-tinted light. To the seductive strains of a neoclassical waltz, a handsome couple in full balletic regalia strolled onstage. He could only be Prince Charming. She was aglitter in swanly white. His hands supported her every move. While she glided. As she bourréed. In gentle ascents and descents. His hands never left her waist.

The music changed. Harmony turned dissonant, and in a whirling crescendo the girl dancer flung her partner's hands from her tutu. Harsh lighting outlined bloodred hand prints that clung to the girl's stiff skirt. As shocked as she, the charming prince reached for her. She turned away from him. He snatched her back and lifted her. The lift became a thrusting. He hurled her into the air. Catching her at the last possible breathtaking second, he pulled her to him with magnetic force. She crumpled to his feet. Tentatively, she began a series of lyrical, lilting steps. He cut off each one in mid-movement. The girl was reduced to small, inward gestures. She could only cringe and shrink away. Was there no way out?

He was as powerless to his violence as she was in helpless pain. He pursued her in the vain hope that she possessed the answer. Relentlessly he surrounded her, eliminating all avenues of escape. Finally she was caught, and his hands fit perfectly over the shocking imprints. She was vanquished. In the moment of his triumph he removed his hands from her, finished with her. But he was never to be finished. As she fell lifeless from his grasp, the red imprints stuck to his hands. In horror and despair, his hands found his own throat, where the imprints again took hold. To the atonal blare of trumpets, the prince ran from the stage and the curtain came down.

The curtain rose for the second time on another couple, swathed in black caps, black leotards, black tights, bare feet. Back to back, they stood motionless. The music continued its dissonant path, and pure white light accentuated the harshness of the dance to come. They marched off the stage, only to reenter from opposite ends. They approached each other, guarded, bodies held stiffly. Lunge. Attack. Parry. Feint. Counterattack. The duel played to a standoff.

The duo circled one another warily. Wider and wider the spiral grew, until they had filled the whole stage with distrust. Retracing the spiral, they wound up touching. They sparked. Ignited. It was spontaneous combustion. Arms wildly gesticulating, their bodies charged out of control. Colliding. Spinning around one another. Bouncing off each other. Blunting one another.

They faced each other, hunched over, contorted. The male grappling for the female. He was clumsy, all bunched muscle and large, undefined movement. She bowed under his weight and then straightened. He came at her and she repulsed him with the firm, strong stroke of her fully extended leg. Then with the other leg. Swifter. Higher. Each time, she broke his hold. He could not dominate her, and in the end she stood over his slumped body, one leg her anchor, the other swept up vertically and held there in hand. The curtain sank in her victory.

Like a rush of fresh air the curtain went up to the romantic motif of the first scene. The same melody swelled to passionate heights, and a couple in contemporary dress, obviously in love, oblivious to all else, strolled on stage. A breeze seemed to ruffle his hair and the hem of her skirt. Their hands touched palm to palm. Tracing the pattern and shape of their bodies, joined as one. Tracing the palpable flesh aching to be caressed. Their arms intertwined. She rested her head on his shoulder.

With a jangle of chords the white prince appeared from the dim rear of the stage, the black warrioress at his side. They stalked the young couple, who were unaware of the threat to their innocence. Like puppet masters, the prince and the warrioress pulled and tugged at invisible strings connecting them to the boy and the girl. In unison the couple twisted. Buckled. Sagged. Deflated.

The avengers showed themselves. The prince raised the girl and dazzled her with pyrotechnic leaps and turns in the air, each time landing within an inch of her feet. At the same instant the warrior-turned-enchantress insinuated herself over the body of the boy, arousing him with angular thrusts of her shoulders, her chests, her hips. Bewitched, the boy was at her mercy. Mechanically, she drove him from the stage, impelling him forward with a series of grands battements, feet flexed and unyielding. At the same time, the prince strode off in the opposite direction, carrying the girl, clutching her aloft. The innocents reached for each other in vain. And to the final, atonal blare of trumpets, the curtain rang down.

There was a scattering of applause and a few discernible clearings of throats. Mattie Wiggins, who held up her vigorously clapping hands for all to see, turned in her seat and glared at those who dared remain reticent. The critics defiantly glared back at her and ducked out of the studio.

The dancers, couple by couple, appeared on stage for their bows. The clapping picked up when all six linked arms, built when the white prince and black warrioress stepped forward, and peaked when the girl in black removed her cap and a sheaf of damp blond curls was unfurled. Nicole bowed deeply, overcome by her accomplishment. I've done it, she told herself. Whether they love it or hate it isn't important. It's my very own. A part of me. And now it's a part of the world.

A small reception was held in the studio foyer. Nicole, still in her damp costume, was bombarded by Manny.

"You definitely got something, kid. I don't know what it is, but you had me by the seat of my pants."

"Very compelling, darling," Gar Fortune pronounced, wresting her away from the fat man. "Such high drama, but don't you think it was a little noisy? Think how effective the piece would be with just the sound of muted gongs setting off each scene. Promise me you'll think of it. And where did you find your young Prince Charming?"

"Alan? You know him, Gar. He's danced with Mattie for years now."

"No, not that old thing. That divine boy in the third piece. Is he taken? Yes? Well then, what about the girl?"

"Nicole, you devil!"

Her fellow gypsy from *Mr. Ambassador* wrapped her in his arms and swung her around.

"Buzz, thank you for rescuing me," she whispered. "I never expected to see you here."

"You're one of the gang now. We gypsies stick together, you know. Pearl's here somewhere. And Jonathan. And Irma!"

"Did they like it? Be honest, Buzz."

"Thumbs down, kid. There wasn't a tap in the whole show."

Nicole had to giggle. She turned away and found herself facing her other three teachers. Their verdicts were in.

Olive McKinnah said, "Youth always lacks subtlety."

Ernest Land said, "Hogwash, Livy. If you don't hit them over their flat little heads, they won't think they got their money's worth. Give 'em blood and guts. That's what it's about."

Mattie Wiggins hugged her and said, "It is a powerful beginning. Now we must hope my critic friends will agree."

She waited up with Nicole for the earliest editions of the next morning's newspapers. The critics agreed on the power of Nicole's dance. That was all they agreed on.

Geoff Tubbs loved the dancers and hated the work. It was diabolical. It was Freudian. It pandered to the lowest forms of theater. He was sure he would hate Miss Varonne's next work.

Jacob Laurensen hailed Nicole's vision. It was disturbing. Intriguing. Many-layered. She was a fresh young talent, a true artist, arriving like a thunderbolt on the scene of contemporary dance. He couldn't wait to see what she was planning next.

"It is the best possible t'ing," Mattie cried. "You've started a controversy. And they've started your career for you. They both talk about your next work. They're expecting something more from you, girl. Something big."

Mattie's studio was packed that second night. Dancers, dance aficionados, people who liked to be seen at the city's hot spots, read the reviews and came to say they'd seen *Skirmishes*. Mattie extended the run to an extra weekend. By the following week Nicole was the talk of New York's modern dance world. She was loved. She was hated. Some people thought she had pushed dance to new heights. Others were convinced she had sunk it to the deepest of pits.

Whatever the opinion, the results were what mattered. Dancers approached Nicole, asking to be in her next work. Nicole was flattered and profoundly touched. Whether she could provide a next work was the question. Nicole couldn't go on accepting charity from Mathilda Wiggins.

"And that's what it is, Mattie. In black and white," Nicole insisted.

Her apartment was more than adequate for the first stirrings of creativity. But she needed studio space for mounting a dance. She needed rehearsal time to work with her dancers. She wanted to rent a small hall to stage her piece. She wanted to pay her dancers for their efforts. Glorified acrobatics at the Chester Academy for Girls was not going to cover the cost of her dream.

Ernest Land came to the rescue. Rather, a patron of his did.

"Don't tell me you don't remember her," Ernest chided. "I introduced her to you the last night of *Skirmishes*. Tall, dark, and hatted. A voice like a submachine gun. Ernestine Pringle. She thinks we were twins in a previous life. I humor her 'cause she's got the bucks."

Nicole shook her head and said, "I met so many people. Ernie, is anyone normal—at least average—in New York?"

"Not that I know. It's better that way. Take Ernestine. She's harmless; she likes artists; I like her money. It's a fair enough exchange."

"But why does she want to give me money?" Nicole asked. "She's your patroness."

"I told her you're a student of mine. I told her you had promise. I whispered sweet nothings in her ear like 'dynasty,' 'patron saint of modern dance,' her name in history books. She ate it up. She's got an ego the size of her—Never mind. Just take the wampum, kid, and whip up a hell of a dance."

"Ernie, why are you helping me?"

"Search me. Maybe I see a lotta me in you. All that anger . . . You are angry, aren't you? Yeah. And I know where there's anger, pain ain't so far behind. Yeah, I see that too. To top it all off, neither one of us gets much of a bang outta men. Don't look so surprised, Nicole. *Skirmishes* wasn't just a pretty little dance you made up one day. It came from your guts. We're fighting the same war, babe. Only yours is internal and mine comes from the ugly old outside world. Now that I exposed myself to you—for God's sakes, don't tell Ernestine—take the damned check off my hands, will ya? And create!"

Nicole took the money. She resigned from the Chester Academy. And she pondered Ernie Land's perceptions of her. Of course, he was right. Without her realizing it, *Skirmishes* had been about Nikki and her . . . and Carlo and her . . . and Vanya and her . . . and even Vanya and Alexandra. Was Margaret in it too? The dance had come so vividly, and yet trying to untangle the relationships, trying to see who played what part in her life—in the dance—was too confusing.

Nicole got a blinding headache just thinking about it. But she thought about it anyway. For the first time since she had left England. She walked about Greenwich Village in the slush and sleet of winter. A heavy wool coat protected her from the harsh elements. Scarves, wound around her head and neck, rippled in the bitter wind. The colors of the India scarves caught her eyes. Teased her. Pulled her away from the mire of difficult thoughts crowding her mind.

Snippets of carmine and coral. Flashes of lapis and lavender. Threads of silver and gold. They blew and bobbed and hovered all about her. She couldn't peel her eyes away. They reminded her of something. Something she'd seen. So beautiful and yet so frightful. She remembered Nikki's butterfly collection. She remembered the diaphanous wings, all the colors of the rainbow. And the pins, those tiny skewers of death. And Nikki, shut up in his room, painstakingly adding to his collection. Studying his collection. Nikki in his own cocoon.

She found herself back at her flat. Throwing off her clothes, she faced the wall of mirrors and began the first pattern of steps for her next dance.

~~ 32

"All right, everyone, let's try it again. *Chrysalis,* from the top."

In the middle of the studio floor Alan wrapped himself in a sheath of gauzy cambric and settled into the curve of a fetal position. Nicole switched on the tape of Ravel as Dominique, a graceful reed who also danced with Olive McKinnah, leisurely, almost carelessly, drifted on to the scene. She discovered the bundle. She touched it. It stirred. Her hand, her arm, her body recoiled. She darted away, glancing warily, and tried to ignore the thing at her feet. Curiosity won out. She was drawn back to touch, to stroke, to stretch herself out, next to, over the bundle. It responded, uncurling, elongating, pulsating. Finally she dared to unwrap the sheath.

Out tumbled Alan, as though weak from the exertions of birth. At first he was like a newly emerged butterfly. Disoriented. Vulnerable. Unaware of the strength he would soon command. The girl treated him like a beautiful plaything. She coddled him. She fed him. She reprimanded him. She led him on. Soon he was too strong for her. He began to respond with a will of his own, with a fever all his own. He grew dominant. She became the toy. The toy to be controlled, to torment . . .

Nicole switched off the tape, saying, "Thanks very much, Alan. You have the makings of an admirable monster. And thank you, Dominique. That luminescent quality is just what I want." She looked about the room at other dancers and added, "Enough for today, everyone. We'll pick up from here tomorrow."

Happily, Nicole closed up the studio. It was still blustery outside, but she deliberately left her coat unbuttoned. The cold air was invigorating. It made her feel full of life and purpose.

During the subway ride down to the Village, the vision of *Chrysalis* filled her mind. The cocoon spilling out a new life, full of potential. The female force burgeoning with love. The love of a mother, a sister, a soulmate, a tease. The delicate balance upset. By whom? Did it make a difference? The resultant treachery, the discord, the hurt. Temporary. But only temporary. As a chrysalis was only a stage in development. There would be a rebirth, a greater rebirth. Not of one but of two together.

The subway lurched to a halt and Nicole got off. The completion of the vision would have to wait until later. The wind had picked up. She hugged her coat to her and set a quick pace along the couple of blocks to her flat. Myrtle Fudderman, in pincurls, a woolly argyle robe, pom-pommed slippers, and cigarette dangling from her lips, caught her as she rounded the first flight of stairs.

"Got a part for me yet, kid? I still got it in me, you know. A few high kicks, a chainé turn or two, a curtsy . . . I still remember the old routine."

Mrs. Fudderman's demonstration had Nicole biting the inside of her cheek. She daren't laugh at the older woman. In a way it was kind of sweet. A woman grown old with her memories but vital because of them. If only Alexandra had had the chance . . . No. Nicole would not allow herself to be caught up in sentiment. Her mother had lived the life she chose. To the fullest extent possible. There was no need for pathos. Just determination. And achievement.

"You're an inspiration, Myrtle. Some day I will mount a dance on you."

Nicole continued up the stairs, went into her flat, threw off her coat and pulled on a thick sweater. Mr. Fudderman had obviously forgotten to stoke the furnace again. She turned on her radio, ignoring the newscast as usual, and searched for some music with a swing beat. The dinner she made was hot, satisfying, sedating. She dragged herself off to bed, listening to the Ravel tape *Chrysalis* was danced to one more time.

Alan, Dominique, and the other dancers were still in their street clothes when Nicole arrived at the studio the following morning. They stood in a cluster, looking helpless and hanging back.

"Come on, troops," Nicole enjoined. "We're wasting time. Let's get to it." When no one moved, she asked irritatedly, "What is going on here?"

The dancers glanced at one another until, finally, Dominique came forward.

"Sit down, Nicole. There's been some terrible news."

"Oh, Christ. Who broke their leg? Or did I forget to pay a bill? Don't tell me Ernestine's been up here."

She looked from face to face for some indication.

"She really doesn't know," murmured one of the dancers.

"You'd think the War Department would have contacted her," Nicole heard another whispering. "Or someone in the family."

The color drained from Nicole's face. Her throat closed up and she could barely draw breath. She knew in an instant. She knew just by those anxious, pitying faces assembled about her. Someone was dead. Her world wasn't safe, not even the corner she had carved out for herself. She could hear her heart beating, pounding. His name came thrashing up from the depths of her core. Carlo. My God, it was Carlo. He's dead, she screamed inside herself. Carlo. My love.

"How do you know?" she rasped. "How did you hear?"

Alan brought his hand from behind his back. He held a copy of a weeks-old London *Chronicle*.

"My cousin sent it. He knew I was dancing with you. I'm sorry, Nicole. I—"

She frowned. It made no sense. No one in America knew about her relationship with Carlo. No one really knew anything about Nicole's private life in England.

She grabbed the thin sheets. WAR OBITUARIES. She closed her eyes and steeled herself. Her eyes opened, stuck on the thick black letters at the top of the page. The ink seemed to bleed into her heart. Finally she tore her gaze from the top and scanned the sad, short items.

Her shoulders sagged and she let out a surprised, little "oh." It wasn't Carlo at all. Nikki's bland face, his eyes confused, not as angry as Nicole remembered them, gazed back at her from an official Royal Air Force identification photo. She blinked. It couldn't be. Nikki in the RAF? Nikki was a dancer. He was only a boy, not yet twenty-three. He didn't even know himself. Nikki was the one who was dead. Her brother.

She was crying. Without knowing when she started. Without knowing how to stop. She was swollen with tears.

Her dancers fluttered about her. Dominique held her hand. Alan and another male dancer went off to make a pot of tea. The other women cooed and cried with her.

"The story said he was very brave."

"Wasn't he shot down over Germany? Those filthy Nazis . . ."

What was he doing? Nicole kept pondering. What was he thinking of? Nobody asked him to be a hero. There were plenty of other people's brothers who could fight in the damned war.

"Your father must be heartsick. To lose his only son. Such a fine dancer, it says he was."

All of Vanya's plans. Down the drain. Nicole almost laughed. Yes, he would be devastated. His precious Prince Charming. His boy wonder. His infant terrible.

"Your dad must be relieved you're out of harm's way."

Her dad didn't even know her address. And these people who dithered about her as though she were a broken plate, these dancers who brought her innermost visions to life, these men and women with whom she spent every waking moment, knew nothing of the truth.

They never had been a closely knit family. Once upon a time Vanya and Alexandra had loved each other. Then Alexandra loved Nicole. Vanya loved Nikki. Margaret loved Vanya. Nikki loved Margaret. But Nikki hated Nicole. And Nicole? She had loved Carlo, but that came to nothing. She had nothing. Now she didn't even have Nikki's hatred.

The world she had built out of spit and grit came tumbling down. There was a war out there, tearing people apart. There were forces causing cataclysmic upheaval. Lives were irretrievably altered. She had been hiding from the real world. Dance was only an excuse. To be too busy to see, and to feel, the presence of war. The war threatening the States. The war raging in Europe. The war within herself.

Dominique, Alan, and the rest continued to pet her and say soothing little nothings. Nicole continued to cry and sink into shock and a deep gloom.

At first she didn't hear them. All she knew was the sound of her own bitter weeping. The timid rapping became louder. It took all her effort to squelch her tears. Hold her breath. Knock, knock. A pause. Fists pounding.

"Nicole? Are you in there? We're worried about you. Are you all right? Nicole, it's been three days . . ."

More persistent knocking. Quiet. Listening. Muffled voices. Then footsteps in retreat. Nicole waited, huddling in a corner of her flat. Silence. She breathed again from under her mound of several sweaters, a coat, blankets, her mother's challis shawl. They had gone and left her alone at last. She would let no one in. Not her dancers. Not Ernest or Mattie or Myrtle. What could they offer her that would change things? Empty condolences. Well-meaning kisses that left her cold. She was cold. The flat was dark and cold. So was death.

The tears started again. She was an endless fountain. She fought for control and gave up. Wildly dabbing at her eyes with her fists, something fell from her fingers. She clutched at it. Crooned to it. Cradled it. It was the one thing she had of Nikki's. The only thing he had ever given her. Morpho Peleides Nikkoli in a tiny glass specimen frame. A wretched corpse of a butterfly sacrificed to Science. Like Nikki, sacrificed to the great God of War. Its delicate wings forever frozen in full flight. Nikki, shot down out of the sky. She brought the glass to her lips and smeared a kiss on it.

It was one thing to walk out of someone's life. Leave him, or her, to go on as if she'd never been a part of it. But this . . . this death. It was final. It was forever. There was no returning. There was no chance to understand. No forgiveness.

Even in the darkened room the glass shimmered and twinkled. Nicole got up from her nest of grief and walked to the window, holding up the frame to catch the glint of light. Looking for one hint of life in Morpho Peleides Nikkoli.

"Nikki?" she whispered half out loud, half to herself. "Are you really dead? If you're really dead, then half of me is too. You're not gone, are you?"

She shook the glass as if the motion would somehow resuscitate the butterfly.

"You're my twin. Why didn't I know it? Why didn't I feel it?"

Some great need urged her to turn on the lights in the flat. She found herself pulling the frame apart. She ignored the thin sheet of glass that shattered onto the floor, and dug the tiny pins out of the backing. Weightless, the butterfly rested in the palm of her hand. So fine and frail. The beautiful wings still iridescent. Splotches of black and red, symmetrical from left to right. She stared, never having noticed before. A pattern like a face. Two faces. One face. Hers and Nikki's.

She raced for the wall of mirrors, studying her face intently. She could see him in herself. He was there. In her eyes. In the shape of her nose. Her cheekbones. Her lips. In the color of her hair. She remembered staring in mirrors— for hours, it seemed like—when she was a child. One half, Nicole. The other half, the absent half, Nikki. Two peas in a pod. Two halves of one soul. Just like the two wings of a butterfly.

Why couldn't it have been true? All those stories and promises her mother had plied her with. She'd believed them with all her heart. And the truth? The real truth had come from her father. Nikki was nothing like her. Bland to the point of numbness when she first met him. Crazed with an uncontrollable anger when she left. Two extremes. What had happened to the baby boy Alexandra gave birth to?

There had only been that brief time when Nikki and she had had any semblance of feeling for each other. Of really finding each other. It had been so tentative. So fragile. Like the butterfly he gave her. So puzzling. Like the Chinese box without an obvious opening. And it was over in a few brief seconds. Brother and sister lost. Damned by their partnership.

If she'd stayed, would things have been different? Would Nikki be alive today if she'd continued to dance with him? Of course he would be, she rationalized. He'd never have joined the RAF if they'd been dancing together.

Nicole's tears stopped. She put the butterfly down and retreated to the mass of blankets and coats on the floor. Guilt weighed on her like a thousand-pound barbell. It was her fault. All of it. Starting with her mother.

Maybe, if she'd been a better daughter, Alexandra wouldn't have died. She should have seen the first signs of disease, Nicole told herself. She would have insisted Alexandra see a doctor immediately. Go to a hospital. Get the finest care. Not have to sit and watch her mother fade away. God, what a punishment. A punishment and a death. Because part of her had died with Alexandra.

The punishments had begun when Carlo left her. No, it was Vanya's fault. No, that wasn't right either. Nikki. Maybe . . . yes . . . it was Nikki who had hurt her. Physical pain equal to the anguish she felt engulfed by. Did he ever know how much? Did he ever realize she was running away from him? From herself? That she had to take herself away before she would die too?

Was that why he had done it? Did he have to get away from himself too? Had Nikki gone to war to get himself killed? Was that to be her punishment too? Wasn't leaving England and disappointing the remnants of her family enough? Was she also responsible for her brother's death?

She loved him so much. She'd wanted them to be so much alike, and they'd been polar opposites. Nikki and Nicole, the two halves. She'd grown up believing that by looking into a mirror she would see him. And in the end they hadn't been able to see eye to eye on anything. Didn't anyone understand? Didn't anyone feel her anguish? Her loss even then? Even now?

Vanya. Only her father would know what she felt, for he must be feeling it now. Her father would understand it wasn't all her fault.

Nicole uncurled herself from the nest she had built around herself. She turned on a light, found paper and pen, and began to write a letter to Vanya.

Dear Father,

I just found out about Nikki. I can't believe he's gone. I got to know him for such a short time. I'm not sure I really knew him, but I loved my brother. I want you to know that, Father. I know how much you loved him. I know he was the light of your life. You wanted so much for him. For me too, I guess. I hope Nikki—Nick—never disappointed you. I know I did. I'm sorry. I really am. But I couldn't sacrifice myself. You never knew . . . you couldn't see . . .

She wanted to tell Vanya about the bruises, the brutality, the cruelty, but she didn't. She wanted more than anything to feel close to her family, to pretend there had been a family. She wanted to pour her heart out to her father. Not her bile. Not now.

Let me try to explain. Yes, Nikki and I were twins. But the similarities you and Mom saw were not what we felt. Everyone assumed dancing would bring us together. It only showed us how different we were. The more we danced, the more we were torn apart. Maybe we were thrilling to watch, but, Daddy, it was terrible. Not fun and not healthy. It was sick. It was making me sick. I had to leave. I couldn't stay. I was losing myself. I'd already lost Mom, and Carlo had gone off to fight his beloved bloody Fascists . . .

She couldn't stop herself. Seeing the words before her, it was suddenly as real as when she was living it. She hurt. She needed to justify her own actions. She needed to blame.

I couldn't let you and Nikki kill what was left of my free will. I had to make a change before I became just another one of those faceless, breastless, technically perfect, emotion vacuums you called ballerinas. That wasn't what Mom was, and it was never what I wanted. If you'd only given Mom more work, she wouldn't have had to go off on her own, where I couldn't take care of her. You and Nikki and Margaret and England killed her as much as that damned disease did. God damn your values! What good is honor and duty and respectability without a little human compassion and understanding?

Now Nikki is the next pitiful victim, sacrificed in the name of pride. Is England happy now? Are you? Did you ever know how much Nikki loathed his mother, his sister, himself? It's true. That's what drove him to dance the way he did. Not your grand, classical training or style. But emotions he didn't know what to do with. Emotions that dear little Peggy never taught him to handle, much less recognize. That's the baggage he took with him into the RAF and up into an airplane and down to his death.

Nicole signed her name, practically stabbing the paper with her pen. She was enraged, infused by the violence of her indignation. She threw on her coat and burst out the door. She had a dance to finish.

That spring, as the first budding flowers broke through Central Park's stiff ground, Ernestine Pringle decided to produce an evening of contemporary dance. She asked a consortium of choreographers to put on their latest, most controversial works. Nicole's *Chrysalis* was featured.

It had become darker, bleaker, more violent. The haunting music of Ravel had been replaced with a jangle of atonal chords. Against the back of the stage hung long graying strips of poorly cut cloth. They gave the impression of having been lately removed from a badly decaying mummy.

The body of the work was the same as Nicole had originally conceived it, except for the mood. Initially whimsical, the accent had been on the sense of play and curiosity between the butterfly/boy and the nymph. There had been a question of dominance. Now the answer was clear.

Doom pervaded each step. There was never any doubt the girl would delve into the secret of the chrysalis. There was never any doubt she would bring out the worst in the creature. There was never any doubt that the weak, too-pretty plaything would reveal its true nature. He was more than commanding. More than monstrous. He was sinister. He was lethal.

As the music roared to its apocalyptic climax, the male crushed the girl as if she were no more than a thin shell, a chrysalis of herself. Plucking her limp body off the floor, he lifted her to his mouth and sucked her dry. Sated and spent, he sank down and wove the lengths of cambric back around himself and his broken love. *Chrysalis* was over.

33

The next year proved to be a creative avalanche for Nicole. *Skirmishes* and *Chrysalis* had propelled her into the forefront of the New York dance world. She formed her own troupe, crystallizing the Varonne style and themes.

She continued to create controversy with each new dance, particularly after Pearl Harbor. With the war effort now an everyday fact of life, her vision struck an underground chord with the women left to fight the battle on the home front. As true for centuries past as for 1941 and '42, women were supposed to feel proud to send their men off to battle. What they really felt were fear, despair, apprehension, profound loss, and desertion. Why, why was there war? Nicole asked through her dances. What was this evil born out of? And why did it flourish in the very nature of men?

The more pieces Nicole choreographed, the less overtly theatrical they became. She turned to Olive McKinnah for guidance, and as a result, Nicole's art grew finely shaded. She focused less on blatant effects and more on innovative movement. The power of her storytelling, the interpretation of her allegories, now came from dance technique.

The female dancers in her works used full, rounded movements. They were creatures of boundless energy and rhythm. Arms and hands were grandly curved and held far from the body. Legs swept the floor in great arcs, swooping outward and upward. The core of strength was in a dancer's waist, from which she could extend her upper body forward or hold herself totally erect. Rarely was a female posed so that she leaned backward. Submission, female submission, was not a part of the dancers' repertoire.

Male submission was another issue. The few men in Nicole's troupe were powerfully built, but they were allowed to move in ironically small, abrupt steps as if fettered by some invisible force. Movement originated from an inward buried impulse. Arms, bent at the elbows, thrust from the chest. Legs, earthbound, jerked in complex combinations of pliés and glissades. Even the neck was given tilted, questioning positions. There was a sense of limitation, of a dim clock ticking away. Men were like time bombs, and when they exploded, almost inevitably, it was left to the women to pick up the pieces. Or ignore the pieces. Or shield themselves. Defend and reconquer. Survive.

Music was still a key for Nicole. She went to the symphony. She haunted record stores. She sat in on informal jam sessions. Her dancers teased her about going so far as to listen at keyholes in music schools. Anything to find the right combination of mood and step.

Unlike her former teacher, Gar Fortune, who would have exposed his grandmother to public ridicule if it meant greater acclaim, Nicole kept her private life to herself. She was known through her works and for her works. Period. Only her dancers saw some of the private emotions she struggled with each time she mounted a new dance. The few who danced for her regularly knew something of the tragedy of her brother's death. The other, newer dancers put it down to artistic temperament. What they didn't know was the scourge that plagued Nicole.

What had Mattie Wiggins said in the early days? Something about the demons that drive a choreographer. Nicole had found her demons. They had faces and names too familiar for comfort. They lashed out at her in dreams. They bobbled up in the soap bubbles of her bath. They peered through subway windows and ducked out of sight when she glanced up. She knew they were always there.

But the demons grew docile in her dances. They hung their heads in shame and behaved like accommodating little imps. She was the mistress and they were her servants. Nikki, Vanya, Alexandra, Carlo. They all had their place in her dances. As did rage and broken promises and the blunt savagery of men and the inherent tenacity of the female spirit. The drama of Nicole's short life was reborn in bits and pieces all women could identify with.

One spring evening after a performance, Nicole was leisurely removing her stage makeup. The small house had been packed.

"What more proof do you want?" Ernestine rumbled. "The country is ready for you, Varonne. It's your duty to go on tour."

"Are you drafting me?" teased Nicole. "Or do I get a chance to enlist?"

Ernestine Pringle had become militant in her own way since Ernie Land had joined the army.

"Listen to me, Varonne. Women need to know where their strength comes from. Women need to know what they're fighting for and against. You could reach such a wide audience. They'd lap it up."

"I'm not ready."

"Who is?" Ernestine demanded. "Promise me you'll think it over. You won't have to worry about expenses. I'll pay for everything."

"Oh, Ernestine, I don't mean to sound ungrateful, but get off my back. Yes, I'll think about a tour. Yes, I don't know what the troupe would do without you. Now go play with your checkbook in someone else's sand box."

Nicole got up, kissed her patron soundly on both cheeks, and firmly pushed her out of the dressing room. Ernestine's harsh rat-a-tat laugh ricocheted off the corridor walls. Nicole resumed her task. She had just slipped on a pair of trousers and a silky blouse when her door cracked open.

"Ernestine," she said wearily. "Go home. I'm really not interested in a tour . . ."

"Good," came a distinctive voice. "Because I don't want you going anywhere."

Manny Schumann stuck his head and then the rest of his bulk into the doorway. "Just give me the word, kid," he said in his best George Raft imitation. "Just one word, and Lady Bountiful is history."

Nicole hugged her former agent and said, "Are you converted yet? Have I made a true believer out of you at last?"

"Kid, I always believed in your talent. I've had my ear to the ground, and I hear you're doin' great things. I hear you're on the verge of makin' the big time. I can give you the break you need to put you over. Make your name a household word. Your face in *Life* magazine. A whole spread." He paused, waiting to see the effect of his words, then added, "You don't even have to leave New York."

"Manny, have you had your ear to the ground or glued to my door?"

"Nicole, you hurt my feelings. I only want the best for you. Just like I wanted for your mother. How'd you like to come back to Broadway, kid? I'm not talking chorus line here. I mean choreograph. Choreograph the biggest musical since *Lady in the Dark* . . . since *On Your Toes*—no, since *Showboat.*"

Nicole felt as though he expected her to stand up and salute.

"I suppose it's very flattering. But frankly, Manny, my work and Broadway are about as far apart as salt and sugar."

"You're not usin' your head, kid. What was *Lady* all about? I'll tell you. Headshrinkers. Psychology. Intellectual stuff. And *Toes?* It had tap and ballet. And *Showboat?* Well, it had everything. Love, marriage, divorce, racism, drink, and unforgettable songs."

"Well, Manny," Nicole said, nodding as though it all made profound sense to her, "that's quite a laundry list."

"Yeah, none of that should go together. But it did. In a big way. You're the next illogical link. Get it? Nicole Varonne . . . priestess of modern dance . . . the battle of the sexes . . . the eternal combat . . . and the Broadway, soon-to-be smash hit musical of 1942 and '43."

"This could be interesting," she said, nodding thoughtfully now. "Tell me more."

Manny settled down in the one comfortable chair Nicole had in her dressing room.

"We're at war, right, kid? And whether you agree or not, this is a good war. A righteous war. I mean we're fighting on the right side for the right reasons. We all gotta do our part. Boost morale. Make Americans feel proud. Show our backbone. Show why we're great . . . as well as right."

"A little propaganda?"

"Couldn't hurt. Look, kid. What is more inspiring, more down home, more corn pone and apple pie than the bigger-than-life men and women of folk legends? You know, like the Pilgrims and Indians at the first Thanksgiving. Or Pocahontas. Or Hiawatha. Or Johnny Appleseed or Daniel Boone or—"

"I get the picture, Manny," Nicole said laughing. "Okay, so which of these illustrious heroes will be the star of the show?"

"Picture this. A man so strong he forges mountains out of valleys and rivers out of deserts. A man so brave he rides lightning bareback and wrestles cyclones bare-handed. A hero with a ready smile who makes jokes and takes them too. A hero who believes he can do anything if he just puts his mind and his muscle to it. A native-born American son."

"Why Manny, you're positively inspiring!"

"I put money in this one, kid. I took one look at the book and heard a couple of tunes and I knew. This show'll make Broadway history. It can crack the box office wide open. Good old Paul Bunyan's gonna do it for a lot of us, kid. You too, if you'll take old Manny's advice."

Of course it was Paul Bunyan. The legends ran through Nicole's mind. The roaring wind from out of the north. The boy child too big for his cradle. Babe, the ox. The blue snow and the queer creatures it gave birth to. Pecos Bill. The mountain of rock candy and the rivers of onions and ketchup. The tall woman he loved and the other woman, just a tiny thing, who told him his work was over.

Nicole could see it. Big and raw and optimistic. Native movements that the audience could recognize. Hoedowns. Rain dances. Virginia reels. Stomping and clogging. Men at their most elemental, at their best. The dawn and the twilight of innocence. No unnecessary flag waving. Just pride to have come from that stock.

"It'd be one hell of a stretch . . ."

"I've got faith in you, kid."

"Okay, Manny. You've got yourself a choreographer. By the way, what's the name of this show?"

"What else? *Tall Timber.*"

Tall Timber was deep into production by summertime. With the musical score complete, Nicole first set the chorus dances that accompanied the songs. She'd finished the full cast numbers and was polishing a couple of featured dances with the ensemble of lumberjacks. An intricate circle dance symbolizing the cutting down of trees. A comic, skating free-for-all on a man-sized, hotcake griddle.

The beasts and birds of the blue snow had a featured dance too. One, two, or three dancers were strapped into costumes with odd numbers of legs, partial wing development, multiple tails, horns, hooves, quills, shaggy fur, and feathers. They bobbled and careened, galloped, and occasionally broke out into an off-balance hornpipe.

Nicole was just beginning to rehearse the dances for the lead roles. She started with the courtship scene between Paul Bunyan and Hattie, the girl who won his heart.

"It's a complicated piece of staging," she explained to the four people assembled in the theater. "That's why we've had to wait for the set to be finished. I couldn't mount this dance until I saw what we had to work with. Work around. So . . . Paul . . ."

Two men looked alertly at her.

"Buzz, we know you dance the part of Paul in the dream sequences, but Mr. Gable has to set the scene. So it's Paul the actor I work with first. It'll be Paul the dancer's turn soon. I know this sounds confusing, but stick with me. I'll try to make it easy. So you, Paul the actor, hear a scream, run to the river's edge, and pull Hattie . . ."

Two women perked up.

"Hattie the actress, not Hattie the dancer," Nicole said patiently. "Hattie gets pulled out of our pretend raging water before she can drown. Got that? Did you bring your scripts? Great. Then the two of you speak your lines. Destiny, blah blah blah, undying love, blah blah blah. And the music comes up.

"Now here's the tricky bit. Hit it," she yelled to the stagehands. "See how the set divides up? The forest and river slide back and we see a vast nighttime sky dotted with moonlit clouds and twinkling stars. Isn't it gorgeous? Now, my two actors will melt into the departing woods. I'll show you some melting steps in a couple of minutes. In their place, dancing Paul and Hattie appear on stage. The point is, instead of singing about falling in love, Paul and Hattie will dance it."

The four professionals nodded in understanding.

"Okay. Actors, let's block it out. Let's start with Hattie. Miss Wyatt?"

The actress, a statuesque bombshell with a voice to match, followed Nicole's direction and was soon floundering adequately in the step-down, recessed trough that passed for a river. She didn't have to be shown how to shake the pretend water off her body in order to display her greatest virtues.

"And now you, Mr. Gable."

"Call me Billy. Everyone does."

He knew just what she wanted. Leaning into Hattie's wailing screech for help. Dashing in and about the jigsaw trees, giving the impression of a forest of great dimension. Churning his arms and shoulders. Finally ceasing all motion to take stock of this female mountain, really looking her over. Making the audience look her over, seeing what he saw.

She taught him how to turn Hattie, slip through the trees, reappear, disappear, reappear, disappear as the set moved aside. He was a fast learner and an excellent partner. He led Gloria Wyatt with a generosity Nicole instantly recognized and admired.

"Good work. I mean it. Now let's run through it again like you've been doing it for eight or nine performances already."

Billy's stage presence was irresistible. Nicole found herself completely absorbed in him. Gloria Wyatt may as well have been a department store dummy. He just seemed to have a way about him. An easy swagger. An inviting grin. He didn't hog the lights or exaggerate the delivery of his lines. He was perfectly natural.

"Once more, please," she requested.

And he didn't seem to have one of those egos in full bloom. Not like that flaming jackass who played Pecos Bill. If she had to submit to one more insufferable lecture about the size of his part, Nicole thought, she was going to take his rattlesnake prop and shove it up his—

"How was that, Miss Varonne?"

"Actually, quite nice, Mr. Gable, Miss Wyatt. Thank you for coming. We'll try a full run-through, cast and orchestra, next week. All right, dancers, your turn."

"Coming, Billy?" asked the actress.

"Nope. Think I'll stay awhile."

He plunked down in a seat in the sixth row, ranging his legs over the backs of the fifth-row seats and a little beyond.

"You mind if I watch? Figure I might learn a thing or two," he asked Nicole.

For some reason she was flattered, but she soon forgot he was there. Dominique, the dancer from Nicole's own troupe, danced Hattie. Buzz, of all people—Nicole's first partner on Broadway—had won the role of Paul.

The dancers obediently trotted through the series of steps Nicole outlined. At first Paul and Hattie were to circle one another, arms locked behind their backs, sizing each other up. Then they were to stand back, arms akimbo, rocking gently on their heels. The two entered into a friendly competition, dancing side by side. What he tried, she copied. What she initiated, he caught on to. At first it went well.

Nicole expanded the competition. It got less and less friendly. Paul and Hattie needed to display their superiority. She didn't like it when he won. He liked it even less when she won. He belittled her, derided her victories, made the next contest harder. What began as a square dance for two was ending as an enactment of the Herculean labors, with Paul dominating and defeating Hattie each step of their courtship.

"Can we take a breather?" Buzz begged, lathered in sweat.

"Just go through that last sequence again. There's something not quite right . . ."

"You see it too," Billy whispered confidentially. "I thought I was the only one."

"I beg your pardon," Nicole said, twisting around in her seat. "Exactly what do you mean?"

"Well, Miss Varonne—can I call you Nicole? Maybe my knowledge of choreography doesn't rank much higher than a grasshopper's leap, but I do know musical comedy. Been in more than a couple over the last few years . . . and seen them all.

"Well, let me put it this way. Seems to me, Paul and Hattie are supposed to be falling in love. Now don't take this the wrong way, Miss Nicole—that sure is a pretty name—but you got these two love bugs locked in mortal combat. The way you've got them going at each other . . . well, forget the marriage bed. I see side-by-side tombstones. Do you really want them that angry?"

Nicole was stunned. Here was this fresh-faced guy punctuating each little dig at her work with a sure, easy smile. His eyes, a cornflower blue straight out of the Midwest, gazed at her artlessly. He genuinely wanted to know, she realized. He wasn't judging or damning her. He didn't seem to be looking for a fight.

What had he said? She ran his words through her mind as she envisioned the dance. He was absolutely right. Love and the marriage bed were getting the short end of the stick. She'd made a charming moment, the heart of the story, into a battle to the death. She could open her mouth and rant and rave. Tell him he was all wrong. He had no vision. He didn't understand.

She might as well ram her head straight at a brick wall. There was only one thing to do in the face of such overwhelming common sense.

"Mr. Gable . . ." She paused as he flashed that damnably reassuring smile. "Billy . . . I can't believe I'm saying this, but you're right and I'm wrong."

"Whoa there, Nicole. There's no right or wrong. It's just a question of what's best for the show."

"Well, Billy Gable, whatever you want to call it, I concede. I'm changing it right now."

Dominique and Buzz were less than enthusiastic, considering the amount of work they had already put in. But when Nicole dropped the gladiator contest for a romantic wandering through the stars, the two dancers found new energy. The friendly rivalry remained. But it developed into a meeting of mind and heart. Where each had taken a turn showing off, they now carefully matched their rhythm until their movements were identical.

The lovers entwined themselves in each other's arms as twinkling beams of light interlaced the whole map of the sky. The earthly giants and their deepening love took on cosmic proportions as they danced, light-footed, among the constellations of the stage set. They even seemed to make their own starry patterns. Nicole devised a sequence in which Buzz lifted Dominique, set her down in such a way that she was then in position to lift him and set him down, and the set repeated itself across the stage. They were equals, catapulting themselves over the breadth of the sky. A constellation of their own making. The lovers seemed to possess superhuman strength and at the same time exude a touching gentility.

"Yeah, that's the way it should be," chimed in Billy again and again. "Love taking a natural course."

"I don't know why I couldn't see that to begin with," Nicole said, nodding in agreement.

It took the rest of the evening to remount the dance. Billy stayed for the duration, cheering on Nicole and the dancers. Finally, it was completed.

"It's beautiful, Nicole," Dominique stated in her breathy quiet voice. "I feel it as I dance. The power is still there, yet it's so different from your other pieces."

"It's gonna be a show-stopper. That's all I know," said Buzz.

"Well, I'm the star of this show, and you know what I think?" challenged Billy, staring down at three expectant faces. "I think I'm starving. Aren't you?"

Both Buzz and Dominique had other plans. Nicole couldn't think of a thing to say. Normally she would have crawled home, made herself some cold beet borscht—Alexandra's summertime tonic—opened the windows and tried to sleep. But tonight she was ravenous. She suddenly pictured a thick steak, potatoes Anna, a Caesar salad, and a thick slab of chocolate cake. When was the last time she'd eaten a meal like that? Not since . . .

Not since she was a young girl . . . was she nine or ten? Alexandra had completed a particularly successful engagement in Chicago. To celebrate, she had bought Nicole a new dress—layers of frills below the drop waist—and a satin bow for her hair. They'd gone to dine at the most expensive restaurant in the city. How they'd stuffed themselves . . .

She found herself smiling at Billy, saying, "I'm so hungry, I could eat a buffalo."

"Well, Miss Bunyan, will a sky-high roast beef on rye make a dent? If I promise a side order of potato salad, onion rings, and a double chocolate soda?"

"You're not from New York, are you?" she said, laughing.

"I'm a Hoosier, ma'am, from the great state of Indiana. My mother's folks raise corn and my father's family raise hogs."

"And you're an actor," Nicole marveled.

"A song and dance man, at least I pretend to be," he said modestly. "Grew up singin' in the fields and in the barn. My old man wouldn't let me sing in the house. Said I might scare the wits out of my brothers and sisters."

"You come from a big family, then?"

"If you think three brothers and four sisters are big . . . I'm the oldest, pushing thirty, believe it or not . . ."

By the time Billy told her everyone's name, age, and 4-H Club accomplishments, Nicole was effortlessly ensconced in a booth at the Carnegie Deli and sipping her second soda. She'd never heard anything like Billy's stories. Not for a long, long time.

 **34**

It was the beginning of Billy always being there. He never intruded. He was more like a friendly hovering presence, waiting for the right moment. Waiting for Nicole to give him the go-ahead signal. She liked it. She liked him. He was easy to be with. He took her to lunch and they talked shop. He brought her coffee during rehearsals. He walked her to the subway, and sometimes he'd ride down to the Village with her.

She came to think of him as a buddy. Someone you laughed with. Someone you exchanged knowing glances with. He was more than a professional colleague. That sounded so cold to Nicole. And Billy wasn't cold. He exuded warmth and sincerity and simple old-fashioned fun. There was a lot of boy in this man approaching thirty. A couple of times she'd caught herself staring hard at his face. Had he started to shave yet? A silly question, but accurate in a funny kind of way.

She saw him as an innocent, untouched by the hell of real life.

"What hell?" he'd asked her. "Real life is what we make of it. Far as I'm concerned, musical theater is real enough."

From her viewpoint, what Billy did was in the realm of pure fantasy if there ever was one. The roles he'd played were so predictable, so true to type, she'd laughed when he recited his resumé.

"I've been a newsboy, a sailor, a teenage vaudevillian. Those were my chorus days. Then there was the time I played a lion tamer. I got to sing—"

"And crack a whip," Nicole had teased.

"That was my audition," he retorted.

It had also been his breakthrough role. That lilting baritone voice made old ladies cry and Broadway angels wax eloquent all the way to the bank. He played second lead, the star's best friend, until *Say It with Roses* came along. The critics couldn't resist the dapper young banker who rescued the Depression era florist from bankruptcy. And a new star climbed the Broadway ascendancy.

After *Roses,* there was *Tell Me a Story,* a farcical rendition of Mother Goose characters let loose in New York City. Too sophisticated for the nursery set and too silly for adults, it had a short run, but Billy had loved it and the audiences had loved Billy. Then *Time Stood Still* opened. The romantic musical about a shy watchmaker who falls in love with a clock-tower figurine he tends was an unqualified hit. A year and a half later Billy was getting ready to play Paul Bunyan, the docile giant who cleared the path for all Americans.

"What's next, Billy? Tom Sawyer or Jesus Christ?"

"That's the funny thing, Nicole. I never really know what's coming next."

It was an uncomfortable moment, revealing a flaw in Billy that she didn't want to see.

"But heck, something always seems to turn up," he added bravely.

That's how life was for Billy Gable.

Indian summer had come to New York. Early one lazy morning, a Sunday, Nicole had planned to waste in splendid idleness, she was awakened by a frantic knocking at her door.

"Nicole! Nicole!" rasped Billy. "Fish are jumpin'. We'll be late."

Billy was here. At her door. How? Why? Her eyes flew open and her hand reached for her alarm clock. She could barely read the time. Five-thirty?

"Yoo-hoo. Nicole."

Good God. Myrtle Fudderman was mixed up in this too? Nicole charged out of bed and threw on a robe. The notion of Billy and Myrtle shuffling off to Buffalo up three flights of stairs was certainly worth getting out of bed for.

The apartment was quiet. Maybe she was dreaming. Maybe it was only a nightmare. A grotesque joke she was playing on herself. Billy would surely laugh when she told him.

"Dungarees, Nicole. You got a pair?"

He was there. A girlish giggle. Myrtle was there too. Nicole cracked open the door. Billy planted a big smacking kiss on the landlady's cheek.

"Oh, Mr. Gable," Myrtle gushed.

"You've been a great help. Couldn't've done it without you."

"Oh, Mr. Gable," she tittered again before glancing at Nicole. "I hope you don't mind. I know he's your friend from the show. Oh, Mr. Gable, I saw you six times in *Time Stood Still.* I cried like a goddamn baby at the end, when Mirabelle finally comes to life. Every goddamn time."

Nicole watched in fascination. Myrtle Fudderman, old enough to be her mother and then some, reduced to utter adolescent jelly. What had happened to the Myrtle

Fudderman she knew? The one with the constant cigarette clamped between her lips? For here was the hard-bitten ex-chorine prancing down the stairs as if she'd seen Santa Claus.

"Shame on you, Billy," Nicole said. "Do you always have that effect on women?"

"All ages and sizes," he confessed. "Only know one who seems to be immune."

More power to her, Nicole thought. Billy was grinning.

"What are you doing here?" she asked.

"Told you. Fish're jumpin'. We'll miss them if we don't hurry. Come on, girl. Wipe that empty look off your face. I'm just taking your advice. Remember when you gave me a choice? Tom Sawyer or our Lord, J.C.? Well, I decided. I'm trying out old Tom for size. See if I like his boots. You're gonna be my Huck Finn."

The light dawned in Nicole's head. This was all about fun and stealing moments from a more sober world. This was spontaneity. This was feeling young and exuberant and carefree. This was Sunday with Billy.

"You're comin', aren't you?" His voice had a slight edge to it. Like a plea.

"You stay there while I get dressed."

"Out here? On the landing?"

"That's what it's there for."

"Nicole?"

"Yes?"

"Bring a swimsuit . . . under your clothes."

A slow blush singed her cheeks. Don't be an ass, she told herself. He's a little boy with big pretensions. It's a line he probably stole from some show he was in. It was a joke and nothing more. He was her chum. A playmate.

They played. A couple of hours out of the city and they were in a different world. Trees with leaves all the colors of fire. A lake so blue it seemed like the sky had fallen into it.

Billy bought a can of bait and showed Nicole the art of hooking worms. They sat on the edge of the dock, pants legs rolled up to the knee, toes dangling in the water, noses turning red from the sun, and fished. And fished. By noon they had caught their quota.

"That was the easy part," Billy said. "Now I'm putting you to work."

He pulled out a knife, some old newspaper, a skillet, and a spatula.

"You clean and I'll cook," he offered.

"You old sea dog!" countered Nicole. "Not on your life. You clean and I'll cook."

"Aye aye, cap'n," he said, and smartly saluted. "It'll be fish-eye stew for the mates tonight."

They worked well together, side by side. The aroma that arose from Nicole's pan was mouth-watering. The fillets were consumed in short order. All of them. Nicole lay on the grassy slope not far from the dock.

"I'm stuffed," she moaned.

"To the gills?" Billy suggested.

"No more jokes, please, Billy. I'll burst."

"Okay. No more. How's this?"

He sat near her head, leaned back on one hand and with the other stroked his fingers through her hair. Slowly working each tangled curl. His touch was so light. Nothing like the strong sure pull of Alexandra's hands inventing hair styles for her daughter the fairy princess or the snow witch or the Indian maiden or the other endless characters of Nicole's youthful make-believe world. Nothing like Carlo, who had grasped her hair in his fists when they made love.

She sat up abruptly. No demons. Not today.

"Was I too rough?" Billy asked.

"I hardly knew you were there. You're so gentle." She got up feeling unsettled, restless.

"Okay," Billy said, and ushered her back toward the dock. "Intermission's over. Act Two begins. This way, my lady."

He'd rented a boat, and now rowed the two of them toward the center of the placid lake. The boat skimmed the surface of the water. Nicole watched the rippling effect of the oars spread across the whole lake. Billy stopped rowing and the boat bobbed gently in the breeze.

"Lie back," he urged. "Close your eyes. You need this day."

He sang to her as though she were a baby in need of lullabies. Whether it was his voice or the rocking of the boat or the result of too many fish, the spell took hold. Nicole felt herself unwind. All the fraught tensions she kept so tightly pent up gave way to the simplest reflex. Breathing in. Breathing out. Letting it out.

She closed her eyes. She drifted with the boat. She floated. Like the cork on Billy's fishing line. Like an ice cube slowly melting. Like Dominique dancing . . . or Alexandra in Vanya's arms before he set her down, that one time Nicole saw them dance together. Floating . . . like a lily flower in a lotus pond. Floating . . . She was asleep.

Shadows passing over her . . . She blinked and opened her eyes. Had a cloud covered the sun? No, it was Billy, shielding her.

"You're so lovely," he murmured. "Golden hair, eyes starry with angel dust, lips smooth as roses. I watched you every second, Nicole, sleeping like a child. Kissed by the sun. I'd like to kiss you . . ."

She was listening to every word he said. Every sweet compliment as the boat floated along. She gazed into his eyes, as blue as the sky above and the water below. The same blue all around her. Coming closer. Closer. His lips brushed hers, staying to sip for just a second. It was . . . nice.

Neither one of them said anything. Nicole didn't know what to say. She hadn't been expecting anything intimate between them. They were supposed to be friends, not lovers. She thought there was nothing physical between them. No hand holding. No caresses. No embracing. She hadn't invited, and Billy hadn't offered. Did it have to change?

Billy studied her as though he were reading her face, hearing the questions racing through her mind.

"All right, Huck," he demanded as he heaved a small anchor overboard. "Last man in . . . Race you to shore."

He pulled off his boots and socks, shirt and jeans, and dived into the water. Nicole breathed freely again. Billy did understand. They were just friends, buddies like Huck and

Tom off on a rafting adventure. She undressed quickly. He was a couple of lengths ahead of her but he swam lazily. Graceful but slow. Drifting wherever the water took him. She was fast enough to catch up with him, and beat him.

She would have too, except that he caught her as she sped by and wrapped her close to him. They flailed awkwardly in the water for a moment, sank, surfaced, coughed, and started laughing. With the sun edging over the treetops, they swam leisurely toward land. Together.

It was another kind of Billy always being there. Smack dab by her side, every free moment they had between rehearsing and more rehearsing. He took her to Little Italy to gorge on spaghetti and Chianti. She passed on the wine. He took her uptown to Harlem to experience the Apollo Theater. He had to restrain her from jumping on stage.

One morning he knocked on her door again. This time for breakfast at the Automat. They climbed to the top of the Empire State Building like a couple of tourists. They watched the sun set over the city from a harbor ferry. They went to a football game. He bought her toasty-hot, roasted chestnuts in Central Park. He surprised her with Chinese fans and Spanish castanets.

He showed up at the rehearsal hall one night dressed as a swami, complete with crystal ball.

"There is a mysterious man in your past . . . no, in your present . . . yes, even in your future," he said in a ridiculous Indian accent. "You and this man . . . he has great talents . . . you bring out the worst—no, the best—yes, the best of them . . . I see you and this blond man are like one. Joined at the proverbial hip, as it were."

Nicole became very quiet. The smile died on her lips. Goosebumps rose on her arms. The male twin. Her other half. Billy didn't know a thing about Nikki. She never talked about family, except for an occasional remark about her mother. How could he know about the blond boy with the best and worst of talents?

"Nicole? It's just a joke. Christ, you look like you've seen a ghost."

Then she got it. Billy was the blond man. He was attaching himself to her. Permanently.

"I have to go home, Billy." She turned to the dance captain and said, "Take over, will you? My mind's gone blank."

Billy hurried after her, ripping his turban off.

"You're not mad at me, are you? I just thought you needed a break. You know, a little fun to brighten an otherwise dull grind."

Nicole kept up her pace.

"Nicole . . . honey . . . I'm sorry. Just show me that sunshine smile once. That's it. The corners. Up . . ."

He went to touch her mouth. She froze on the spot and grabbed his hands away.

"Stop it, Billy. Just stop. I don't need games right now."

"Do you want me to go away?" he asked forlornly.

"Oh, for heaven's sake. Stop acting like a little boy. I'm just tired."

"Of me?"

"No, goddamn it. Of working out the kinks in this damn musical. And come to think of it, yes. I am tired of constantly playing with you. Can't you do anything but entertain?"

"It's my best trick."

"It's not your only trick. That time in the woods. At the lake. You were . . . different. Look, sometimes I want . . ." She paused, searching for words to fit the feeling. "Sometimes I want someone who understands. Who knows not to push me. Life's crazy enough without adding more pressure."

"I know, honey. I just want to make you happy."

"You do just by being my friend. It doesn't have to be all circus magic and Christmastime with me."

"You want the quiet times. Like when we went out in the rowboat. Just you and me . . ." Billy said softly.

". . . and the sun and the water. And the quiet. Yes."

Billy slipped the swami's turban back on his head.

"Merely speak and it shall be done."

35

Nicole had worked hard on the final dance in the show. It seemed to her that a great statement could be made. If *Tall Timber* was about the legendary spirit of America, it was also about the collision of naturally opposing forces. Here was Paul Bunyan, big enough, strong enough, likable enough, superhuman enough, potent enough to change the face of the earth itself. He paved the way for lesser mortals to farm the land, build the cities, live off the gifts of this great land. Yet the inevitable march of civilization spelled the death knell for someone like Paul. He was obsolete. He had served his function. It was time to pack this atavistic marvel off to the great forest beyond. The age of innocence was over.

Everyone associated with the show came to see Nicole present her vision of the finale. The scene opened with the loggers at work as usual. But the air was different. The men were sloppy. Even Paul, danced by Buzz, was careless. The intricate circle dance Nicole had created in an earlier scene was repeated but with awkward little variations. Mistakes put in deliberately. Steps missed. Axes going off in wrong directions. Axes dropped. There was something in the air. Something was changing.

Then Paul heard it. Was it a distant waterfall cascading downward? Bells tinkling from the necks of mountain sheep? A teasing breeze? He recognized it. Laughter. The soft sound that came from a confident woman. Was Hattie back?

He followed the trail until he found the woman. It wasn't Hattie at all, but a tiny slip of a woman, hardly man-sized. When she saw Paul, she laughed even more. She beckoned to him, enticed him, enthralled him. The giant was under her power. She showed him the world built in the shadow of his footsteps all across the land. It was almost complete. But not yet.

She led him back to the edge of his camp. With the cleverness of a pied piper she gathered the loggers together. Between the magic of her laugh and the web her sly feet wove around them, they were her men now. She paraded them past Paul, past the edge of the last great forest, toward her world of cities and machines and women waiting with their arms open. The men went willingly. Paul tried to go but he wasn't allowed in. He didn't fit. The female sprite pointed in the opposite direction and laughed. One last soft tinkling taunt of a laugh. And she was gone.

Paul was left on the empty stage. The music swelled to a poignant peak. Paul remained motionless. When the music died down, he lifted himself taller, straighter, grander. With head held high, he swung his axe over his shoulder and set out for the next frontier.

The dancers applauded wildly. Billy hugged Nicole to him before letting her scramble to the stage. Scanning the first few rows, she knew she was in trouble. The producers sat stony-faced while the director of the musical bit his lip. The applause stopped and a heavy silence filled its place.

"What the hell is she thinking of?" one of the producers demanded of another. "This is supposed to be an upbeat, patriotic show. For this I gave up my poker night?"

The other producer shrugged and said, "You wanted drama."

"Drama," agreed the first man. "Not Greek tragedy. Peter," he said, addressing the director, "what are you gonna do about this fiasco?"

Nicole burned with embarrassment and fury. Those dopes. Those ignoramuses. Those pompous asses. She wanted to take a prop axe in each hand and heave them at their empty heads.

"Well, gentlemen, you can't ignore the power of Nicole's choreography. It conveys some real feeling here. We never wanted fluff. Nicole's given us some real art here."

"Thank you, Peter," Nicole began. "If I may—"

"Art!" scoffed the first man. "If I wanted art, I'd go to a museum. We want to sell tickets. We want to sell New Yorkers and the rest of the country on Paul Bunyan, lovable lumberjack, symbol of our fighting forces—"

"That's just what's going to happen."

Billy leaped to the stage and put an arm around Nicole's shoulder. He squeezed her reassuringly. She found herself leaning into him.

"You gentlemen know you're making Broadway history with this production. The marriage of music, dance, and story in this show is out of the ordinary. It's extraordinary. You didn't want another fluff show. Power and guts and glory packaged into two and a half hours of memorable moments. That's what you wanted.

"Well, you have your memorable moments, gentlemen. Look what Nicole's done. She's worked like a champion, bringing art and life and a message to the dances. Gloria and I and the rest of the cast will have 'em rolling in the aisles. And they'll be humming every tune on their way out the door. You can bet on it.

"But the ending of *Tall Timber* has to be memorable. More than memorable. Unforgettable. Who's gonna forget Paul Bunyan going on to greater glory, knowing he's done his job the best he can? Who's not gonna think of Uncle Fred or Cousin Bobby doing his bit overseas? Who's not gonna feel pride in collecting metal scraps and conserving sugar and flour and buying a war bond as often as they can? No one. Not after Buzz goes off stage and I come on in front of the curtain and sing 'Going On.' There won't be a dry, unpatriotic eye in the house!"

Billy launched into an a capella version of the song, keeping Nicole at his side throughout verse and chorus. He sang of the beauties of this land, the eternal frontiers to be conquered, the pride and perseverance inside each of us. He sang of the greatness of this country and the spirit of individual achievement. As long as the laws of nature and human nature prevail, all would be well.

"What's true for the land is true for me, and true for all of us. The promise and the dream is always there. I'm going on. I'll never stop. I'll fight the fight. Work day and night until the struggle's won. I'll sing my song. I'm going on. I'm going on."

It was thrilling. Spellbinding. She could feel the reverberations of his voice and emotion ripple out of his body and into hers. Out of hers and through the dancers, singers, actors, director, producers . . . the entire theater. Unifying. Healing. Inspiring. It was a true marriage . . . her dance and Billy's song. She looked at him with tears spilling from her eyes. It seemed as though Billy were bathed in the white glow of a hundred spotlights. And the heat extended and embraced Nicole as well. She mouthed a fervent thanks to him.

"You can't beat a good team," he whispered back, as though he'd known the outcome all along.

Everybody present leaped to their feet, cheering and applauding, including the recalcitrant producers.

"All is well, children," beamed the once-obstinate producer. "Billy, you're a million-dollar baby. And Miss Varonne, I beg your pardon most humbly. Now," he said to his partner, "can we get back to poker?"

The cast departed. Billy and Nicole were the last to leave.

"I'm not very good at being grateful," Nicole said, "but I owe you for this. You stood up for me. They wouldn't have listened to me. Not if I was Nijinsky or Fred Astaire. Well, maybe Astaire, but sure as hell not Varonne. I . . . I want to thank you. Show you my appreciation."

She was squirming now, uncomfortable with this feeling of being indebted. Even for the best of reasons. She needed to even the score as soon as possible. Tonight.

"How about dinner at my place tonight?" she offered. "I'd like to cook for you."

"Dinner at your place? You mean I finally get to come in? Or are you planning alfresco on the landing?"

Billy's lighthearted touch was just what she needed to relax.

"It's time you saw how the other half lives," she teased.

"Just what half is that? Female? Pagan? Vegetarian?"

"Modern dancer."

At seven-thirty, not a minute before or a second late, Billy was knocking at Nicole's door. As prepared as she thought she was, she was still startled when the moment arrived. She took another quick glance into the pots bubbling and steaming away, shrugged, and crossed her fingers. She ducked into the bedroom to glance frantically, once more, into the mirror. Her hands flew to her hair, tucking obstinate tendrils back into place. Again she shrugged, and walked the length of the flat to the door.

It seemed to take forever, and yet she was at the door in no time at all. Why did she feel like a death-row convict taking those final steps from the safety of the cell to the unknown of the execution chamber? She extended her hand. Grasped the doorknob. Turning. Opening.

"Nicole! Honey!"

Billy burst in like a robust winter wind. He swept her up in his arms, which were filled not only with her, but with flowers, a box of candy, two bottles of wine, and the city chill on his coat. Nicole shivered.

"It's too much, Billy. I mean you didn't have to go to all this . . . trouble."

"This isn't trouble, baby. I wanted to. It's fun. You wouldn't deny me—us—a little fun?"

She broke away from him and looked toward her kitchen and dining area. What she found more than adequate for one now seemed as tiny as a postage stamp. Especially for two. Particularly for Billy and herself.

"I think dinner's almost ready," she said tentatively.

"Great! Let me help. I'm gangbusters in the kitchen."

"No," Nicole cried. "I mean you're my guest. I . . . I want you to make yourself comfortable. Let me take your coat and . . ."

She had to extricate him from his muffler. Then there was an awkward exchange with Billy loading one arm with his gifts while Nicole pulled at one sleeve of his overcoat, and the trade of gifts and available hands for the other sleeve. Somehow, finally, the coat was off and the flowers and candy were in her arms. Billy held onto the two wine bottles. He was laughing, and Nicole felt exhausted.

"You'd think we were a couple of puppies, not knowing which end was up. Boy, this is some way to start a date."

An alarm went on inside Nicole. Date? This wasn't a date. She and Billy went out. They did things together. Crazy, fun things. That didn't mean anything. Not the way he was talking.

"It's just a simple dinner. I haven't gone to much fuss," she said, knowing she lied as she spoke.

"Smells special," he said, sniffing the air. "I didn't know what you were making, so I brought a red and a white. We can drink one with dinner and save the other for the next time."

The next time. She wasn't sure whether she liked his presumption or not.

"This is a nice place, Nicole. Very original. Artistic."

"Why don't you look around while I get everything ready."

"Great."

Nicole succeeded in putting a little distance between them. She puttered about in the kitchen, draining pasta and serving up the spaghetti sauce. She had borrowed a few things from Myrtle Fudderman, who had been more than enthusiastic when she heard Billy Gable was coming to dinner. Myrtle had even suggested that she and Billy eat in her apartment. Myrtle had a real dining room. A star like Mr. Gable expected class, she'd said.

As Nicole tossed the salad, she peeked over at Billy. He was inspecting her record albums. It had been hard to think of Billy as a star until this past afternoon. He was so genial, so happy-go-lucky. There didn't seem to be a mean bone in his body. After his defense of her at the theater and his wonderful rendition of "Going On," she began to understand what his attraction on and off stage was.

He believed. He believed in everything he sang about. He

believed in the timeliness of *Tall Timber* for its message as well as for his career. He believed in finding and taking joy in life. He believed in his own talent. And he seemed to believe in her. Because he believed with all his heart, he convinced those around him. It appeared as simple as that.

Belief and conviction. It was so logical and illogical at the same time. Nicole searched for the right label. It was so . . . American! It was what she was looking for when she left England. It was what she had found in the freedom of modern dance. Doing it on your own. In your own way. Knowing it's right.

She glanced at him again. He'd come nearer, standing slightly behind her, to stare at the objects of Alexandra's past, enshrined in the built-in cabinet.

"So delicate," he was saying. "And exotic. That little cup and saucer. And that carved bird. They look like they belong in a museum. Makes me think maybe you were a cat burglar before you took up dancing," he teased gently.

"They were my mother's. The tea things were given to her by an Austrian king. And she bought the bird in Peru before I was born. There's a story for each one."

"And you could tell them all," he added. "Say, that's not a bad idea. When the show's into its run, you could make up a set of dances about each item of your collection."

Nicole stiffened. Collections were for poor souls like Nikki. Dances about collections. The notion made her shudder.

"I'll tell you what, Billy. I promise not to tell you what shows to be in or how to sing, and you promise not to tell me how or what to dance," she said, trying hard to sound lighthearted.

"But I already have, baby. Paul and Hattie's dance, remember?"

She remembered. The courtship she'd turned into a trial instead of a love affair. Billy had made her see the errors of her way. And Billy had saved her finale for her. He'd made the others see what she was after. Here it was again. Billy's strength and his appeal. Belief and conviction.

"Mr. Gable, I'll yield this once."

"A miracle!" he cried.

"A phenomenon never to be repeated," she retorted. "Now let's eat dinner before it's spoiled."

Time passed swiftly at the little table. Billy and Nicole ate, listened to Gershwin, drank Billy's bottle of red, had seconds, and washed the dishes together. Afterward they sat on Nicole's sofa, which now served to separate the dining area from the studio. They listened to more music. In a light moment Billy sang along with the record, and Nicole danced a frivolous waltz about the room.

She ended up in Billy's arms. She could either rest her head against his chest or stare up at him and dare to read the message in his eyes. Either one was risky. He wasn't letting go. She dared to look up at him. Tenderness. A question. Longing. Waiting. Waiting for some sign from her. She couldn't give it. She pulled back and took his hand instead.

"Billy, I want to say something to you. I need to thank you for today. Really for the past several months. It's been a long time since anyone's been in my corner. The way you've been."

He covered her fingers with both of his hands, holding her hand as though it were a coveted prize, and said, "Don't you know how I feel about you? I've been in your corner since the first time I met you."

"I know," she murmured.

"I've been waiting for you, Nicole. I'd wait a long time for you if I had to."

"I haven't known what I wanted. I never really thought . . . I owe you so much . . ."

"Consider any debts canceled," Billy insisted. "I just want you to be happy, honey. I know we can be happy together."

He pulled her close to him again and cradled her.

"You try so hard, Nicole, and you're so good at what you do. You want so much to be accepted. I know 'cause I want it too. Well, I accept you, Nicole. There's such a sweet little girl lurking underneath that hard-working professional.

"You make me want to love you. All of you, baby. From the tip of your head and those flyaway curls to the soles of your feet. Let me love you, Nicole. Let me cherish you and cling to you. Let me show you the sweetness. The glad times. I want to give you so much . . . ."

Was it possible? Could Billy love her the way she was? Could she be who she wanted to be with him? If she believed enough . . . and Billy believed it. Maybe they could make it possible.

Nicole looked into his eyes. There was that cornflower blue. Stalwart. Unchanging. She could see her own reflection in them. She was already a part of him. Did he see himself in her eyes too?

Then their eyes were closed to each other and their lips met. She could hear his sharp intake of breath. She could feel her breath fall on his cheek. And their lips were still together. Pressing. Clinging. Caressing. Covering.

Billy treasuring her. Billy holding her. The demons fading. Fading. The pain and the fury remote. England, Vanya, Nikki, Carlo far, far away.

Billy's kiss. Nothing else mattered.

~~~ 36

Tall Timber was on its way to being a triumph. The opening night audience roared with laughter at each joke. They rocked back and forth in their seats with each winsome ballad and kept time, jiggling fingers and feet at the up-tempo numbers. They interrupted the dances over and over with bursts of applause.

As Billy predicted, the finale brought down the house. When Paul the dancer strode off to seek his future, the uproar was deafening. The audience hushed as, a moment later, Billy appeared to sing "Going On." By the end of the song they were stamping and whistling, crying and clapping.

The entire cast joined Billy in a reprise of the final chorus. To their utter delight and surprise, the audience added its mixture of voices to the last echoes of "Going On," changing the lyrics to "We're going on, we're going on."

The cast flung up their arms. Bow after bow was taken and still the audience would not leave the theater. Again the chorus appeared before the curtain. The featured players, including Dominique and Buzz, took their turn. Gloria Wyatt was called for repeatedly. But it was Billy Gable who was besieged with adoration. He brought out the director, the conductor, the librettist, the tunesmith and lyricist, and Nicole.

Giant bouquets were brought onstage to all the principals. Billy presented Nicole with hers. In the best of stage traditions, she extracted a single flower and offered it to Billy. The audience went crazy again.

"Keep that stuff up and we'll never get out of here," he warned her.

Finally the curtain came down to stay. Backstage the cast and creators shared in another whoop of victory. Nicole cheered wildly for Buzz and Dominique and all her dancers. Then Billy grabbed her. They hugged and kissed like a couple of kids attending their second boy/girl party.

"You've got stars in your eyes," he whispered in her ear.

"Those are bubbles I'm blinking away. This champagne tickles."

"There's more in store at Sardi's. The producers reserved the big room for the cast to celebrate. I'll go change. Will you wait for me?"

Nicole curled her arms around his neck. "I'm getting kind of fond of that lumberjack shirt. It's more you than your tuxedo."

Billy smiled. "You promise to wait for me, and maybe I'll surprise you."

"It's a deal," answered Nicole.

Within twenty minutes Billy reappeared, fresh-faced and apple-polish clean. Paul Bunyan makeup removed, he looked all-American handsome with his best and brightest

toothpaste smile. Nicole burst out laughing. Billy was a
dear, willing to do just about anything to please her.

"I don't understand," he said, trying to keep a straight
face.

His tuxedo was pressed and impeccable. His cummer-
bund trim. His handkerchief folded elegantly. But missing
was the boiled white shirt and starched collar. In its place,
impossible to miss, was Paul Bunyan's red-and-black plaid
lumberjack shirt.

"You'd better think twice about this, Billy. You just might
start a fashion trend."

Sardi's was aglitter with first-nighters and cast members.
Champagne flowed. Rave reviews abounded. Dollar signs
flashed in the eyes of the ecstatic producers and angels of
Tall Timber. One in particular hailed Nicole as if she were
his long-lost daughter.

"These dances I understood," beamed Manny with a
twinkle in his eye. "You done good, kid."

He held up two fingers in a vee-for-victory sign and then
crushed her in a bearlike embrace.

"As for you, you big palooka," he said to Billy, "well, you
are Paul Bunyan. You convinced me. I'll never doubt again.
Cross my heart and hope to kiss a lumberjack."

Manny released Nicole, and the men shook hands. Billy
ushered Nicole around the room, stopping to introduce her
to well-wishers and old pals of his. The couple table-hopped,
thanking and congratulating members of the cast. The star
and the choreographer were toasted, saluted, and compared
to stars in the almighty heavens. At the first opportunity,
they left. Billy was taking Nicole home. To his penthouse.

She snuggled against him in the taxi, letting him kiss her
temples, the lobe of her ear, the line of her jaw, the length of
her neck.

"You're warm," she murmured, and snaked her hands
inside his coat.

"You're getting warmer," he breathed back. "Let's not
shock the cabbie too much."

She settled herself in his arms and leaned her head on his shoulder. "Tell me a story, Billy. Tell me what happens next."

"Well, little girl, it's like this. Once upon a time, there was an orphan, all alone in the world. She worked real hard and did her best. And her best was pretty good. She had enough to eat and a place to sleep. Sometimes she even smiled. But sometimes she stuck out her tongue at people and they got the wrong idea about her. Thought she was ornery, angry, a real nuisance. She said she didn't care, but she did. Now this orphan was a proud little orphan. People had to take her as she was or they just didn't have to take her at all. Some people admired her for her spunk, but few told her so.

"Then one day, a prince of the land, a fair-haired lad with a bellwether eye, came along and was thunderstruck by the orphan. He'd never seen such industry, such energy, such passion. 'Why, you have everything I've been looking for. This land needs you. I need you. Consent to be my princess or I'll die!' The orphan looked at the prince and saw a nice, if very ordinary, man. 'You're too dramatic,' she said. 'Straighten up.' 'I will,' vowed the prince. 'Just say you'll give me a try.' 'I might,' said the orphan, 'on one condition.' 'What's that?' asked the prince. 'I'm really not all that brave,' said she. 'I'm really quite shy. Promise you won't scare me.' 'Done!' declared the prince. The orphan came to love the prince as much as he loved her, because he kept his promise. And in time, not too much later, all the people loved her too."

Like a child lost in a favorite storybook, Nicole hadn't moved or breathed or blinked. Did he really understand how she felt, or was he just spinning a yarn? She turned to face Billy and smoothed the hair that had fallen onto his forehead.

"What am I going to do with you? Subtle you aren't, but sweet, so very sweet, you are."

"I promise I'll make it easy, Nicole."

"I know, Billy. I'm here, aren't I?"

The taxi pulled up to the curb, next to a twenty-four-story

building. Billy whisked Nicole out and into the lobby, up the elevator and through the door of his penthouse. He turned on the lights.

Nicole was surrounded by ultramodern Scandinavian. Black laminate and natural blond dominated the seating arrangements, the obligatory cocktail cabinet, the picture frames. The draperies were of pale yellow raw silk. Here and there the room was punctuated with small abstract sculptures of chrome.

"You . . . decorate the place yourself?" Nicole asked.

"Hell, no. I wouldn't've known where to begin. The department store sent someone out to fix the place up. I just gave them my name and my address . . ."

"And they gave you what every Broadway leading man should have."

"Guess so. Kind of nifty, isn't it?"

He showed her the rest of the apartment. The dining room, the kitchen, the den, even the bathrooms were uniformly glossy and lacking in personality. Nicole didn't see anything that remotely suggested that Billy Gable, nice young man from Indiana, lived there.

"Wait. You'll see what I like about this place. With the right music and the right mood . . ." Billy suggested, and led her back to the living room, dimmed the lights, and put on a record of Frank Sinatra. "Dance with me, Nicole."

It was only a simple two-step, but Nicole couldn't find the right rhythm. She felt awkward in a man's arms, held so close.

"This is so silly," she tried to explain.

"Try it this way," he said in a voice, low and calming.

He shifted her around so that her back leaned against his chest. His arms embraced her and he rocked her slowly to the music. Nicole relaxed, giving herself up to the seductive tempo.

"There, Nicole. Look. That's what I like about this place."

She became aware of the view pouring in through the pale, silken drapes. The lights of the city. Twinkling. Beckoning. Billy left her for a moment, just long enough to draw the drapes aside. It was breathtaking. It reminded her of *Tall Timber*'s starlit set. Nicole could just imagine Paul and Hattie dancing their way through the midnight hour of Manhattan's starry streets.

"Oh, I like it too, Billy," she murmured, holding tight to him.

It was the right moment. He nuzzled her hair, lifting the weight of it from the back of her neck and brushing his lips over the exposed skin. He whispered his message again in her ear.

"Baby, I'll make it easy for you. I promise. So good for both of us."

She nodded. Squeezing out of his embrace, she turned to face him. Billy, her friend. Maybe it was the right thing. To make love with your best friend. She took his hand and they danced slowly toward the bedroom. He lifted her into his arms, opened the door and laid her on the bed. While he took off his clothes, she glanced about and breathed a sigh of relief. Billy Gable the star never entered this room. Here was a bit of home. A bit of the man she thought she knew.

Overstuffed pillow shams with tassles on them. Family photographs of young Billy and an older man—his father—with fishing poles and a string full of trout. An afghan only a grandmother would crochet. A jumble of cuff links littering the bureau top. Stacks of letters, probably from all those brothers and sisters. And on the bed table an unfinished pencil sketch of a girl with a tangle of hair, large expressive eyes, a sharp little nose, and a Mona Lisa smile. It was Nicole.

Slowly, she unbuttoned her blouse and slipped off her skirt. Off came the shoes, stockings, garter belt, and panties. Billy had gotten under the bed covers while she removed the last of her clothes. He held up the blankets for her to join him.

He was nodding and said, "I was pretty sure you didn't wear a bra. That's sexy, Nicole."

She found herself blushing and forced herself to reply, "It's got nothing to do with sexiness. I'm just small."

She slid under the covers, pulling them up to her neck. Stretching an arm across her body, he gently uncovered her.

"I think you're perfect."

He fondled each breast and lowered his head to suck, first from the right one and then from the left. He rained kisses on her, starting at her face and ending down the length of each leg. Nicole lay on her back, pliant, willing, content to let Billy do all the work.

The fire in her built gradually. She could feel each part of her wake to his touch, comply with his demands, and finally spark to life. She reached for him. She needed to feel the skin of him, the arc of his muscles, the power of his thighs.

"Yes," he encouraged her. "There. And there. Yes."

He slid easily into her and, without conscious exertion, she gripped him, tightening and releasing, tightening and releasing, as he stroked her to orgasm. Finding the rhythm, they climaxed together. It was . . . nice. Textbook perfect. And when it was over, he brushed his lips over hers, like their first kiss.

"It was good, Nicole."

She heard the need in his voice.

"Yes, Billy, it was good."

In another moment he was asleep. Like a little boy, his mouth was slightly open and his hair had fallen into his eyes. One hand clutched Nicole and didn't loosen its grip. She leaned over him and kissed his closed eyes. He'd made it easy for her, as he'd promised. She'd felt safe with him. Unthreatened. And it had been good. Not great. Nothing like Carlo.

Carlo's lovemaking had always been powerful, passionate, unpredictable. One time he might be the courtly lover, a slave to the needs of her body. The next time he'd been the brooding pirate, taking what he demanded. It wasn't safe with Carlo. She hadn't wanted to be safe then. And he'd hurt her, leaving her when she had needed him the most.

Billy began to snore. Gingerly, she prodded him. The snores stopped. He shifted and made sucking motions with his mouth. The reflexes of a baby, Nicole thought. Such innocence. This man wouldn't hurt her. She imagined him as Paul Bunyan. Baby Paul. As big as a grown man. Asleep in his giant-sized cradle, rocking in harbor waters.

The image didn't quite work. Billy wasn't really an overgrown tot. He was a man. Safe and gentle. Like the harbor. That's it, she thought as she nestled down among the blankets. Billy was the harbor. Carlo had been the restless open sea. She needed the harbor. The haven Billy offered. She caressed his sleeping form. Stretching out beside him, she held tightly to the hand still grasping hers, closed her eyes and went to sleep beside her lover.

~~~ 37

Nicole felt as though she were on vacation. Billy showered her with gifts. Every morning was like Christmas. She'd wake to a gewgaw, a toy, a silly stuffed animal, some memento of the night before or a surprise for the new day dawning.

He squired her everywhere, and, apparently, he knew everyone in Manhattan. Shopkeepers, maître d's, doormen, Broadway luminaries, New York politicians, newspaper reporters and photographers. They all seemed to light up with pleasure when Billy came around. It was a constant stream of "Hello, Mr. Gable." "Hiya, Billy." "Billy boy, join us for a drink . . . stay to dinner." "What can I get for you, Mr. Gable?" And Billy's immediate reply: "I'd like you to know my dear friend, Miss Nicole Varonne, the famous choreographer." To Nicole's surprise, their faces stayed lit for her.

Life was a breeze. Rising by noon. Making love. Or getting ready for some excursion Billy had concocted. Going to the theater to rehearse her dancers, get rid of any flaws, incorporate any changes. Watching the performance. Partying with Billy to the wee hours of the night. Falling into bed at dawn. Sleeping soundly. Dreamlessly.

The next month passed quickly and painlessly. Nicole moved into Billy's penthouse. She became an integral part of his sunny circle. Regardless of what went on in the daily grind of the war, Wall Street, and the White House, Billy made life simple. Fun. Carefree. With his arm always around her, the scent of him clinging to her clothes, the sound of his laugh a gladsome echo in her ears, Nicole believed she was changing.

The bitter memories, the mocking torment, had lost their bite. It was hard to hold on to hatred and hurt, yearning and desolation. The domineering father, the long-absent lover, the dead brother, even the lost mother. How could they compete with generous, adorable, uncomplicated, and very much alive Billy?

It was possible to let the sting of her adolescence fade. It was possible to recapture the sheer joy of childhood, of being alive and glad of it, of caring only for today. As Billy said, tomorrow would be here soon enough.

Tall Timber took its final form. No more changes were required on a nightly basis. Nicole's role as choreographer went from active participant to a printed line in the program. She was at best an observer, albeit an enthusiastic one. It was time to go to work again.

She was lucky. Most of the members of her troupe were available and willing to work with her again. They gathered at the studio she had rented before *Tall Timber* claimed her life.

"Let's take a couple of weeks as class time," she told her dancers. "A time for reacquaintance and renewal."

The dancers exchanged glances. Nicole Varonne spending days, weeks to get reacquainted? Renewed? What had gotten into her?

"And bend . . ." she ordered, starting the old routine at the barre.

The dances she would create! What with Billy and all this happiness propelling her, the world would see a new Nicole Varonne. As the class moved on to its center floor work, Nicole began to put steps together.

"All right. First group."

Two men and a woman glided forward and performed the combinations. Nicole was pleased. She signaled for the second set of dancers, three women, to try the same movements.

"Yes," she said. "We'll use that bit."

"Wait a minute, Nicole," said one of the women in the second group. "Are we 'reacquainting' ourselves with the Varonne technique or are you setting a new piece?"

"Well, maybe a bit of both."

Nicole sounded confused and uncertain. She knew it and they knew it.

"Look, Nicole," one of the men said, stepping forward with a conciliatory air, "maybe you need a little more time to plan . . ."

"Jesus, it's only a couple of steps. What difference does it make?"

"Because," said the woman, pointing to the man who just spoke, "Teddy and I went to see *Tall Timber* last week. This sequence is right out of the second-act opener."

Nicole reddened. Her mind flew to the show. She ran through the dance. They were right. She was repeating herself and she hadn't even known it. The phone in the foyer rang. Saved by the bell.

"I'll be right back. I brought the music from *Chrysalis*. Turn on the tape and see if you can remember it."

She fled from the studio and slammed the door shut. Hard. This was ridiculous. She felt so creative. She was so happy. The phone kept ringing, insisting to be answered. She grabbed at the receiver.

"Hello."

"Nicole? Thank God I found you."

"Billy? What's the matter?"

"Oh, honey, I woke up and you weren't here."

"Billy, you knew I'd be with the troupe today. And I left a note on the pillow. With the phone number which you obviously found."

"Yeah, you're right."

Nicole could just imagine him hanging his head sheepishly.

"It's just that this is the first morning we haven't . . . you left before I could—"

"Billy, I'm kind of busy here. Is there something . . .?"

"Well, without you, Nicole, I just don't know what to do with myself. I miss you, baby. So much."

She didn't know whether she wanted to shake him or kiss him. Patiently she asked, "What did you do before we . . . before me?"

"I can't remember what life was like before you. Can you cut it short today, baby? I need you."

Maybe it was just as well. She needed time to think. To look inside herself and pull a dance out of her heart and soul. A quiet day, today. Billy could stroke her hair, and she'd lie in his arms and dream.

"Give me another hour. I've got to run the dancers through their paces. Get them used to me again . . . and me to them."

"I'm waiting, honey."

Nicole walked back into the studio. "Okay, let's see it," she said with the old snap in her voice, "and then tomorrow we'll start fresh."

She ran home to Billy. She soothed and petted him. He demonstrated his need for her. And then it was time to go to the theater. Time to watch Billy play Paul Bunyan. Time to make the rounds of the restaurants, the bars, the nightclubs. Time to put Billy to bed. And the circle completed itself as it had for the past several weeks and as it looked like it would into the dim future.

The next day, the next week, and the week after, Nicole was pitched into a limbo. Billy was devoted to her. He demanded her presence and her attention. Nobody had ever needed her like Billy did. It was more time-consuming, overwhelming, and touching than Nicole could imagine. But what she needed was inspiration. Billy wasn't giving it to her.

Her dancers were getting restless. Damn it, she was

getting restless. Her technique was as sharp as it had ever been. But her choreography . . . hell, she couldn't call it choreography—her dance sequences were pitiful. At best they were like a vague recollection of something almost interesting. At worst, they were a parody. Flabby movements that didn't flow together. Meaningless combinations that refused to make sense.

"Come on, damn it," she screamed, pounding the floor with her fists.

The radiator hissed in response, and the clunk of worn-out pipes echoed through the wall. The dancers laughed nervously. Nicole looked up, listening. Chortles. Chuffs of air. Giggles. Tinny reverberations. She pounded the floor again. With her fists. With her heels.

"Roger! Teddy! Do this for me. Keep it up at this tempo."

She launched into a percussive pantomime. She was building. Erecting something. From the ground up. A shelter? A statue?

"Follow me, girls. That's it. Now take over. Build it higher. Take the time. Take the care. Yes. Now for the counterpoint."

She wove in and between the women. At the same tempo. With similar gestures but an altered spirit. While the women built with their implements, Nicole destroyed with hers. Her body was a weapon. Getting in the way. Tearing down. Destroying. Once again the male principle at work.

"Okay, boys. There's your lead. Go to it."

She stomped on the floor, jumping hard with both feet. She grabbed a chair and ran it along the length of the wall. She clapped her hands, her hips, her knees. She felt alive. The challenge was back.

"Drop, everybody."

The dancers fell in a heap. The room was still.

"I think this dance has a chance," Nicole sang joyfully.

Bricks and Mortar, as Nicole called this piece, underwent vast changes. She needed just the right sound to get her point across. She started with tribal drums, then discarded them. Too monotonous. She tried viola and trumpet, traditional instruments to mirror the female and male impulses of the dance. Mistake. She turned to twelve-tone music. Chaos. She chose composers against type. Gottschalk's romantic ragtime. Fauré's soft lullabies. Wrong. Wrong. Wrong. The music. The steps. All wrong. The dancers were worn out. She was worn out.

"*Bricks and Mortar* my ass! No matter what I try, all I'm left with is a pile of bloody rubble!"

Nicole stormed out, grabbing her coat and bag. Black fury propelled her home to Billy's penthouse. She threw down her keys and purse, practically hitting Billy, who lounged on the couch. Billy put down his copy of *The Saturday Evening Post*. Her coat flapped behind her as she paced the living room.

"Mindless pap! That's all it is. Why can't I figure out what's wrong? Is it the dance? The music? It's me."

She threw herself at Billy, who opened his arms to her.

"What the hell's the matter with me?" she cried into his shoulder.

At first he whispered sweet nothings to her, getting the coat off her, patting and petting her until the storm of rage subsided. He cuddled her and she sat on his knee, her torso curled against his chest.

"Now honey, I want you to listen to me. You don't need to prove anything to anybody. Not even yourself. I can tell you everything you need to know. Are you listenin', baby? Here's the story. Nicole Varonne, a looker and a comer, is a first-rate, class-A choreographer. She's just come off a big Broadway show and she did a helluva job. And she's gonna do a helluva lot more. But not just yet. First, she's gonna spend some time with the person who's mad about her."

"But Billy, I know myself. My life is dance. What am I if I've lost my talent?"

"Honey, you haven't lost anything. You're just drained. It can happen to an actor, a writer, a painter, or a composer. Now is not the time to push. Look, are you happy? Do you feel you're a better person for going through the struggle?"

She whimpered.

"Bingo, Nicole. Just let it go."

There was no denying how miserable she was. Billy needed her, and she was neglecting him. For a switch, she was the one doing the deserting. Another first: she had to face the fact that *Bricks and Mortar* was a disaster. She'd suffered her first defeat in modern dance. Her creativity, even her judgment, seemed to have deserted her. Something was truly wrong. Maybe Billy was right. Maybe what she needed was a rest. A rest to clear the cobwebs from her head.

"I will, Billy. I'll really try."

She lazed in bed until noon or later. She picked up novel after novel and finished them in long uninterrupted sittings. She had wine-sloshed dinners with the wives or girlfriends of Billy's cronies and listened to their catty tales. She'd manage to catch the last act of *Tall Timber,* greet Billy's friends and admirers in his dressing room, and spend the night at Billy's beck and call.

She became personally acquainted with Conga lines. Coney Island. Radio broadcasts. Rooftop gardens. Audiences heckling comics and comics heckling right back. Goodwill appearances at charity balls and USO canteens. Band leaders. Private casinos with seminude girl dealers. Champagne and more champagne.

It was an impossible dream. It was a fool's paradise. It was a bore. Nicole stood it for a month. She woke up one morning to a half-filled box of chocolate littering the bed, a sour taste in her mouth, and a headache that wouldn't quit. Billy was leaning on one arm, watching her open her eyes.

"Happy, honey?"

Was she happy? She was busy . . . living the idle life. She was numb . . . from too much liquor and rich greasy food. Her head was filled with noisy chatter and not a single new idea. She was complacent. She was getting fat. She was restless.

"I want to be your girl, Billy. Really I do. And you've made life very easy for me. But I'm going nuts just being your playmate. I've got to be my own woman too. I'm just not cut out to be a hausfrau or one of the idle rich. I need to dance and choreograph again. I think I've got to give it another shot. Can you understand that, Billy?"

He kissed her on the forehead and pulled lazily at her curls.

"Fine with me, baby. Do anything you want. Just don't push so hard."

He pulled her to him and pressed himself over her so that she could feel his arousal. She accepted his weight, preparing herself for another exercise in textbook sex. He kissed her. Caressed her. Entered her. Thrust in her.

Frequently Billy would murmur some little endearment during the buildup to climax.

This morning he smiled his secret clubhouse, members only, smile and grunted, "Doesn't make a damn bit of difference really. Who the hell's gonna have heard of either one of us in a hundred years?"

Nicole froze. She couldn't have got it right. "What did you say?" she asked.

"What I mean, baby, is we won't be around to know about it . . . or care, for that matter. So do your bit now. Do what you need to make yourself happy."

He lowered his head to her breasts and continued to pump away at her constricted core. She stared over, past his shoulder, at the dark shadows lurking in the corner of the bedroom. Billy didn't have the solution. He couldn't even recognize the problem.

"Oops. Sorry, honey."

He'd climaxed without her.

~~~ **38**

A couple of weeks later Nicole stood before the dwindling remains of her troupe.

"Tina, Bobby, Cile, Kiko, thank you for agreeing to try again. I know we'll do some great things this time. I'm all fired up with ideas . . . I've got some new music . . . I think I figured out what was wrong with *Bricks and Mortar . . ."*

Did she sound convincing? She wasn't sure, but she smiled bravely.

Bobby rubbed his hands together eagerly and walked toward the barre. The other dancers followed suit.

"Let's get to it."

Encouraged, Nicole set to work.

"Limber up, everybody. And bend . . ."

Nothing had changed. Her dances were all disasters. Movements flung madly, maddeningly, into the void.

Nicole felt she was a disaster. Her vision was blurred. She didn't know what she wanted or what she was after.

Every day was a disaster. The dancers hurled themselves about the studio, trying to interpret her muddled sign language. Invariably they ended up huddled in a corner of the studio, muttering.

Tina massaged the arch of her foot and glared in Nicole's direction. "Even if I had three legs, I couldn't give her what she wants."

"I heard that, Tina," Nicole said through gritted teeth. "Look, I'm not asking the impossible. I'll show you again."

She launched into a series of spins and turns, her arms stretched out, seeking, seeking. She veered off into a sideward descent like a yawing airplane. She rolled around the floor in a tight awkward ball. The pain of a fetus experiencing birth. Did it ask to be born? Slowing, she stuck one leg up into the air, then an arm, then the other leg, the other arm. Finally she lay flat. A starfish gone belly up.

Her head bobbled toward the dancers.

"Got it?"

The dancers looked helplessly from one to the other to the next and back again.

"Try it, damn it."

Nicole picked herself off the floor and started the music again. She turned up the volume. The dancers counted the beat, unsure when they were to start.

"No," she shrieked at them. "How many times do I have to tell you?"

She grabbed at the needle, scratching the record as she started it again. Louder. She danced faster, congealing some of the movements. She lost her balance at one point and reversed two sequences. Bouncing up from the floor, she ran back to the phonograph.

"Now let me see it done right this time."

The dancers went to work, performing the steps doggedly. Then Cile dropped out. Kiko and Bobby bumped into each other. Tina stopped cold.

"Chaos!" screeched Nicole. "I give you form. You give me turmoil. What the hell is going on with you?"

"Maybe if we understand," Kiko said in her halting English. "What is purpose? What is dance supposed to mean?"

"Right," prompted Cile. "What are we supposed to be feeling?"

"Yeah, what do formless blobs feel anyway?" Tina muttered.

"For Chrissakes, use your brains. You're the dancers. You figure it out."

Tina exploded, shouting, "That's right, Nicole. We're the dancers. And you're the choreographer. It's your fucking dance, and you can't even do the same set of steps twice in a row. If you don't know what you're doing, how the hell are we supposed to figure it out?" She threw down the towel from around her neck. "I quit."

Bobby, Cile, and Kiko looked down, away, any place other than at the scene in front of them. Nicole waited. The dancers didn't rise to her defense.

"I see," she said icily. "If any of you had Tina's guts, you'd be walking too. Perhaps that's one thing I can demonstrate properly."

She turned on her heel and stalked out, blind with fury.

The midnight hour was approaching. Billy's penthouse was dark, light switches off and the drapes drawn shut.

Nicole sat brooding on the couch, staring into the half-empty glass she held before her. She tipped the goblet slightly from side to side, then with more agitation. Answers. Where were the answers? The liquid sloshed obediently back and forth, coating the glass and beading up to slide down into the depths. No answers. Only dank quagmires sucking her down. Abruptly she reached for the decanter at the edge of the coffee table and spilled more scotch into her glass. She filled it to the brim.

Suddenly there was light. Billy was home. He walked over to her, rubbing the back of his neck, and kissed the top of her head. He dropped down on the couch next to her.

"Oh honey, what a night. Act Two was a real killer. Pecos Bill came to the theater loaded. Staggering drunk. Insisted on going on. Practically fell on top of me. I wrenched my neck pretty hard. Here, honey, see the knot back here? Give me your hand . . ."

Nicole stared at him, glaring at him. Didn't he see the pain she was in? How could he go on and on and on? What was a stupid charley horse compared to the creeping paralysis jeopardizing her whole existence?

"Do you feel it, honey? Massage it for me, will you? You've got the best hands in the world. Here, let me show you the spot again. Wait a minute."

Billy took the drink out of her hand, plunked himself down on the rug, pushed the coffee table out of the way of his long legs, and took a sip from her glass.

"Ahhh," he groaned. "This is just what the doctor ordered. Scotch for the inner man and Varonne for the outer. Okay, honey, go ahead. I'm all ready."

Nicole sat farther back into the recesses of the couch and folded her arms.

"Go on, Nicole," he prodded her.

"Billy Gable," she said, seething, "has it ever occurred to you—just for a single second—to think of someone other than yourself?"

Billy put down the drink and twisted around. "What'sa matter? Did my little girl have a bad day?"

She felt like slapping the wide-eyed concern right off his face.

"That's just great. I've been living with you for weeks—months now—and you have no more regard for me, for my life. . . . I'm sitting here in the dark for my health, you fool. It's my secret pleasure, you know, flailing at my soul with an invisible cat-o'-nine-tails. And each little cat with a whip for a tail has two eyes that burn into my guts.

"But don't worry your pretty little shallow head, Billy boy. Your precious loving slavey will wipe the tears from her eyes and the blood off her breast and rub Billy boy's widdle achey-poo. Come to Mama, you sweet insensitive son of a bitch," she crooned snidely.

"Whoa," said Billy, scrambling to his feet, knocking the scotch over. "Sounds like you need a rubdown more'n I do. Come here, sweetheart. Let me knead all that frustration away. So you had one bad day . . ."

He went to touch her. She slapped his hands away. Billy frowned.

"Nicole. Honey."

He tried to put his arms around her. She pushed him back. Pushed hard.

"I don't want your shitload of platitudes," she rasped, glaring at him with eyes afire.

Billy stepped back. "So the pussycat wants to claw and scratch and screech a little."

"A little?" she said with eyes aglitter, her nostrils flared.

"All right, a lot," he conceded. "Seems clear to me you're looking for a knockdown, drag-out fight. Although I can't see why. Lots of other ways to skin a cat."

"Will you stop talking about cats?" she screamed.

"You brought 'em up," he said sulkily. "All I wanted was a little tender loving care."

"All I want is to stop feeling like the bottom has dropped out of my world."

"Well, honey, if I could do it, I would. I'd do almost anything for you, Nicole. But I won't fight. It's not in my nature. I can't humor you."

"Humor me?" she said, getting to her feet. "You think I'm doing this for kicks? You think I enjoy misery? You don't know me at all, Billy Gable."

"I know what you could use. How about a good roll in the hay? That'll knock some wind out of your sails."

"My God, Billy!" Nicole shrieked. "Now you're gonna dole out sex like a dose of cough medicine? Poor Nicole," she mimicked, "one screw and she'll be good as new."

Billy shrugged, saying, "I guess I don't know what to do for you, Nicole. I just want to keep it friendly."

"Friendly. I see. Who do you think we are, Billy? Jack and Jill going up and down a hill? Raggedy Ann and Andy having adventures outside the toy box? Go out, Billy. Go find some of your friends and take them for a nightcap at Mocambo's. Better yet, I hear the Ferris wheel at Coney Island is working again. Maybe you'll get lucky and get stuck at the top."

"This is my house," Billy said softly.

"This is my nightmare," Nicole cried, "and you're only making it worse."

Billy's face crumpled. He nodded and left, switching off the lights before closing the door. She was alone again. In the dark. She sat down. Then she jumped up, turning on the lights and pacing the room. Nervous. Formless. Meaningless. She went to the phonograph and put on some music, the first album her fingers lit on. It was a Rachmaninoff concerto. It made her cry and her nerves calm down.

She cleaned up the puddle of scotch. The ordinary task made her think straight. She didn't like what was happening. She was hurting her dancers . . . and Billy. It wasn't their fault. She was the one who was screwing up. So I won't have a great season this time, she told herself. But I'll have a season. I'll work myself out of this slump. And next season, or the one after that, it'll come together. I know it will.

The following morning, with bright sunlight flooding through the windows, Billy tiptoed home. She was in bed, drifting half asleep, half awake, as images of dances floated just beyond reach. The fetid smell of liquor pervaded the room. Her eyes flew open as Billy came in. His clothes were disheveled and he looked like he'd been crying. He knelt down at the bedside and rested his head against her arm.

"I'm sorry, baby. I'm sorry. I just can't fight like that. I can't handle it."

"I know," she murmured, petting his hair. "You can't be what you aren't. Life doesn't come out the way we want it to sometimes."

He looked up at her all puppy dog and wistfulness. "It'll be all right. I know it will."

"If you say so, Billy."

He crept up beside her and tentatively opened his arms to her. She cuddled into him, expecting a kiss or a whispered message of love. But Billy was instantly asleep, a dead weight surrounding her from which she could not pull away.

Nicole swallowed the bitter pill, and, over the course of the spring months, she compromised. She apologized to her dancers. She revived her works prior to *Tall Timber,* and she made *Bricks and Mortar* work. She worked hard on perfecting the original elements of the Varonne technique. Though her new dances were mediocre according to her own set of standards, every step was crisp, synchronized, and meshed well with her dancers' abilities. Where the vision failed her, she repeated sequences that had worked in prior pieces, giving each one a twist, a new turn, a new variation.

Nicole thought the work was indifferent and lackluster. But Ernestine raved, as did her former teachers. And the audiences who knew the name of Nicole Varonne from her Broadway show stoppers flocked to the recitals Ernestine produced for her. It was a source of wonderment to Nicole that when she felt the least creative, she was winning the greatest acclaim.

"What's the matter with them, Billy?" she asked, scanning the critics' reviews. "Have they all gone blind, deaf, and dumb?"

"Um, er . . ." he mumbled over the columns in the sheaf of newspapers, occasionally making coherent noises. "Uh-uh, you can see right here . . . this part about your germinal period, if you'll excuse the expression. See what this guy says? This thing about the force and statement of the early dances. He says it's clearer now. And stronger."

"Don't they realize I'm stuck? I've gone nowhere," she wailed.

"Honey, as far as they're concerned, now they understand you. You've 'matured.' See? Look at what this other guy writes. 'Miss Varonne has come into her own.' "

Into her own hell. That's where she'd come to.

"Isn't that great, honey? You should be so happy!"

Nicole managed a weak smile. It felt more like a grimace.

She began to wake at odd hours of the night. Mindful of the day's hard and heavy work that lay ahead, she would try getting back to sleep. She tossed and turned. She kicked off the blankets. She covered her head with a cool pillow. She threw the pillow down on the floor. She considered waking Billy but rejected the idea immediately. He'd only want to make love to her, and the thought of being touched made her skin twitch. She was twitching. Itchy. Uncomfortable. Unsettled. Bed was no place for her. She needed to move, to get rid of the restlessness.

Getting out of bed, walking from room to room in the penthouse, moving turned into movement and the need to dance. Night after night she found herself turning on the record player and moving to the music. Dancing until she dropped with exhaustion. Until the churning fever left her body. Until she had gotten rid of that full, bloated feeling that her body was not really hers but possessed—by old demons, new demons.

Some nights she was danced out in thirty minutes. Other nights it took hours.

~~ **39**

She woke up with a start, pouring with sweat. It was a humid summer night and the latest dance was not going well. But Nicole sat bolt upright for another reason. Carlo. Carlo caught in the hellish tentacles of war. Carlo in some sort of pit . . . and she was there with him . . . yet she wasn't . . . yet she knew everything that was happening to him. Where was he? Where was she? She glanced quickly about. Billy's bedroom with its funny homespun touches. Billy, snoring, sleeping like a log, beside her. And outside . . . the familiar ghostly lines of New York's skyscrapers. An occasional twinkling light. From a window. From the sky.

Nicole knew now. She'd been dreaming. Vivid. Real. Ugly scenes of torture and terror. Carlo, her beloved, caught in a trap. Suffering. Dying. Eyes wide open, she pictured the dream all over again.

Yes, it was Carlo all right. Chains or leather straps biting into his skin. Those flashing angry eyes. The muscles bunched like a cat on the prowl. The proud sneer of his whole posture. Even in chains. He was in some dark hellhole. He was waiting to be interrogated. She felt his fury and his dread at what lay ahead. The air was close, thick with suspense. Nicole had a feeling of being suspended. Of Carlo hanging, twisting, in a cruel wind. Of Carlo waiting for the dragon, the dragon who shattered bones with its roar.

The dream had been full of noise. Aimless, atonal noise. Then it became clearer. There were voices making guttural sounds, and the beat of marching feet. *Eins . . . zwei . . . drei . . . vier. Eins . . . zwei . . . drei . . . vier.* Military boots. The goose step. Nicole knew then that Carlo was in the hands of Nazis. And the roar she heard, the dragon, the counting, the pounding boots, the scream stuck in her own throat, dissolved into a wild howling of all humanity in pain.

Suddenly she had been back with Carlo in the inky pit. Out of nowhere, a hot white light flared in his face . . . her face. He couldn't see at all. Nicole saw it all. He was pinned by the light, pinned by his shackles. And in the background the relentless marking of time. *Eins . . . zwei . . . drei . . . vier.* Like angry thrusts of a dagger. Counting. Stabbing.

Then silence. His neck pinched by invisible fingers. Hoisted. His head thrust in water and held down. Carlo sputtering. Coughing. Fighting for breath. Gasping for air. Taking water into his lungs. Screaming. Lapsing into unconsciousness. The light dimmed. Darkness. Carlo, can you hear me? Carlo, are you there? Carlo, where are you? I need you. I love you. Nicole's voice hammered in her head.

The dream vision faded. Nicole clutched herself, caught in the shivering release of an adrenaline surge. The dream had been so real. She felt as though she had stood right next to Carlo. Felt all that caged strength. Felt that indomitable presence. Felt the hunger for him race through her body. She wanted him. Out of danger. Back in her life. She wanted to be back in his arms.

Nicole felt herself blush red hot. Four years he'd been out of her life. She thought she'd cured herself of him. Why had he resurfaced, if only in her dreams? She got out of bed and roamed the penthouse, haunted by the dream, by Carlo's vitality. She found herself at the phonograph . . . for the hundredth time. Music was the answer. Music would drown out the frightening nearness of the dream. Debussy's "La Mer." She let it sweep over her, taking her to the sea, through its storms, its stillness, its depths, its passion for life, the source of all life.

She let the swelling tide embrace her and carry her into its mystery. She danced. Unleashed. Passionately. She leaped and soared. She felt free. Carlo's spirit danced alongside her, urging her on, inspiring her to greater heights . . .

"Jesus Christ! It's three-thirty in the morning!"

Billy rubbed his eyes and gazed blearily at her. She stopped in mid-stride, cutting a tour en l'air into a short stilted hop. Her arms flew across her chest, as though she'd been found naked. Billy stumbled toward the record player and lowered the volume.

"You're dancing? At this hour?"

"I've got to," she said, pressing her point. "I've got to fill the void."

Billy cocked an eyebrow at her and shook his head. "No, baby, you don't need to do this now. You'll have plenty of time to dance tomorrow. Don't make breakfast for me. Go in a little early. You won't forget your little idea. I promise."

He reached for her, slinging an arm around her shoulder. "Come back to bed, honey."

"No, you go back to bed. Just leave me alone."

"Baby . . ."

"Don't call me that. You don't understand."

"You're right. I don't understand."

She turned her back to him and fiddled with the knobs. "I'll keep it soft so you can't hear."

She didn't turn around until she heard the measured tread of his footsteps retreating, and then she danced until dawn.

Nicole's secret was out. Now Billy not only knew about her insomnia but, worse still, her latest obsession. It worried him, and he didn't understand it. Wasn't it enough that she spent all day at her studio? How many times had she forgotten the hour, only to rush home and find his note . . . sometimes angry, sometimes hurt, sometimes with no feeling at all. Left for the theater. How he yearned for her to be with him. But she'd taken to skipping his nightly performances altogether, leaving him to his friends and his champagne or scotch. And then, when he did get home, she was out like a light. If he tried to touch her, she turned away from him, pulling the covers over her head.

Billy took to pretending he was asleep. And when she rose, hounded by hysteria, devils—he didn't know what to call it—he'd sneak out of bed to follow her and watch what she did. All she did was dance. Move crazily about the living room like she couldn't stand being in her own skin. It hurt him to watch her. He wanted to reach out to her, fold her in his arms, lull her back into the sweet stupor of sleep. But he couldn't, not after she caught him spying on her.

At first Nicole had seemed angry. Then the blaze in her eyes sputtered and the set of her jaw slackened.

One night she asked, almost teasingly, "Dance with me, Billy?"

When he shook his head, her voice became harsh.

"Dance with me," she demanded. "It won't come right."

She pulled him into the room and swayed her hips at him. It was a seductive movement. Nicole had closed her eyes. Her arms snaked upward along the curves of her belly, breasts, shoulders, neck, and head. Sinuously. She was a siren, calling to him, singing to him with her body. She was irresistible.

This time the record player was wailing the blues. Low, earthy lamentations of women gone wrong and whisky-soaked men. Saxophones reaching deep inside the soul. Drums pulsating like broken hearts.

Billy followed her lead. She bent and curled in shame with the girl who lost her man. She shimmied in slow motion, sending languid ripples across her arms and torso, like the ricochet of a mournful cry. Her bare feet punctuated the carpet with agitated brush steps as the tempo picked up. He tried manfully to capture the mood. To keep pace with her mercurial shifts. He couldn't. He stopped.

"Enough, Nicole. It's late. We've got to get some shut-eye."

"I can't stop. I haven't worked it out yet."

"Honey, there's all of tomorrow and the day after that and then some. Nobody's putting a gun to your head."

"That's just it," she said excitedly, "it feels like Russian roulette. Cock the trigger and *poof.* No bullet. No dance. Cock it again. *Poof.* Still no dance. And then *bang!* The payoff. Everything clicks and I have a dance. Don't you see, Billy? I've got to keep going to beat the odds . . . before they beat me." She clawed at his pajamas, adding, "I think I'm losing."

Billy hugged her fiercely. "You just need your rest, Nicole. You're a fighter. Never met a more stubborn female in all my life. Your routine's upset, that's all. All these crazy hours. Make anyone think they're going nuts."

"You think I'm acting crazy?" she demanded.

"Well, honey, how many people do you know who do their best work in the middle of the night after working all day? I mean, let's face it, it isn't exactly normal."

"I'm a choreographer, not a plumber."

"I'm just trying to help," Billy said in defense.

"I know what'll help."

Nicole dashed to the volume control and drowned out the sound of Billy's voice. Defiantly, she strutted before him. Twisting the links between song and dance. Exaggerating each sensual step into an absurd parody. Destroying the beauty. Driving Billy back to bed. Alone. Leaving her to search for her muse. Alone. With her demons.

It went from bad to worse. Nicole was up every night. Billy tried ignoring her. He bought earplugs to deaden the rage of music catapulting through the penthouse. He moved the bedroom clock out of sight so he couldn't watch the minutes and the hours pass. It wasn't worth pretending to be asleep. Nicole was so wrought up, she barely noticed him. He could stand it no longer.

"Not again!" he yelled. "Not tonight too. God damn it, do you have to ruin my sleep too?"

So the unflappable Billy was human after all, Nicole thought. The perennial sunshine boy had a mood or two in him. His nauseating cheerfulness had its limits. She felt a wicked thrill of satisfaction course up and down her spine as he raved on.

"Stop punishing me, Nicole. It isn't my fault you've lost your lousy inspiration."

It was the line she'd been waiting to hear. She went on the offense, delivering the salvos that had been boiling inside her for months.

"It *is* your fault, Mr. Billy Gable! Before I met you, I knew how I felt. I knew what I wanted. Where I was headed. My vision was *clear*, goddamn it! I could give form and substance to my feelings. My dances were vital and dramatic and energizing. There was a purpose to them—and to me. My dances were me."

"You think I'm some kind of devil? Made you sign your name in blood . . . turned you into some kind of zombie?"

"All I know is, since I've been with you, I don't know who I am anymore. I'm sure as hell not Nicole Varonne, ace choreographer. What do my credits include now? A dumb musical comedy and a bunch of trivial, rehashed dance sketches. No, I'm Billy's girl. Billy's maid, Billy's cook, Billy's mistress.

"Well, Billy's girl has had it! I won't let you hold me down anymore. Petting me like an old lap dog. Trotting me out like an expensive fur coat on display. Stifling me. Keeping me from what I need to do. I'll dance when I want to dance. I'll feel what I want to feel. Whether it's acceptable to your middle-class ideals or not. I'm an artist, for Chrissakes. This is my life, not some cute little hobby!"

"You forget pretty easily," Billy cried. "Who stood up for you in preproduction? Defended your dances and your precious vision to the money bags? Convinced them you were right? Have I stood in the way of your career? Hell no. 'Go back to work,' I told you. I encouraged you. You were miserable, remember? I begged you to take time off till you were ready. Maybe you're still not ready, Nicole. Maybe what you're fighting is yourself. Maybe you just don't have it anymore. I don't care if you do or not. I'll still love you. Don't you see? It makes no difference to me."

"Well, it bloody well matters to me, Mr. Gable. If you cared for me, really cared, it'd matter to you too. You don't love me. You love some image you concocted. Some innocent little girl who's happy to play games from dawn to dusk. You don't want me, Billy. You don't even know who I am."

"You're not being fair, Nicole."

"Fair? What does 'fair' have to do with anything real? Life isn't fair or nice. Life is pain and fear and anguish. Everything you're afraid of. Well, I'm sick of your pretense. Refusing to see the ugly side. Covering over the lumps and bumps."

She dug at him. She wanted to hurt him just like she was hurting inside. Break him down. Make him burst. She wanted to see what was under all that smooth skin. Was it raw and bloody like hers?

"Smile, Billy. Dazzle them with your pearly-white teeth so they won't see your shifty feet. Sing, Billy. Fill their ears with lilting words of love before they figure out how shallow you are. Stand tall, Billy Bunyan. Wave your magic wand before they see you flinch. You're a joke. You don't know when you've been had."

He stood there, taking every last stinging barb, letting them land where she aimed them. And with each succeeding curse, he seemed less and less ruffled.

"Are you done?" he asked, completely calm. "Really, Nicole, this isn't any way to handle your problems. Name-calling is for kids."

Nicole couldn't believe his reaction . . . lack of reaction. She'd expected him to go on a rampage. Hot with fury. Icy cold in his wrath. What did she get? A watered-down version of sticks and bones, breaking bones, and names that couldn't hurt.

"People don't act this way and get what they want," he continued. "You're saying things you don't mean just to provoke me. Well, it won't work. Not with me. Now if you want to be reasonable—"

"Who wants to be reasonable? It's the middle of the night. I'm talking about the irrational, the illogical, the unspeakable. Impulses and temperament. Emotions that make the blood boil. Jesus Christ, Billy! If I wanted a Sunday sermon, I'd have gone to church."

He stared at her. She glared at him. She wanted to slug him. Right on his righteous, smug, perfect face. And at the same time she was disarmed. Billy's passion, which rang true in the theater, was hollow in real life. Fighting with Billy Gable was as safe as having sex with him. No fear of recrimination. No dangerous, exciting exploration. No imagination. No tempests. Just control. Concrete limits. Dull. Billy wasn't what she needed at all.

She walked past him, went into the bedroom, took off her nightgown, slapped on some clothes, and walked back out. Past him. To the door leading out of the penthouse.

"Where are you going?" he demanded.

"Let me spell it for you, Billy. O-U-T!"

She slammed the door shut. Now where was she to go? Down the elevator. Out of the building. Walking. Walking. The subway. Christopher Street, her old stop. When she emerged from underground, somehow the Greenwich Village air seemed fresher, easier to breathe.

Nicole made straight for her flat. She'd continued paying rent for it despite having moved in with Billy. Had she known it wouldn't work with him? Did she know anything anymore? She threw herself down on the musty sofa, wrapping Alexandra's challis scarf about her.

Of one thing she was certain. This nonsense of being Billy's girl was at an end. Leaving her apartment and moving into his had been a mistake. The wrong thing to do. Staying so long with him had been worse. She could no more be Billy's girl than Carlo's lover or Nikki's partner or the kind of daughter—or dancer—that Vanya had wanted her to be.

The list, the procession from man to man, regardless of the relationship, seemed endless. And doomed. Nicole wove the scarf through and around her fingers, thinking. Hadn't she learned anything from her mother? It wasn't that Alexandra loved a man and then left him. Rather, she loved a man without needing him. Without needing to prove something about herself. There lay the strength. The resolve. The answer.

For the first time in a long while, she felt as though she weren't grasping at invisible straws. She stretched out, letting the first ripples of serenity and confidence penetrate her roiling spirit. She saw her path clearly. Just ahead. Within reach . . . she fell asleep and hours later, when she awoke, she gave the flat a thorough scrubbing. She wanted to start clean.

That afternoon, she went back to the penthouse for the

last time. She was shocked by Billy's appearance. He had obviously gotten no sleep. Still in his pajamas, he hadn't shaved, and cigarette butts jammed the ashtrays. Telling him was going to be hard. But not impossible. She had to do it.

"Billy, I—"

"Before you say it . . ."

He knew that it was over between them. Nicole let out a sigh of relief. Maybe it wouldn't be so hard. Maybe they could part as friends.

". . . Look what came for me today," he said, waving a sheaf of papers in front of her. "Look's like Uncle Sam's offering me quite a deal. 'Course, he doesn't say anything about Hollywood, but I might stop there on my way to the Pacific theater."

"You've been drafted?"

"Not exactly. Seems my draft board, back home in Indiana, sort of forgot about me. I love this country, Nicole. Wouldn't be right not to fight for her. So, I kind of signed up a few weeks ago."

"Without telling me?"

"When was that supposed to happen, Nicole?"

He didn't say it accusingly, just sort of resignedly. The notion of Billy having to make weighty decisions was as foreign to her as the thought of her giving up dancing. Guilt and shame spread through Nicole like sticky, slow molasses. When, indeed, had she been there for Billy? Just to sit and talk. Just to listen.

"No recriminations," she muttered to herself.

"What was that?"

"Uh, when do you go?"

"Two weeks. You'll stay here with me till then, won't you, honey?"

He was pleading. The pain in his eyes was too much for her to bear. She sat down next to him and stared at her hands.

"Will you play one last game? We could call it 'Keeping up a front for Billy . . . with Billy. Until he goes to the front.' Just for two weeks, Nicole. Fourteen lousy days."

God damn it, she owed him. For being her friend and her lover. Her champion and her wailing wall. And yet it was the same damn thing all over again. Another man demanding that she sacrifice her life and her needs for him. It was on the tip of her tongue to refuse. It went against the very resolve she had just come to. To leave. To stand on her own. To find herself again.

"Help me? Please? I'm scared, Nicole."

Fourteen days. She couldn't imagine getting through the next hour, let alone two weeks of riding an emotional roller coaster with Billy. She glanced at him. He was gazing at her with those cornflower eyes. His hand crept into hers. This boyman going off to war. It was ridiculous. It was tragic. It was as wrong as when Nikki joined up. She couldn't let Billy leave, shattered, as Nikki must have been. Oh God, the wounds. Old and new. Barely healed. Bleeding anew.

"All right, Billy," she said in a whisper. "We'll take it one day at a time."

"Thank you, Nicole. I swear I'll never forget this," he said, gathering her into a clinging embrace. "I'm just gonna believe I've got someone to come home to. I don't think I'll make it otherwise."

"Believe whatever you want, Billy."

She didn't expect him to come home.

The cold hand of reality slapped Billy hard. It was easier for her, Nicole thought. In a way, she had already said good-bye to him. But Billy was giving up everything he knew. When Billy's Broadway cronies found out he was off to do his patriotic duty, they gave him a whirlwind of parties. Far less complicated to be swept up in these last hurrahs than to face the depths of emotion. Wine and liquor flowed heavily, and Billy drank way too much. He rationalized it as building up his courage. She saw it as anesthetizing. Whatever the label, they both accepted its consequences. Masking reality got them through the days and the nights.

Sex was another veiled event. Even drenched in scotch or

bourbon or whatever he had tanked up on, Billy made love to her. It was the same old reliable routine, but there was a ghostly patina to it. Each time was like their first encounter. The tender, slightly uncertain brushed kisses. Fingertips just breezing over tingling flesh. Worshipful hesitation as he entered her. Careful balancing of weight and fit as she was stroked to orgasm. And when he slipped out of her, the sadness, the inevitable awareness that they were closer to the last time. That they were slipping away from each other toward their separate fates.

The night before Billy was to leave, Nicole had another dream, one as distinct and frightening as the nightmare about Carlo. At first she could barely make anything out. Everything seemed so gritty. So dark. Then she saw a lifeless yard surrounded by high stone walls. Wooden soldiers filed in. No, they were human. It was their faces that were wooden. Expressionless.

A second unit of men marched in, hands tied behind them. Their clothes were ripped and muddied. They were stumbling . . . as if they couldn't see where to go. Of course they couldn't see. Grim horror filled Nicole as she realized each poor soul wore a dark sack over his head. And those wooden soldiers . . . they were kneeling. Pointing and aiming long gleaming rifles. Their bayonets caught the glint of the moon. Her eyes darted to the ragtag herd. Now she knew. The dark sacks were hoods. Executioners' hoods.

She couldn't cry out . . . not a warning . . . not a farewell as the firing squad performed its grisly task. She stared, transfixed, at the bullets speeding death through the air, piercing their targets. The hooded ones jerked and fell as neat puddles of blood seeped into the barren dirt. She stared, transfixed, as one of the soldiers moved out from the squad, striding to the bodies spewn on the ground, ripping off the black hoods one by one.

Nicole gasped at the dead faces. Their names came tumbling out of her. Nikki! Carlo! She was crying. Screaming their names out loud in the dream. Louder. Billy! She wrestled with the nightmare, tangling with its images. She

had to get out. Wake up. Death. All of them dead. Push.
Shove. The rifles. The bodies. The blankets. *Nikki. Carlo.
Billy.*

She was talking in her sleep.

"Billy!" came the muffled shriek. "Dead . . . No, not
dead . . ."

He woke up and pulled her close to him. "Hush, honey,
hush. It's all right. You're just dreaming."

Half awake, Nicole buried herself in his arms, muttering,
"Firing squad . . . all of you . . . You . . . Billy . . .
killed . . . So worried . . . I couldn't stop it."

He hugged her more tightly. "Oh God, baby, you do care.
I love you so much. I promise, honey, I swear. I'll make it
back."

He plied her with kisses and more whispered vows. Nicole
let him. What was the point in telling him the truth? The
whole truth? It was her goodbye present to him.

The next morning Billy packed a small bag. Nicole hung
back, dreading the last uncomfortable moment.

"Will you promise me something, Nicole? Will you keep
the home fires burning?"

She couldn't imagine what he meant. Was she to roll
bandages and knit socks? Was she supposed to promise she
wouldn't enlist in the WACs?

"I want you to stay here, honey. In the penthouse. It's
your home as much as mine. I couldn't stand to think of you
back in that little rat trap in the Village."

She could feel the bile start to rise. Billy, the tyrant with
the best of intentions, was on the loose again. Did he care
what she thought? What she wanted? No, it had to be his
way. Butter them up. Slide their pants down and tell them
it's all right. Then pow. The double whammy. It was his way
or nothing. Every time.

"Come on, honey. What do you say? You'll have room
here. Do whatever you want with the place. Hell, you can
mirror every wall if it'll help you dance again."

"I don't think that's such a good idea," she said in a low
voice.

"Why not?"

"It's your place, Billy. Everywhere I turn . . ."

She looked at him, pleading with her eyes. She didn't want to say it. How could she tell him she felt like a captive and hope he'd go off to war with a smile on his face?

"I get it, baby. Too full of memories."

"Something like that," she said, relieved he'd supplied his own answer.

"Promise you'll come by once in a while? I'm gonna write you every day, Nicole. I'll send every letter to this address."

Nicole on a leash. Heel, Nicole. Her neck in a noose. Tightening. She gulped and forced a small grin.

"You do that, Billy."

He smiled. Big. Open. Sunny. She nodded. He glanced down at his wristwatch. The smile faded. He looked nervous.

"Guess it's time to go."

She went to pick up her purse. He stopped her, putting his hand over hers.

"I don't want you to come with me. You'll cry. I'll cry. What would people think if they saw Billy Gable, leading man, bawlin' like a baby?" He shook his head, adding, "Bad for the image."

"You're human, Billy. Nobody would mind."

"I would, Nicole. Maybe I need the image."

She clasped him in a final hug. He clung to her. Then the image must have snapped in place, because he was suddenly strong, stronger than she was. He kissed her full, hard on the lips, and went out the door. She couldn't believe her ears when she heard the strains of a whistle emanating down the hall. Billy was warbling the chorus of "Going On." Billy, the true believer. Where did the actor leave off and the man begin? Or was it the other way around?

She turned around and a shiver sprang from her. The penthouse suddenly seemed cold. She went from room to room, extracting her clothes, her toilette articles, the few magazines she'd bought, and dumped them in a satchel. She paused and looked around once more. There was nothing more of hers. There was no reason to stay. Quickly, she made Billy's bed, cleaned up his dishes, straightened his albums. She drew the drapes and locked the door behind her. In the lobby she left her key with the doorman. She had no plans to return.

On the way home to the Village she stopped for groceries and splurged on a huge bouquet of flowers. My reward, she told herself. Obligation to one William Gable of Indiana and New York paid in full. Now she was ready . . . God, she was champing at the bit. It was her turn again. She would devote herself to her art with all the conviction of a religious zealot. Away from the confusion of men. She was no good with them, and they were no good for her. Confining. Constraining. They brought sorrow with each footstep. They carried death in one pocket and destruction in another. Carlo, Nikki, Billy. It was true of all three. Gone off to a war where men could kill more men.

Up the three flights of stairs. Into her own tiny flat. Home. Safe. She put down the satchel, the bag, the flowers, and faced her mirrors. Men the bringers of sorrow. Men as wreckers. Men destroying men. She began to dance. The images and the movements flowed from her as though the well had never been dry. The female purpose. The male element. Her dreams. Her feelings. They all came together in a torrential outpouring, and *Carnivore* was born.

It was performed for the first time in the height of the winter season and reignited the controversy that had always bloomed around the Varonne name. Back in form, Nicole put together a new company, dancing a full repertoire of Varonne choreography: *Skirmishes, Chrysalis,* the courtship pas de deux from *Tall Timber* as well as the blue snow dance, *Bricks and Mortar,* and two of the reconstituted pieces from her previous season that Ernestine and the critics had liked.

She had corralled the diehards of her former troupe into dancing for her again, and hired extra male dancers for *Carnivore.* Adding to Nicole's happiness, Dominique joined the group, having left *Tall Timber* after dancing Hattie for more than a year.

PIROUETTE

The opening performance of Nicole's new work was like a homecoming. Her old friends and teachers packed the front rows. It was a modern dance crowd. Avant-garde. Ethnic. More exotic than ballet or Broadway. The lights in the hall dimmed. The audience quieted. The curtain rose.

The merry tootle of a fife signaled the entrance of a quartet of women. Clad in pastel skirts of rose, lavender, lemon butter, and powder blue, the dancers resembled budding flowers. Fragile. Young. Fresh. Their steps were lively, full of spritely bounce. Graceful, harmonious, one by one and in unison, their dance was a joyous ode to springtime. The flowering of life. The fife ended its paean. The women continued to dance in silence while the muffled drumbeat of a dirge echoed louder and louder.

A cadre of nine men marched in slow motion onto the stage. They were all in charcoal gray. Executioner hoods covered their heads, except for eyeholes. They danced in cadence opposite the women. Big leg movements, grand battements swept the floor. To the front. To the side. To the rear. Sweeping the women about. Disrupting their patterns. The men moved as though the women weren't there. The women flitted in and among the linear columns of men like garlands of delicate light.

The drum pulsed, throbbed, palpitated like a heart overworked. The men tightened and compressed their lines. Closing in on the women. Trapping them. Each woman boxed in by a wall of men. Rat-a-tat. Rat-a-tat-tat. Up went a woman. Down came a woman. Up, down. Up. Down. With pistonlike precision the cadre marched the women off the stage, frozen in lift position.

The drum maintained the rat-a-tat spit. One at a time the men walked onstage and took their place within the cadre. Three by three. No more of the broad sweeping steps. They performed an intricate series of steps. One-footed hops. Skips and jumps in place. Slapping the floor with the heels of their shoes. Arms jutting forward and back. The motions reminiscent of soldiers practicing with their rifles.

The drumming ceased. The men stopped in mid-motion.

A mournful bugle replaced the drum. The men marched slowly, hypnotically. Then one man was excised from the cadre. He fell to the ground, was stepped over and pushed away. The cadre reformed. Another man excised. Fell. Stepped over. Pushed away. The cadre reformed. Then the next. And the next. Until all the men lay dead on the stage and the bugle wailed "Taps." As the last note blared, the curtain came down.

~~~ 41

Nicole was in her dressing room, removing stage makeup.

"I'm listening, Ernestine."

Ernestine Pringle tapped a cigarette against the butt of her hand. She lit up and drew in the smoke. After a long moment the smoke jetted out from her nostrils and the corners of her mouth.

"Don't fight me on this, Varonne."

She was still in her military mode. With the latest in padded shoulders filling out the jacket of her suit, she could easily have taken command of the Allied forces. By dint of her appearance alone.

"Okay."

"Lord knows I've got your best interests at heart."

"I agree."

"I have everything lined up and ready to go. You just have to say yes . . . and mean it . . . and do it."

"Yes. I mean it. I'll do it."

"This is the right time to leave New Y— What did you say?"

"I've already talked to the company and they're all willing to go. Book the tour, Ernestine. It's time to hit the road."

"Oh, darling!" croaked Ernestine, her arms flying around Nicole. "I'm going to make you famous! Well," she added, slightly mollified, "you already are famous. . . ."

"That's all right, old girl," Nicole said, patting her friend's substantial arm. "I'm ready for the rest of the country. It's time to see if they're ready for me."

"They are, if I have anything to say about it."

Nicole and company set out on an extensive national tour. Ernestine had them scheduled to perform at colleges, small-town halls, and community theaters. The tour started in New England, where Nicole's name was more or less recognized. She found herself the darling of the local intelligentsia. And she was surprised to find her performances playing to standing room only. Whether the audience agreed and cheered for her works was secondary to the fact that they came to see and think and ponder her vision. Even in wartime, controversy was the spice of life.

For the first time in years she felt justified. Her vision was clear again and she was able to communicate it through the power of dance. Nicole felt true to herself. The restless nights were a thing of the past. She slept well. In fact, she never felt better. She was positively blooming with health and self-satisfaction.

The tour progressed to the Midwest. Her works continued to brew controversy. Sometimes the audience loved her dances but the critics hated them. Other times the audience sat in stunned silence but the critics raved. It was perfectly normal, as far as Nicole was concerned, but she began to worry. Something was different. Something had changed. She was changing.

She was hungry. Ravenous. All the time. If she didn't eat, she thought she would throw up. And, of course, she was gaining weight. Dominique, the slimmest reed among the company, had taken Nicole aside and tactfully suggested letting out her costumes. It was embarrassing.

She ached, or her breasts did. They seemed fuller. It was an odd time to be developing. She'd never heard of anybody past adolescence getting bigger . . . unless the woman was pregnant. The thought stopped her cold. It was impossible. Wasn't it? Like most dancers, her menstrual periods were irregular. When was the last time? Just a couple of months ago. Or was it three . . . or four? Could she be pregnant? If she was . . .

The next stop on the tour was a college town in Iowa. Nicole looked up the name of an obstetrician and made an appointment that very day. It was painless. A urine specimen in the office. A phone call at her hotel the following day. The rabbit died. She was pregnant.

"Good luck and much happiness," she was wished, "and by the way, congratulations to Mr. Varonne."

Nicole hung up the telephone in a daze. There was no Mr. Varonne. There was no husband. There was only Billy. Gone off to war. Not likely to return. As if she wanted him to come back to her. He was the father of this baby.

She lay down on the bed in her hotel room and stared up at the ceiling. Billy had had the last laugh after all. If she'd only stayed away. Not gone back to make a clean break. They'd both known it was over. It was never really right between them. Billy needed a full-time admirer. She wanted no restraints.

It must have happened during those last two weeks. She let him make love to her regularly, repeatedly. As though it were his God-given right. As though she were allowing him last rites. Now she was never to be free of him. Even if he were killed, even if he made it home and fell in love with somebody else, he had planted his seed. Left his refuse behind. The wart growing in her womb was Billy's. His monument. His reminder. Her burden.

What the hell was she going to do with a baby? She was a dancer, a choreographer, a professional artist. Not a wet nurse. Not a nanny. She had no time to be a mother. Some day, maybe, she'd want a child. When the time was right . . . with the right man.

She daydreamed of a warm, sunny day along the shore. No, a crisp, autumn day with the wind tossing leaves higgledy-piggledy. She'd be pushing a baby buggy. Just the tip of a pink bonnet would be visible from under the voluminous folds of soft angora blankets. And her husband would be holding the chubby hand of their son. They were the spitting image of one another. A thatch of dark hair. Wickedly sparkling eyes that pierced her heart. A mouth that wouldn't stop. But no Italian accent. Not like his father. Carlo would have to content himself with teaching the boy other—

Nicole sat up with a start. What the hell was the matter with her? Carlo, the father of her children . . . Carlo, her husband! Is this what pregnancy was going to do to her? Make her dream of things that could never be? Dreams that had been twisted, stunted. That had died stillborn.

She took a deep, angry breath and pounded her thighs with her fists. Stop it, she told herself. Stop playing games. Stop imagining. Stop thinking, period. Better to concentrate on pickles and ice cream, catsup on pancakes, and marmalade slathering a thick, juicy steak. Her stomach turned over in protest and she ran for the bathroom, getting there just in time.

She knelt before the toilet, heaving and sobbing. She hated everything. Billy. Being pregnant. Her runaway thoughts. Food. Throwing up. Herself. The only thing in her life she didn't hate was dancing and creating dances. She would never give them up. The dance was her anchor and her safety net. Dance was life itself to her. It defined her.

A rush of determination sped through her veins. She still had purpose. A stupid little thing like having a baby wasn't going to stop her or slow her down. Nicole got up from the floor, washed out her mouth and rinsed off her neck and face. She went back to the telephone and made several calls. Within minutes her dancers trooped into her room, flopping down unceremoniously on any available piece of furniture.

They all spoke at once. "What's up? You scheduling an extra rehearsal? Something the matter with the hall? Is the war over? Don't tell me we've been invited to another dinner? If I see chicken, peas, and mashed potatoes one more time . . ."

Nicole shook her head. She surveyed her troupe. They were eager, relatively happy, tremendously talented, fairly open-minded. She decided to give it to them all at once.

"I'm pregnant. I just found out."

Silence. Like at the end of a bad performance. The men cleared their throats, smiled uncomfortably and looked elsewhere. The women exchanged glances. One or two looked shocked. A giggle escaped from the youngest dancer. Dominique stood up and went to put her arm around her old friend.

"Billy?" she whispered.

Nicole pursed her lips and nodded.

"Were the two of you planning . . ."

"To make a baby?" Nicole scoffed. "It never entered our minds. My mind."

"I was talking more about marriage, Nicole."

"Never!" she said vehemently.

"But if he knew there was a baby coming . . ."

"I'd never marry Billy under any circumstance."

"Well, when he comes back—"

"No, Dominique. I wouldn't go back to him. Anyway, we were separating when he got his orders. It's over between us."

"Do you know what you want to do?"

The unspoken question hung in each of her dancers' eyes. What was going to happen to the troupe? To the tour?

"I'm going to ignore my condition for as long as I can. I'm going to dance, and we're going to continue this tour. Nothing means more to me than that. When the time comes to have the baby, then I guess I'll have it. But that's months away. We'll be back in New York by then. . . . Well, what do you say, gang? Will your morals permit you to associate with a scarlet woman like me?"

There was a long pause. Nicole looked straight into the eyes of each of her dancers. Most looked right back. But not Tina, who always found an excuse to argue with Nicole at the slightest provocation.

"Art is one thing," the dancer said with a sneer. "But this . . . I won't have my morals questioned because you made a mistake."

"Then you'll be leaving us," Nicole said, her jaw clamped tight in an attempt to control her churning emotions.

"If you'd like me to stay for tonight's performance . . ."

"I wouldn't dream of asking so much from you," retorted Nicole.

"I'd better pack too."

It was Renée, the giggler. She was barely sixteen.

"If my father found out . . . well, he didn't want me to come at all. You know what he thinks of dancers, Nicole. One step up from hoochie-koochie girls." She giggled, glancing at the men of the troupe. "You know what I mean, guys. But Nicole, you do understand, don't you? I can't—"

Nicole nodded. "Go home, Renée. You've had enough of an adventure."

The two girls slunk out, leaving Nicole with the others.

"Well, any more rats deserting this sinking ship?"

She tried to sound bright and sophisticated, but so much was at stake. She only heard the fear in her voice. Were they all going to abandon her?

"I don't care if you had sex with a bull elephant and gave birth to Dumbo," said Bobby. "As long as I have a job dancing."

The remaining group laughed. The terrible tension was broken.

"Whatever you want, Nicole. We're with you a hundred percent. Just let some jerk say something . . . I'll clobber 'em one. I think you're supposed to drink lots of milk."

The tenor of the discussion changed.

"We're your family now," Dominique said softly. "You've stood by us . . ."

"Sometimes over us, with a horse whip," quipped Joe, the other male dancer.

"It's our turn to stand by you."

Tears of gratitude leaped from Nicole's eyes. "You make me believe it'll be all right."

The dancers huddled around her, some patting her, some hugging her.

"Now if I can just get my appetite under control, I'll still be able to pay you all."

* * *

The tour went on. After the Midwest the troupe went southwest into Indian country and then zigzagged north again into the Rockies. It was in Denver that Nicole realized she had no choice. This bulge of hers was making demands. She had burst the seams of her clothes one time too many, and it was too late to get by with a few blouses and skirts in larger sizes. The moment had come to shop in the maternity department.

She didn't like it. It made her feel embarrassed and self-conscious. Although several of her dancers volunteered, even begged, to accompany her, she insisted on going by herself. She found a Sears, Roebucks, with the maternity section off in a small room by itself, away from the mainstream of shoppers. A limbo between ladies' lingerie and the baby department. What could they be hiding in there the rest of the world shouldn't see? Nicole wondered. She took a deep breath, threw back her shoulders and crossed the threshold.

Items of torture from another era. Brassieres that looked like Valkyriean breast plates. Bony corsets capable of strangulation, if not the guts of the mother-to-be than surely those of the fetus. Full slips designed to hide the truth the other undergarments couldn't disguise.

And the clothes! Nicole thought they were the ugliest she had ever seen. She could hardly bring herself to touch the dresses. More like giant potato sacks, they hung on the racks, shapeless, lifeless. In black or navy blue. One after another. Then there were the housecoats. Myrtle Fudderman would have been in heaven. Washed-out spring floral prints. Bright, clownish colors accentuating huge floppy pockets. Nicole pictured an army tank dolled up for a tea party.

As she wandered from rack to rack, it only got worse. She shook her head at the incomprehensible panels across the fronts of skirts and pants. Clips, ties, fasteners, and unfasteners. The hours it would take her to learn to attach these clothes to her . . . And the maternity blouses—horrid exaggerations of little girls' clothes. Crisply cute Peter Pan collars. Rows of rickrack. Bows. Ruffles. Impossible. How could she walk down the street, go to the theater, talk to people, and expect them to take her seriously looking like that?

When a saleslady approached her, Nicole took off in the opposite direction. She paused at the edge of the department. She really couldn't leave without buying something.

Two women, arm in arm, strolled past her into the room. They browsed through the same racks she had just left. Only one of them was pregnant. Nicole inched forward. The two women were talking, and Nicole had an urge to hear what they said. Maybe it would unlock some mystery for her.

"Darling, you're so much luckier than when I was pregnant with you. The styles we were forced to wear."

"Oh! Look at this one, Mom. Isn't it adorable? I could wear it for Harve's birthday. And after the baby is born, I can get it altered. It could last me a good couple of years."

She was right, Nicole thought. There were mysteries she didn't begin to understand. She squinted at the dress the younger woman held up. Adorable? Alterable? Who in hell would ever want to see, much less wear, these clothes again?

The older woman had her arm around her daughter. The two whispered and gurgled. The same pitch. The same beat. Sharing. Delighting in all this froufrou. It was sickening . . .

Yet there was something about it. Something that drove Nicole closer still. The mother put her hand over the daughter's blossoming belly. The daughter stood there, offering herself to her mother. No words were necessary. The linking of generations spoke through the gentle touch, the gentle acceptance. It was unbearably sweet.

Nicole ached in a way she hadn't felt for years. She ached for her own mother's touch. To share her own pregnancy with Alexandra. An opportunity stillborn. Never to be. Alexandra would never know her grandchild. This baby would have so little family—less than she had.

Her hand covered the mound of her belly like a shield. Varonne blood ran deep. This baby, her baby, would know its heritage, its enormous legacy. Alexandra, dancer and mother. Nicole, dancer, choreographer, and soon-to-be mother. It was her turn to extend the chain another link. She patted her belly, caressing the tiny life within.

"My little daughter!" she whispered to her baby, suddenly knowing she wanted a girl, desperately hoping it would be so. "Will you dance for your mama?"

When she got back to her hotel, she ditched the bags and boxes of clothes she had bought and took up paper and pen. Dear Vanya, she wrote, scratched out her father's name, and crumpled the sheet of stationery. She started again on a fresh page.

> *Dear Father,*
>
> *Words have always been difficult between us, but I owe you this letter. You're going to be a grandfather. I hope the news gives you a sense of joy and satisfaction. Please tell Margaret about the baby. She might be happy for me and the thought that her beloved Nick would have been an uncle. While the family name died with him, the line will live on in this child.*
>
> *I'm on tour with my own company now. You'd be proud of me, I think. I guess you're still in pain over Nikki's death. I am too. I understand the menace the world must deal with, but I hate the war. I hate all war and what it does to all our young men. That's one of the things I make dances about.*
>
> *I go to California next. I'll be back in New York when the baby comes. At the same address.*
>
> *Nicole, your daughter*

~~ **42**

Another month came and went. Nicole took to chatting amiably to the other soul that occupied her body. It was surprising how utterly comforting it felt. Such an easy intimacy. One she hadn't known since the days of her childhood, in the company of her own mother.

As for her troupe . . . well, they were troupers! She had come to look upon them as her traveling family. They continued to pamper her, making sure she took time to rest, to eat properly, and to drink glass after glass of milk.

"I swear," Nicole taunted her band of old biddies, "if I ever see a cow, I'll shoot the damn thing!"

But the dancers, male and female alike, just cooed and billed at her as though she were a swollen, ruffled, exotic bird needing tender handling. They fluffed her pillows in her hotel rooms and helped her in and out of stiff, unforgiving chairs, moaning and groaning empathetically at her newly awkward body. They gasped in awe, sharing the joy of the tiny kicks "their" baby gave its mother in increasingly constant reminder of its existence.

"Petits battements," gurgled a few of the dancers, whose hands placed over Nicole's belly received the outward thrust of new life.

"Grands battements," argued others, "if you want to get technical about it."

"The kid's gonna be a prize fighter, and that's the end of it!" declared Nicole.

The troupe even juggled roles night after night as Nicole felt less inclined to dance. Give up dancing. Nicole couldn't believe she was agreeing to it. But she had no choice. Her body sent her undeniable messages to stay off her feet.

The critics were sending another kind of message. Tough Nicole who had braved so many adversaries—be they fellow dancers, choreographers, booking agents, Broadway producers, family, or lovers—was undone by the catty treatment of the San Francisco critics.

She thought she was prepared for the innuendos sure to crop up about her pregnancy. She was ready to fight back the insinuations of immorality and bohemianism hurled at her across the staid panorama of small-town America. But to find the smallest, most closed minds in cosmopolitan San Francisco was more than she could handle. Hot tears of rage and embarrassment flowed as she read the reviews in the major newspapers.

"Who the hell do they think they are?" she cried. "Walter Winchell? Hedda Hopper? The United States Supreme Court? What does the name of my baby's father have to do with the creative process?"

"Nothin', of course," soothed Mattie Wiggins, whose company was also on tour and playing in San Francisco. "But they think of us as women, not as choreographers. Here, girl, read what they've said about me. It's no different. They think our brains are in our wombs."

"It's not true," Nicole sobbed passionately.

"Of course not. What is true, though—what we women know for certain—is where their brains are located."

"It sure as hell isn't anywhere north of their necks."

"On the mark, girl. More to do with where they sit, I think."

Mattie had Nicole laughing. To demonstrate her new disdain for critics, she tore the review sections out of each newspaper, shredded them, and tossed them into the air. Mattie applauded.

"Now drink your milk."

Nicole groaned. "Not you too. After this baby is born, I'll never look at that stuff again. You know, I never actually saw a dairy truck in Manhattan. Certainly not in the Village," she added hopefully. "Maybe there's a law against it in the city."

"You still got a lot to learn, girl, about New York City . . . and children. You've got to get settled, girl, before this baby comes. When are you due?"

"Oh God, Mattie, I don't know. Maybe another month. Maybe six weeks."

"Nicole, you've got to go home. What is Ernestine thinkin' about? How much longer does she have you tramping around this country? Talk about proof that a woman doesn't think with her womb. She doesn't have the least notion—"

"We're going home next week, Mattie. I'll have plenty of time to lick my wounds."

Mattie raised a disapproving eyebrow, saying, "What wounds? You've had a marvelous tour. Your halls were filled, yes? The people saw you. Argued about you. The works, I mean. What more do you want, Nicole? Hand-delivered valentines? You'll see. Next year, they'll be calling Ernestine and begging for a return engagement. Have I ever been wrong?"

"Not where I'm concerned," Nicole concurred.

"Well then, girl."

"Well-then-girl yourself. All right. If you'll help me up from this ridiculous position, I guess I've got a theater to get to, packing to start, and a nest to feather when I get home. And a baby to have."

"And to love . . . and teach to dance," Mattie said, continuing the logical progression.

"Mattie," Nicole asked, hesitating, "do you know much about babies?"

Mattie took a deep breath. She placed both hands over Nicole's sweet protrusion, gently moving her fingers, prodding the bulge.

"This is what I know, Nicole," she said finally. "You better be travelin' soon . . . and fast. Your baby will be born in five weeks, maybe four or four and a half. And you'd better be buyin' a lot of frilly little pink things. This baby's a girl. I'll stake my whole reputation on that."

"I knew it," Nicole murmured through a big smile, and hugged her old mentor.

Two weeks later Nicole came home to New York and to her little flat in the Village, faithfully kept up by Myrtle Fudderman. Her dancers met daily in her old studio to practice, rehearse, and wait with their leader for the birth. The days dragged on into a week. Two weeks. Two and a half weeks. And then, in the midst of a series of leg extensions circling the ground, Nicole's water broke.

For a brief, mad moment or two, it was Keystone Kops time. Dancers, suddenly clumsy, flew about the studio, bumping into one another. They tried to dial the hospital but fluffed the number and had to call again. They stuffed useless articles into an enormous suitcase. They mopped up Nicole and the floor while attempting to sort out just which of them would ride in the cab with her.

Nicole, like the eye of a storm, calmly surveyed the madness. This cartoonlike display had nothing to do with the birth of her child. It was outside. Extraneous. And it had to stop now.

"Dominique, send everyone home. I would like it if you came with me in the cab. Then you go home too. I love you all, but I need to have this baby by myself. And soon."

Everyone came to immediate, orderly attention.

"Nicole," said Bobby, "we don't mean to contradict you, but we've gone the whole course with you, and we're not giving up now. Don't argue. That's how we feel and that's how it is. We'll behave; we're all adults. It's just that none of us have had a baby before and it's so damned exciting."

His voice rose several notches before he could regain control.

"Please . . ." he began, and looked frantically at Dominique.

She interceded, telling Nicole, "You know how we feel. It's our baby too."

In the face of so much love, Nicole could only surrender. In a short time a caravan of cabs honked their way uptown and the maternity waiting room fairly overflowed with anxious dancers. They had to wait until the wee hours of the morning for the news they wanted to hear, and then went home with the milkman to plan a celebration.

Five days later Ernestine—the only one with an automobile—escorted Nicole and her tiny wrapped package home. Opening the door, Nicole was besieged by her dancers and close friends from the dance world with congratulations and gift boxes. The guests were rewarded with a lusty cry emanating from the delicate baby blanket. Everyone laughed and Nicole beamed.

"That's wight, sweetums," babbled Gar Fortune in his best baby talk. "Let 'em know wight off the bat who to put the spotwight on."

"Well, girl," Mattie said, "aren't you goin' to introduce this beautiful bundle of joy?"

Nicole obediently took center stage in the overcrowded apartment.

"Everyone, thank you so much for coming to meet my daughter. I'd like you all to know Alexis Varonne. I named her for my mother, who was a great and generous woman."

"Also temperamental, highly dramatic, and tremendously talented. Not a bad set of genes to inherit," came a hoarse voice through the door behind Nicole.

"Manny, you old devil," Nicole cried with genuine pleasure. "How did you know?"

"You know me, kid. Always listening at keyholes. You didn't expect me to miss a debut performance of yours, did ya?"

It was all a little too much, and Nicole found herself laughing and crying simultaneously. In another moment a glass of champagne found its way into one hand as Alexis was extricated from her mother's trembling grip. In place of the baby, a gift was firmly clapped into her palm.

"The gifts! Time for the gifts. Open the loot," came the next series of demands.

The decision was made. Nicole was made busy opening presents. There were practical ones—like a free month's diaper service. Extravagances—like the silver spoon and fork. Sublime ones—the softest sweater with matching booties. Even the absurd—a pair of silk stockings, and fire-engine-red lipstick.

"For the little darling's hope chest," insisted Gar in his own defense.

"I sincerely hope not," her mother retorted.

"Okay. For yours then."

More laughter. More champagne. Through it all, Alexis slept peacefully, despite being passed from one awed person to the next, each of whom exclaimed over the absolute perfection of her long fingers and toes. Then, at the hint of a yawn from Nicole, everyone filed out, depositing a last kiss or hug for the new mother and child.

Finally Nicole and Alexis were alone. Nicole listened to

the blessed silence. Then she wished for noise. Because the time had come. She was not just a woman or a dancer. She was a mother. *A mother.* And she didn't have the slightest notion what to do.

Right on cue, the baby began to howl. Urgently. Unignorably. The wisest thing, Nicole thought desperately, was to put Alexis down. Some place soft would be fine. Or was the firm floor better? And then . . . run like hell out of the flat. Run for Myrtle. Or Mattie. Or just away.

Nicole stared at the angry little bundle in her arms. Alexis was staring right back, her adorable pink face screwed up in the most ghastly expression. Gargoyles. Imps sent by Satan. That's what babies were. They tested and taunted and made their mothers sick with worry . . .

And made their mothers damp! That was it! The source of the horrible problem. Alexis needed her diaper changed. Nicole squared her shoulders. She knew how to do that. In moments the baby contentedly closed her eyes and made sucking noises. Aha, another clue! thought Nicole. It wasn't going to be so hard after all. If she just paid attention, this miracle of miracles would teach her all she needed to know about being a mother.

Instinctively, Nicole began humming. It was an old tune of Alexandra's. She picked up the baby and rocked her at arm's length.

"Alouette . . . Gentille Alouette . . ."

As she danced her daughter into the tiny bedroom they would share, Nicole switched to "Aloha Oe," then a rousing version of "Swing Low, Sweet Chariot," and as the bottle of milk heated in a sauce pan, "Dark Eyes."

"Soon, my darling," she cooed, "Mama's gonna make it all better."

~~ 43

The world was changing again. The second war to end all wars had been over for three months. The men and women who had served their country and lived to tell the tale swarmed through New York City. Reunion scenes seemed to clutter every busy corner, or so Nicole thought as she scurried through the streets, Alexis in constant tow. Now, with the advent of Christmas, the city seemed to be bursting with joy. Every store displayed nostalgic scenes of carolers, skaters, mannequin families intent on devouring the plumpest of papier-mâché turkeys.

In the little theater where Nicole was hard at work performing her latest creation, the scent of pine dominated. Every last nook and cranny was bedecked with fir and holly. Even Nicole's dressing room hadn't escaped the touch of Santa's elves. Someone had left a tabletop-size tree there, complete with ornaments and candy canes. It was all Nicole could do to keep Alexis from devouring the entire spectacle. More than once the little dickens had marched right over to the table and, in full view of her mother, pulled the tree down to the floor.

"That's it!" shrieked Nicole, lunging for her child, who persisted in giggling. "Backstage is no place for a little girl. On stage, much better. Yes?"

Nicole often caught herself falling into the stylized speech patterns of Alexandra. She found them immensely comfortable. As though her mother were there with her, helping to raise this fifteen-month-old, irrepressible pixie. Her perennially bouncing ball of energy found this funny way of talking most sensible.

"Dance, Mama? Me? Like dis?"

Alexis launched into a dizzying spiral of baby steps which sent her sprawling, once again, onto the floor.

"Something like that, you dervish." Nicole laughed and plucked her daughter's fingers away from yet another candy cane. "Let's take you to Greta and see if we can alter the doll's dress in the finale to fit you."

As usual, it was bedlam backstage. The stage manager was scolding the prop men; backdrops shot up and down with alarming frequency and not much logic; dancers in all modes of attire chattered and warmed up wherever they could. Here and there the ubiquitous military uniform was receiving a welcome-home kiss or hug or slap on the back. Who was it this time? Nicole wondered. A cousin? A brother? A fiancé? God knows she had no one coming back to her. If it hadn't have been for the pudgy little hand that squeezed her so indelibly, she would have been overwhelmed by feelings of aloneness. But she had Lexie, and that was enough. Her heart was filled to capacity.

Nicole left her daughter in the nimble hands of the seamstress, who promised to have the company's newest member in place and properly trussed up for the last act. With only moments to spare, Nicole completed her makeup and slipped on the diaphanous Grecian tunic she wore in *Eternal Spring,* her version of the classic Demeter/Persephone myth. On stage she took her place as Demeter in the opening tableau of her first full-length dance.

Her version was primeval, reaching into the naked core and heart of the story. She brought to life the closely knit relationship intertwining the ancient goddess of fertility and her daughter. Symbol of earthly fruit. Child of the goddess/ mother's loins. Through their dance of life together, they crossed the fecund face of the earth, blessing it with each trace of their footsteps. A chorus of females—girls and women of all ages, suggesting the span of procreative power—wove a chain about the two immortals so that they appeared to be continually enwreathed, enshrined in flowers.

Time and the dance were eternal until the earth shattered. Split. Gave violent birth to the tyrannical and destructive male force. The spirit of Hades, king of the mysterious and impenetrable underworld, wove his own spell on the goddess's faithful followers, breaking the magic that bound mother to daughter. Powerless, Demeter was forced to watch as Hades stole Persephone. Raped the land. Robbed the goddess. To Demeter in her grief, they were all the same.

She was left to scour the earth. To weep. To mourn. To search. Demeter felt barren. The earth became barren. The chorus of women trudged about her in rags. Withered. Stunted. They were the barren earth itself. Bleeding.

Cracked. Open . . . to reveal the hall of Hades and Persephone as his Queen.

Nicole danced Demeter's descent into the underworld as though she were sleepwalking. As though another part of her were still aboveground. Waiting to be awakened. Demeter's women followed her, trancelike, populating this hell with their lifeless presence. Demeter and Hades met in confrontation. Cosmic in proportion yet intensely personal. The unholy wedlock of the fertile mother earth and the baneful lord of ghosts. They fought. They linked . . . were linked together. To bargain. To strike a deal. To give birth to an answer. Persephone was to return with her mother for nine months of the year, but the remaining three months belonged to Hades. So the seasons were born.

For now Persephone was free. Freed of her curse. Free to bloom. Herself to give birth. With her mother at her side, she ascended to the blooded world of warmth and energy and life. Faithful still, the chorus of women recapitulated their flowery dance, celebrating the return of the goddesses and the rebirth of spring. As the fertile spirit reflooded the land, Demeter and Persephone appeared one more time, accompanied by the infant spirit of Spring.

"Hold tight, Lexie," Nicole mouthed to her fearless toddler. "Follow Mama and Aunty Dominique. Good girl."

Nicole breathed a sigh of relief as the curtain lowered.

"More, Mama?" Alexis asked, taking a step forward.

Nicole whisked the child up into her arms just as the curtain calls began.

"Little ham," she scolded with an indulgent tone in her voice, wondering to herself what, indeed, she had started. "Smile, Alexis. That's right. Now curtsy. Good girl. Off we go."

Lexie shrieked with laughter as her mother galloped her off stage the second the curtain finally stayed down.

"Fun, Mama."

"We do have fun, don't we, my darling?"

Nicole continued to hold the child, balancing her on one hip while attempting to get to the dressing room without too many interruptions. But there had to be a moment for Olive McKinnah, who was enthralled with the nuances of her former pupil's dance. And Nicole had to be gracious to a refugee mother and two hideously thin children who offered the star a bedraggled bunch of violets. Then there was Ernestine with a pile of notes she'd taken on the performance.

"Brilliant as usual, Varonne. What little voice of genius told you to put Alexis in as Spring? Wish I'd thought of it. Keep her in. It brings an odd dimension of reality to the end. Simply brilliant. Can't wait for Ernie to see it. He'll be home next week. I've missed him so much. What'll I wear? And my hair . . . it's a mess."

It was strange to hear Ernestine sound so girlish. All these women who had taken up the slack. Shouldering the burdens of war as well as their own. Taking on the mannerisms of being in charge, making decisions, mastering fate. What was their fate to be? Nicole mused. She could already see the change. Women giving up their jobs. Surrendering to frilly aprons. Slaving for men again. That was a life Nicole would never agree to, much less take part in. Lexie and she were independent. Unbeholden to men and determined to remain so. And just what was that child up to now?

"Please don't put those in your mouth," Nicole said, snatching the ragged bouquet from her daughter's lips.

She kissed the pouting lips instead and winked, reverting to Alexandra talk. "Pretty flowers are for smelling. Not eating. Can you sniff flower?"

Alexis nodded, promptly grabbing some carnations from the mass of bouquets a stagehand was carrying from the stage.

"Let's go to the dressing room, sweetie. Is time to take off costume. No? Yes!"

Thank God for timing, Nicole thought. With the right timing, life could be so simple. She stepped aside to let yet another man in uniform walk by. But he stopped. Directly in her path.

"Excuse me—" Nicole began.

And stopped. Then stared. At Billy. Billy Gable. Alive and standing on his own two feet. In front of her. In New York City. In her theater. Staring at her with an intensity that promised to devour her.

"Sure are a sight for sore eyes, Nicole."

She could say nothing to him. She stared back, clutching their child to her bosom.

"Don't I rate a kiss hello?"

He took a tentative step forward but halted when she backed away. Was he expecting a hero's welcome from her?

"Guess I kind of took you unawares, huh?"

His tone was sheepish. Was he acting, Nicole wondered, or had he reverted to the country boy from Indiana she'd first known?

"Cat got your tongue?" he asked playfully. "Come on, Nicole. I don't look that bad, do I?" His gaze fell on the pretty child at Nicole's hip and, smiling, he said, "Am I some kind of monster?"

He hid his face with his military cap. Then, pulling it away, he mugged outrageously, making the silliest faces for the little girl. Lexie seemed mesmerized. Terribly interested yet not quite sure why this man was making such a fuss. Finally he stopped and offered the child a finger to shake.

"Kitty cat got your tongue too, little mouse?"

One performance demanded another. To oblige the stranger and to show she understood, Alexis did the only acceptable thing. She meowed back at him and buried her head against her mother.

Nicole felt utterly helpless. She'd never expected Billy to return, much less survive the war. In her lowest moments, when she dared let the possibility surface that she would see him again, that she would have to explain about Lexie, it was certainly not in this setting. Maybe when she was more prepared. On her terms. Not like this.

"Mama!" wailed Alexis.

Nicole realized how tightly she was gripping her child, and released her hold.

"I'm sorry, darling. Mama didn't mean to squeeze you."

It wasn't going well at all. As she hugged and kissed the hurt away, she felt an arm placed solidly across her shoulders. Protective. Heavy. Bearing down.

"I think we need to talk, Nicole. Where's your dressing room?"

She had no choice but to invite him in. At least whatever was said would be between the two of them, without curious ears and inquisitive eyes lurking in the shadows backstage. What was she going to say to him? Think fast, Nicole.

Not fast enough. Billy took charge.

"How old is she, Nicole?"

Barely whispering, she answered, "A little over a year. Fifteen months."

"Well, well, well."

He sounded excited to Nicole. Not resigned. Not perturbed. Not angry. Not judgmental. Not yet. He was pacing the small room, cutting it into smaller increments with each step.

Perhaps she ought to sit down. Affect nonchalance. No, better to stand and face him, she decided. Tell the truth head on.

"I can count as well as the next man. She's mine, isn't she?" he said, grinning.

From the moment Nicole accepted her pregnancy, she'd felt as though the baby were hers. Alone. Unaided by male participation. Alexis and she had done just fine without a father. Without Billy to get in the way. But now, even in the few short minutes since Billy had walked back into her life, she saw how much of her precious daughter came from the man who fathered her.

That wide, engaging smile that won everyone's heart was Billy's. The natural tendency to mimic came from Billy. That hammy quality Nicole had just seen on stage was all Billy. Varonne and Borcheff blood ran in Alexis's veins, but so did Gable. Alexis was Billy's child, undeniably.

Unwillingly, Nicole nodded and said, "She's yours."

With a smile as warm and inviting as sunshine, Billy turned to his daughter, stretching out his arms to her. The innocent child went to him. He picked her up and held her gently, securely.

Nicole thought her heart would break. For the first time she saw how fragile the bond was between mother and daughter. Splintered so easily, this thing she had come to build her life around. Not granitelike at all. But delicate. Like the wings of a butterfly. And all the more dear. Her eyes filled with tears.

Here was the tableau she had yearned for. The complete family. Something she had dreamed about and never really known. Mother . . . father . . . child. Always out of reach. Or slightly off balance. Alexandra . . . Vanya . . . Nikki . . . herself. The bonds cruelly severed. She never wanted Lexie to know that kind of estrangement.

Lexie seemed fascinated with him. She tugged at the visor of his hat. She fingered the medals on his uniform. She stared straight into his eyes and glanced back at her mother.

"Dis?" she asked Nicole, pointing to Billy.

Billy toyed with the little finger, curling it around one of his own. "Daddy. I'm your dad-dy."

Lexie did her best to approximate the new word. "Da-da? Da-da."

Nicole watched as father and daughter made friends and fell instantly in love with one another. It was achingly sweet. It was horribly ironic. Billy, of all men. Why hadn't she just slept with one of her dancers? Or Gar Fortune? Or one of those critics who loved her work?

But it had to be Billy. Billy who suffocated her creativity. Billy who really needed a nice girl from back home to take care of and worship him. Billy who believed. And Billy, goddamn it, who of all people didn't desert, but came home to her!

"Something will have to be worked out, Nicole," Billy sang in a voice meant just for enchanting little girls. "Everything's changed now that Daddy's come home."

He'd never said a truer thing. Lexie had a right to know her father, whether Nicole loved him or liked him or could even abide him. Everything had changed. There was

Lexie . . . a bona fide miracle to Nicole. And of all crazy things, Billy had returned. Stepped out of her lexicon of male behavior. She couldn't blame him for walking out. Walking away. Deserting her in her hour of need. Not that she ever really needed him. But Lexie might . . . And he was actually here. If Vanya had only—

"I went straight to the penthouse, hoping to catch you at home."

A warning light went on inside Nicole. Not even two minutes and they were already steeped in the mire.

"I don't live there, Billy."

"That was pretty obvious. The place was thick with dust. How long did you stay? A couple of months? A year? You must have been lonely."

It was painful to be forced to hear his wishful thinking.

"I've been very busy. Actually, I left soon after you did. I never promised to stay."

"I guess so," came his deflated response. "Well, where have you been living?"

"In the Village. When I wasn't on tour."

"And now?"

She could tell he was hoping for something better. A sign of her success. "Same old place. The baby loves it there. I don't know what Myrtle would do if I took her away," Nicole babbled, retrieving Lexie. "Oh God, this is going nowhere, Billy. Let me just . . ."

She opened the dressing room door, hailing Dominique on her way out. Before she could hand Lexie over to her friend, the little girl twisted toward Billy and waved.

"Da-da bye-bye," she said with great seriousness.

One dagger aimed perfectly at her heart, Nicole thought, taking a deep breath and facing her ex-lover. The expression on his face as he waved good-bye to his daughter was pure rapture. Another dagger stabbed Nicole. She wanted to scream something about conspiracies, but held herself in check. There was too much more to have out with Billy.

"Look," she began, "did you honestly expect me to stay at the penthouse after everything that happened?"

"I hoped you would," he said, the look of bliss fading into

sadness. "I needed to believe you were there. That's the only thing that kept me going in combat. God, it was awful, Nicole. Worse than anything I ever imagined. Shells exploding all around me . . . my buddies dying in front of my eyes. Picturing you puttering around the penthouse was all that kept me sane."

Her puttering . . . it was quite a fantasy.

"That's nice, Billy. I'm really glad it did the trick for you. But, you see, that's all that was necessary. I didn't really need to be there. What I do doesn't really matter . . ."

"It does now . . . now that I know about . . . what is my daughter's name anyhow?"

It was hard to tell him. As if she were giving away her privacy. Or a secret. It made her feel intimate with him. She couldn't look at him.

"Alexis . . . I call her Lexie."

"Aahhh," he said, sounding satisfied. "For your mother. It's beautiful, Nicole. Our daughter is beautiful."

He went to hug her. For Lexie's sake, she let him.

"See, honey? I came back," he whispered, nuzzling at her earlobe. "I got back because of you. We can find the magic again. And now that there's Lexie—there's so much to share. . . ."

Nicole panicked. The conversation was going in exactly the wrong direction. Right back to where they'd been two years ago.

"Wait a minute, Billy," she said, pushing him from her. "Let's not get all muzzy with sentiment. Remember who I am—the woman whose needs you couldn't handle. Look, I hate to be brutally frank . . . Christ! You just made it back from Hell . . . but you've got to face facts. You wanted me to be a sweet little girl. I'm not and I never will be. I'm a complicated woman."

Billy sank back into the one comfortably stuffed chair in the room.

"Two weeks after you left, I was on the creative path again with good, really good work. I made it happen, Billy. I've got my own troupe of dancers. I built a solid reputation. I had a baby by myself, and I'm raising a happy child. I know how important fathers are . . . I don't want to deny you Lexie or Lexie her father . . . but frankly . . ."

She couldn't say it. Maybe motherhood had given her more compassion. Maybe it was easier to see the other side of the argument. Maybe it was the utter dejection or the slight quiver of his lips. She couldn't tell him she didn't need him. No matter how true it was. She didn't feel the need to hurt him.

"Frankly, well . . . it's us, Billy. We've hardly had what anybody would call a good track record. We really haven't been very good for each other."

Billy just sat there, resigned, nodding his head. "Can't argue with a single word, Nicole. You've always been dead honest . . . even if it hurts. And it does, baby. Real bad." He paused, rubbing his hand over his mouth, and then asked, "Let me just ask you one little question. Is there anyone else in your life?"

Nicole almost laughed. "I don't have the time or the inclination. All I care about is Lexie and my career."

"Then there's hope," he said, smiling at her.

In disbelief, she stared at him. "I've got to go, Billy. Lexie will be waiting . . ."

She got out of her dressing room as fast as she could and leaned heavily against the door. My God, she thought to herself, Billy the Believer has risen again. She stood there, heart pounding, still in her Demeter costume, as the old familiar feeling seeped into her bones. Hemmed in again.

 44

Other ghosts resurfaced for Nicole, as if Billy's resurrection weren't enough for her to contend with. One day she received a package in the mail, its addresses and postmark all but obliterated. The poor box looked as though it had been shipped via dog sled. Or maybe just via dog. She opened it and discovered an elegant white baby's bonnet. At the bottom of the box was an envelope with her name on it. A sheet of notepaper fell out, inscribed "M.D.B." at the top. She quickly scanned to the closing lines of the letter.

> *Do keep in touch, dear. Your father may grumble but that's to be expected.*
>
> > *Fondly,*
> > *Peggy*

M.D.B. The hair on Nicole's arms rose in protest. So, thoroughly respectable Vanya had finally made an honest woman of his little English hen. It was Margaret Dunstable Borcheff now. She had won the long battle. Or had Vanya merely given up in defeat in the face of so much death?

Nicole returned the bonnet to the box, placed the letter within, and closed up the package. Out of sight, out of mind, she told herself. Seven years had passed. She was a different person. A twenty-eight-year-old woman. A professional. A mother. She didn't need reminders of an earlier era.

Then the thought of Lexie someday asking questions crept into her mind. Took hold. Shook hard.

"Tell me about my granddad, Mama," she would say. "Was he a wonderful dancer? Did his hair really look like a lion's mane? Did he love you as much as I do?"

Echoes from Nicole's own childhood filtered through her hardened heart. Tell me more, Mama, Nicole remembered asking Alexandra. Tell me everything and more about my father . . .

Slowly, Nicole reopened the box, took out the letter and began to read.

Nicole dear—

I must dash this little remembrance off to you with some haste. What with the post operating as it does these days, I can't be sure when you'll receive our little gift. Sometimes I think we were better off during wartime. Except for those awful ration books. Did you have them too?

But I mustn't dither so. I can't begin to tell you how

grateful I was to receive your letter from Denver, Colorado. Your news was so terribly exciting. Van, of course, didn't say much. But I must tell you, dear. His eyes filled with tears and he was forced to blow his nose several times. Such an emotional moment for both of us.

It was lovely to know how much you care about carrying on the family line. Especially after your last letter. I must say, that one was very hard on your father. He was already in the deepest slough of despondency. To be fair, we were all terribly upset. The pain of losing Nick was excruciating. But I understood how you felt.

Does that surprise you? I always knew how difficult it was for you here. Our little household didn't manage very well with all those Borcheffs and Varonnes mixing it up. But all's well that ends well . . . so Shakespeare said. Life's tragedies have a way of dimming over time. Even the darkest of moments must give way to a ray of sunshine.

For Van and me, it was finally marrying. Believe me, dear, we are happy together in our own quiet way. For you, it will be in raising your beautiful child. And he or she will be beautiful, as you and Nick were.

Then came the closing lines Nicole had already read. It was a long while before her eyes were dry. When she managed to compose herself, she called Lexie in from the tiny bedroom.

"Look, darling. A present for you," she murmured. "From your granddad and . . . from your grandparents."

The bonnet still fit the little girl later that spring when Billy took Nicole and Lexie to the zoo in Central Park. He gave Lexie an extended piggyback ride from cage to cage, naming each of the animals and imitating their calls.

"For heaven's sake, Billy," Nicole complained. "She was born with two good legs. She can walk, you know."

"But Daddy enjoys it so," he whined, deliberately putting on a sad face, so sad that Lexie gurgled with glee. "Mommy says down, baby."

PIROUETTE

But she clung to his neck and started to cry. "No, up," she demanded. "Daddy carry."

And Billy picked up the tune, begging Nicole in the same heartrending tones as his daughter.

"All right, all right," Nicole conceded. "But only till lunchtime."

"Hurray!" cried Billy. "Let's go, Lexie."

He whirled her away past the big cats and headed in the direction of the monkeys. Nicole could only follow.

"Big ape," she called after him, but along with irritation, there was a hint of affectionate humor in her voice.

Billy was good with Lexie. In fact, he was downright wonderful. She couldn't have come up with a more attentive, more patient, more entertaining father for her child. It was gratifying to see the two of them together. And she didn't mind the occasional family outing that Billy concocted. As long as he didn't push for more.

After their picnic lunch in the park, Lexie asked to see the elephant one more time. Billy and Nicole sat on a wooden bench, watching their daughter try to feed peanuts into the willing, outstretched trunk.

"Stand on tippy toes, Lexie," Nicole said encouragingly.

"She's got stage presence, Nicole. Look at the crowd of kids around our little girl," added Billy proudly.

"Look at the concentration on her face. She's not going to give up until that elephant gets a peanut."

"She's determined all right," Billy agreed. "Takes after her old man. I'm determined too, Nicole."

"Billy, don't start," Nicole demanded. "Please give up this crazy notion. Don't spoil what was a nice day."

Billy seized her hand, undaunted, and said, "It's been more than a nice day. It's been perfect. Don't you see, honey? We could have days like this all the time. You . . . me . . . Lexie. It's what life's all about. Marry me. Say yes, Nicole. Say you'll think about it."

Nicole quietly removed her hand from his grasp. "Don't ruin the little we do have between us, Billy. Let me go now. Lexie's calling. I've got to go to her."

* * *

Billy didn't give up, and neither did Lexie, who embraced her new playmate wholeheartedly. With a vengeance. She sobbed big, desperate tears whenever their time together came to an end. She took to begging Nicole to let Daddy stay and play a little longer . . . to stay for dinner . . . to spend the night. And Nicole found herself giving in by inches. Soon the inches grew into feet that were walking all over her.

She didn't know what to do. Billy was opening in *Riley Loves Rosie,* another surefire hit show. Audiences were going to love Private Riley O'Dell, who came home from the war just in time to rescue Rosie from the rivet factory. Billy loved the premise. It was something he could believe in, and he was at the peak of his form. On stage and off.

"I promise you," he vowed each time he could successfully corner Nicole, "I can respect you for who you are, not who I want you to be."

Perhaps it was the methodical repetition that wore her down. Perhaps it was the numerous advantages of having a full-time father for Lexie. Perhaps it struck a certain empty chord deep inside her. But there was something so right about seeing Billy and his child together and happy. It made Nicole want to love him. She could imagine loving him. Living with him. By summer's end she consented to marry him.

Billy wanted to go all out. Purchase a grand estate. Live high on the hog. But she objected. They compromised on a picture-perfect, vine-covered cottage out on Long Island. Triumphantly, he toted Lexie into their new home, astride his shoulders, letting his bride walk over the threshold.

"We're three peas in a pod," he exclaimed. "We'll be snug as three bugs in a rug."

They settled into family life. Theirs was a typical, New York, successful, show-biz ménage with two parents, two active careers in the arts, and a nice lady from Harlem who agreed to keep house and child in order.

Billy and Nicole were busy. All the time. Billy rode home on his nightly wave of standing-room-only adulation. Knowing Nicole and Lexie were tucked in their beds.

Waiting for him. Well, usually fast asleep. So what if sometimes he took a bottle of booze to bed with him. He had to come down from his cloud somehow. . . .

Nicole went off each morning to plan another season of new works, confidant in the direction of her dances and in her vision of Lexie's happiness. She was relieved that she no longer had to play at being Billy's girl, and more than content to let Lexie fill the role. As long as Billy had his daily shower of attention, what difference did it make if the source was wife or daughter?

Gradually, the idyll showed signs of erosion. Nicole's hours in the city became longer as her new works pulsed into life. Sometimes the housekeeper stayed late to put Lexie to bed or make a late supper for Billy when he came home from the theater. Sometimes Nicole spent weekends in town, taking Lexie with her and leaving Billy to thrash and wriggle about the house like a lone sardine in its own tin can. Billy's drinking became the rule rather than the exception. His usual harmonious complacency was replaced by unexpected rolling thunder.

On a Monday night—when Broadway theaters were customarily dark—just after the first snowfall, Nicole came home to find Lexie hot with fever and crying. Billy was banging around in the kitchen, trying to make soup.

"Where the hell've you been?" he shouted. "I've been trying to reach you all day."

"In the studio, as usual. I never heard the phone ring," Nicole said. "Where's Beulah? She knows what to do when Lexie's not feeling well."

"Of course Beulah knows," Billy said sarcastically. "She's the only one who's ever here all day. I wouldn't be surprised if Lexie started calling her 'Mama.'"

"Where is Beulah?" Nicole demanded through gritted teeth.

She could smell the liquor on Billy's breath all the way across the room.

"Sent her home. No use spending good money when the man of the house is in charge. I can handle anything."

"Right, Superman."

He was making no sense at all. Half drunk, territorial, and miserly. Here was a Billy Gable Nicole had never met and didn't want to know.

"I'll clean up this mess," she said wearily. "You take Lexie upstairs and put her to bed. Dinner will be ready in fifteen minutes, and we'll all feel better."

"That's my mother's recipe for pea soup," he whined. "You better treat it with the dignity it deserves. C'mon, Lexie. Daddy'll sing you a song."

Nicole listened from the doorway to make sure Billy successfully maneuvered the stairs to the bedrooms. She turned and faced the pots littering the stove. In a matter of seconds the contents were dumped down the sink and flushed to oblivion.

"Thank you, Mother Gable, for your contribution this evening," she muttered.

She set some trays on the kitchen table and grilled cheese sandwiches. Opening a can of Campbell's, she hurriedly heated it up for Lexie. A tiny devil whispered in Nicole's ear to open another can for Billy. A few minutes later she was on her way to Lexie's room with a tray of soup . . . a bowl of chicken noodle for the sick child and a bowl of green pea for the father.

Lexie took a couple of spoonfuls and promptly went to sleep. Billy sat guard by her side and cleaned his bowl.

"Best damn soup Mother ever made," he said, frowning at the burst of giggles from Nicole.

Unofficially, war had been declared. Billy, Nicole learned, was capable of fighting after all. And he didn't fight clean. So life wasn't perfect. They were still a family, weren't they? That was all she wanted. It had been what Billy said he yearned for. Yet he wasn't satisfied. Lexie remained the ideal playmate, but Billy longed for something else. Something more. He had never hidden his desire for Nicole. Now it became his cause célèbre.

His drinking became more overt—as though he dared Nicole to say or do something about it. At first she tried to avoid the subject. Avoid him. Then she realized he was using the liquor as a crutch. It gave him the courage to provoke her. He whined. He nagged. He complained. He pleaded. It was always on the same subject.

"Damn it, Nicole," the argument would start. "I won't even mention how you neglect Lexie."

There. He'd pushed the first button.

"A little girl needs her mother. Who's gonna darn her socks? Or wipe the tears from her eyes? Or give her cookies and milk? Or a good, hearty dinner?"

Oh, the pathos. The heart strings he tried to pluck.

"You're never around when I need you either."

Button number two. Forget the heart strings. Now he was going for the throat.

"I want a real marriage, Nicole."

"You wanted a family, Billy. You got one."

"You know that's not what I'm talking about. I want you to be waiting up for me, not dead to the world and snoring like some old alley cat."

Button number three, not just pushed but shoved.

"I work a long, hard day," she said as her jaw tightened.

"Pardon me, Your Majesty," he sniped. "I forgot just how difficult it is to figure out when to put your left foot in front of your right."

"You bastard. That's what you think I do all day long? Play footsy with myself?"

"I don't know what I think," he cried. "I just know you're driving me crazy. You're starving me, Nicole. I need to feel the passion with you. I need you to want me. To want it. Damn it, we had plenty of sex before we got married."

There it was. Finally out in the open.

"You didn't walk into this marriage blind, Billy. Don't blame me if there's trouble in this paper-thin paradise. You're the one who wanted all the home-grown, ginger-bread, gimcrack nonsense. I told you how important my career is to me. You've always known dance was my life. I warned you, and you promised to respect that. Now grow up. I won't take this spoiled little-boy crap."

"But honey . . ."

He was deflated so easily. It almost hurt her to see it. She reached out her hand to him, the way she would to Lexie.

"I can't turn my feelings on like a faucet, Billy," she said, trying to soften some of the stridency in her voice. "You know what we got married for. We both love Lexie so much . . . We want the best for her. Can't we at least show her that her parents are friends?"

"Best buddies," he echoed, attempting some enthusiasm. He clutched her hand, adding, "Buddies can be lovers too, can't they?"

"Yes," she said after hesitating. "They can. But Billy, cut the drinking down, okay?"

"Promise, Mommy," he said, nuzzling his head against her breasts.

 **45**

Nothing was solved. The situation only seemed to worsen. Nicole made an effort to show more interest in Billy, other than as the father of her child. It didn't work. Rather, it worked too well. Billy's response was to put more pressure on her. His occasional calls to the studio with cute messages of love were well-meant, but a source of irritation and interruption to Nicole. And when they didn't work, Billy escalated, calling daily with ridiculous demands.

"Where's my new golf sweater?" he would ask.

"Doesn't Beulah know?" Nicole asked back.

"I can't find it anywhere," he pouted.

"You've got more than one, Billy."

"I want this one."

"I'll look for it tonight when I come home."

"You always say 'tonight,'" he sulked. "But you're never there when I need you. It's always tonight or tomorrow or some other time. Well, I'm sick of it, Nic—"

She hung up on him. Repeatedly.

When Billy and she were at home together, he couldn't leave her alone. He tried to choose her clothes for her. Brought her perfume, flowers, and candy. Suggested elaborate plans for outings to the country, complex menus for intimate dinner parties. Filled her bath to overflowing with strongly scented bubbles. Filled her glass to overflowing with imported champagne. And made a complete nuisance of himself.

The pleasure Nicole got from watching Billy with their daughter began to evaporate. If it weren't for that single tie of blood connecting them, she would have left him. But she couldn't. Not as long as Lexie loved her daddy and he loved his little girl. That split was more painful to contemplate than she could bear. But not by much. And Billy knew it.

Alone in their bedroom in the middle of the night, after a half-hearted session of making love, Billy suggested, "Let's go away together . . . for a week. We both need a rest."

"We need a rest from each other," Nicole said soberly.

"No, honey. We need to get away from the pressures. You know how the city can get to you . . . make you do and say things you don't really mean."

Billy was trying to make amends. Again. Her heart sank. How could she refuse him? She owed him the chance. Didn't she? For Lexie's sake . . .

"The mountains . . . the seashore—you name it and we'll go."

A different vista. Time to relax. Time to think. Or not think. Just be. It was so tempting. It sounded good. But was it possible?

"Okay, Billy," she said with a degree of reluctance. "Let's try some place we haven't been to before."

"A fresh start. I like that, Nicole. It'll work, honey. You'll see. How about Cape Cod? There's an inn I heard of . . ."

He was off and chattering about getting back what they had once had. She tuned him out. She couldn't listen to the naive optimism. But at the same time she hoped he was right. Because something had to give. Or burst.

They were lucky. A break in the cold weather provided perfect springlike conditions. For a frantic three days Billy and Nicole ransacked the peninsula. They pillaged every olde shoppe in quaint little village after quaint little village. They stuffed themselves with clam chowder, lobster stew, and navy grog. They snapped photos of each other in front of weathered cottages and deserted lighthouses. They bicycled up and down winding roads, along the high cliffs of South Wellfleet and past ponds and open heath. They hiked to the white cedar swamp and to the spring of fresh water at Pilgrim Heights and stood at the bracing shore, taking in great gulps of salty sea air. They pointed out the blueness of the sky . . . the burly whiteness of the mashed potato clouds . . . the shifting of the sand dunes . . . the wild beauty of the beaches . . .

They did everything but talk to each other. Touch each other. And when there was nothing more to do, when they were reduced to polite and completely meaningless conversation, Billy remembered a shop or two he wanted to go back to. He muttered something about fishing tackle and buying a pipe . . . maybe. Nicole suddenly thought of an ocean view she wanted to see again. She took her warmest jacket in case she wanted to stay and watch the moon climb over the bay. She stayed, returning to the inn late. Billy was sound asleep with a companionable bottle of rum.

The next morning, waking to the clang of church bells, they faced each other warily. Apologetically.

"What do you want to do?" one asked the other.

"I don't know. This air makes me tired," came the reply.

"I know what you mean."

"Well, do you have anything in mind?"

"Not really. Maybe we'll go somewhere later."

"Sure."

They didn't go anywhere. Together. Eventually, Nicole washed her hair and started reading a thick book. Billy walked to a neighboring village in search of the trade papers. By the time he got back, she had taken a bike and the camera. He nursed another bottle of rum until she returned.

"Where you been?" he asked sulkily.

"The dunes. I was watching the shape and swirl of the sand. It gave me some great ideas for a dance . . ."

"We said we wouldn't talk business. Remember?"

"Sorry, Billy."

"You're not the only one."

"What's that supposed to mean?" she asked, unable to keep from bristling.

"I don't want to argue with you, Nicole."

"Good. Because I don't want to either."

Silence. Nicole picked up her book and Billy filled his glass. Then he lifted it and threw it against the wall.

"Damn it, Nicole. This is supposed to be our second honeymoon."

She stared at him, devoid of emotion.

"When did we have our first?" she said, and returned to her book.

Without Lexie as a magnet, there was nothing between them. Except the burden of knowing. The bond of parenthood had little to do with the boundaries of love and marriage.

In Billy's case it seemed to be a matter of ignoring the truth which rabbit-punched him in the face. Later that night it became apparent that nothing was going to happen in bed either.

"Let's just go home, Billy," Nicole suggested. "Let's pick up Lexie and take her into the country. We could go out to that pony farm." When he didn't answer her, she added, "Look, I'm willing to try a family outing. Maybe if we work at it as a family—"

"No!" he barked. "This isn't about Lexie. It's about you and me." His mood shifted and he was begging her, "Don't give up on us, honey. You don't know how much I need you. It's not just Lexie. It's having a home and someone you love to come home to. It's proving to the world you're somebody special . . . important. It's proving to yourself you're not alone. . . . You don't have to be alone."

Nicole was overwhelmed by the need in his voice. His

face spoke it. His whole body showed it. Poor Billy, she
thought. To have been brainwashed so throughly. To believe
with such fervor and such pain. She couldn't help aching for
him. This grown-up man with the emotional maturity of a
nine-year-old boy. This man who could put himself up for
public examination any night on stage, who had survived
the horror of war—this man had trouble with the notion of
being by himself. My God, Billy, she wanted to scream at
him, you have so much to be proud of.

"Don't you know," he asked her, voice trembling, "you're
the only prize I ever wanted to win?"

She remembered the prizes she had set her heart on. Her
father's devotion. Her brother's acceptance. Carlo's love.
All impossible to hold on to. She'd had so much to learn. So
much to give up before realizing the prize was her own
independence.

"Billy," she said softly, pulling him into her arms, "don't
put me on a pedestal. I'm just an ordinary mortal of flesh
and blood."

"We have two more days here, honey," he whispered
while blowing hot air against her ear. "Let's make tonight
count."

But Billy couldn't, even with a willing Nicole. He blamed
the rum. The salty sea air. That they'd fought too much.
That Nicole was cold. In fact, it was Nicole's fault altogether. He took his wounded pride and his limp penis into the
bathroom for a long hot shower.

The following day they found little to say to one another.
Billy occupied the bedroom. He made himself busy with his
fishing tackle and came out only to announce that he was
taking a nap. Nicole continued to plow through her novel.
She was reading the words but not concentrating on a single
one. Why had she bought the book in the first place? she
asked herself. Who cared whether Napoleon was more
successful on the battlefield or in the beds of his wives and
mistresses?

Affairs of war . . . affairs of the heart . . . Her mind
wandered, eyes blinked, and she drooped . . . The book fell

out of her grasp, into her lap. Without thinking, she picked it up, closed it, and put it on a table beside her. Twisting in her chair, she stared out the window at the distant sea. The vacant beach. The isolated clump here and there of tall, windswept grasses. The empty road that had brought her to this place . . .

No, not empty. Someone was walking down the road, taking purposeful strides. He had the steps of a man who knew where he was headed. But graceful. Powerful. Surely not a sailor, she mused. Or a fisherman. There was too much command in his gait. As if he had no time for the caprices of nature. Here was a man who would dare the wind to blow him down.

He was closer now. She could see that he was tall for a dancer—her standard of measurement—and muscular. His hair, dark and wavy, bristled against the stiff breeze. Yet he never seemed to avert his sharp gaze . . . which bore down, on her. All he needed was an eyepatch and a saber and the vision would be perfect. The pirate king descending on his victim. The dark, sleek panther prowling stealthily toward his prey.

Nicole's heart stood still. It was impossible. She shook her head and rubbed her eyes. Pirate king . . . panther on the prowl. Was she dreaming? Was she mad? Could he be real? Carlo? Was it Carlo?

In a daze she moved to the door and flung it open. The man was running, loping toward her. In a moment she knew. Carlo Domenici was alive. In her arms. She was kissing him. She was in his embrace, held prisoner by those arms of his. Strong. Sinewy. Broadly covering her back. His lips swooping down onto hers. Demanding. Devouring. Taking. Leaving her breathless, as his kisses always had. Breathing her name wherever his lips touched . . . her eyes, her cheeks, the hollow of her throat, her earlobes, and again her lips . . . Nicole . . . Nicole . . . Nicole . . .

But this was now. Eight years since he had made his choice. Eight years since she had last seen him. Eight years since he had walked off toward his train and left her desperately, terrifyingly alone. To face her mother's death and her brother's vengeance. At the mercy of her father. Eight years to hate him and miss him and learn to live without him.

After all that time, he'd come back to her. Too late. She wasn't available to be his anymore. She was Mrs. Nicole Varonne Gable. Wife and mother. And Mr. Gable was only a few feet away. Pulling away from Carlo, she shut the front door.

"The beach," she said. "We can talk there."

He nodded, murmuring something in Italian. The last time she had heard Carlo speak his native tongue was with his parents at Trattoria Bari. Stefano and Francesca . . . when was the last time she'd thought of them or their cozy restaurant? Were they still alive? Happy? As warm and thoughtful as they'd always been to her mother and her?

The questions were on the tip of her tongue, but she wouldn't let herself ask. It would only encourage Carlo. Make him think there was hope when there wasn't any. Hope was dead. As dim and distant as London itself.

"What?" she asked, caught in her web of memories.

"Forgive me, cara . . . sweetheart. I've been in Italy so long. I forget the rest of the world doesn't think, speak, and dream in Italian too. What I was trying to say was that we have so much to say to one another. It's been a lifetime, Nicole. The thought of you was all that kept me going sometimes."

Oh God, Nicole thought, echoes of Billy. Or was it just that every boy sent a long way from home felt the same yearnings? And dutifully reported them the minute he got back. Was every girl who suffered so keenly through absence and worry and enduring supposed to swoon in gratitude at this declaration?

How many had come back as strangers? she wondered. How many had been met by strangers? Did she know this man walking beside her? Was he really the same boy . . . man . . . who had turned her world upside down? Made her see through his eyes? Feel through his touch? God knows, she wasn't anything like that girl now. Naive. Trusting. Vulnerable.

"Nicole? There was no way for me to communicate while I was underground. You understood that, didn't you? I've come to you at the first real opportunity."

Yes, he was speaking English now, but it still wasn't in language she knew. He didn't sound a thing like the Carlo who had mastered the tough streets of London, who argued with Vanya like his equal, who showed gentlemanly deference to her mother, and who had talked straight to her.

"Look at me, Nicole."

He grabbed at her and held both her hands in one of his. He cupped her chin with the other so that she had to stare into his eyes. Ah . . . yes. There was Carlo. In those insolent, burning, piercing, dark eyes. There the message was unmistakable. Nothing has changed. Nothing will ever change. You are mine. I am yours. Nothing else matters.

"You went away," she whispered, still staring into the well of his eyes.

"I'm here, aren't I?"

"Not when I needed you, you weren't."

"There was a war."

The spell that broke the enchantment. She backed away from his grasp, glaring at him with a will of her own.

"This is 1947, Carlo! The war's been over for almost two years. Three in Europe. Christ! 'First real opportunity,' my ass, Carlo darling. Sounds more like convenience to me."

He grabbed her again, embracing her stiffening body. To Nicole's chagrin, he was grinning . . . laughing at her. She wanted to slap him. Slap that face that had sneered with impudence. Glowered with gloom. Smoldered with passion and life. Damn him!

"God, Nicole, I love you. You're as stubborn as ever. I knew you wouldn't change."

"Damn it, Carlo. Where have you been? Let go of me!"

"Okay, okay. Hands off. See? There's a lot to tell. You want the short version or the long, complicated one?"

Already he sounded more like himself, less like a throwback to a dandified duke. Or a zealot on unfamiliar ground. She looked back toward the inn. She looked at the footsteps, side by side, that Carlo and she had tracked in the sand. Separating her from Billy. Setting herself and Carlo apart from the rest of the mundane world.

"I want to know everything," she said.

~~ **46**

Carlo nodded, saluting her smartly. He squared his shoulders and stared down the long strip of beach, as though his story ran the length and breadth of it.

"It was easier than I expected to get into Italy. Of course I had about a six-month jump on Hitler. By the time most of Europe fell in '40, I was firmly entrenched in the Italian resistance movement, or what I could find of it. Little pockets of peasants . . . ladies of the manors . . . professori . . . the occasional policemen . . . and lots of boys. Oh, God, Nicole, so many boys. Half-starved ragamuffins with dreams of glory. Misplaced bullies who knew how to handle guns. The timid ragazzi who'd already seen more death and destruction than they should have known in a lifetime. There was no organization, nothing holding them together except a hatred for the enemy and a common battle cry. Freedom and revenge! Sound familiar?"

Nicole nodded, remembering the boy she'd fallen in love with. The passionate declarations. The fire in his eyes. Loathing so strong, sometimes it had seemed to direct his arms upward, his legs outward, in some fearsome kind of dance. Angry punctuations to the rhetoric of philosophy and politics. Carlo would have fit in well with his compatriots.

"We were a joke," he continued. "Taking potshots at trains. Trying to blow up old wooden bridges with homemade dynamite. Stealing food from commissaries. We weren't making a dent, weren't even of nuisance value. For form's sake, the Fascisti would periodically round a band or two of us up, beat us black and blue, and send the babies home to their mamas. So much for freedom and revenge."

He kicked at the sand, sending tiny clouds of grit scudding ahead.

"When France surrendered, everything changed. We began to hear about the Maquis. They knew how to resist. So I took a little trip west and learned the subtle art of sabotage at the masters' knees. When I returned to Italy, I was ready; I was trained; and I had my instructions direct from Allied HQ: destroy the network of secret munitions factories. Piece of cake, I thought. All I had to do was gather my merry band of boys, and the Italian Robin Hood was ready to lead the way to victory."

There was a new tone in Carlo's voice. One Nicole was unfamiliar with. A hint of mockery. Of irony. Aimed at himself. Had the man changed? she wondered.

"It was hard work. A lot of the boys didn't want to learn; they just wanted to know where their next meal was coming from. But I was lucky," he said, squaring his shoulders. "I took with me a dozen or so ragazzi, and we settled in a little town north of the Apennines and south of the Po. The townspeople were more than cooperative. They embraced us as heroes, as if we had already liberated all of Italy."

Nicole thought she caught the briefest hint of a smirk crossing his face. She could just imagine him wanting to strut down the main street of town. Wanting to preen like a peacock. Yet holding himself in check. Wanting even more for the enemy to reveal himself. She stared at him openly, hungry for more of the tale.

"We melted into the daily life of the town. I posed as the younger brother of a widow, Signora Maroni, who had four small sons. I got work at the local newspaper and slowly began nosing my way around town. It was always amazing to me what a free glass or two of the local vino would produce.

"My boys and I were ready for action within a couple of months. We chose our target twenty kilometers away and secreted our cache of explosives in the sacristy of a church, thanks to the sympathetic priest. We did the deed and were back in our beds before dawn. We were jubilant but careful. Our first success! And our first true blow for freedom and revenge."

Carlo was staring into the waves that crested and crashed onto the shore. For a moment he was silent, listening to the ferocity of nature at work and likening it to the roar of cannon fire.

"We hit three more factories in '41 and five in '42. Our plans worked perfectly. Then the next time . . ." He paused, shuddered, made himself continue. "One of the boys got sloppy and blew himself up instead of the target. The time after that, another boy got caught by a guard."

Nicole stiffened, feeling Carlo's pain. She needed to touch him, quietly put her hand in his.

"All we knew was that he was turned over to the police and somehow a German officer got involved. We had to leave our little town or put everyone in jeopardy. By spring of '43 I'd sent the boys on to their next posts. I stayed behind with a plan of my own. I wanted one last parting shot. For the boy who was killed and the boy who was captured. Just a little revenge."

Revenge? Nicole wondered. Or perhaps a little compassion? She read the toll in his eyes and knew the answer. The young man who had thrived on principles had learned to take chances. He had risked himself not for honor, but for the sake of humanity. For a couple of lost souls. She could feel him tighten against her, then stretch to break the building tension. When he spoke again, he was in control, simply recounting a story.

"I took more precautions than usual. Maybe that's where I went wrong. Maybe I was too obvious. Or maybe my time was up. Whatever the reason, I went back to the factory we had failed to blow up and walked right into a trap. The Fascists were waiting for me with an invitation to come with them for questioning. They mentioned the name of the boy who had been caught and what an agreeable lad he had been.

The poor kid had squealed, and then they'd killed him, the bastards. I knew then that they'd have to kill me too, because they weren't going to break me."

"Wait a minute," cried Nicole. "They took you off to prison camp . . ."

"It was a rotted old jailhouse—a medieval torture chamber, really, although the local Nazis liked to refer to it as their interrogation center."

"Nazis—" she began, and faltered.

Her face took on a tortured look. She knew what was coming next. That awful nightmare . . . When was it? Four years ago?

"Carlo, when did this happen? What time of the year was it?"

"Summer of '43. Midsummer night."

The time for dreams and magic to entangle and come alive. Her nightmare had been real.

"It was dark . . . dank . . ." she entoned, seeing again the deeply buried images. "There were chains. And noise . . . shouting or screaming or both. Harsh light. Blinding. Choking. Torturing you with light and water. Stabbing at you. I didn't know whether you were alive or dead."

"What are you talking about, Nicole? How do you know so much about it?"

"Oh, God, Carlo, I lived those moments with you. Our minds were linked . . . our souls . . . I don't know how to explain it. I just know I saw the whole thing in a dream. I was there with you. Suffering. Oh, this sounds ridiculous!"

"Not so ridiculous, cara mia," he said, staring deeply into her eyes. "I give a lot more credence to the unexplainable these days, having lived through the war and after. Compromise and survival—that's what it came to, often enough. You were there with me, you know."

She looked at him incredulously. Now who was talking nonsense? But she felt the blood rushing to her head when he produced from his wallet a battered snapshot of her looking incredibly young and deliriously happy. She remembered. The picture had been taken only a short while after Stonehenge. After the first time Carlo had made love to her.

"You were with me when I escaped," he continued. "I pulled the stunt every good prisoner dreams of. When they were done beating me, they threw me into a cell. I was able to haul myself upright so that when a guard came to check on me—see if I was dead or not—I threw myself on him, dashing his head against a wall. I stripped him, put what remained of my clothes on him, dressed myself in his uniform, and marched out of the building. I made it back to Signora Maroni's. She hid me and nursed my wounds, but at great cost. The Germans had trailed me back to town. They hounded the poor woman, broke every stick of furniture in her house. When she wouldn't budge, they tore her four sons from her. Good sons of Italy make tasty fodder for the better sons of Germany, they told her.

"I never knew her sacrifice until she had made me well again. I vowed then and there to find her children and bring them home to her, no matter how long it took. It wasn't just a debt of honor. I owed her my life. I owed those boys of hers a chance to grow up in their homeland. I owed my ragazzi, who, right or wrong, had given their lives. I wanted to have made a difference."

"Very interesting, Carlo," she remarked. "The Fascists couldn't break you down. The Nazis couldn't. It took Mama Maroni to melt down your armor. It's about time you joined the human race!"

"I'm still an arrogant bastard at heart," he said, laughing. "But even I had the sense to realize that war, like life, doesn't always follow the rules. Sometimes there is no right or wrong. You do what you do because you must."

"And you had to keep your promise," Nicole said, veiling the reproach she felt rising up inside her.

"I did. And suddenly Mussolini fled from power. The Allies landed, regained Sicily, and made for the mainland. I went south to join them. When the war in Italy was over, I set out in search of the Maronis. It took me a year and a half to find three of the boys alive and verify the death of the fourth. Then I took them home to their mother, and at last I was free to go home to you. Debts paid. Promises fulfilled. You've led me a merry chase, Nicole. London. New York. Thank God the dance world is inundated by gossips. But even if you'd given up dancing, I'd have found you. I could have waited for you at your studio, but I ran out of patience. As it was, I grilled a couple of your dancers till they cried uncle. I guess I can be kind of intimidating. So here I am."

Nicole just stood there. What could she say to him? Congratulations on a job well done? You've always been my hero? Waiting has made it all the better? The hell with that mush! She was mad. Furious.

Carlo and his damn-fool priorities. The glory of Rome! Family honor! Choosing to play tin soldiers over love. Opting to give up his life in the tarnished name of duty. Offering chivalry to a widow instead of winging his way home to her. God bless the lady for saving his life, but goddamn her too. If Carlo hadn't gotten himself immersed in her life . . . if he'd only come back in '43 . . . she wouldn't be married to Billy. Carlo and she would have had a chance. Damn him!

"Proud of yourself, aren't you?" she taunted. "Stood right up there for God and country and saved the day. Bravo," she said, stepping back, clapping her hands, bowing before him. "And now you're ready for your reward. Not a medal or an oak-leaf cluster. Oh no. It's Nicole you want pinned onto your lapel. At *your* bloody convenience. So sorry to disappoint you, but it can't happen. You're too late. I married somebody else. We have a child."

She did it. The big, confident grin was wiped from his face, replaced by disbelief, anger, betrayal, hurt, loss. She saw each emotion, one by one, take hold and sink in. She was satisfied. Now he knew what she'd felt eight years ago when he announced he was leaving her.

He gave her a measured look and asked her quietly, "Do you love him, this man you married?"

"Going deaf, Carlo? Let me repeat. He is the father of my child."

"I know you, Nicole. You're not lying, but you're not telling the truth either."

She couldn't hide the downcast flicker of her eyes. He'd caught her; he always could. She might as well be standing naked before him. Exposed. Hung up on a cross. She wouldn't respond. She wouldn't look at him.

"He got you pregnant and did the decent thing. Married you so the baby would have a name."

She had to glare at him. "You'd think that, wouldn't you? Thank you, Your Supreme Holiness, for the high regard you have for my morals. Well, you're dead wrong. He loves me. He's never deserted me and he never will. I love him for that," she said, realizing she meant every word.

"For a woman in love," Carlo said slyly, "you have an interesting way of greeting an old flame."

"An old flame," she retorted, "that's exactly what you are, Carlo. Sputtering in the wind. Gasping for breath. Extinct."

"It's not over, no matter what you say. We both know it."

She started to stalk off, but found herself twisting in his arms.

"Let go of me," she cried. "You're too late . . ."

"Never, cara. I never stopped loving you, and you've never stopped loving me. You can't deny our memories . . . the picture of you next to my heart . . . your dreams . . . We've never really been apart . . . I won't let you throw us away now."

He was kissing her. Hard. Slow. Electric. She was yielding. She had to fight. She yanked herself from him. From his seduction. Away from the danger. Away from the truth. She ran full speed for the inn.

Carlo was right behind her, grabbing her as she reached for the door to her rooms and pulling her to him as the door opened. Billy stared. His wife was in the clutches of another man. Nicole thought fast.

"Thanks for catching me," she said, slipping away from Carlo. "My ankle twisted on this darn step. Just like yours did the other day, Billy."

She glanced from one man to another. They were sizing each other up. Defining the stakes: Nicole. It was obvious in the way they both hovered over her without touching her. It was a war of wills. Of territory. Billy took control first.

"You okay, honey? I can get some ice. Or perhaps your friend here wants to fetch some from the bar."

Billy put a protective arm around her, drawing her closer to him. Nicely done, Billy, she thought. She meekly followed his lead and cuddled into his possession of her. Take this picture home with you, Carlo, she telegraphed silently.

"Billy, isn't this the funniest coincidence? Of all places to run into an old acquaintance. This is Carlo Domenici. He used to dance for my father . . . a long time ago."

"I went away to war," Carlo said.

"Didn't we all?" Billy replied.

"A lot has changed since then," parried Carlo.

"Not everything," thrust Billy.

Another standoff.

"What brings you to the Cape?" Billy asked, suddenly genial, as though Carlo were his long-lost friend.

"Unfinished business," snapped Carlo.

"I think it's finished," said Nicole softly.

"Well, look us up in New York, why don't you? Next time you're passing through. We'll swap war stories . . . have a couple of drinks."

Enough, Billy, Nicole urged silently. Carlo nodded curtly and gave Nicole a final piercing look.

"You can bet on it," he said, and walked away.

With that same purposeful stride. Up the road. Out of her sight. Billy closed the door, and Nicole immediately disengaged herself from him.

"I want to go home, Billy. Now. This very minute."

Billy complied without an argument.

~~ **47**

Taking Lexie up in her arms, Nicole felt strong again. Here was her reason for going on. For making something more than a masquerade out of her relationship with Billy. This little girl loved her. That was motivation enough to forge ahead.

If Lexie was her anchor, dance was her elixir. Dancing out the frustrations and pain. Molding them into steps and symbols that gave her life a whole different meaning. Perspective. Snatching the positive, the creative out of a seemingly negative force. The gold from the dross. Choreography as alchemy. Dance made Nicole feel magical and powerful, and right now, after the disaster of Cape Cod, she needed to feel in control.

She headed into the city a few days later, at a time when her studio would be vacant. Dressed in simple leotard and tights, with her feet bare, she selected a couple of records and several tapes and dimmed the light. Music filled the room. Deep, luxurious resonance. Reverberating off the walls. Penetrating her. Filling her with harmony. Energy. Dimension. Inspiration. She closed her eyes. Her body began to sway, her arms float, her legs twirl and swirl about the room.

She was the shifting sand, spellbound by currents of the wind, by the pull of the tide and gravity. She was airy and light. Frenetically swift. Her feet flashed upward. Downward.Her body spun and tossed with the music. With the images. Of sand. Sea. Air. The elements and the dancer. As one. Alone.

No, not alone. A shadow in the doorway. Watching. Invading. Nicole froze. The mood was broken. Quickly she stopped the music, adjusted the light, and saw Carlo, clapping and shaking his head in semblance of disbelief.

"My God, Nicole, you haven't lost anything. You're as good—as great—as I knew you'd be."

"I was letting off steam. Didn't even know what I was doing," she mumbled, confounded by his approbation. "I had this idea . . . watching the dunes at the Cape. I was just trying out a few movements. It's nothing the company would do."

"Forget the humble pie, Nicole. It's a virtuoso solo piece."

She lapped up his praise as though she were fifteen again.
Ignoring the volume of work she'd produced. The critical
acclaim she'd earned. The confidence she'd built in herself.

"You really think I'm good?"

"I'll tell you over dinner."

"Dinner! What time is it?"

She'd only planned on spending a few quiet hours there.
To reflect. To plan. To dream of new dances. To be back
home in time to see Billy off to the theater and make dinner
for Lexie. But it was late. Billy had had to see himself
off . . . again. Beulah must have fed Lexie and put her to
bed . . . and was probably fuming about where that crazy
missus was . . . again.

"I've got to go home, Carlo. I'm late."

"Late for what?"

It was a perfectly good question. Typical of the Carlo
she'd known, it went straight to the heart of the matter. The
truth was, she was probably too late. Too late to make
amends for this evening. With husband gone and child
asleep, it didn't seem to make any difference if she were five
minutes late or three hours.

"Everyone's got to eat, Nicole. Even dancers."

"You're pretty damn sure of yourself, Carlo Domenici. In
fact, you've got a hell of a nerve showing up here at all. I
thought Cape Cod made it pretty clear . . ."

"It did. Now how about dinner? I made reservations at a
place in Little Italy."

"What makes you think I'd go anywhere with you?"

"Because you're a pro and I need to ask your advice."

Surprise, Nicole. Touché, Carlo. Be on guard, she told
herself. The pull of the past could be deadly.

"Nothing personal? You promise?"

He held up three fingers, saying, "On my honor."

"When were you ever a Boy Scout?" Nicole retorted.

"I'll tell you over dinner," teased Carlo.

Nicole called home to tell Beulah she'd be even later, and
soon found herself ensconced in the familiar red vinyl booth
with a checkered, soiled cloth covering a rickety table that
came with every spaghetti house this side of Italy. She didn't

trust him. She thought he would barrage her with intimate, impossible questions she couldn't and wouldn't begin to answer. But he didn't.

Over bread sticks and antipasto he brought up old times. Classes with Mademoiselle Paisy, Andreyev, and the impossible Demsby-Worth. Nicole chuckled over Carlo's imitation of Mademoiselle's fluttering eyelashes. She choked with laughter when he smashed a bread stick to smithereens right there on the table, mimicking Andreyev's compulsive use of his cane. She gasped for breath and held her aching sides as he reenacted the affected lisp of Demsby-Worth.

"I can do Miss Archway," she offered, sending her fingers into a perfect rendition of the class pianist valiantly trying to keep the dancers on tempo.

"Gladys was a sport," Carlo recalled fondly.

"Gladys was in love with you," Nicole retorted. "You were the only one who ever gave her the chance to play presto allegro."

"Until Andreyev would stop us."

They were silent for a moment, sharing in the memory. It made Nicole angry. She found herself feeling as bitter as though it had happened yesterday.

"God, it was stifling. All we ever wanted to do was dance. Our way. But no," she said, floodgates unleashed, "talent wasn't enough. Drive was too much. All the English wanted was subjugation. Do it their way. Faceless, disembodied, lifeless. Vanya should have been honest enough to call the company 'Borcheff's Puppet Show.' Come one, come all. See the life-size dolls do the master's bidding."

"Whoa! Nicole! Where's your perspective? I know we got the short end of the stick, but British Court was—is—a great ballet company. It was the wrong place for me and for you. Vanya had his vision. It was just too small to contain dancers like us. We needed to set the world on its ear. We wanted to explode the limits. Dance as birds flew. Free. Far. Do you remember the time . . ."

Nicole remembered. Vividly. The turbulent days of London. Falling under Carlo's spell. Feeling truly alive only when she was with him. Stealing moments with him while

Vanya and Nikki plucked away pieces of her soul. Clinging to him while her mother receded into the distance. Precious times when they danced like the wind. Like fire. Like the sea in a storm.

"That's what dance has always meant for me," he was saying. "To push oneself to the absolute end and find the strength to go beyond."

Yes. Yes. He was right. That was the secret to dance and to life. Carlo knew it as well as she did. But then they'd discovered it together long ago.

"You were brave, Nicole. To cut all ties and strike out on your own. You've made a place for yourself, a name for yourself. I want the same thing."

"Oh, yes, Carlo. You should have your own company," she said enthusiastically.

"I should, but it won't be here in the States."

Was she disappointed? Had she really expected him to stay? No. The ghost would return to the grave; the past wouldn't haunt her. She was relieved.

"But I'm thinking of staying for a year to study, pick up the latest trends. I need to see where I fit in. You understand, Nicole?"

"Yes, I do, Carlo. I really do. That makes such good sense."

Relief again. He was staying. She could see him from a distance. A nice safe distance. He wouldn't leave right away. She'd have him for a year. Oh God, she cried, only one short year.

"I can't wait to get into the kind of thing you do, Nicole. The strength. The subtlety. God, it was invigorating to watch you. What you do with that body of yours . . . you're in great shape."

"And you, Carlo?" She couldn't help a wicked thrust or two, adding, "Aren't you just a trifle out of shape? Eight days away from the barre is hell. Eight months an eternity. But eight years! That's death to a dancer."

"Don't count me out yet, Nicole. You'd be surprised at the physical discipline spying and sabotage take. Seriously, you remember my unorthodox barres in the alleys of

London? Well, I did the same kind of thing in Italy. Stealing an hour here, an hour there . . . While the boys thought I was busy dishing up Molotov cocktails in Signora Maroni's basement, I made sure I never let go of my technique. I still filled my quota of explosives. I've always been a fast worker. But the war wasn't going to last forever. I knew I'd be back. Given the chance, I think I can still shake a leg. That's what they say on Broadway, isn't it? So, do you know someone who would take me in?"

There it was. Baldly put . . . bold. He was asking to be in her company. Put up or shut up. She couldn't. It was one thing to reminisce. Open up the past for one brief peek. But it was quite another issue to let Carlo into her life now. It was complicated enough. Skirt the issue, she told herself.

"I have plenty of contacts," she said, hiding behind her profession. "I think I could find you a spot. Gar Fortune might have room for you, although Ernie Land would be a better choice. There's a new guy, from out West. Yancy Marklin. He's in the market for strong male dancers. Your type exactly."

"So I have a chance?"

"Oh, I don't see you having any problems."

"Of course, I'd love to dance with you, Nicole."

Alarm bells went off, screeching inside of her. Dangerous territory had been entered. Beware. Go back. Get out.

She slid out from the booth, purse and coat in hand.

"It's later than I thought, Carlo. They're waiting for me at home."

"Of course, Nicole, I understand," Carlo said with just a hint of condescension. "We wouldn't want to keep the little man waiting."

"Good night, Carlo."

She was home in record time. The lights were burning. Billy was already back from the theater. And waiting up for her.

"Share a nightcap with me, honey?"

"No, thanks, Billy. I'm kind of tired. I think I'll just slip up to bed."

"No. Stay and talk with me. Please."

"Bring your drink upstairs, Billy. We can talk while I'm getting undressed."

"Okay, sounds promising."

She wasn't promising anything.

"Box office better tonight, Billy?"

"Nah, receipts are still falling off. Manny stopped by with the news. The show's closing."

"You'll get another one. Soon," she said, giving him a hug. He held on, burying his nose in her hair.

"Mmmm. Smell so good, baby. Make your Billy boy feel better. How's about it?" he begged, steering her toward the bed.

"Oh, Billy, I have such a big day tomorrow. I've got to be up early. Get Lexie to nursery school. Then a full day at the studio."

"Sure, Nicole. That's just great. Where do I fit into the schedule? Do I get five minutes tomorrow?" His voice turned petulant. "Can't I have a lousy twenty minutes of your precious time now?"

"No, Billy. I'm sorry. Good night."

She got into bed and turned her face to the wall.

"Your busy day tomorrow didn't keep you from staying out till all hours tonight."

"I didn't plan it that way, Billy," Nicole said quietly.

"When the hell do my plans count?" he yelled, and threw himself under the covers.

She closed her eyes, but sleep wouldn't come. Only images of Carlo. Carlo bearing down the road to the inn. Carlo sweeping her up in his embrace. Carlo bringing three war-shocked children home to their brave mother. Carlo applauding her dancing. Carlo back in her life. Like gangbusters.

He hadn't deserted her. And he wanted to dance with her. If she only said yes, she could be dancing with him. God, she was tempted. But the dangers. His arms . . . his eyes . . . his mouth . . . He reduced her to an inarticulate teenager. Longing for love and romance . . . and kinship. The dreams of her girlhood came flooding back to her. Carlo and she soaring. The passion they had had. The sparks they had ignited.

Lying next to her, Billy tossed and turned in his sleep. There were no sparks between him and her. Never had been. Their love . . . their sex . . . their being together at all was based on safety. Bland security. Guilt. She yearned for the spark again. And Carlo.

Apparently Carlo didn't waste time. By the end of that same week Nicole got a phone call from Yancy Marklin. He sounded like he was bursting.

"I knew the dance world takes care of its own, but this is overwhelming. You're overwhelming. Your generosity . . . well, there aren't words."

"I'm happy to get a pat on the back, Yancy. But what did I do to deserve it?"

"Carlo . . . Carlo Domenici. He's fantastic. He's fabulous. I've never seen anyone with his fire. My God! The raw talent. And the endurance! The man must be made of iron. He never stops. There's no limit to what he can do. What he'll do for my company. I don't know how you could pass him up, Nicole. But thank you, thank you."

"That's all right, Yancy. He . . . just wasn't my type."

"Well, God bless you, Nicole. And God bless his type. I'll send you free tickets for Domenici's first performance."

Two months later she received them in the mail. Only two months! she thought. Eight weeks to get in shape. Learn the new vocabulary. Mount a dance. Rehearse it. Iron out the kinks. Rehearse some more. Be sure enough to present it.

Carlo debuted in *Whirlwind*. He was the whirlwind. With all its power. Energy. Chaos. Risking everything. Daring the laws of nature as much as personifying them. Occupying the air above the stage as well as the stage itself. Saving nothing for the end. Giving his all every second, every step of the dance. He was magnetic. Galvanizing. Utterly sure of himself. Completely open to his audience.

It was a tour de force. Nicole, like the rest of the audience, was mesmerized. Her eyes followed him everywhere. She had no choice because his artistry demanded it. He brought to his dancing what a shaman brings to his magic. The gift of himself. His body and his soul. She felt jealous. Angry. She was filled with longing for him. Wanting him so much. Wanting what he did to be hers again. Hers alone.

When the dance was over, she sat still for a long time. Thinking. If she felt this way about Carlo, what the hell was she doing with Billy? Billy, who used the stage to hide from himself. To cloak himself in someone else's words and actions. Who could never understand that for her and for Carlo art was a means to uncover oneself. To discover oneself. The answer was staring at her. Screaming at her. She could not pay attention. Carlo had come back on stage to dance again.

She went home in a mental fog, her thoughts aswirl and her emotions roiling. The house was dark. She opened the door and tiptoed in. One lamp was on in the living room, casting a soft glow on an object at its base. Nicole walked over and picked up a single red rose. Under it lay a card which read, "For my own true love." Oh Billy. He could be unbearably sweet. But his sense of timing was never more off. What was she going to do with him?

She passed on into the dining room and gasped. Spotlighted on the rosewood table was a stout little easel, displaying an old theater poster of her mother. Alexandra, the ideal soubrette, complete with flowing ribbons, flowers at her bosom, and that dazzling smile. Instinctively, Nicole reached out her hand to touch the picture, tracing the youthful face of her mother. She remembered the love and the sharing. Alexandra's generosity to her little girl. To her company. To her audiences.

Nicole felt suddenly small. As though she weren't living up to the standards her mother had set. Sure, she danced at her peak and gave it her utmost, Nicole thought about herself. But did she give enough to the people who really mattered? Oh Christ! she wailed inwardly, realizing who should matter to her. Tears sprang up in her eyes, dimming the view before her.

"Do you like it?" Billy asked softly, stealing toward her. "I'd been hunting for something special, and when I saw this . . . well, I was pretty sure I'd found it."

She couldn't speak or the tears would overflow. They spilled over anyway. She flung her arms around her husband and kissed him. Once. Twice. He responded gently, treating her like a fragile flower.

"You do like it. I'm glad."

"I love it, Billy," she murmured. "You're too good to me."

"I can never do enough, baby, to show how much you mean to me."

He was so damn well-intentioned. Giving so much of himself. Unfortunately, he expected as much in return. She so rarely could reciprocate. She'd given her hand in marriage to him and the right to love their daughter on his terms. And that was about it. And then he'd turn around and do something wonderful for her. Like the rose and the note. Like the picture of Alexandra. Tonight she owed him, and she would pay up.

"Billy, I . . . I've been so caught up in my work lately," she began. "I'm sorry—"

"Hush," he said, covering her lips with his fingers. "Tonight is just for you."

He led her to the rear terrace, where a candlelit dinner awaited them. He seated her, placed her napkin in her lap, and recited the menu in his worst French accent. Over steak tartare and asparagus tips he plied her with fine burgundy and yarns about the constellations overhead.

"Now that one there," he said, "has been known to be called after the Gemini. Twins, you know. But they've got it all wrong. See, long time ago, this earthly giant—some thought he was immortal—fell in love with a giantess. Paul and Hattie, their names were. Perhaps you've heard of them. I think their last name was something like Binyun, Bunyan—you know what I mean. Well, when the great grand Goddess of Choreography found out about them, she had to do something. Seemed their stompin' was sendin' shivers and shakes all through the land. So she set them a dance to the top of the highest mountain and beyond into the stars. And there she kept them so's everybody could remember a love bigger than all Earth."

Billy was completely charming and funny, and Nicole remembered why she had come to love and trust him when they first met.

She found herself saying, "You were my best friend."

"I want to be again, honey. Will you let me?"

Tears again. Always getting in the way. Blinding her when she most wanted to see and think clearly.

"I'll try," she said, and held out her hand to him.

Without another word he lifted her up, carried her into the house, up to their bedroom, and lay her on the bed. He was tender with her. As he'd been the first time he'd made love to her. Promising he'd make it easy. This time she clung to him. Eyes shut tight. Reaching for the mountaintop with him. Blotting out everything else in the world. Trying to put Carlo out of her thoughts. Trying. And not succeeding.

~~~ 48

Time stood still for no one. Not Billy, who couldn't sustain the sweet moments that degenerated into bitterness at best and jealousy at its worst. Nor Nicole, who couldn't limit her life to an orbit around Billy. She had to dance and make dances or stop breathing. She had to have the best for her company. Within months she had plucked Carlo from Yancy Marklin's tenuous grasp. Certainly, time flew for Carlo, whose aim, all along, had been to dance with Nicole.

By the spring of 1948 he'd become the unconscious leading force of Nicole's company classes. He stood at the most conspicuous barre. He executed center floor work with the first group of dancers. Nicole, along with everyone else, found it difficult to conceal her admiration for the way he pushed himself toward greater goals, for his concentration and intensity, and mostly for the sheer powerful beauty of his class work.

Deliberately, she did not dance with him. Knowing it was the last barrier to keep them apart. Knowing, if he partnered her, his touch would be like Pandora's box. She would open, revealing the urgency, the need, she had for him. The bond she already felt with him.

She knew now that the attraction she first felt for Billy came because they had worked together. He'd been the healing balm she'd needed to soothe the raw wounds Nikki had inflicted. And her partnership with her twin had been a warped version of what she had yearned for with Carlo.

Always it had been Carlo . . . Carlo who shared her love for dance. Carlo who shared her artistic values. Her dreams. Carlo who argued with her. Carlo who prodded her. Carlo who made her feel alive. Who made her feel complete.

Yet Carlo it could never be. Not the way life had turned out. Not as long as she had a husband who doted on her. And a child who tied them together.

So Nicole told Carlo, "Not yet. You may think you're ready, but I don't. Not for what my company does."

A month later she had to say, "Okay. You've got the skills. But not the discipline. Not yet."

Knowing everything she said was a line, a fraud, a postponement of the inevitable. But not yet. She wasn't ready.

How could she be ready? Billy called her three, four times a day at the studio. He hadn't gotten another show. Golf had kept his interest for about three minutes. After taking Lexie to school, there wasn't much to occupy his time. Beulah had threatened to quit if he followed her around the house one more time. And he was trying to keep his promise not to drown his sorrows in drink.

"Come into the city with me," Nicole had begged.

"And be reminded of where I should be? Never."

So he sat by the phone, waiting for his agent to call. When Billy couldn't stand it anymore, he'd picked up the receiver and dialed her. He'd stay on the phone. Letting it ring.

Knowing she would eventually hear it or be hounded into answering. He never had anything to say that mattered. She could always hear the desperation in his voice.

"Am I alive?" he seemed to be asking. "If I yell and scream and carry on and act like a spoiled brat and bother you till you go crazy, will I have proven I love you and need you? Will you love and need me just a little?"

"Not now, Billy," she invariably answered. "This isn't a good time. Can I call you back? I see. You don't want me to tie up the line in case you get a call. Well, what the hell are you doing then, calling me?"

In seconds the spat had escalated so that she sounded like a drill sergeant. Then a nagging bitch. Then a resident of the nearest funny farm.

The phone calls all ended identically with harried screams, a slam, and a white-faced Nicole bursting through the door, apologizing to her troupe for the interruption. They politely brushed aside her excuses, looking at their feet, out the window, never at her. Except Carlo. He was always watching her. Never more intently than after one of these marital skirmishes. She threw herself back into her work, and by the end of class she and the rest of her company were lathered with sweat.

After one such session, punctuated by seemingly nonstop calls from Billy, Nicole headed for the shower, needing to stand under scalding hot water and let it burn the anger out of her. Helplessness too. Torn between wanting to do something for Billy—find some way to put him out of his misery—and to give her complete attention to her company. She was on the verge of an idea. An important one. For another full-length dramatic piece.

Carlo was in front of her. Sauntering his way to the men's room. Exuding confidence. Even in his walk. Slow, sure, and overtly sexy. She found herself staring. At his narrow hips. The firm bunched muscles of his buttocks. Eyes up, she commanded. And her eyes were filled with his sinewy back. Rivulets of sweat descending from the back of his neck down the taut line of his spine. She felt the urge to bring her fingertips forward, to trace the path each bead was taking. Steaming downward. Touch the heat . . . Abruptly she turned away, fingers clenched into a fist. God, how she needed that shower.

She took an exceptionally long one. Long enough, she hoped, for the rest of the company to have left the studio. Turning off the water, she listened for sounds of lingerers. None. She shook the big heavy drops of water from her hair. Wrapping herself in a huge Turkish towel, she padded out of the ladies' room. Only to be startled. Carlo was leaning carelessly against the outer wall of her office.

"Didn't work, did it?" he asked.

"I don't know what you're talking about," she snapped.

"You're still wound up, tight as a watch spring. I can see it even in your hair," he said, lifting a finger to catch a moist curl.

She backed away fast, not wanting his touch. Not wanting to have contact with any man after a day like this one had been.

"Look, I'm tired, Carlo. I've been working hard. I've got this dance to finish . . ."

He stepped toward her. His eyes pinned on hers. Smoldering. Playful. And there was that damned irrepressible grin of his.

His eyes traveled down the towel, stopping at her breasts. "I know what used to work," he said suggestively.

"Don't," she said in a flat voice.

She did not want to play this game with him. She was too old. Too tired. Too weak to keep him from sweeping her up in his arms. Too worn down to shut out his murmurs, soft in her ear.

"Cara," he was whispering, "you're like a wild bird trapped in a cage. Just let me open the door a little. I want you to fly free again. Remember when you used to come to me? So much rage and frustration for a little girl. So many tears. I knew how to make it all go away, if only for a little while. Remember, cara?"

Nicole remembered. Couldn't forget how he listened.

How she'd wanted to hammer her fists on his chest. How he cradled her. Just held her. Till the storm abated. And the passion changed colors. And he'd make love to her. God, how she'd needed him to love her.

It was no different now. He was here, with her. On her side. Understanding. Not fighting. Wanting her. She wanted him. She could touch him. Reach out to him. Be with him.

Carlo reached for her and kissed her. She felt herself responding just as she had when she was young and needy. His kiss blotting out the pain then. His kiss healing the ache in her now. His lips demanding. Hers answering. His arms encircling her. Hers entwined about him.

It was all right. She was all right again. Aware of how her body felt. Her heart pounding. Her skin singing . . . just the towel separating her from him. The touch of him. The smell of him. Her hair entangled in his hands. His lips coursing down her neck. Not by the book this time, she prayed. Not by the . . . Billy. It was Billy who made methodical love. Her husband. What was she doing? She pushed Carlo away and grabbed at the towel before it could fall from her breasts.

"I can't do this, Carlo. Don't ask me to do this," she whispered, pleading with him. "I'm married . . . My husband—"

Carlo shook his head and pulled her toward him again.

"No!" she said.

"You can't let that louse come between us, Nicole. Not now. Not when we've gotten this close."

"He's my husband," she breathed, pleading with him to understand.

"What's he ever done for you I haven't?" demanded Carlo.

"He came back to me," she cried.

"So did I!"

"He married me."

"He just got to you before I could. He got to you in a weak moment."

"For Chrissakes, Carlo, I had his child," she screamed,

and slipping through his grasp, ran for the safety of the bathroom.

"It should've been my child," she heard him yell after her. "God damn it, she should've been mine."

Nicole covered her ears, her whole head. She slid down next to a toilet, her head in her hands, and didn't move. She didn't come out until she was sure Carlo had gone. Until she had heard the studio door close and no more footsteps echoed in her ears.

From then on Nicole made sure she was never alone with him—even when it made sense, like speaking to him in her office. She kept Dominique by her side or Bobby or another of the dancers. Because she knew what was at stake. And she knew that he knew.

She kidded herself into believing there was only one way to take control. One way to be with him yet dominate the relationship. She decided to mount her next dance on Carlo. In public, at least on stage, she could pull his strings the way she knew it must be.

Nicole went into creative seclusion. She spent hours at the studio when no one else was present. Early hours. Late hours. Hours when Lexie and Billy didn't need her.

She turned the reins of conducting everyday class over to the troupe. Each member in turn led the group through the usual exercises and combinations. Each member got the opportunity to add a personal brand. To try a hand at choreographing. The old-timers, such as Dominique and Bobby, were veterans, leading the dancers through bits and pieces of the Varonne repertory. The newcomers were less certain but equally willing.

Except for Carlo. From all reports, Nicole heard that he was sure of himself. Filled with derring-do. He led the class like a master and was an inspiration to everyone.

"You should see him," Bobby said to Nicole one late afternoon as he was leaving the studio and she was just arriving. "There's nothing the man can't do. I'd like to hate him, but he's too damn good. I think I'm in awe."

Another time, Dominique left a note for Nicole. In her

quiet way, the dancer let her boss know that Carlo had passed all tests as far as she was concerned. He was on the right side of marvelous. In fact, he was extraordinary. To see him was a treat. To dance with him . . . Dominique hinted at divinity. Or at least dying and going to heaven. Nicole was a visionary, her dancer thought to point out. But Carlo ranked right up there too. Perhaps Nicole might want to see what he was doing in class. . . . Perhaps it might alter the dance she was composing . . .

Nicole threw the note into a wastebasket. She didn't want to see Carlo in action. Her intent was to contain him. The dance coming out of her latest vision turned on that very point.

The opening curtain would reveal a bare stage with only a single figure on it. But a mighty figure. An omnipotent figure. A totem of many faces and many hands and many powers, appearing as one goddess to mankind.

Each aspect of the goddess would come to life to show the male creature his fallibility, his inferiority. Be he boy, warrior, lover, old man, the lesson was the same. The lesson was inevitable. The dance would have a fatalistic, otherworldly quality pervading every movement. The goddess in any of her forms could act without seeing. The mortal supplicant could see but was reduced to pitiful motions and limited gestures.

In the end, the goddess would triumph as she always did. As she had to.

~~ 49

Nicole returned to the troupe, ready to present the new piece.

"The dance suggests the oneness of the goddess. The fragmentation of the male persona. Because it does, we will populate it in the reverse. One man will take the four parts of the male. Four women will take a different face of the goddess."

Time to name the cast members. Time to let Carlo know she was showcasing him. Her way. She was scared. She couldn't look at him . . .

"Joe will understudy Carlo . . ."

She glanced up from her clipboard for just a moment. He was smiling broadly. Happy. More than happy. Like a cat who had a canary unexpectedly fall from the sky and land between his claws. She gulped and retreated to the unemotional order of her notes.

"Marya, Dominique, Sharon, and I will dance the goddess. I'm thinking of Marya as the Mother, Dominique as the Warrior, myself as the Inamorata, and Sharon as the Primal Dowager. At this point, I'm going by physical type. But I may make changes as the dance progresses. Any questions?"

Carlo's hand shot up. "When do we start?"

"You don't start for another week," she said pointedly. "I plan on starting with the figure of the totem. We four women must learn to think and move as one."

"You're asking too much," came a teasing soprano voice from the back.

"I always ask too much," agreed Nicole. "And then you give it to me. Right, gang?"

The meeting rapidly degenerated into an excited babble of voices. Nicole loved this part of the process. Right before the hard work set in. When the excitement and the anticipation was at its highest. Electricity seemed to crackle through everyone's veins. Not just her own. The stuff of creation was in the air. And success within her grasp.

Carlo was at her side.

"Thank you," he said in deep sincere tones.

"For what?" she asked, still avoiding the eyes that could spear her.

"For giving us a chance."

He considered himself in her debt. It was an interesting concept. The dance she had started between them was going to work. Keeping him in line, on the shortest of leashes, was the only answer. She looked straight at him without hesitation.

"Don't thank me yet."

The four women worked easily together, using full-length and handheld mirrors to maintain the discipline they sought. They studied pictures. Assumed poses. Of Indian and African masks. The implacable face of Buddha. The whole pantheon of Hindu gods and goddesses with their multiple heads, limbs, and functions.

Finally they focused on the wife of Shiva, who, as the divine mother goddess, was known by a thousand names. She was both benevolent and cruel. Womanly yet bloodthirsty. Graceful yet fierce. The giver of life and the bringer of earthly suffering. There were ways to appease her. Gifts. Dancing. Sacrifice. Purification by fire. She was dangerous, unknowable, alluring, and untouchable. She was the very figure Nicole wanted Carlo to contend with.

A few weeks later the entire troupe gathered together to watch the first meeting of the goddess and Carlo. The goddess figure stood atop a great pedestal from which a long string of steps descended. The four dancers who made up the goddess were lined up, one behind the other, tallest in front. So that there appeared one head and one body. With eight arms. And eight feet, fan-shaped, turned inward and out.

When the first goddess separated from her sisters and descended to the floor—the earthly level of man—the totem figure remained, seemingly intact, with a different mask, six arms, six feet. And so on. The goddess figure was wonderful to look at, all the dancers agreed. Any audience would be spellbound.

Then it was Carlo's turn. Bobby had rehearsed him, using Nicole's dance notation. The movements were to be explicit. Not subtle. Of the earth. Big, yet clumsy. Powerful, yet heavy. Passionate, yet vulnerable. Animalistic. And inadequate.

He took his place on the floor, demonstrating a portion of each of the four faces of man. The concentration on Nicole's face slowly turned to concern and then pinched into a frown. It was all wrong. The boy showed all the bright promise of manhood instead of dim-witted brutishness. Carlo gave the warrior intelligence and cunning where Nicole had meant none to be. The lover had become subtly erotic. Nicole could just imagine the press she'd get over this sequence. And the old man had a dignity the goddess was to have shredded long before.

Carlo's interpretation was dead opposite to hers. His male was vibrant, strong, thrilling. More than a worthy opponent. Unconquerable. The fatalism was missing. The subservience was gone. The vision was all askew.

Dominique was the bravest of the dancers.

"The two roles are wonderful, Nicole. Individualistic and compelling. But the unity . . . how will you pull them together? And the theme. It doesn't look much like what you talked about."

It didn't at all.

Nicole beckoned to Carlo, saying to the group, "Maybe it's because we learned the parts separately. Carlo has such stage presence . . . it's hard to imagine the interaction. Let's just get down to work."

Marya, dancing the Mother goddess, and Carlo began their part of the piece. The goddess of all children transcended motherhood. She was bountiful. Beneficent. All loving. And for the life of her didn't seem to notice, much less care about, the single man-boy who bowed down to her. Who offered her beautiful gifts. Gave of himself. Gave his all. She was cold to him. She glided by him without a single ounce of divine humanity. She ignored the boy who only wanted to love his mother, veiling his spirit with her own blindness.

"That's enough," Nicole called out to the struggling duo. "Let's move on."

Come on, Dominique, Nicole prayed silently. Marya was just too inexperienced. Nicole would make a cast change, tone down some of Carlo's emotionality, and the first section would be fine.

Nicole's heart sank. The second section, depicting goddess and man as warriors, was a disaster. Slim as an arrow, fast as the flick of a whip, Dominique was bent on blind revenge. But with Carlo as the blazing samurai, the white knight lusty with honor and might, she looked stupid. Silly. Like a rodeo clown knocked from her perch. The effect Nicole had been after was lost, long before tittering, poorly muffled, escaped from the rest of the troupe. Where was the goddess warrior? Nicole wailed internally. What had happened to her vision?

Carlo had happened. The suppressed quality of movement she generally pulled from her male dancers—that limited, suggested latency that came naturally to Bobby and Joe—was foreign to Carlo. Alien. His physical strength, the way he seemed to occupy a whole room, his surprising buoyancy, had nothing in common with the direction of her choreography.

What was she to do? Abandon the project there and then? Do what Yancy Marklin had done? Provide a showcase for Carlo on Carlo's terms? Let him go? No!

"Everyone," she began, addressing her company, "I apologize. The piece isn't as ready as I thought it was. Not all dances come easy. Especially those that really matter, that have something different to say."

She saw heads bobbing up and down in acknowledgment.

"We'll continue to hold class, but don't plan on rehearsal time for a while. Carlo? Can you make yourself available full-time for a week or two? You and I have a lot of work ahead of us."

What else was she to do? She'd have to work with him alone if the dance were to succeed. If he were to be a part of her company.

They worked nonstop for several days. Nicole endlessly changed his gestures, his combinations. Anything to reduce him. To limit his vibrancy. To maintain the superiority of the goddess. And Carlo tried. He diligently attempted every alteration Nicole thought up. He struggled valiantly with them. By week's end she and Carlo were exhausted and had made no progress at all.

"Give it up, Nicole," he urged. "We'll do something else."

"Never," she cried adamantly. "I never give in."

Carlo grabbed a towel and wiped the sweat from him. He plunked down on the floor, apparently settling in for good.

"Three cheers for principles," he said with open sarcasm. "Look, Nicole, face it. This is not working."

"You think you have to tell me that? I know it's not working. What's eating at me is why. I've never had trouble like this before."

"I know," Carlo said quietly. "The dancers always conform to the choreographer. It's the unwritten rule we always said we'd break, remember?"

She stared at him, her mouth agape.

"We were going to dance free. Remember? Well, I still do. If you're choreographing for me, you've got to start from there."

How could he sit there, lazily, on the floor, *her* floor, and say those things to her? She could feel her blood start to boil.

"Choreographing for *you?* You're dancing for *me.* In my company."

"But I'm not like the others, am I? It's not me you're trying to control. It's yourself. Admit it."

He was egging her on, hoping she would burst and become so emotional she'd cave in, asking him to fix it for her.

"What's happened to you, Nicole? You used to like me the way I was. Don't you remember how good it was between us?"

Damn him. He was remorseless. Relentless. I should just turn on my heels and walk out, she thought. I should—

He picked himself up off the floor and in a flash was lifting her off the ground. Swinging her. Spinning her in the air. Tossing and catching her. Holding her high above him at the mercy of his strong arms.

"Put me down," she demanded.

"Like this?"

Slowly he slid her down so that every part of her body touched a part of his. When her feet had touched the ground, he didn't quite let go. He slipped his hands from her waist up the sides of her breasts. Over the round of her shoulders. Along her neck and under her chin so that her head was tilted toward his. She could feel his breath heat her skin.

"I know you want me," he said, with the hard quiet edge of absolute certainty. "I can feel you wanting me."

In an instant she broke away from him, slapping him across his impudent face.

"We may dance together, and I emphasize the word *may*, but that's all, Carlo Domenici. I've made vows. . . . You remember that word, don't you? Vows of matrimony. Unlike some people who happen to be standing in this room, I keep my word."

Carlo didn't give her an inch.

"Those vows aren't meant to keep two people together who make each other completely miserable . . . no matter what the Church says. Don't try to tell me you're not miserable. I've seen the man and I've heard the phone calls."

She slapped him again. As hard as she could.

"How dare you!" she screamed. "You self-righteous bastard! It's all right for you to leave the woman you supposedly love for years on end to satisfy your vows. But mine can go in the toilet as soon as you're satisfied and ready."

"Playing the same record, again?" he goaded. "Aren't you bored with it yet? I know I am."

He was obviously enjoying every second of their argument. She wasn't. She hated him for making her blood run hot, but she was damned if she'd let him know. She'd show him that ice ran in her veins.

"Mr. Domenici," she stated, coldly formal, "if you want to stay in this company, you'd better show me the same respect all my dancers show me. I direct this troupe. No one manhandles me. No one."

Carlo, never undone, responded with a swift military salute.

"I can follow orders . . . if that's all you really want from me."

50

The rehearsals continued, and went nowhere. Carlo gave her precisely what she asked for. Gentlemanly, cool professionalism. Nicole talked about the emotions in her dance as though she were dissecting a steer for the butcher shop. She intellectualized and analyzed each sequence of steps to death. The results . . . there were no results. Just exhausting rehashes. Exercises in frustration.

Carlo and she were working on the third segment, where Man played the lover to the goddess. They were sprawled on the floor, seemingly in mortal—or was it immortal?—combat.

"Think of it this way," groaned Nicole. "The goddess is the queen bee and the mortal is her drone. Her worker. Her slave. There to do her bidding."

"I'm trying," he replied as calmly as possible. "It's just hard to find the motivation, much less the interest, in playing a brainless idiot spraying seed on command."

"Just follow my lead. Okay. Where's your arm? It's supposed to be stretched back over your head. There. Now bend that leg in deepest plié. Lean into me. Don't loom. You're supposed to be begging the goddess. Reverently."

"Nicole," Carlo grunted, "you're squeezing blood from a pretzel. There's only so much even I can do." He broke away from the unnatural position, arched his back for relief, and sank back to the floor, adding, "Let me show you something I thought of last night . . . after we threw in the towel."

He flexed himself over her, entwining his legs about her torso and raising her off the ground. With a quick flip she was bound in his arms and . . .

"No," she said adamantly. "We'll do it my way."

They rolled about the dusty floor, grinding sweat and grit into Carlo's flesh-colored tights and Nicole's flesh-colored leotard. They were locked in conflict. Locked in unearthly embrace. Two heads. Assorted appendages. One torso molded onto the other. Unaware of anything but the dance. The struggle. The tension they were building between male and female.

They were unaware of Billy, who had walked into the studio and stood there. His mouth was wide open. His eyes were narrowing. His feet were frozen, paralyzed by the scene before him.

"Can't take me for a goddamned fool," he mumbled. "I know what I see . . ."

He was moving. Running. Hopping. Wedging himself between the body parts on the floor and pulling at Nicole, yanking her to her feet. His face was lobster red.

"This isn't dance. It's shit! No wife of mine is doing this in front of an audience," he roared, his voice cracking with embarrassment. "Do you know what it looks like? The two of you naked . . . humping before the whole world. How could you do this to me, Nicole? How long've the two of you been screwing around like this behind my back?"

Nicole was furious. She tore herself from his grip, glaring at him as though he were criminally insane.

"What the hell are you talking about? This is modern dance! We're fully clothed, for Chrissakes! We're working on the goddess piece."

"Don't try to pull the wool over my eyes," Billy snarled. "I'm a song and dance man. A hoofer. You think I don't know the difference between dancing and fucking?" He turned on Carlo next, jabbing a finger at his bare chest, shouting, "Tell me you haven't been to bed with her. Tell me you haven't had her right here on this fucking floor!"

Carlo's eyes hardened and he flicked Billy's hand away. In an instant he seized the lapels of Billy's coat and jerked him forward.

"You're way out of line, buster. Apologize to the lady."

It was Nicole's turn to intervene. She brushed the clenched muscles of Carlo's arm and signaled him to leave.

"I can handle this," she said. "You'll only make it worse."

"I can wait."

"No."

Carlo left reluctantly, tossing several backward glances before closing the studio door. The room became deathly still, except for the sound of Billy's breathing. Impassioned. Soblike. Nicole took a deep breath of her own, seeking calm.

"Look, Billy, I can only think of two things to say to you right now. One you want to hear. One I have to say. First, I have been faithful to you. Either you believe me and trust me, or you don't. Second, I am a professional. Dance is my career. Not my hobby. I'm working my brains out trying to meet a deadline on a project, and I'm stuck. I've got a sequence that won't work, and it just happens to be a love scene. How many love scenes have I seen you in, Billy? Did I tear your costar's hair out? Did I come raging into your rehearsals like a wounded cow?"

"I know what I saw," he said stubbornly.

"You mean you know what it looked like," Nicole suggested. "You've got to get a grip on yourself, Billy. I've put up with the phone calls. The ridiculous requests and the stupid fights you start. The constant interruptions. I'm telling you right now—are you listening?—I won't put up with it anymore. One more stunt like this and we're through. I'll take Lexie and—"

She had to stop. Billy had raised his hand as if he were going to hit her. She stared at him. At his upraised arm, full of suspended rage. If he exploded . . .

But he didn't. Slowly the hand came down. His head lowered and he was muttering to her.

"I thought you'd be glad to see me. I thought if I came into town when you weren't expecting me, if I surprised you . . . Then I saw you with that guy. I didn't know what else to do. The two of you looked so intimate . . . I was jealous. I'm afraid we're not . . . that way anymore."

"Why do you torture yourself?" she asked, shaking her head at him.

She adjusted his coat, straightened his tie, and smoothed his ruffled hair. "Let's just go home, Billy. It's been a long day."

She took his hand and led him out as though he were a little boy. She drove them home, pretending not to notice the slugs he stole from his pocket flask. By the time they reached Long Island, he was helpless. She had to put him to bed. Exhausted, she went to bed too. But not to sleep. Billy took possession of her hands, holding them tightly even after he'd dropped off.

She couldn't find a place for herself. Taut with frustration and a growing despair, she managed to slip out of bed without disturbing Billy. Oh hell, she thought. Nothing was going to bother him tonight. She tiptoed past Lexie's door and went downstairs. Like the old days, she turned to her music. She riffled through the large selection of albums and tapes, but she really had no choice. There was one thing weighing on her mind, and she had to resolve it.

In a moment the all too familiar biting whine of an Indian raga slithered into her ears in the dark room. It seeped through the pores of her skin, penetrating and igniting her. She danced the role of the man the way she had envisioned it. The movements should have worked. They fit the mood and rhythms of the music. Why weren't they right? Why couldn't Carlo dance them right? She repeated the steps and made up variations of them, trying any old combination.

She ended up on the floor, caught in the same web of gyrations she'd been trying to perfect for hours . . . days. Then she was flailing her limbs. Kicking outward. Trying to break away. Break out. Surrounded by the frustration. The limitation. The strangulating of her work. The vision was fading. Her creativity was enchained. Not again, she wanted to yell and scream. I won't go through it again.

"My God, Nicole, I'm sorry."

Billy. At her side. Down on the floor on hands and knees. What was he doing there?

"I know it's my fault," he was saying. "Just get up and dance. Lemme help. I'll dance with you. 'Member how you used to ask me to dance with you the last time . . . before the war? I wasn't any good to you then, but I wanna help now. I'll do anything, baby."

He thought it was all about him. The earth . . . and Nicole . . . still revolved around Billy Gable. Good or bad or indifferent.

"Please, honey, dance any way you want. I won't interrupt you anymore. I promise. Just don't leave me."

A tiny part of her was touched by his conciliatory attempts. But she was so riled up by the damn puzzle that wouldn't crack, Billy's presence only irritated her.

"It's got nothing to do with you. It's this godforsaken thing I'm doing with Carlo. It won't come right."

"Carlo," Billy repeated.

In the dark, Nicole didn't see his jaw tighten.

"I see. So I was right the first time."

Nicole flopped flat on the floor, sighing, "Billy, I'm tired. Stop being such an ass and go to bed. This has nothing to do with you and me."

Hoisting himself up, he muttered, "It better not," and left her alone.

She watched his lonely figure climb the stairs in retreat. In the background the raga was whipping itself into a frenzy, building to the point of orgiastic release. In the dance Carlo and she—she meant Man and the goddess—were supposed to be heaving to the cosmic vibrations of a great orgasm. That was Orgasm with a capital O. She rolled herself up into a ball. Orgasm be damned. Nothing was coming tonight.

Nicole gathered up the tattered bits of her dance and decided it was now or never. If her dancers approved of the work, then it would be all right. Carlo had done the best he could do. Maybe the problem was with her. Maybe she just couldn't be satisfied. Maybe she just couldn't see clearly.

She called it a workshop but it felt like opening night. She felt sickeningly nervous. As bad as the first time she'd presented a dance. Taking complete responsibility, she dismissed the other women from their roles. The damn piece would live or die because of what she alone could imbue in it.

She and Carlo began the dance of the Mother Goddess. Despite the mature dignity Nicole gave to her role, Carlo's flashing upstart of a boy jangled with the message. He was no more in awe of the goddess than a thief with a penny. The dance made no sense. The battle of the warriors was another mismatch. By the time the seduction in the third part had started and it was impossible to tell who was seducing whom, Nicole surrendered.

"That's it," she said grimly. "Just forget it. I can't do this anymore."

She trudged across the studio floor and dragged the needle across the record. Then she stomped out and raced to her office. She banged the door shut and sat at her desk with her hands covering her face. In a minute Carlo entered and quietly sat opposite her.

"What are we going to do?" he asked.

She lifted her head and looked at him. Just looked. She was fresh out of answers.

"It's not going to work," she admitted wearily. "I can't make it happen between us."

"No, it's not. Not as long as you're hung up on these fantasies of yours."

"Fantasies?" she said. "What the hell do you mean?"

"Don't you see, Nicole? You're stuck on one theme with a dozen little variations to it. All about the suffering majesty of earth mothers who are constantly beleaguered by lots of bad little boys."

"Excuse me for wasting your time! Excuse me for thinking that I could offer something of value. Like a dramatic vision of the way life is."

"I can't dance it with you, Nicole. I can't because I don't believe in it. There are plenty of dancers who can give you what you want. They separate their personal identities from their professional ones. We don't do that, neither one of us. You and I dance who we are."

He was absolutely right. He'd grown. Matured. Experienced life, love, and war. Yet Carlo, at thirty-two, danced with the same verve, the same joy and abandon, she'd first seen in him as a teenager. He'd been able to steer his own course past obstacles and disappointments. He'd triumphed despite them. As for her, each twist of fate had turned her further away from the child she'd once been. The innocent girl who'd laughed, soaring in Carlo's arms. They both danced exactly as they were. A world apart.

"If you can't," she said slowly, realizing the message she was conveying, "then . . . I guess . . . you're out."

"It's too bad, cara. Too bad you've stopped challenging yourself. The Nicole I know—I knew—would never have settled for threadbare fairy tales. Or a lukewarm husband," he added.

"Thank you for that tidbit of Domenici wisdom. It comes straight from the clouds. Where your head always was. Stop dreaming, Carlo. This is the real world. You know? The one where we don't live happily ever after."

"That's not my world. I won't accept it that way."

"And you say I live in a fairy-tale world."

He stood up, leaned over the desk, took her hand and pressed his lips to her fingertips. "Then this is goodbye, cara."

"What do you mean goodbye? You're out of the dance. Not out of the company."

"I don't think so. There's not much of a future in being the star of the class."

She was losing him again. This time by her own design. He would fly away, free of her. And she was left behind. With her albatross of a dance to comfort her.

"Merde," she muttered after him, and she really didn't mean "good luck" at all.

Carlo went to the men's room to clear out his belongings. Nicole returned to the studio.

"If you'll indulge me one more time, we're going to try it again," she told her dancers. "And Joe, I want you to play the role of Man. Marya, Sharon, Dominique, please take your places too. We're going to do it the way I first intended it. Complete with the totem goddess. Who's gonna help me haul out that damn pedestal?"

The piece worked. The goddess triumphed in each scene. The mortal was properly slavish. Nicole had another bravura drama on her hands. Despite her dancers' congratulations, she felt empty. As though she had settled for something less than perfect. Something that barely satisfied.

51

Nicole closed her eyes. The dance worked and that was that.
It was presentable. A more than acceptable addition to the
Varonne repertoire. If Carlo couldn't handle it—had to
judge it, find it wanting, find her wanting—then too bad.
That was his problem, not hers. She had no problems, she
told herself. Not when it came to dance. If she were
clear-sighted about anything in her life, it was her dances.
What she wanted to say. How she said it.

That's what she told herself when she first woke up in the
morning and the only image in her head was Carlo shaking
his head disapprovingly, the slightest hint of pity crossing
his face. She'd drown him out with visions of the next dance
piece she was working on by beating time on the edge of the
sink with her toothbrush or staring into the mirror, erasing
his eyes where hers should have been.

That's what she told herself. At the studio, with her hand
clutching the barre too tightly, gearing up to set her newest
steps into the flow of her dance and worried if they would
work. If her dancers could execute them. Finally feeling the
fear dissipate as she danced. And her dancers faithfully,
skillfully, brought her latest conception to life.

That's what she told herself. When she was too tired to
move or think. When all she could do was lie down on the
leatherette sofa in her office as her mind played tricks on
her. Conjuring up Carlo. Dancing like the whirlwind. Clut-
tering up her life. Confusing her. Making her doubt herself.
Making her wonder if he was right.

No. He was wrong. As wrong and blind and pigheaded as
any one person could be. She'd prove him wrong. Better yet,
she'd ignore him. Forget him. After all, she reminded
herself, when had she ever let anybody's opinions influence
her? Potshots. That's all they'd been. When he didn't know
how else to explain his inability to follow her lead. There

was no excuse. No reason to let his parting potshots affect her.

She'd show him. She wasn't settling for second best. Her choices, her decisions, were justifiable. Mature. They showed wisdom. And a knowledge of how the world worked. She had learned well how to manage her life. How to make compromises and adjustments. She'd show them. Show them all. Carlo . . . her audiences . . . Billy . . .

If there were rips in the fabric of her life, she determined to darn them too. And redarn them if necessary. For the rest of the year Nicole adjusted her hours to regular, shorter ones at the studio. What bristling new idea didn't get choreographed one day got worked on the following day. When the next performance season rolled around, she was ready with three new pieces. Maybe not as many as she might've had if she'd gone at her normal breakneck speed, but solid. Presentable. So she told herself.

In the meanwhile, with her orderly extra time, she cooked breakfast daily and dinner nightly for Billy and Lexie. Lexie was the star of the table, making eyes at her daddy and poems for her mommy. Nicole became the one to plan little excursions for the family, including a summery week's getaway to one of those resorts in the Catskills.

Billy immediately fell in with a crowd of first and second bananas, all of whom had long since made the transition from vaudeville to Broadway to radio. One old friend was looking for an emcee who could sing for his new variety hour. Billy landed the job on the spot. He was never happier. His clever wife was managing to have a fine little career and be a first-rate homemaker too. He sighed with relief when he learned through channels of his own that the wife-stealer, Domenici, had gone back to England. All was safe and well on the Gable home front.

Except for Nicole. She was doing everything she thought she was supposed to do. The way it was supposed to be done. Billy was thriving. He'd cut out the liquor entirely, and it was nice to see him enjoying his life and his daughter again. Lexie, of course, was blooming with all the attention she got. Nicole couldn't help feeling that Lexie would have bloomed if the sun forgot to rise. She was just that kind of child. The kind Nicole had once been when Alexandra called her "sunbeam."

But Nicole felt . . . flat. There was no other word for it. Like a dimension was missing to the world or in her. She woke up each morning and went through the motions of her daily routine. Once a week she dutifully tussled with Billy under the covers, usually the night after his broadcast. She slept. Dreamless. Then woke up to do it all over again. And again. Flat. Deflated. The days, weeks, months piled up. Weighing on her. Preying on her.

It wasn't only the monotony of her life that made her feel as though she were in prison, shuffling from cell to cell under the ever-present, watchful eye of Warden Billy Sunshine. She felt tight in her own skin. Like a pupa stuck overlong in its cocoon. Or a snake that forgot to shed its last coat of scales. Something inside was holding her down. Holding her back. Keeping her from the challenges. Diverting her from the course of life. Her life was slipping away. Her life. Her way.

Even during the course of the fall '48–winter '49 dance season. Her works were heralded. As usual. Her fans seemed to become more fanatical. Her detractors more appalled. The critics evenly split on the contribution she was continuing to make to modern dance.

Walking on stage to receive her plaudits should have thrilled her. Made her feel the most alive. Here in the home of the arts where inspiration and creativity were revered . . . Where she assumed the mask of a goddess . . .

Something vital was missing. Something unplanned. Disorderly. A little tumult. A fresh breeze . . . wind . . . storm. Bringing the breath of life. New ideas. Spirit. She needed a change or she would drown in the dust that seemed to pervade her life.

She felt little more than a wooden doll when Billy made love to her now. But how could she feel more when it was always the same?

Maybe she would have put up with it longer, looking for the canker in herself and settling for each disappointment,

Nicole thought. But she knew she had to bring this pain to an end when it erupted from another source. One she would not endure.

Lexie was a busy sleeper. Tossing her blankets off. Turning this way and that. Often ending up at the foot of the bed or splayed out sideways so that her limbs hung over the edge. But she slept all night long and always woke refreshed. Until the performance season had begun. When Billy thought it would be fun to play with his little girl all day long. And longer, when Nicole couldn't make it home to tuck Lexie into bed. At first Nicole thought she was waking her daughter up. Making too much noise when she got home.

"I'm sorry, baby," she would say. "Mama wore her elephant shoes home by mistake."

But after several nights of still finding her child fitfully, fretfully awake past midnight, Nicole had to take action.

"What's the matter, darling?" she finally asked.

"Dunno," Lexie answered, rubbing her eyes with balled-up fists.

"Maybe it's just a bad dream," Nicole said, trying to reassure her daughter. "Lots of children have them for a little while. Then they just go away."

"I haven't been to sleep yet, Mommy. I can't sleep."

She moved restlessly under the covers.

"Can't get comfortable, Lexie?"

Another shrug. A sigh. A frown.

"Tell Mommy what you did today," Nicole prodded. "What happened at school?"

"Daddy didn't take me to school today."

Nicole was dumbfounded.

"Didn't take you . . ." she echoed. "Well, what did you do?"

The list began. Breakfast at a pancake house. In New Jersey! Then a race back to Billy's country club for a tennis lesson. And a golf lesson. For a preschooler! Then they had lunch . . . well, they shared a hot dog aboard the Staten Island ferry and grabbed another on their way to the zoo. Except Lexie fell asleep in a hansom cab and woke up on the living room couch. And there was her daddy with an

armload of games and toys and dolls. They played Candy-
land and dominoes and Mr. Potato Head and built all kinds
of strange things with Tinker Toys and all kinds of forts with
Lincoln Logs. Dinner was late, but it was a tea party with
Raggedy Ann and Andy and Raggedy Billy and Lexie. After
dinner they toasted marshmallows and danced. Something
called a Jitterybug. Or was it a Lindy hopper?

"Why do Daddy's dances all sound like insects?" Lexie
wanted to know, yawning and curling up against her mother's warmth.

"I don't know, sweetie. But what a big day you had!
Daddy must have spent all week planning such a special
time for you."

"I don't know, Mommy, 'cause we've been having big
days for a long time."

An uneasy feeling spread over Nicole.

"When's the last time you went to school, baby?"

Lexie yawned again, saying, "Weeks and weeks ago.
Daddy said I was his best girl and his best friend. Best
friends are supposed to play together all the time. But
Mommy," she added earnestly, "couldn't I just be his
daughter? Do I have to be his best friend too?"

Nicole clasped Lexie tightly and rocked. It was too much.
Billy was too much. Overwhelming his little girl with his
own need. Leaving his mark on Lexie. As he had on her,
Nicole thought. How she had paid. She'd be damned if she'd
let the same thing happen to her daughter. She'd stop him.
One way or another.

When the season came to an end, she gathered her
dancers together.

"This coming summer marks a personal milestone for
me. It will mark the beginning of a new decade for me,
eleven years that I've been back in the U.S. They have been
solidly creative years that I'm immensely proud of . . . years
of very hard work. I've been thinking it's the appropriate
time to take the company on tour. A major retrospective of
my work and a showcase for you who've brought my ideas to
life. I need you all. Will you come?"

The response was unequivocally positive. Now all she had

to do was break the news to Billy. Tell him his world was about to shatter. What time was the right time to deliver that kind of blow? Right away to give him time to prepare? Time to carry on and make life miserable until she left? Or not until the last second when, like a bomb, the truth exploded and he had no time to feel the pain? Just the shock.

She began to lay the groundwork. First, she let him know she was thinking about a tour. The next time she mentioned it, she casually suggested the summer months as a strong possibility. Then as a likelihood. Finally as a fact. She would be leaving in early June.

Their last night together, Nicole planned a quiet dinner at home for two, with Lexie fed and popped into bed early. She made Billy's favorite meal. Not the restaurant food he pretended to fancy. But honest, home-style food that Mother Gable had reared him on. Pot roast with mashed potatoes. Cooked carrots. Strained applesauce flavored with cinnamon. An ice cream sundae for dessert.

He loved every second, every smidgen of it. When she told him she wanted to talk to him about something important, about the tour, he got downright excited.

"Let's go into the living room, honey. Put our feet up on the sofa like two old folks. Better yet, sit on my lap. Or would you like me to give you an old-fashioned foot massage?"

"No, Billy, I think we're better off here at the table."

"Anything that makes you happy . . . Now, what do you want to tell Papa?"

How to start? Where to start? She'd had weeks to rehearse her speech. Choose just the right words. There were no right words.

"Billy, I know you've been happier—"

"Happier!" he burst in. "I haven't felt this swell in nine or ten years. 'Cept when I found out about Lexie. And when you said you'd marry me."

"Well, Billy, I've tried. I really have. To be happy. With you and Lexie. Balancing a career and a marriage—"

"I never thought it would work either," said Billy, interrupting again. "I always wanted you to choose one or the other. Well, really, only one. Me. But you've pulled it off, honey."

"No I haven't," she said quietly. "That's what I have to tell you."

"You mean you're giving up this silly tour?"

The sheer ecstasy on his face was like a dead weight sinking into her heart. Ball, chain, and all. Then the chain snapped. She'd been beating the life out of herself for this man and his idea of what a family should be. For nothing. He'd never understood her. Never valued her for herself. Took her for granted. Expecting her to be the constant satellite around his star. The story was so damned familiar. She'd recognized it and purposely ignored it. Billy and she were the next generation's Vanya and Alexandra. The decision Nicole had finally reached was the same one her mother had come to years ago. She found herself chuckling and then roaring with laughter.

"Did I say something funny?" Billy asked, his brow knit in confusion.

"I'm sorry; it's not funny at all," she said, wiping the bitter smile from her face. "Look. There's no easy way to say this. So I'll just say it. I'm not happy. I haven't been happy for a long time. Nothing is working for me. The dance. The marriage. I'm empty, Billy. Just going through the motions."

"It's that Carlo character," Billy yelled, jumping to his feet, upsetting wine goblets, water glasses, his chair. "It's his fault. Everything was fine before he came along."

"Billy, sit down. Please. Just think back. Our marriage was on the rocks long before Carlo came back into my life."

Billy loomed over the dining table, gripping it with both hands. His knuckles grew white with outrage. The table quivered beneath his grip.

"He wasn't just one of your dancers. Admit it, Nicole. Tell me the truth this time. You were having an affair with him. Right under my nose."

The same old ground. Nicole was so weary of it. Billy always translating her problems into his personal injuries.

"No, Billy. I never did. I haven't been unfaithful to you,

although God knows you've given me enough reason to. Now sit down. Please. We can discuss this like grown-ups. I don't want Lexie to hear us arguing."

He glared at her belligerently and paced the room, not taking his eyes from her. "What the hell has the last twelve months been about, Nicole? Soften old Billy boy up for the kill?"

"I'm not assigning blame, Billy. I'm finally trying to take responsibility for my mistakes."

"Oh, right. Mistake number one: our marriage. Or is the first name on your list Alexis Gable?"

"Billy, I know you're shocked and hurt, and I'm sorry. But I've thought it all out and this is how it's going to be."

He stopped midstep, saying, "Wait a minute. Wait just a goddamn minute. You're telling me I have no say here?"

"I mean there's no other way," she said.

She reached out a hand to him as if to soften the blows to come. Then retracted it when she saw his eyes. The pain darkening and twisting into a storm.

"The tour is really convenient, you see. We'll be apart a couple of months. Till the end of summer. It'll give you enough time to get adjusted to our absence."

"Our absence? What do you mean 'our' absence?"

"Lexie's coming with me, of course. She'll just miss a few weeks of nursery school and—"

Billy stalked toward her. The thought flashed through her mind he might hit her.

"You bitch!" he snarled. "You can't take my daughter away from me."

He wanted to hit her. She saw it in his eyes. In the way he loomed over her, wanting to strangle her. Not wanting to touch her at all. Nicole felt his heartbreak as though it were her own. This is what it had been like when her own parents had separated, she realized, each wanting to keep some semblance of family intact. Each ending up with half a family. One child allotted to one parent. And in Billy's case, no child with which to pretend all was still right with the world.

"What can I say, Billy?" she whispered, her heart breaking for him. "We have no choice. If we stayed together, we'd both end up miserable, hating each other and giving nothing to Lexie. Isn't it better that we find what's best for each of us? So that we can give Lexie the best parts of ourselves?"

"I want her," he rasped. "I want her with me."

"I know you do," she said, trying to sound soothing. "I know how much this hurts. But I'm her mother."

"Well, I'm her father," Billy retorted, "and I have just as much right—"

"No court in the world would take a child away from its mother. You know that, Billy."

Billy began to pace again. His tone changed from outrage to deep concern.

"My God, Nicole, you know what the road is like. A different motel room every few nights. If you're lucky, a hotel. If you're not, a boardinghouse, for God's sake. And she'll be eating God knows what at all sorts of odd hours."

Billy paraded through his list of domestic nightmares as if he knew them by heart.

"You won't even know if something happens to her. You'll be performing . . . she could be trapped in a burning building . . ."

And on and on and on.

"Billy, Billy . . . no," she said, finally getting a word in edgewise. "It won't be like that. I promise you. Touring is a wonderful life. I never had so much fun or learned so many different things than when I went touring with my mother."

"A wonderful life," he scoffed. "Oh yes. How stupid of me. After all, it made you what you are today: a woman incapable of committing herself to anyone or anything. A rootless, heartless bitch."

She had pushed him. Caused him to spit the venom at her. But it hurt just the same. And it made her hate him a little bit more. Made her backbone all the stronger.

"Then you won't be missing me very much," she said woodenly, pushed her chair back and walked out of the room.

"You can go with my blessing," he yelled to her back. "But don't think you can take my flesh and blood away from me and get away with it."

Nicole went straight up to her bedroom and packed her bags. Then she packed suitcases for Lexie. She slept in the spare bedroom and in the morning woke her daughter up at dawn.

"Mama's taking you on a special trip, darling. Just the two of us. And Mama's dancers."

"Is Daddy coming?" the little girl inquired anxiously.

"Not this time, sweetheart. But next time, you and Daddy can go someplace very exciting together."

"To Gramma Gable's house?"

Nicole kissed the top of her daughter's head and whispered, "Lexie's such a clever girl. Daddy would like that very much, I think. Now you get dressed while Mama calls a taxi."

"Should I kiss Daddy goodbye?"

"I don't think he's awake, dear."

But he was. Standing grim as a stone sentinel by the front door in yesterday's clothes.

"You'll be sorry, Nicole," he muttered.

"I am sorry, Billy, but there's no other way." She turned to her daughter and caught her hand, prompting, "Say bye-bye to Daddy."

Lexie was suddenly shy, and hid her face in her mother's skirt. Nicole hustled the child outside and into the waiting cab.

"You're not sorry enough, Nicole. Not nearly sorry enough," Billy grumbled to himself as he watched the yellow car drive away.

When it was completely gone from view, Billy headed for the telephone and dialed.

"Scott's Detective Agency? Mr. Scott, please."

He doodled nervously on a pad of paper beside the phone. Bold x's filled the page and then another page.

"Mr. Scott? This is Billy Gable. I'm fine, thanks. I have another job for you. No, nothing to do with Mr. Domenici this time. It's my wife. I want her followed. I want proof that she's an adulteress, a degenerate, an unfit mother. Do whatever you have to do. I want evidence that's gonna stick. Yeah, that's right. For a divorce and custody case. And Mr. Scott? Send out your biggest guns."

He hung up. His mouth was dry. Ransacking the liquor cabinet, he lugged his quarry upstairs to the bedroom. Throwing the bottles onto the bed, he unbuttoned his shirt and took off his shoes.

"If ever I deserved to get blind, stinking drunk, it's now," he muttered.

~~ **52**

Three days later and stone sober, Billy met with his attorney.

"This isn't my area of expertise," George Barlow said. "I can recommend a good man in the field though. A savage, if that's what you really want. But let me give you some common sense advice, Billy—get you thinking the way a divorce lawyer might handle a case like yours these days."

"You think I have a case, then?" prodded Billy. "I don't just want to win. I've got to win."

Barlow pushed his horn-rimmed glasses down toward the tip of his nose and leaned forward over his desk.

"Then you're going to need more than whatever garbage a private eye can dish up. Sure, maybe you'll be lucky. The guy will come back with steamy pictures of your wife in bed with a Negro. Better yet, three Negroes, at the same time. No judge can overlook that. But what if you're not so lucky? How can you provide for a minor any better than your wife?

"Let's look at the evidence," Barlow continued, counting off point by point on his fingers. "You're in the arts. A Broadway and radio personality. Negative. You work at night . . . when you're working. Sleep by day. Two negatives. You come equipped with a housekeeper and maybe a chauffeur. Big deal. You've got servants. It doesn't quite fill the bill. It may be your idea of the all-American dream, but it won't wash with a judge who believes in mom-and-pop stores or nine-to-five jobs or a neighborhood school within skipping distance.

"If you want your daughter, you're going to have to make some sacrifices. Respectability, son. That's the name of the game for the 1950s. Hell, what do you think we fought in the war for? So dear old Mom can safely and securely bake her apple pies. So little Junior can grow up with a nice savings account and go to college. So little Babs can marry the boy of her dreams. And you and I, old-timer, can rest on our laurels and congratulate each other at the golf course with a five-iron in one hand and a dry martini in the other."

Billy nodded, his eyes narrowing. "I get the picture, George. I know what I have to do."

While Nicole was on tour, Billy went on his own plan of attack. He put the Long Island house up for sale and began to cut his ties with the New York entertainment circle. He let his agent go. He broke his radio contract, citing personal crisis.

He told his friend who'd given him the job, "You understand, don'cha, Buddy? I gotta fight for my kid. I'd do anything for that little girl. She's a part of me. If I lost her . . . Well, I just can't lose her. I'm gonna take her back home where it's safe for a kid to grow up."

Luckily, Buddy understood. He'd lost a couple of kids himself. With the proceeds from the sale of the house and the bonus Buddy gave him for staying on an extra month, Billy had a tidy nest egg. Four days out of seven he spent in Indiana, living with his family on their farm. He took his money and invested it. In housing developments that were springing up all over the Midwest and mid-Atlantic states. In his own town of Harmony Grove and half a dozen little towns along the White River. And in building the sweetest house a little girl could fancy at the edge of his family's property.

By the time he had to go to court, he'd be ready to offer the ideal American dream that no judge could turn down. Small-town life. Grandparents, aunts and uncles, cousins climbing out of the woodwork. A rural public school. As normal a life as anyone could have. An apple pie of a life, served up on a tray with a scoop of ice cream, a squirt of whipped cream, and a cherry on top. Billy could imagine George Barlow pointing to each finger on his hand. Positive . . . positive . . . positive . . . Unbeatable was what Billy hoped for.

Meanwhile, Nicole led her version of a normal life. The tour was a success. Lexie had a ball and was never left alone. It was old hat to Nicole. Alexandra had taught her well. When the tour was over, mother and daughter went home to Greenwich Village. Nicole rented an entire floor from Myrtle Fudderman, who still insisted on wearing loud housedresses, high-heeled mules, and curlers in her hair.

"What's the point in changin'?" she said to Nicole. "I'm never out of style for long. The day Macy's runs outta models' coats and slippers is the day I retire."

The Varonnes' life went on. Lexie was enrolled in kindergarten for the fall semester. Nicole repaired to her studio to work on the next season's worth of dances. She did nothing else to alter the way she lived or cared for Lexie. Except to hire a lawyer to represent her side in the pending divorce and custody hearing. Someone she considered would be fair. Her other concession was to ask Dominique to stay with the child during the courtroom proceedings.

The first day, Nicole went alone, meeting her attorney at the courthouse. Billy showed up with an entourage. Lawyers. Reporters. Secretaries. Photographers. The opening argument came as a shock to Nicole. It had little to do with the plain facts of incompatibility. Less to do with Lexie's happiness. Nothing to do with balancing the scales of justice. Billy's attorney was on the warpath. Nicole's attorney was forced to play catch-up.

Entering and leaving the courthouse became an Olympian event. With each edition, reporters filled their newspapers with all the gossip, innuendo, and biased statements they could find to pitch. It was clear from the beginning that Billy was the press's pet. He was always referred to as "the wronged father."

Day by day the threats, the complaints, the claims grew wilder and uglier. Nicole, in court and in print, was labeled an unfit mother who'd put an innocent child in the company of "suspect" people. Driven away the ever-popular father. And had the bad taste to make no secret about her choices.

Who in their right mind, the tabloids wondered in their inimitable way, would allow foreigners, dissidents, immoralists—amoralists, for God's sake, bohemian artists, no less—to surround and brainwash a tiny tot? Not a loving mother. Not a mother concerned with instilling the right values in her child. Only an unfit mother. A social outcast herself. A woman with no morals, who had actually simulated the sex act on stage and dared to call the travesty a dance. The tabloids deemed all her negative reviews fodder to feed from and news worthy to reprint.

Billy's attorney took a slightly less sensationalist tack, but one meant to raise the same questions in the mind of the presiding judge. It was fact, the attorney proclaimed, that little Alexis Gable had been neglected. Left alone. Put in precarious situations. It was downright criminal. But one could understand, even forgive, Miss Varonne her laxity. After all, she herself had been the victim of similar atrocities. A product of a broken marriage. No choice but to undergo a peripatetic childhood at the whim of a flamboyant, often bankrupt, belly— No, make that ballet dancer. Torn from her native country to travel halfway around the world. Forced to live the meanest, cruelest of existences . . . until Billy Gable came into her life and changed everything . . . for the good.

The attorney's exaggerations were insupportable. When he called Billy to the stand and her soon-to-be ex-husband began to paint the roseate picture of the promised land he would provide for his daughter, it took all of Nicole's willpower to restrain herself from standing up and screaming at the man. Both men. But if there was only one lesson Nicole had learned from the world of dance, it was discipline. And she applied it now. Soon it would be her turn. The dam gates would be slammed shut. The flood of wrongs would be righted.

Nicole took the stand. Her testimony was simple and direct.

"I am Lexie's stability. If you take her away from her mother, her stability is gone . . . no matter how many apple-cheeked grandmothers you substitute. My daughter's never been apart from me since the moment she was born. I love my daughter and would do nothing to endanger her life. Nor would I dare to influence the love she feels for either her father or me. That is her right, as it is her parents' right to cherish her."

Not a word against Billy. Not a word attempting to defend herself, much less acknowledge the charges purported by the other side. As far as she was concerned, the case was closed. Verdict . . . to be issued the following day.

Nicole glanced about the courtroom. In the gallery behind her were Ernestine, Mattie Wiggins, Nicole's troupe, and an overflow of her colleagues and supporters from the dance world. They had all come at one time or another during the course of the trial to help in whatever way Nicole would let them. Billy, dapper as ever in a dark blue suit, was smiling and talking to his lawyers and their staff. He was saying something about not being able to wait to go back home to Indiana and Mother Gable. Nicole had to look away. Tear her eyes and ears away. Billy's need to win was painfully obvious.

The courtroom quieted down as the judge took the bench.

"Case of Gable vs. Gable," droned the bailiff.

"Reconciliation appears never to have been a possibility in this marriage," declared the judge. "It becomes my sad duty, therefore, to render this union, which God supposedly made permanent, sundered. Decree of divorce granted to the plaintiff, Mr. William Eugene Gable. Mr. Gable, I further order that you pay Mrs. Gable two hundred and fifty dollars a month in alimony."

Pandemonium threatened to break out around the area of Billy's side of the courtroom.

"Shut up," Billy yelled. "He hasn't said anything about Lexie yet."

"Thank you, Mr. Gable; however, I don't need your assistance in managing my court. That is what this gavel is for."

The judge proceeded to wield it mightily.

"If I may continue," he said, "I have some remarks to make to Mrs. Gable, er, Miss Varonne."

Nicole stood up to face the judge. It was happening so quickly, she thought. Already, she was divorced. In another second, just one more second, Lexie's fate would be determined by this stranger.

"It is the opinion of this court, Miss Varonne, that Mr. Gable is a wonderful example of what fatherhood should be. His love and devotion to your daughter is to be admired. I can only impress on you the serious responsibility of ensuring that the child in question not be kept from seeing her father."

What was he saying? What did it mean? Nicole's eyes darted to Billy. Did he understand? Billy was staring, open-mouthed, at her.

"Mr. Gable," continued the judge, "you have presented yourself admirably to the court. You should be commended for taking such a great gamble in fighting proven statistics. Mothers, after all, have been the traditional custodians of their minor children 99.9 percent of the time in this country. Frankly, Mr. Gable, it is a fact of nature, human and animal, that a child belongs with its mother. What you've proven to the satisfaction of this court is that Nicole Varonne may be an unconventional mother, but hardly an incompetent one.

"I therefore award you, Miss Varonne, full custody of said minor child, with liberal visitation privileges granted to Mr. Gable. Further, Mr. Gable is to pay child support in the amount of five hundred dollars per month. Court is adjourned."

It was over. The courtroom erupted over the decree and the exorbitant settlement. Nicole was pounded on the back and hugged by people whose faces she hardly recognized. Tears ran down her face unchecked. She shook hands with her lawyer. Somehow she was carried along with the crowd from the courtroom outside to the busy street. All she cared about was getting home. Getting the hell away from the courthouse and racing to Lexie. They'd go out for ice cream. They'd go to the top of the Empire State Building. They'd . . .

"No pictures. Please. Move those cameras out of the way. No, my client will not be making a statement."

Billy's attorneys were standing on either side of him like bodyguards, fending off the curious. The rabid. The reporters and the fans. Nicole stood there, in the middle of the raucous crowd, alone. It was Billy Gable the world wanted to know about. Billy Gable, the wronged father. Billy Gable, Broadway and radio star. Billy Gable, openly distraught and broken by the verdict. Billy Gable, who needed the whole world's sympathy to survive the crushing blow.

Nicole felt herself propelled forward. Moving by instinct to Billy. Inching between the bodyguards. Touching his sleeve. Feeling his pain.

"It never had to go this far, Billy," she murmured. "We could have talked . . . reached some agreement . . ."

His face contorted. Twisted. He couldn't speak. Just look. And bleed. Agony. Chagrin. Misery. Shock. Revulsion. There was hate in his eyes. For her.

"I've done nothing . . ." she said, confused, squirming, averting her eyes.

"You won," he spat.

Nicole couldn't answer him. All of a sudden there were a dozen reporters flinging questions at her, and Billy was being led away.

"How does it feel, Nicole? Will you put your daughter on stage with you? Did you ever really love Billy Gable? How will this affect your dancing? Is there another man waiting in the wings? Is it true the disease your mother died from is hereditary? How does it feel, Nicole? How does it feel?"

Nicole took the bullets and finally stated, "All I have to say is this: I will never keep Billy . . . Mr. Gable . . . from his daughter. They may see each other, be together, whenever they like."

Then Ernestine, Mattie, Ernie Land, and Bobby and Joe

from her company, rushed her away to a waiting car. For once the drive to the Village was speedy. Dominique opened the door to Nicole's apartment, and Lexie was in her mother's arms.

"Mommy, you're squishing me!" croaked the little girl.

"Well, squish me back," Nicole cried.

There was the explosive pop of a champagne cork. Glasses were passed all around. Awkward toasts were proposed and drunk to by an assemblage of Nicole's supporters.

"Victory sounds a trifle hollow. How about 'To the Varonne girls. May they prosper,'" suggested Gar Fortune. "And now, kiddies, gather your things. The party can continue at my place."

"Gar, didn't you once say timing was everything?" teased Nicole. "Well, it's true. Thank you for coming and thank you for leaving. Thank you, everybody, for sticking with me."

It wasn't even noon yet. Nicole felt as though she were ready to throw the covers over her head and not come out for a week. But that wouldn't do. Lexie had to have lunch. After lunch mother and daughter went to the park to feed the pigeons. Lexie fell asleep on a blanket Nicole had laid on the grass. She sat there, watching her child. Promising she would know her father. Promising to tell her the truth. Promising never to let her down.

By mid-afternoon Lexie woke up. Nicole took her hand and they walked slowly back home. They stopped to pick up some apples and to peek at the new puppies in the pet shop window. They stopped to pick a dandelion that grew in a crack of the sidewalk and to give Mrs. Fudderman an apple.

Nicole started to make dinner. Out of habit she turned on the radio. It was tuned to the program Billy had been on. Lexie sat at a miniature table, scribbling with crayons.

"Why isn't Daddy singing?" came the first innocent question.

"Daddy isn't on that program anymore, sweetie."

"Why not?"

Innocent but not so easy to answer.

"Because Daddy decided not to sing on the radio for a while."

"I want to hear Daddy!" Lexie demanded.

"We can put on one of Daddy's records. Which show do you want to hear? *Tall Timber? Riley Loves Rosie? Tell Me a Story?*"

"No! I want to talk to Daddy. I want him to sing to me!"

Oh God. Why tonight of all nights? Nicole picked up her daughter and cuddled her.

"Okay, Lexie. You go wash your hands for supper and I'll call Daddy on the telephone."

"Okay."

She dialed his hotel and waited while his room was rung. And waited. No answer. Lexie came out of the bathroom.

"We'll try again after we eat," Nicole suggested. "During dinner we'll listen to Daddy on a record. You can even sing along with Daddy. With your mouth full."

Lexie grinned at the offer. She smiled all through dinner, showing plenty of teeth and chewed-up chicken and string beans. Afterward, Nicole tried calling again. Still no answer. She tried at Lexie's bedtime and after the little girl had given up hoping and gone to sleep. She even tried well into the late hours of the evening. No answer.

"Where are you, Billy?" Nicole kept wondering.

He was in a tavern on the lower East Side getting drunk. And when he was thrown out of that one, he weaved across the street to the next bar. And the next. And the next.

 **53**

Nicole tried repeatedly to reach Billy during the following few weeks without success. He was not in his hotel room. Or he was not answering the phone. He was not picking up his messages. Or he was ignoring them, even the ones on which Nicole left Lexie's name.

"Mr. Gable, please," she requested for what seemed like the hundredth time of the hotel operator.

"I'm sorry," droned the nasal-twanged woman. "No one by that name is registered at this hotel."

"Mr. William Gable," Nicole prodded. "Billy Gable, room 1459?"

"Mr. Gable checked out last night."

"Did he leave a forwarding address?"

"I'm sorry. I do not have that information."

Nicole hung up the phone. What was she going to tell Lexie this time? Daddy's disappeared, sweetie, and we don't know when we'll see him again. Just the message to give a child whose life had already been bounced around. What the hell was going on in Billy's mind? Didn't he realize the effect his absence would have on his daughter?

After dropping Lexie off at school, Nicole riffled through her personal directory, making a list of people to call who might have seen Billy. To whom he might have turned. First, she called the dance studio to leave the message she would be late that day. Then she got down to the business at hand, starting with the A's.

She was lucky. She only had to go as far as the B's. George Barlow told her where Billy had gone.

"Gone home, Nicole. Back home to Indiana to lick his wounds. I hope you'll pardon me for saying so, but you hurt him very much."

"George," she admonished, "that's crap. I've had to sit and listen to my name impugned, my family history abused, and my choice of career maligned. All in the name of justice and fair play. Well, it wasn't just or fair, George, and you know it. Billy hurt himself. That's the truth."

"Really, Nicole?" the attorney said snidely.

"Really, George. That's how the judge saw it, and that's how I see it."

"Maybe there's a grain of truth in what you say," Barlow conceded. "But he loved that little girl of yours, enough to go as far out on a limb as he did."

"The sad part is, he didn't have to."

"Did you tell him that?"

"He never gave me a chance. I tried to. Right after the judge's decision. I don't know if he even heard me."

"Maybe you should try again, Nicole. He needs to know he hasn't lost his child."

"That's what I've been trying to do for the last three weeks. I'll call Harmony Grove right now—"

"Wait a minute, Nicole. Maybe you ought to give him a little time. He's pretty depressed. You never know how he might take hearing your voice. He might be filled with all sorts of false hopes, or it might take him down even further."

"Like I was rubbing his nose in my victory . . . I understand, George. All right, I'll wait. Time at the farm and the old fishing hole and some of Mother Gable's home-cooked meals may just be the right kind of medicine. I'll call in another week or two."

"Now you're using your head, Nicole. If you like, if at that point you feel an intermediary would be useful . . . well, I'd be glad to help."

"How generous of you, George," Nicole said, trying to hide the irony seeping into her voice. "I'll let you know."

Why hadn't the pompous son of a bitch offered to help when it really could've made a difference? Before the hearing. During it. Of course he hadn't seen fit, Nicole thought. He was just another one of those controlling male bastards. Intent on herding women into their tiny insupportable niches. Damn him. She grabbed up her purse. Damn all of them. She grabbed her dance bag too. May they all rot in hell, she fumed to herself. She slammed the door of the flat behind her, hurtling down the stairs. And may Billy Gable rot in Indiana too.

Rot. The smell of wood rot haunted Billy. He stalked through the shell of the house he had been fixing up. The one he was going to live in with Lexie. It was empty, cold, sterile. Like all the clean fresh air had been sucked up and replaced by . . . nothing. He'd never known "nothing" could stink.

But there was a dank, soiled dryness . . . moistness . . . something . . . that surrounded him and threatened to invade him too.

He took a giant swig from the bottle of bourbon he held. His only friend, that bottle. Giving him the only kind of comfort that seemed to sink down deep enough to make a difference. To make it different. To make him forget and not feel the pain. The knots of agony that ripped through his gut and his heart whenever he thought of his little girl.

He'd had a bottle in hand since the day of the decision. He couldn't seem to do without it. It had become a part of him, as important as his right arm. With it, he managed to get through the days and the nights. He managed to forget what he'd lost. For an hour or two or three. He managed to fake the dream. Fool himself into imagining he hadn't lost her. Imagine what he'd do when he finally got Lexie back. What they'd do together. How he'd hold back the mountain of feeling he had for her. That threatened to crush her. Both of them. Hold her to him tenderly so that she would never break. Or get scared and run away. Like Nicole.

The thought of his ex-wife drove him to take another belt. It tasted awful. Like rot would taste. He spit out the venomous liquid, spraying the walls of the house he and Lexie were meant to live in.

"Oh God!" he groaned, and slammed himself out of the house.

He was walking aimlessly, toward his mother's farmhouse. She'd have peach cobbler waiting for him. Or a sky-high ham sandwich on homemade bread, hot from the oven. Or a glass of lemonade, chilled with thick chunks of ice. Tasteless. He wouldn't be able to taste any of it. His senses had stopped working. Billy Gable just wasn't working. As if to prove his point, he stumbled and fell. He didn't bother to catch himself, and welcomed the dirt heaving into his eyes, nose, mouth, lungs. He let himself lie there. As if that were his rightful place. He closed his eyes and dozed off.

The sun beat down on his back. Hours later he awoke, hungover. He couldn't even lift his head. Dizzy, nauseated, he made himself turn over to feel the sun on his face. Why was he so damn cold? Involuntary shivers ran from his shoulders down his back and his arms. A hot bath. Scalding. Turning his skin red. That's what he needed.

He stumbled home and fended off his mother's worried questions, pleading a headache. Later that evening, like all the other evenings since he'd been home, when sleep refused to quell his anguish, he flipped a coin.

"Heads he walks; tails he drives," he mumbled to himself.

Six nights in a row he'd walked till dawn. Walked through the farm lands, along the banks of the river, reliving his childhood, up and down the main drag of Harmony Grove, all the side streets too. Nice neat little neighborhoods with nice neat little families tucked into their nice neat little beds living their nice neat lives. God, how he envied them and hated them for what they had and he didn't.

The coin jumped, twisted, leaped into the air and fell. Deciding Billy's fate for yet another night. Tails. The long spell of heads was broken. Tonight he would drive. As he had dozens of times from age twelve on, he tiptoed into his parents' bedroom and stuck his hand in the rear pocket of his father's pants which hung on a peg behind the door. Bingo. Keys to the prewar, mid-Depression hulk of an automobile.

He snuck out of the house and headed for a small side barn that doubled as a garage. In a minute the car leaped to life and chugged down the country road. Within fifteen minutes Billy was far beyond the outskirts of town, heading for the highway. He made a brief stop. Couldn't go anywhere without his friends. He stopped at an all-night roadhouse and bought some bourbon. An armload of bottles. Before starting the car, he guzzled half a bottle without stopping for breath.

One hand on the steering wheel. One hand clamped around a bottle. Driving. Anywhere the car pointed. He began to sing.

"Oh ho . . . Where have you been, Billy boy, Billy boy? Oh ho, where have you been, darling Billy? I have been to seek a wife; she's the joy of my life. She's a young thing and cannot leave her mother."

There was a joke if ever he'd heard one. He finished off the first bottle and opened the second, taking his hand off the steering wheel to do it.

"Billy, Billy, come and play, while the sun shines bright as day. Yes, my Lexie, so I will, for I love to please you still."

Damn it to hell. His mind was playing tricks on him. He for sure didn't want to think about Nicole, and he couldn't think about Lexie. Not the sweet, mischievous smile on her face. Not the songs he'd refashioned so they were just about him and his little girl. Something else. Anything else.

He'd had triumphs in his life. Plenty of 'em. "Going On" sprang into his mind. There was an anthem for him, by God. How did it go? The words lurched jerkily out of his memory.

"What's true for the land is true for me," he chanted, hesitating over each word before spitting them out. "And true for all of us."

The chorus came rushing back.

"The promise and the dream are always there," he sang in his beautiful deep baritone. "I'm going on. I'll never stop. I'll fight the fight. Work day and night until the struggle's won."

He was in tears and felt so damned sorry for himself. He'd tried so hard. Believed he was doing the right thing. Still believed it was the right thing to've done. Couldn't accept that he was wrong. How could he have lost? It hurt. God damn it, how it hurt.

"I'll sing my song. I'm going on."

The tears rained down unchecked, blinding him. The car swerved. Where was the lane? Have to stay on the right side of the road, he told himself, although why he had to was beyond all power of reason. He slowed down and infused himself with bourbon.

"Steady as she goes," he mumbled. "Aye aye, Captain. Now where was I? Oh yeah. I'm going on," he proclaimed.

He sang it at the top of his lungs. Screamed it.

"I'm going on. Go-ing on."

The car swerved again. Again he fought for control.

"Go-ing on," he sang, his voice broken with emotion. "Why? What the hell for?"

Ahead, down the road a few hundred yards, Billy saw the lights of an approaching vehicle. They were higher than a car's and on their brightest exposure. Hadda be a truck, he thought, blinking, putting an arm to his face to blot out the light. Then he stared straight at it. Wondering. A dairy truck? A jeep? G.I.'s packed like sardines going who knew where? Pigs on their way to slaughter? Ah, what the hell. A hundred years from now, who the hell would know . . . five minutes from now . . . who the hell would care . . .

Billy could've driven right by. Passed the truck. Gone on to get even drunker. Eventually weave his way home. Sleep it off. Start the process all over again. But he didn't. Instead he stared into the lights of the oncoming truck. Stared at them as though they were some sort of beacon. Beckoning. Promising. Stared at them until they were all he saw. All he thought of. And aimed the car right at them. Until he was consumed by them and the world went dark.

Nicole sat up in bed, rubbing the sleep from her eyes. It was still dark. Why was the telephone ringing at this hour of the night . . . morning? What time was it? she thought foggily. She reached for the alarm clock, groaning when she read a quarter to five.

"I'm coming," she said, as if the telephone could answer itself. "For Chrissakes, stop ringing."

She raced to the living room. Thank goodness Lexie was a sound sleeper. Like her father, nothing seemed to faze her once her head hit the pillow.

"Okay, okay," Nicole said, and reached for the receiver. "Hello?"

"Nicole?"

"Who is this?" she demanded.

"Nicole, it's George Barlow. Sit down, Nicole."

"George, I was lying down just a minute ago."

"I'm sorry, Nicole. Terribly sorry. But I just got word from the Gables . . . Billy's family. Are you sitting down, Nicole?"

Suddenly she felt cold. Bone cold. She sat down and pulled Alexandra's old challis scarf from the back of the sofa around her shoulders.

"What's the matter, George?" she whispered.

"It's Billy. He's been killed in a traffic accident. Just a few hours ago. Seems the family flivver had an altercation with a truck. . . . They assured me he must have died instantaneously. Never felt a thing, Nicole. He was sloshed on bourbon. You know Billy. He probably didn't even know he was on the wrong side of the road. Nicole? Are you there?"

In a daze she hung up the phone. She sat in the dark, making pictures of the collision. Of Billy's face. Billy holding his daughter. The look of pure ecstasy on his face. Radiant with pride. Dead. No. She saw him shouldering his axe, going on to greater glory in *Tall Timber*. Saw him coming home the conquering soldier boy in *Riley Loves Rosie*. Saw him coming home to her after the war, as though her very life gave him meaning. No, Billy Gable couldn't be dead.

She got up from the couch and wandered about the room, turning on one lamp. Another. All the lamps until the room blazed with light. Still she saw Billy. Driving the car. Drunk. He must have been upset . . . out of his mind . . . looking for answers that would explain . . . No answers . . .

All she could hear was the thump of her own heartbeat. Regular. Strong. Pounding in her ears. All she could see was Billy behind the wheel, driving himself to his death. Then she knew. As surely as though she had sat next to him in the car. As surely as she knew the man-boy she had married. He had believed and been judged lacking. If he were wrong, that wrong, then what was there to believe in? Nicole knew Billy had killed himself.

She hugged herself and rocked back and forth, trying to cope with her revelation. Billy committing suicide. It was horrendous . . . horrific. An incredible waste. And preventable. Like the hiss of a snake, the idea penetrated, reverberated, inside her. Billy didn't have to die. She could have called him. Insisted on setting things straight. Gotten Mother Gable to intercede. She could have put herself and Lexie on a train or a bus and gone to Harmony Grove. She could have just handed Lexie over to him . . .

She stopped. Billy's death was not her fault. She wasn't the one who put drink after drink in his hands. She hadn't torn him from his daughter. The truth played over and over in her head till it made sense and calmed her. Guilt and shock turned into a dull ache in her chest. Such unnecessary tragedy. Billy's desire to love and be loved was overwhelming. Had overwhelmed him at times. Her all the time. And Lexie? How she had tried to handle her father . . . to love him on his terms.

There was the greatest tragedy of all. How was she to tell Lexie about Billy's death? Lexie had had him for such a short time. Shorter than she'd had Vanya, actually. She could still go home to her father. If she wanted. But Lexie? Never.

Nicole had a sudden need to hold her baby. She went into the sleeping child's room and gently scooped her up. Tiny beads of sweat marked her forehead and upper lip. Living was such a hard thing to do sometimes, Nicole thought, remembering her own youth. Even the easiest of things, like sleeping, took effort. Nicole rocked the little girl against her breasts.

"It'll just be the two of us," she murmured softly. "Just like when you were born. We had a good time then, and we'll have more good times, my sweetheart."

Without Daddy. Billy would become a tiny beam of light in the vast array of memories Lexie and she would store up.

Tears came to Nicole's eyes and fell on the child's nightgown. How would she ever be able to make it up to her child? Not with storybook lies, as Alexandra had. And this time, not the truth. There would be no discussion about suicide. Nothing about Mama and the men who left her. Whom she drove away. Maybe when Lexie was older, she would talk to her about sorrow and sadness so deep, you forgot that people really did love you and need you. But for now, she would say nothing about these curses.

She'd concentrate on the blessings. The good that came out of bad things, even when it was hard to believe. She could tell Lexie about angels and heaven, where Billy would always be singing. About the love she felt for her little girl, which Lexie could always depend on. About one man who loved her like no man ever had and ever would.

~~ **54**

The newspapers called Billy's death a tragedy too. Nicole was more than relieved to find no hint of suicide. But there wasn't a single account that didn't tie the Gable divorce and custody suits in with the accident. Nicole's picture was splashed all over the paper. From page one to the obituaries. From the gossip columns to the arts critic, who deemed it obligatory to look back on the careers of the Broadway star and the scandalous choreographer.

The only bright light in the ugly rehashings of Billy and Nicole's life together was that Lexie's picture did not appear. Although her name and the circumstances of her birth did. In Lexie's best interest, Nicole took her out of school and kept her under her loving eye. The little girl missed her classmates for a little while, but Nicole made sure she wasn't alone. There were the dancers of the troupe and Myrtle Fudderman, and songs to sing and drawings to scribble in brilliant strokes.

Public reaction was equally intense. The upright, moral citizens of New York weren't going to support a divorcée who'd hounded her husband to his untimely death. Or a shameless hussy who'd had a child out of wedlock and thought nothing of it. They'd had all they were going to take of the woman who demeaned the proud spirit of American men. The first few nights of her next set of performances were a nightmare. Those few who attended, who had already purchased season tickets, booed and heckled her, bringing her dances to a standstill.

"Go back where you came from," shouted the pests.

"Pinko!" a few brave ones cried out. "Slut!"

PIROUETTE

The darling of the modern dance world had finally committed the one sin the public couldn't forgive. She stood alone on the stage in makeup and costume, bewildered. What was the matter with these people? Why was her personal life more important to them than her art? It was as bad as the time she'd been in San Francisco and gotten drubbed by the dance critics because she had the audacity to be pregnant.

No, Nicole decided. It was worse. Then, at least, she'd had public support. Her audiences had still flocked to performances of the Varonne Company. She'd been thirsty for some show of approbation, and there it was. Their applause had been like the sweetest wine. Intoxicating. Thrilling. Reaffirming. Now she was getting whistles and catcalls. As though the very sight of her was license to judge her. Damn her.

Well, damn them! Nicole concluded unceremoniously. She continued to stand tall on the stage. Silent. Glaring straight ahead. Staring them down. Till the noise died down to a whisper. Then a nervous twitter. Then to silence. A handful of people walked out of the hall. A handful stayed. To them and for them, Nicole danced. When she finished, she walked off stage, not returning for a bow.

In her dressing room she stared into her mirror. Looking to her reflection for wisdom. For an explanation. The first night she'd tossed it off as an anomaly. Thrill-seeking lowlifes who'd go anywhere to spread the dirt. Dig in it themselves. The second night, after the reviews and the reports came out, she knew it would be worse. She could only liken it to a circus with the audience waiting for the freaks to appear.

When the third night proved no different, she was ready to throw in the towel. If the whole season was to be turned into a tawdry sideshow, she'd have no part in it. Simply remove herself, as she'd done with Lexie and school. She could no more put her dancers through this nightmare than her daughter. Than herself.

In the midst of this mess and out of the blue, she received a fan letter.

Cara,

Hold your head up high and ignore the bastards, every last one of them. You've got nothing to be ashamed of. The situation with Billy was impossible. Anyone who really knows you knows the hell he put you through. Love was never an issue between the two of you, Nicole, just a question of possession. You know that, don't you? You are not to beat yourself up over his death.

You know what I think. If you're even one tenth the mother Alexandra was, your daughter is a lucky little girl. I don't care what the scandal sheets say—here or there—and they're having a field day here. I've made my position clear. Any reporter comes near me gets a kick in his fat ass!

If I know you, you're thinking to yourself, it's none of his fucking business, or sugary words to that effect. Well, I think it is, cara. Maybe we didn't get along so well in New York. Maybe a little too much water has passed under the bridge. But you're under my skin, Nicole. Always have been and always will be. So if you need me, if you want me, forget about pride. Let me know and I'll be there like a shot. There's still time for us.

Carlo

For some unexplanable reason, Nicole began to chuckle. To laugh outright. To guffaw till the tears erupted from her eyes and rolled down her cheeks. Carlo, as insufferably arrogant as he could be, was offering to come to the rescue.

The image flashed before her of a young Neptune. Trident in hand. Striding across the ocean. Visiting waves of tidal proportions upon the fourth estate. And in the midst of wrack and ruin, he would snatch her up. Save her from the yawning bowels of public turpitude. Before she was forever swallowed up and forgotten. Perhaps to emerge once in a millenium from the dim recesses of a history of dance textbook. If she were that lucky.

He was expecting her to cave in. Give up without a fight. Why else would he tell her not to? Mr. Domenici, she thought to herself, reading the letter a second time, you don't know me at all. But then she frowned, realizing everything he had written was true. Except that bit about her pride. Which was still intact. And that line he threw in at the end. There would be no more men in her life. Not with her track record. But there would be dance. If not in New York, then somewhere . . .

Nicole decided to get out of the city. She asked Ernestine to set up a tour. It made little difference where. Only the length of the tour mattered. She gathered up Lexie and swept up her dancers, bouncing from city to city.

The tour was a fiasco. Billy and Nicole were more than big-city news; their story had connotations that seemed to apply to every person in every burg in America. Nicole was forced to confront mostly empty auditoriums, hecklers, even pickets. House managers canceled the company's engagements. City after city declined to have her perform. She resolved to forge ahead, but it was pointless. She was left with only one answer. Give it up. Go home. Lay low until the flack stopped flying. Even her dancers agreed.

"At least we'll have our hides intact," offered Bobby.

"It's all right, Nicole," Dominique tried to reassure her. "We've had difficulties before . . . for other reasons. We can weather this one. Sometimes it's better to wait out the storm."

If Nicole had ever felt like tangling with a storm, it was now. Buck the tide of resentment that threatened to engulf her career. Unfair! she wanted to cry. She wanted to shake each booking agent, each theater manager, each newspaper critic, each one of the legion of fans who only, the previous year, had applauded her till their hands were raw. Judge her dances on their own merits, she wanted to demand. Not on half truths, speculations, gossip, out-and-out lies.

But with few places to dance and fewer dollars coming in, she was forced to yield. She went home, played dutifully with Lexie, and turned to choreography for solace—where her anger and pain and frustration stirred the creative pool, giving birth to a new dance.

She danced about Billy having the last laugh. Destroying her career. She danced about Lexie being left fatherless. She danced about Nikki and Billy. How they left her to be consumed by questions, never to be answered. How Vanya and Carlo had given her answers she could only question.

She danced about the bravery of women. Danced about herself. Idealized the spirit of Alexandra. And the life force of all mothers who tied the family together till the very end. Who persevered despite the ugly divisiveness of men. Binding the wounds. Not causing them.

It was the male who brought dissension and chaos. It was the male who killed. It was the male in Nicole's dance who came to wear a Medusalike mask, capable of turning all those he encountered—loved and hated—into lifeless, frozen stone.

In her studio she danced the role of the Medusa as though she were a man. Hulking. A hunter. Defiant. Deceptive. Blind yet with piercing vision. Filled with hate. For others. For himself. Doomed.

An old familiar figure stood in the doorway of the studio and clapped.

"Jeez, Nicole. I think I'm beginning to understand this stuff."

Startled, she threw off the wild-eyed, snake-kinked mask. She was so much into the character of the male Medusa, it took her a moment or two to stumble back into reality, stumble forward and shake Manny Schumann's hand.

"I always knew an old dog could learn new tricks," she teased.

"It's good to see ya, kid," he rasped, taking out a cigar. "May I?" Nicole nodded, and he went on between puffs, saying, "Been through the ringer, haven't you?"

Nicole nodded again, adding, "And the mangle."

"But you landed on your feet, I see. Still crankin' out the sausage."

"That's one I haven't heard. Is it a compliment, Manny?"

"You bet, kid. Never let 'em getcha down. That's the ticket."

"Well, I haven't sold too many of those lately," said Nicole disparagingly.

"But you'd like to again. Wouldn't ya, kid? Knock 'em dead at the box office? Laugh all the way to the bank?"

"Is it me?" she asked, laughing. "Or are the clichés for your benefit?"

"Just tryin' to make a point, kid. Look, it's no secret. You're washed up here. You couldn't get an audience or a critic on your side if the President himself gave you a handwritten invitation. But they're clamoring for you over in Europe. Those limeys and frogs and the rest of them over there eat and breathe scandal. They're dyin' to see Nicole Varonne."

"Nicole Varonne the modern dance choreographer? Or Nicole Varonne the man-eater?" she posited.

"What difference does it make if it's one or the other? They want you. Lock, stock, and ugly barrel. Do you know what that means? With the way your life's been going, they'll make you a millionairess in no time flat. And they'll appreciate your dances too. You know what snobs they all are on the outside. But on the inside, kid, they're dyin' for the juicy stuff."

"You make it sound like the freak show at a circus, Manny. Is that what I've become? The bearded lady? The two-headed monster?"

"C'mon, Nicole," he said, placing a fatherly arm around her shoulder, giving her a good shake, "you and I know it ain't true. When they see your work, they'll know it's not true too. The accolades'll really start to pile on. So . . . whaddya say? Cash in while you're a hot item."

How she wanted to believe it were true. There was a future for her dances, for Lexie and her . . . somewhere out there. But Europe? England?

"Going back there . . . I don't know, Manny. I never thought I'd set foot there again."

"You remember when you first came to me, kid? It was twelve years ago, but I can remember it like it was yesterday. I never saw such a wild-eyed ragamuffin in my life. But I took a chance on you. Not for your name. Not even for your mother's sake. Because I saw somethin' in you, kid. I saw spine. Spunk. Not just a will to survive, but an urge to make it. A need to make it big. I was right, wasn't I?"

Nicole nodded, unable to speak.

"Well, I'm still right. It's still there, deep inside you. So do what Uncle Manny says. I've got big connections, kid. And your name is on the top of everybody's list 'cause they already know you from before the war. They're dying to see you; their tongues're hanging out. I tell you, Nicole, I can get you a tour on the continent just like that. If you thought of going back to England . . . well, hell, you could dance there for life. So, what's it gonna be?"

Everything Manny said had the ring of truth to it, as much as she hated to admit it. She was finished in the States, at least for the time being. She'd be a fool not to realize that. To stay meant hibernation. Stagnation. For God knows how long.

And there was Lexie to think of. As well as the dancers who'd stuck by her through thick and thin. She owed them. She owed her daughter. She owed it to herself. Her career was paramount, and it only made sense to go where the work was. Paris. Rome. Vienna. London. Yes, even London.

Maybe it was time to face all of it. All of them. Face the old lion in his den. And his prissy bird of a woman. Maybe even the panther. She chuckled to herself. The animal shuffle. Vanya, Peggy, and Carlo. What a dance she could make of it all.

"What the hell, Manny. I'll go. You can book us first in London."

Part III

~~~

LONDON

1951

It was different, Nicole insisted. Not at all like the crossing Alexandra and she had made almost twenty years ago. The obvious change was in the mode of transportation. Then their journey across the Atlantic took days ... weeks. Enough time to build up all sorts of expectations. And hope. Now she and Lexie would be in England in a matter of hours. No time for impossible dreams to be dreamt and shattered.

She leaned over Lexie, who had claimed the window seat for her own, and stared downward into the mass of pillowy white clouds.

"Wouldn't it be fun to walk right out of this old plane," Nicole whispered conspiratorially to her daughter, "and bounce up and down on the clouds?"

"Sure, Mama," Lexie said in her most grown-up, world-weary voice. "And the moon is made of green cheese."

"Well, it is, you know," Nicole said soberly, poking at Lexie's sides to make her laugh.

"Is not!" insisted the child, breaking down into giggles. "It's made of purple cheese."

Nicole sat back in her seat, marveling at her luck. Lexie still laughed with the wonderful ease of a child who knew she was loved. It had been a hard road for the two of them. Especially Lexie. The shock of losing Billy and mourning him were bad enough. But to be uprooted too . . . to lose the newly made friends from school. To leave New York. The whole United States! It was a lot to ask of a little girl.

But there was a plus side to the unhappiness and the chaos. One Nicole knew well from her own experience. One she saw in her daughter as well. Lexie had loved her father and missed him. But now she slept well at night. No nightmares. No disjointed crying out. No anxiety about the next day. In short, Lexie was relieved. She didn't have to be Daddy's perfect little girl anymore.

She talked about him. Sang his songs. Laughed when she chose to remember a silly story he'd told her. But the intense expectations were gone. Erased. With luck and her mother's sensitivity, Billy's sad disappearance from his daughter's life would be but a short chapter, outweighed by the good memories the child would have. At least this daughter would remember her father at his best, Nicole mused. Unlike her. She'd never conquered her need to please her father. All she'd ever achieved was failure. And here she was, going back for more.

No, not true, Nicole told herself. This time she had no expectations. No outsized need to prove herself to him. She wasn't coming back to him because she needed a man to help her. Unlike her mother, she had the bookings. Had the company. Had a guaranteed future . . .

"Mama," chirped Lexie, interrupting Nicole's thoughts, "tell me again about the time you and Grammy Shura came to London to visit the queen."

Nicole smiled. Family history and nursery rhymes were easy enough to confuse.

"Actually, there was a king then. Now there's a queen. Then there was a fierce old lion named Vanya. He's your grandfather. And a well-meaning little bird. That's Pi— Peggy. She's the lion's wife."

"Does that make her my gramma, too?" Lexie asked innocently.

For a moment Nicole closed her eyes, stealing a moment to yearn for her mother. Alexandra would've made the most wonderful grandmother, sweeping up yet another little girl and weaving her mantle of magic. It was not to be. Lexie would have to be content with stories.

"Yes, honey," she was forced to answer. "Gramma Peggy. But then she was just Peggy. Just like a little brown hen, she loved her garden and she loved her kitchen."

The story told itself. Soon Lexie was asleep and Nicole was left to remember what really had taken place. Then there was no time to remember or think. The plane landed. The company bustled off to its hotel near the Strand in London's West End. With everyone assigned and settled in rooms, Nicole raced off to the theater. It was a small, sound building with old but still flexible floorboards. The dressing areas were adequate. The box office receipts looked promising. The company was sold out for the first five nights of the engagement.

"Complimentary tickets, miss. How many will you require?" asked the brisk house manager.

Customarily, Nicole always reserved tickets for her old teachers and fellow choreographers. And of course for members of the troupe not dancing any given night. And their families. And Lexie, if she wanted to sit out front, rather than backstage.

This time there were no cohorts. Every member of the troupe was dancing in one piece or another. She would insist on Lexie being backstage at least the first few nights, until she grew familiar with the surroundings. And no one else had brought family along.

Family. Vanya and Margaret. When was the right time to reintroduce herself to them? Would they feel slighted . . . miffed . . . if she didn't send them complimentary tickets? Or would they think it presumptuous of her? Typically American? A wild Indian kind of stunt?

"Two tickets for opening night, please," she said.

It was the professional thing to do. The English dance world might attend out of courtesy. Or curiosity. She surely couldn't accommodate them all. Nor should she. That smacked of bribery. But offering freebies to Vanya Borcheff, to whom she had personal ties also, seemed the correct thing to do.

Carlo. There was the other thorn.

"Wait a minute. I might need three," she said to the manager.

What to do about Carlo? Her head swam with possibilities, indecision, the whole range of emotions. She wanted to show him she was undefeated. Her dances were more powerful, more dramatic, truer to her vision than ever. She also wanted to avoid him completely. He'd been right about every man in her life. Vanya. Nikki. Billy. Consistently she had made the wrong choice. And lived to regret it. Every damn time. And he'd told her so. Cheerfully too, damn him.

"I'm sorry. Two tickets will be just fine. Will you send them to this address, please?"

Carlo would have to wait. She wasn't ready to face him and Vanya too. Maybe she'd never be ready.

The audience was riveted to their seats. The climax of *Male Medusa,* the final dance on the evening's bill, was taking place. Prowling the stage among the litter of death he had wrought, the Medusa figure turned with agony. Writhed in the air. On the ground. Contorting into the same twisted shapes as the snakes frozen on his mask. The end was near. Had to be near. The destruction had to stop. Had to be stopped. No one had proven powerful enough to stand up to the Medusa.

Who could possibly stand up to such a creature? Vanya wondered. In the midst of the audience he sat next to Margaret, who clutched his hand tightly. It was a marvelous bold image, ungodly and yet human too. This his daughter had created? That spitfire of a mouse who alternately trembled and stomped her way through his house and his stage? This daughter, estranged from him, who chose to remind him of her existence through an impetuous letter or two?

He had never known her, never understood her. He had been right to think of her as Alexandra's child, not his. Alexandra . . . her talent, her presence . . . her spirit . . . always bigger than life itself. Like this male Medusa character of Nicole's. It took a mind different from his to build ballets out of this improbable, probing stuff. The stuff of dreams and nightmares. Not the stuff of clean lines and order.

A wrenching clang of chords beat through the hall. From the soul of the Medusa. Through the ears of the hushed audience. Echoing the beat of the heart. In the beast. In each man and woman. At last, center stage, the male figure tore the mask of Medusa from his face and turned it on himself. Metamorphosing into stone. Satisfying the curse to its ultimate, inevitable conclusion.

Margaret and Vanya looked at each other in stunned silence while the audience, all around them, broke out in a storm of applause.

"It's very different. Isn't it, Van?"

"Is too modern for my taste," he said dryly. "But the drama, the emotion," he added, thoughtfully nodding his head, "is superb, is gripping. I couldn't take my eyes off the stage during any of her works."

"That's very true, Van dear. I agree. I just wasn't too sure I'd survive. I don't know about you, but I'm all played out. Van?"

He was on his feet with the majority of the audience, clapping his hands in measured cadence for the dancer/choreographer, who appeared before the curtain for her bow. His face was a study of conflicting emotions. Pride for his blood that flowed in her veins. Resentment for the pain and the embarrassment she had caused him, leaving him without a word . . . just a chicken scratch of a note. Envy for her talent, which was so divergent from his. And an enormous gladness in her accomplishment.

He had to sit down and compose himself. There were too many emotions wreaking havoc with his self-imposed sense of harmony.

"Everything all right, Van?"

"Yes, thank you, Piggy."

"Will you go backstage to see Nicole and congratulate her?"

"No," he said. "Will be madhouse. I think it better to send a note asking her to tea tomorrow at home. Will be all right with you?"

"Of course, Van. Whatever you want. Won't it be lovely to see dear Nicole again?"

He frowned, glaring at his wife. Lovely was the last word he would have chosen. Exacting, challenging, torturous, exasperatingly necessary, were closer to what he expected.

~~ **56**

"Now, listen to me, Lexie. If you're at all unhappy and you want to leave, just give me the high sign. Okay? Wink at me or pull my skirt or just come sit on my lap. And we'll go. We'll get out of there faster than—"

"But Mama, why wouldn't I like it?"

Because I didn't, Nicole wanted to tell her child. Because that house and those people had made her feel inconsequential. Lonely. Because her mother had died in that house, and she was afraid she'd smell death the second she set foot in there again. Because of all the places she'd been to and lived in, that house never felt like home.

"It's just a feeling I have," she said to Lexie. "I just want you to be happy."

"I always am, Mama."

Then they were in front of the brick house. Nicole stood at the base of the steps and gazed up toward the shiny black door. Brahms, always Peggy's favorite, wafted out the open window of the parlor. Colorful splashes of rambling rose wound about the iron railings. It could have been 1933 again. Nicole could almost hear the ghostly rippling of Alexandra's melodic voice, singing out to Vanya and Nikki to bring in the trunks. She was brought back to reality by Lexie's bright little chirp.

"It's pretty, Mama."

Pretty? Nicole had never looked at the house aesthetically. From her first day to her last, she'd only thought of it as a dreadful sort of prison. Dark. Grim. Unwelcoming. Now she could see it was just a house like every other one on both sides of the street.

"C'mon, Mama," urged Lexie, tugging on her arm.

Give me another minute. Just a few seconds more, she pleaded silently.

"All right, all right. Race you up the steps. First one to the door can ring the bell."

Nicole made sure Lexie won. Anything to forestall the inevitable. But Lexie was already on tiptoes. One dainty finger furiously working the buzzer. Already footsteps at the other side of the door. Vanya's? Margaret's? A hand opening the door. The sound of a soft, fluttery, tittery kind of voice.

"My, my. Who have we here?" Margaret inquired.

"It's Mama and me, Gramma Peggy."

"Why I never expected—" Margaret began and stopped, suddenly having to dab at her eyes with her apron.

They were fixed again on Lexie. Margaret couldn't seem to tear her eyes away. Nicole had gotten used to seeing the mix of Billy and herself in the child. Now she realized Peggy was seeing a piece of the little boy she had raised. Mirror images echoing through the generations. Affirming life. Denying death.

She folded Nicole in an embrace. Holding her within the circle of her arms without really touching her. Both women a trifle awkward. Unsure. Like two birds having to reestablish the pecking order, Nicole thought. Which of them had the upper hand?

"Peggy," Nicole said, searching for the right words, "you . . . you haven't changed a bit. Not at all really."

The older woman colored slightly, self-consciously patting her hair and adjusting the bow of her apron.

"One tries to keep fit, dear. But Nicole," she exclaimed, "you have changed. You're a woman . . . and beautiful," she added, examining her inch by inch.

Again Nicole knew what Peggy was up to. Looking for

Nikki grown-up. For some semblance of the dead boy magically returned to life in his twin. At what would have been the prime of his life. It made her uncomfortable, but she understood the need.

"I hope you don't mind that I brought my daughter. You were so kind . . ."

Stop stumbling over the words. Over the sentiment. You're here because you chose to come, she told herself. After all, she had received an invitation. Not a summons.

"You were so kind to send the bonnet when she was born."

"Nonsense, Nicole. It brought me pleasure. But do come in. Van is waiting, and we wouldn't want the tea to get cold, now would we? Would you like to help me bring the tea tray in?" Margaret asked the little girl.

"Yes," Lexie answered shyly.

"Well then, come along . . ."

Margaret cocked her head at Nicole questioningly.

"Her name is Lexie. Short for Alexis."

"Alexis," Peggy repeated. "Of course it would be for your mother."

Why was each simple exchange charged with tension? Nicole still felt as though Peggy was teaching her lessons in life she had mysteriously avoided learning. Although now she could see it was just the woman's way. No invisible cannons firing off demerits for poor etiquette. Yet there it was. She seemed to be taking the same old aim at Margaret. Little potshots. Like Lexie's name. It carried weight. It had a history. It made a decisive point.

"And you're my gramma too," prattled the child. "Mama says so."

Thank God for children, Nicole thought. Lexie knew how to make a point too.

Peggy raised an eyebrow and glanced at Nicole. Then her face relaxed and broke into a smile. Almost girlish, Nicole noted.

"If Mama says so, then it is so. So, come with me, Alexis. You can carry the biscuits to table . . ."

It was 1933. Nicole was certain Margaret had uttered those very words to Nikki the day Alexandra and she had arrived.

". . . and Nicole dear, your father is waiting for you in the parlor. He would have come to the door, but his leg's bothering him today. You remember the old injury. . . . He's missed you, dear."

"Vanya's missed me?" Nicole echoed, as though she hadn't quite heard right, as though it weren't really plausible.

Taking hold of Lexie's hand, Margaret leaned toward Nicole to whisper conspiratorially, "You'll find dear Van a changed man."

Nicole suppressed a giggle at Peggy's unintentional rhyme.

"It's true, sad as it is. I've done my best to make life jolly for him, but the loss—the double loss, triple really—of Nick, you, and your mother—well, it just took so much out of him. I was very worried for a time there. He wouldn't talk to anybody. Even I couldn't get but a grumble from him. He seemed to go inside himself. Refused to go anywhere or do anything. He wouldn't go near the company: his office, classes, the stage. Nothing."

Alarmed, Nicole asked, "He isn't still like that, is he?"

"Oh no, dear. I got him to come 'round. He was better after I proposed to him. And much better when he learned you were with child. But you go see for yourself, dear," she added with a smile, her eyes cheerfully mysterious.

Well, maybe it was 1951 after all. People only spoke with such ease when there was history . . . intimacy between them. When there was a sense of family. Nicole took a deep breath and stepped through the door. She watched her daughter disappearing with Margaret into the infernal depths of the kitchen. Be careful, she wanted to warn the little girl. But of what? A bird of a woman who clucked and chirped? The rules she would impose? Nicole shook herself. The rules no longer applied.

She wandered toward the parlor and paused at the

doorway, struck by the feeling again. It truly could have been yesterday. All the yesterdays she spent dragging her heels in that room. Crowded by the bric-a-brac. Dwarfed by the furniture. Smothered by the ever-constant fire which was still burning in the fireplace.

There was a difference though. The room seemed smaller. Less threatening. Cozy in a cluttered sort of way. The antimacassars, the framed pictures on the mantel and on the walls, Margaret's knitting bag, even the music, all seemed to be relics of a bygone era now filled with sentiment. Genteelly shabby in an endearing sort of way. Like a comfortable chair with the stuffing flattened from overuse. Like a lion who's lost his roar.

There was the old lion himself. Vanya. Sitting. Not seeing her yet. Pipe in hand. Eyes closed. Pipe beating time to the symphonic swell. Foot tapping. Wheaten hair grizzled with time. Silver and gold intertwined. Father, do you want me? More echoes of the past beating in her heart . . . even now. On the tip of her tongue. Propelling her into the room.

"Father?"

Vanya opened his eyes and let them sweep over his daughter, returning to her face. His face. Nikki's face. With Alexandra's eyes staring back at him.

"Some things never change."

His voice was formal. Crusty. As though he hadn't spoken for a long time. He cleared his throat.

"I'm pleased to see you, Nicole."

"How have you been, Father?" she asked, choosing the same safe distant formality.

"Piggy keeps me well for the most part. The company gives me headaches. But you know about that from your own experience."

That was nice. Being treated as his equal. Father and daughter, both directors of dance troupes. It gave them a mutual interest. A starting point. Nicole took a seat on the couch across from him.

"I'm thinking about retiring," he added.

"No, Father. You?"

She leaned forward with an expectant look. For some reason the idea was dismaying. A shock. What would Vanya Borcheff do without his company? Take knitting lessons from Peggy?

"We all grow old," he went on, warming to his topic. "Is duty of the young to replace us. We expect it after a while. You made it clear to me last night."

"I did!" She sat back. "How?"

"I saw power of your dancing and your choreography. You had audience in palm of your hand. Is like old story of Pied Piper or Dr. Mesmer."

Nicole was surprised and touched. That he should compliment her—that he could—after all that had passed between them.

"Oh, Father, you don't know what it means to me to know you liked my work. I wasn't even sure you'd come, much less approve—"

"Piggy and I were quite pleased to receive tickets. Was honor you did to me. But don't get wrong idea. Admiration and approval are world apart. I've never thought much of dance created for sake of exploitation. Is circus of the emotions you are putting on stage. Is too naked. Why, Nicole? Why is it necessary to put all that on stage?"

"All what?" she asked through gritted teeth, knowing already what he would say . . . knowing she would hear the British Court party line on appropriate dance subject and form.

"All that raw sewage. Is not just pain. Is personal hell. Is not just suffering. Is drowning in misery. Is not just madness. Is tornado of vengeance. Where is purity? Where is subtlety? Where is beauty?"

"So if you're not wearing toe shoes, it's automatically wrong," she said dryly.

"It's got nothing to do with pointe shoes or bare feet. But with the ballet, at least you have drama . . . without melodrama," he said with conviction.

"You don't understand, do you, Father? What I show isn't melodrama. It's my life. It's me. My vision of the world."

"No," he cried. "Who feels life with such pain, so much cruelty inflicted? Not even Russians have so much melancholy. This cannot be life you have lived, Nicole."

"But it is," she said quietly.

"Never one happy moment? Never an island of calm in midst of maelstrom?"

"There've been moments," she reflected. "My dances have made me happy. And Lexie has brought me the greatest joy."

"This Lexie . . . is man in your life?"

"No, Father. Lexie is Alexis Varonne. She is your granddaughter. Peggy's got her busy in the kitchen—"

"The child is here? My granddaughter is in my house!"

His face told Nicole everything. If she'd been an abject failure in life, her worth was still redeemable. The Varonne-Borcheff succession was secure.

"Will she dance?" he whispered, almost reverently.

Her answer was important to him. He had edged forward in his chair, gazing hopefully at her. What was it about those of us in the world of dance? Nicole asked herself. Why was that one question the point on which life itself turned?

"If she wants to," came the measured response. "If it means more to her than anything or anyone else."

Vanya reached out his hands to his daughter, searching her face, looking for clues in the language of her body. He caught her and brought her close to his chair.

"Is that what happened to you, daughter?"

Nicole felt a deep pulling. Something was rousing itself inside of her. A magnet drawing her to her father. An alarm clock finally ringing. It was time to confide. To confess. To shed the great millstone that hung in her chest, next to her heart. The need grew into a desire. Into an urgency. She was bursting. Be sure, cried a distant voice of warning. Don't let yourself be hurt.

Perhaps it was the location. England. That particular house. Perhaps it was the man. Her father. Knowing he'd been hurt. Finally reaching out to her. Finally asking the right question. Wanting to know. Wanting to care? She dismissed the tiny voice and joined hands with her father.

She knelt beside him, gazing up at the blue eyes. Where had the sternness gone? Where was the impenetrable wall? Faded with age or with concern?

"Was it wrong to want it all?" she murmured, asking herself as much as her father. "To dance. To go as far as one possibly could . . . living, breathing, dreaming, making dances. To love someone who could love me because I was me . . . because I danced . . . because I wanted so much."

"Is good to want much," Vanya asserted. "Is good to aim high. Is better when you can share with one you love."

Instinctively Nicole jumped on his words, crying, "Then why did you split up Carlo and me? We were the perfect duo. Maybe not perfect for the British Court Ballet, but perfect for one another. And we loved each other so very, very much. We could have added the missing dimension to the company. You knew something was missing, didn't you, Father?"

"Perhaps I saw something else which you did not."

"You saw what you wanted to see. I've had long, lonely years to figure it all out. I've dwelled on it. Reliving every moment. Made dances about it. Oh yes, Father. You saw something else. The opportunity to replay your life and your mistakes. Except this time they were supposed to work out the way you wanted. Nikki and I were just an echo of Vanya Borcheff and Alexandra Varonne. A warped version of husband and wife, with the husband always winning the perennial battles. A far cry from reality, wouldn't you say, Dad?"

Vanya was dreadfully uncomfortable and trying not to show it. He wanted to jump up and defy the ingrate. Justify himself by putting her in her place. But his leg throbbed like the devil. All he could do was sit still and tall, spine straight, and lock eyes with his adversary.

"I gave you and Nikki the chance to dance together. How else were brother and sister to come together after lifetime apart? I gave gift to world . . . well, at least audiences in London. Would have been world if you had stayed with us. There was uniqueness between you two like I never saw before or since. Yes, there was electricity with Carlo partnering you," he said, as if it were inconsequential. "But when Nikki danced with you, was revelation. He became different person. You unleashed a force in him I never knew was there."

"He didn't either," Nicole whispered, remembering the fiercely glazed eyes, the grip that wouldn't let go, the punishment he needed to exact.

"Is true. With my Nikki there was sense of never knowing what to expect. There was sense of imminent danger. I made choice. I was director. I chose Nikki for you. He would have been partner for life. He was your brother. He would have loved you as he loved me. All Carlo cared about was defiance. Is why he wanted to dance with you. Was another way to get back at me."

"You didn't see anything at all, Father," Nicole said bitterly. "Your vision was blind. Inward. Carlo and I belonged together. On the stage and in life. You—and the war—and I ruined it. Botched every chance there was."

"You? You ruined it? You saw Carlo again?"

"After the war, Father. Long after the pattern was set."

"What are you talking about patterns, Nicole?"

"My pattern with men. God, I don't even know if it started with you or Nikki." Nicole stood up and began pacing the room. "All I know is that whenever I've tried to love a man, it's ended in terrible destruction. Maybe it never had anything to do with you, Dad. Maybe it was always me. Something terrible locked inside of me. Just look at my history," she demanded, facing her father. "Carlo ran from me twice! Carlo and his scourges . . . it's almost funny. First Fascism. Then my choreography."

She took a heated step closer to Vanya.

"And poor Nikki. I was the key that unlocked all his anger so that it overpowered both of us. I had the bruises to prove it, though I could never bring myself to show you. I thought you'd blame me! So I left. A simple act of self-preservation. And then I heard about Nikki's simple act. Switching his skin for an RAF uniform. Which was worse, Dad? Dying inch by inch on stage . . . because he couldn't understand what he was becoming? Or performing suttee in the name of king and country . . . because he couldn't face what he had become?"

The painful memories knifed to the front of Vanya's mind. He covered his head with his hands to blot out the sight, the feelings, the helplessness of those horrible days. Both children gone. Nothing he could do. What had he done to his golden twins?

Nicole wasn't done. She was on her knees before him, pulling his hands from his eyes. Making him look. Pulling his hands from his ears. Making him listen.

"Then there was Billy Gable, Lexie's father. You probably would have liked him. A happy-go-lucky kind of guy with dreams of his own. He wanted me to share them with him. But I couldn't. I wouldn't. They say it was my fault he drank. My fault we got divorced. My fault he lost his daughter. My fault his life was cut short. You wonder why my dances explore—what did you call it? The circus of the emotions. The raw sewage of life."

He was spent from her tirade. But behind the weary eyes and the hangdog shoulders was a glimmer of strength. A gleam of understanding.

"Has been poison running around inside you. Yes, Nicole? Has found its way out now maybe? We're both still here, you and I, unharmed. The bite of the fang may sting like hell, but it doesn't have to kill. You understand, dievushka?"

Dievushka. Little girl. Nicole stared at him in wonder. After all was said and done—screamed, howled, and buried six feet under—to discover that she was his little girl. Suddenly it was all she wanted. To feel like a daughter. Vanya's daughter. Tell me it's not true, she wanted to beg. Tell me I've been a fool or I'm nuts.

Tentatively he smoothed the skin of her cheek, touching her as he had when she was first born.

"If these men, any of them, blamed you, Nicole, it was only that they could not face their own inadequacies. Carlo was young. A firebrand. With something to prove to himself. Perhaps many things to prove. You know, Nicole, achieving manhood is difficult and complex thing. Same as becoming a woman. With Carlo, it wasn't just the dance that goaded him. It was winning back family honor. Was making up for what his family lost. Maybe, when he'd done that, then he had to prove what kind of dancer he was. First he had to be true to himself. Does this sound familiar?"

It was plausible. It could've been that way. But the rest of her life . . . how could he explain the mess she'd made?

"As for this Billy, well, I have to admit, I've read all the accounts . . ."

Nicole's eyebrows shot up.

"You are surprised. Piggy and I don't talk about it, but we've managed to keep up with your career, illustrious and otherwise. Is little secret. She brings home the trade papers and the scandal sheets. Leaves them in inconspicuous spot. I sneak them off to read in private and then return them to identical spot. She takes them away to line rubbish bins, to use at her potting table, saves them for the charwoman. Of course, I know she's read them too."

Nicole was forced to giggle.

"But about this Billy fellow. He was good at what he did. Big star on Broadway and the wireless. But not so good with life. I've seen it happen in the ballet too. A person who's all stage presence and no substance. No one, you or anyone else, can give a person what is missing inside. No matter how hard you try. Fix one thing and something else goes wrong. Was his problem, Nicole, not your fault. Like Nikki. Was nothing you did. Was deep inside him. Like sleeping volcano. Pressures mounting, maybe for his whole life, containable for only so long. Resistances melting, evaporating. Then boom. Volcano erupts."

Vanya and Nicole were both silent for a while. Heads turned aside. Feeling the pain fresh again. Pushing it away.

"I put myself at head of list."

Nicole jerked her head in his direction.

"I was sick when your mother left me. I had never meant for her to go. I had never meant for her to be unhappy with me. But there it was. Done. Wife and baby daughter gone out of my life. I thought forever. But I managed to hold on . . . like never signing divorce papers. I had my grudges to nurse."

Vanya raised himself out of the chair. It was his turn to pace.

"Maybe you recall small discussion your mother and I have when you first came here. She saw my limp. I told her was accident. Dancing with bad ballerinas. Dancing one night like I don't give a damn. Next night like my life depended on giving greatest performance. Carelessly letting myself fall. Not healing right. Was partially true. Rest of truth was I didn't want to dance without Alexandra. Believed I couldn't dance without her, and went about proving it. Until I damaged myself so severely, I couldn't dance at all. I could have closed my eyes, folded my arms, and blamed your mother for my lameness. I wanted to. But I knew I stopped dancing because of something in me, not her."

Vanya paused in front of his daughter, lifted her to her feet and planted gentle hands on her shoulders.

"I loved your mother and I know she loved me. Till final breath she took. I will never forget time we were apart, or be sorry for life we each made. But I will never regret that in the end, when it mattered, we were together again. In the end we knew there was no need for forgiveness. You understand why I'm telling you this, daughter?"

Nicole's heart was bursting. Deep releasing sobs filled her throat. In a moment she had thrown her arms around her father and he was clutching her to him.

"Welcome home, Nicole," he murmured.

 57

Their embrace lasted for several minutes, purging the years of doubt and delusion. Finally, Margaret and Lexie came into the room, laden down with tea things. Nicole broke away from her father, but he took up her hand in his and beamed.

"That's as it should be," the older woman said approvingly.

"Thank you, Peggy," said Nicole with all her heart.

"Mama," Lexie chimed in, "guess what I've been doing?"

"Visiting the queen?" asked her mother playfully.

"Something even better, Mama. I've been making cucumber sandwiches!"

"Oh!" cried Nicole, dropping into a chair in mock swoon. "To think that I've deprived you all these years. Next thing you'll tell me you like kippers."

"What?"

"It's just a joke, dear, we shared with your mother a long time ago," said Peggy, winking at Nicole, to her utter surprise.

"Lexie," Nicole prompted, "why don't you offer your grandfather one of those sandwiches you made."

"Is he the old lion?"

"Passing on the same heresy as your mother, I see," Vanya said, arching an eyebrow.

Then he bent down on one knee and opened his arms to the beam of light who rocked on her heels, artlessly appraising him. In a flash Lexie leaped forward. Vanya clasped her tightly to him. Over the little girl's head he glanced up at Nicole.

"She'll dance," he affirmed. "I can feel it in her bones."

Nicole started to chuckle. Margaret joined in. And then Vanya and Lexie were laughing too. Margaret settled down behind the tea cart.

"Something to drink, everybody? And I have your favorite, Van dear. A nice digestive biscuit with just a spoonful of jam . . ."

The tea party was under way. When it was over, there were prolonged farewells at the front door.

"You'll be in England a good long while, won't you, Nicole?" prodded Margaret. "Wouldn't it be lovely, Van, if Nicole and Alexis stayed with us instead of in some stuffy hotel."

"Well, I don't know what my plans are exactly," Nicole said hurriedly. "I'll be in and out of London quite a few times over the next several months."

One delightful tea did not a family make. Not quite yet, thought Nicole. She stole a glance at her father to measure his reaction. He was stroking his chin and watching Nicole. Their eyes met.

"I think Nicole knows she is welcome here, any time she wishes. Come . . . go . . . stay . . . leave. Is her decision to make."

"But you're coming for early supper tomorrow," Margaret pressed.

"I will, Peggy."

Lexie piped up, "And me too."

"Especially you, squirt," Nicole said, picking her daughter up. "Say 'bye now."

There were hugs. Kisses. The lingering touch of fingers. The door opening. Closing. A backward glance. Faces in the window. Smiling. Hands waving. Walking on.

"Did you have a good time, Mama?" asked Lexie.

Her mother was holding her hand. Twirling her down the street.

"Yes, baby. I really did."

After a brief ride on the Underground and another short walk, they were back at their hotel. Too little time for Nicole to absorb everything that had taken place. Between Vanya and herself. Between Peggy and Nicole. Lexie with her grandparents. And there was no time to think now, because she needed to prepare for her performance that evening.

"We'll change clothes real quick," she told Lexie, half running, half walking through the lobby. "I've still got to check on the lighting. Set up the music . . ."

Her mind was everywhere but on the path her feet were beating. She plowed into a gentleman who was waiting at the elevator.

"Please excuse me," she said automatically. "I'm so terribly sor—"

Carlo Domenici, hat in one hand and a formidable box in the other, grinned and bowed.

"I never thought of you as clumsy, Nicole. Forceful, yes. But clumsy? Never." He continued without letting her get a word in. "I brought you a peace offering," he said, thrusting the box at her. "Consider it an homage to *Male Medusa*. These are fresh . . . I ate the ones I bought last night. When I saw how the performance was going, I knew it would be madness to try to get to you backstage. So I waited. It's been hell, Nicole, but I wanted to see you alone."

She was in a fog. A daze. The earth was shaky beneath her feet. In one fell swoop of an afternoon to have to confront every demon she'd ever known. And here was Carlo, completing the list, with this ridiculous box that smelled. Timidly she peeked inside and sniffed. Then she inhaled deeply. Glorious, steaming samosas. Deliciously warm, as though they had just come out of the oven.

"Vegetable or meat?" she couldn't help asking.

"A dozen of each, signorina, to satisfy even your appetite. When I bought them, Kali insisted . . ."

Nicole remembered. Their first date . . . rendezvous . . . escape from the confines of Vanya's house of correction. How free she'd felt racing through the London streets. Dodging the cars, the people, the constraints. With Carlo at her side, leading the way. Showing her the shortcuts. Speeding faster and faster, so that she felt as though her feet barely touched the ground. Or so it had seemed to a fourteen-year-old. So it seemed in memory eighteen years later. They had feasted on samosas then, served by Kali.

"Don't tell me it's still our Kali," Nicole exclaimed. "She was ancient then."

"It's our Kali's daughter, Kali Junior. Or is it Kali the Third? But this," he said, looking down at Lexie, "must be Nicole the Second. For you, little one."

He put his hand into his hat and extracted a bouquet of paper flowers.

"Ooh, Mama," Lexie cried, cradling the blooms. "He's a magician!"

"You could call him that," agreed Nicole dryly. "He can do a mean disappearing act when he has a mind to."

Carlo managed to look hurt. "You're not still mad at me after all this time, are you, Nicole?"

She took the bouquet from her daughter and handed it and the pastry box back to Carlo. Firmly. Leaving no room for speculation. She took Lexie's hand and marched into the waiting elevator.

"I don't have time to play games."

"Right," he said, mimicking her stern tones and dogging her steps. "You've got a company to run and a performance to give and a daughter to tend to and—"

"Were you put on this earth to pester me?" Nicole demanded as the doors closed behind them.

"Whenever and wherever you need it," he retorted glibly. "Now let's get down to the facts. You're at the Princess for two weeks. Then you're going north for one week, and back again to London for another. Then—"

"I know my schedule, Carlo. I don't remember hiring you to manage my career. Or is that another little surprise you've got tucked up your sleeve?"

She turned her back on him, fussing with Lexie. Unbuttoning the child's coat. Straightening her dress. Smoothing the bow in her hair. Anything to ignore him.

"The point is," he persisted, "I want some time with you. We have a lot to talk over, and I want you to see what I'm doing."

"I want, I want, I want," she spat through gritted teeth. "Well, I don't want! I would have thought New York made that clear."

"I thought New York, as you so cleverly refer to our last magnificent collision, made it clear that the desire was there. It was just the mechanism that was lacking. Plus the presence of a rather large encumbrance."

The back turned against him grew increasingly stiff.

"Aargh!" he gurgled, and fell against the side of the elevator, holding his hands to his heart.

He accomplished his purpose. Lexie peeked around the wall of her mother and giggled.

"If mamas were porcupines," he rasped, "I'd be quilled to death. Quick, help me pull them out."

Fascinated, Lexie hopped over and obliged. Nicole stood and glared at him, arms akimbo and face in a frown.

"Stop being so damned amusing. You don't own me, Carlo. And you're not going to get to me through my daughter."

"I know, Nicole. That's already been tried and it failed miserably."

Damn him. He knew too much. Damn him for even obliquely bringing up Billy. He'd done it twice in the last thirty seconds. She wanted to throttle him. No, not touch him. Any kind of physical contact was a fatal mistake. How long did it have to take for the damn elevator to get to her floor?

"There's only one way to get to you, Nicole. Come see my company. I know you'll love what you see."

"You have a company?" she asked in a tiny voice, at once curious, surprised . . . no, not surprised at all.

"I would have mentioned it in my letter, but it didn't seem right. I was concerned for you, Nicole. You did get the letter, didn't you? I never got an answer."

Finally the elevator came to a stop. The doors opened and she could escape. But now she had to be civil to him. To thank him. Why did he always demand a response from her? Why did she keep responding to him?

With Lexie between them, Carlo and Nicole proceeded down the hallway to her room.

"I couldn't answer then," she said, telling the truth to him, admitting it to herself. "It was a very hard time. I did blame myself—just for a little while—just like you said. But then I stopped. I knew I had to go on with my life. Make sure her life went on too."

Nicole paused to caress the blond head of her daughter.

"Actually, I was thrilled to get your note. I thought of it as a fan letter. The only one I received. I guess I needed someone to be on my side without being at my side. Does that make any sense?"

Carlo nodded, saying, "That's how I hoped you'd feel. I knew if I came rushing to your rescue, you'd push me away.

I could see you stamping your foot, shaking a finger right in my face. 'I don't need anybody,' you'd have said. 'Especially you,' when just the opposite was true."

"But the opposite wasn't true. I needed to stand up for myself."

"And let the rotten tomatoes fall where they may," he taunted. "Very noble, Nicole. But goddamn it, totally unnecessary. If you'd sent an answer, given me any hope, I would have been there—"

She couldn't help interrupting, adding "With trusty sword and shield . . . imprinted with the Domenici coat of arms."

"I didn't think it was funny," he said indignantly.

"It isn't, Carlo. It was really very sweet and very wonderful," she said, unlocking the door to her room.

Carlo had handed Lexie the box of samosas, and now she raced in ahead of the adults, the big box firmly in hand.

"Put those down," her mother reminded her. "You can't possibly be hungry after Peggy's tea."

"Just one, Mama, while I wash up and change my dress? Please?"

It was an acceptable compromise.

"One," said Nicole. "Before you wash. You can take it into the bedroom."

The little girl promptly removed two samosas from the box.

"I thought we said one," Nicole said.

"She meant one of each kind," inserted Carlo, winking at Lexie, who winked back at her new compatriot before running off.

"Damn it, Carlo. This is a perfect example of what I've been trying to tell you. I can't afford to depend on you or anyone else. My strength is in me."

He punched his hand against the open door, sending it flying to slam shut.

"Oh, God, Nicole. Who's talking about dependency?" He pushed past her and took possession of the sitting room. "I'm talking about love and partnership. Don't you remember how it was between us? Together, we were going to conquer the world. Make our own private, perfect place. Sure, we were kids then. We could afford those big dreams. Now we're grown up . . . or at least older and, I would hope, wiser. Now we know how to make those dreams come true. Don't you want to make them real, Nicole? Cara?''

A flood of feeling swept over Nicole. She felt the stirrings of her own dreams. Felt the passion of his. His passion. It had always swayed her. From the first moment she saw him dance. From the first moment he swept her up and away into his world. Into his arms. When they'd made love. When they'd fought. Through his moods. His defiance. His arrogance. His pride and honor. His persistence. His obstinacy.

He was obstinate now. Holding on to skeletons. Shadows. For Nicole the dreams were dead, youthful ambitions withered. Wispy castles in the air that evaporated with a single sigh.

"It's not possible . . . after all these years," she said, stumbling over the words, the thoughts. "I don't deserve . . ."

In a moment he had crossed the room and folded her into his arms, holding her so tightly she couldn't breathe. She flinched and closed her eyes, preparing to resist his onslaught. His kiss.

Instead his grip relaxed. He was cradling her, though she couldn't break his hold. She didn't want to break it. She felt the warmth and the rhythm of his breath on her face. Meeting hers. Quickening. Like hers. Heated. Like hers. Then his lips were on hers. Slow. Seductive. Tender. Pulling her back through the years to when hope and trust still flourished in her heart. She kissed him back, as she had when she was fifteen and sixteen and seventeen. Offering the promise. Offering herself.

Carlo broke away from the kiss to stare into her eyes. She saw herself reflected in his eyes, the mirror into her own soul. Asking how much she wanted. Asking how far she would go. This far, she responded, lifting her head to touch his lips again. This far, she thought, caressing the velvety smooth, moist skin. This far, letting him sip from the sweet recesses of her mouth. Then she didn't bother to think about it anymore. She forgot to count the obstacles. Measure them. Mount them on pedestals. She gave herself to the kiss. Freely. Completely.

When it was over, he buried his face into her hair and whispered sweet nothings into her ear. Old familiar ones. New exciting ones.

"Ah, cara, what you do to me," he murmured.

A smile lingered on her lips. Lit her face. Buoyed her heart, making her feel as though she had found her way home. Making her feel . . . happy.

"Oh, Carlo, I want to, but I don't know. All the years. All the problems. We've become so different."

"We always were. That was part of the excitement, even then. My God, Nicole, you feel it as strongly as I. Do I have to beg you?"

"But we're not the kids we were then. There's my company, my choreographing. My daughter."

"There's the rest of our lives, Nicole. We'll handle it. All of it. The company, the dancing, the past."

"And Lexie?" she asked, slipping out of his embrace.

"She's a part of you, isn't she? That makes her irresistible, in my book."

"We'd fight," she warned him. "Constantly. I don't give in anymore."

"I've noticed," he replied. "Look, Nicole," he added, taking her hand once more, "we've waited a hell of a long time. It's our turn now. But I understand your qualms. So don't give me an answer yet. Don't say anything until you've seen my company. Come to my studio tomorrow and then make up your mind."

She stood there shaking her head. "I don't see how that will make any difference."

"I know you don't. But it will. Trust me, Nicole." He drew her back into his arms and kissed her again. "Tomorrow," he reminded her, and was gone.

58

It was absurd for her to have come to Carlo's studio. She didn't know what she was doing there. What had happened between them the previous day was no more than a dream. A momentary delusion. A mistake. She could no more go back to him—go on with him—than he could dance with her. The kisses they had exchanged were a ruse. To tantalize the body and make the mind forget.

Yet here she was, going through with the empty gesture. Giving in to conveniences. Letting Peggy and Vanya take Lexie to Kensington Park for the day. Shaking hands with Carlo's dancers. Smiling at him. Being so damned agreeable. Setting themselves up for disappointment and rejection. Because it was inevitable. Because Carlo was fooling himself the way she had fooled herself. Because it was impossible. Wasn't it?

Nicole sat in a straight-backed wooden chair toward the front of the studio, where there was a small stage. The curtains were drawn open, revealing a plain backdrop tinted daylight blue. On the stage floor a woven line of bodies curved and arched, ebbed and flowed, as the tide itself. In the air was the sound of a breeze, blowing into a wind.

Then the backdrop darkened to violet. The rush of air became a howling at gale-force intensity. Darkening to the blue black of midnight. Then the background brightened. Slices of orange, vermilion, cherry red, brick red, blood red, oozed and spread like a violent sunburst, highlighting the urgent, frenzied motion of dancing bodies. Tossing white like angry crests of waves. Churning blue like the deepest water forced to the surface.

A huge fiery ball, black and red, plummeted from the heights down the length of the backdrop. Exploding the human waves apart. Sinking. Into the depths. The storm of fire, air, and water ceased. The undulating bodies lulled into temporary repose. The light returned to a cerulean blue. The air was alive with the flurry of wonder. Questions hissing. Reeds chanting a quiet alarm.

From out of the waves a scorched figure pulled itself up. Himself. Appeared to float on the back of the waves. His chest undulating. Sucking air into his lungs. Flailing for life. Catching it. Possessing it. Floating with the waves. Until he became strong enough to lift himself forward. Dragging his burden with him. His once beautiful wings. Now singed and broken. The wings of Icarus, melted by an angry sun. Consigned to doom. But not death. Icarus was not dead.

He pulled himself to dry land. Behind him the waves seemed to recede as the dancers moved farther and farther back, and finally offstage. He was left alone. Deserted. No father to fashion a gift of the gods. No god deigning to offer or grant a boon. Icarus in exile.

He strove to make the wings work again. Slaved over them to restore them to their former glory. Ran with them to catch a flutter of air into the wilted feathers. Lifting them high overhead to feel the thrust of wind as he had felt it, when first he wore the mighty wings. Leaped and soared as high as a mere mortal could. Higher, for he was no longer an ordinary mortal, having tasted the ether and known its ecstasy. Hoping the wings would magically remember, revive, rekindle the magic of flying as high . . . higher than the birds.

Refusing to give into exhaustion. Willing the wings back to life. Rewarded with empty air. Limp, lifeless wings. A rage that such beauty should be annihilated for his mistake. For believing in the gift instead of the giver. Was there no way to alter destiny? Was the gift truly lost?

As though bidding farewell to a lover, Icarus buried himself one last time in the body of the great wings. Enfolded within them. Embracing them within the cradle of his arms. Then tenderly he lifted them, carrying them to the arms of the ocean. And then gave them up, watching as they drifted from surge to surge, dancer to dancer, farther and farther beyond his grasp. Till they were gone. The sacrifice made.

Icarus landbound. His curse and his fate. Broken. Bowed. Ashamed. All these he should have felt. Yet he held his head high. His body straight. His neck arched. He looked upward. Toward the sun. The bringer of life and destruction. He was surrounded. Eerie white light, as white as his wings had once been, embraced him, urging him to move.

He felt the power within him. The swell of thrust and movement. Building. Surging. Peaking. He stepped forward. Walking. Trotting. In a gallop. Unable to hold himself back. Unable to hold himself down. His fingers quivered with anticipation. His arms began to beat at the air. Stronger, swinging them. Finding the currents. Lashing through the breeze. Creating his own wind.

He leaped. Soared. Flew. Upward. Higher. Higher. Never to come down. Creating the illusion of sky and open space. Making it his kingdom. He had no wings. Yet he could fly. He was only a man of muscle, flesh, and blood. Yet he was no mortal. He was weightless. Powerful. Light. All in one. He was flying. Flying. Out of sight. Offstage. And then Carlo's modern ballet was over.

Nicole gasped for breath. Unexpected tears rose in her eyes. Carlo had done it. Defied the laws of gravity. Made her believe he had fallen out of the sky and fought his way back up. Earned his triumph by sheer dint of will, beating insuperable odds. She applauded fiercely, ignoring her stinging palms, overcome by his vision that ascension was not only obtainable, but a certainty.

Carlo emerged from a side door and prowled toward her. He was dripping wet and wrapping a towel around his neck, grinning with pride at her reaction. He was never more attractive.

"It's a little different from what you do," he noted.

The smile on Nicole's face vanished. The contrast was never more obvious. Bits and pieces of her works flashed before her eyes. Earthbound, heavy, angry pieces. Bleak pictures of souls in torture. The ancient tug of war. Domination versus submission. Where the victor and loser were givens.

"You stayed true to the dream," she said, her voice flat. "I . . . went another way."

"You got lost in the anger. You let it overwhelm you, Nicole. You think it defines you. But deep down inside of you, the dream, our dream, is still there, waiting."

Nicole shook her head. "What you do takes my breath away," she admitted. "But is it real? Is it true to life? Overcoming all obstacles. Bursting beyond all limitations. People don't do that in my world. Don't you care about concentration camps? The bomb? Christ! Look at Nikki's wasted life . . . and all those other boys who died with him . . ."

"Of course I care," he insisted. "I see the ugliness. It makes me angry too. But I believe we are here to overcome the obstacles and the limitations. To transcend them. To illuminate beauty, even when you think none exists. The dross can be transmuted into gold. The negative into positive. We can make that happen . . . through our art."

"Maybe yours can, Carlo. Not mine."

"Let me prove it to you," he urged. "I want you to be my partner."

Nicole's mouth fell open. "You want me to dance with you? Toe shoes and all?"

"Maybe not toe shoes right away," he said with a grin. "But eventually. What do you say? I tried your stuff. The least you can do is try mine. Afraid you'll like it, Nicole?"

Damn him. She was afraid. Afraid she'd like it and afraid she would fail. Afraid she couldn't dance that way anymore. But admit it? Never.

"I can keep up with you, Carlo."

"Would I have asked you otherwise?"

For the next two weeks Nicole performed with her own company at night and rehearsed with Carlo by day in his studio. Just the two of them. She was never more aware of her own body. Overly sensitive to how she moved. Constantly analyzing. Nitpicking.

"Stop forcing it, Nicole," Carlo cautioned her. "You're trying too hard. Loosen up, cara. Let the tension go."

But she felt rigid. Like steel pins had been inserted in her bones, leaving her at a loss. No timing. No fluidity. At best a marionette making a mockery. She felt dulled. As though she were just emerging from a long enforced sleep. Conscious for the first time of the driven, inescapable heaviness of her art. Stunned and stimulated by the endless surge of possibility in Carlo's.

"Let it come," he urged her. "Give yourself to the music, to your feelings. Don't just follow me. Go with me."

He put her in the mood by bringing on stage a backdrop suggesting the midnight-blue sky, punctuated by moonlit clouds. He set the music. A choir of stringed instruments wafting grand baroque concerti through the air, giving way to a flute and a harp, singing in glorious harmony. Heavenly music for cherubs and angels. Music that cheered the soul and sent it soaring. As the dancers were to soar. Carlo and Nicole. Free to dance the triumph of the human spirit, at one with the firmament.

Carlo danced the work for her, and she ached with its richness, its freedom. Beauty, above all, was the key and the message. The sheer beauty . . . of bodies in motion. The sublime beauty . . . of airborne freedom. The inspirational beauty . . . of Carlo's joyous choreography. It was everything he and Nicole had imagined dance could be.

She vividly recalled the endless discussions, the variety of steps, the hours of dreaming they had shared so many years before. She could remember the two of them leaping through the air side by side. She could remember flying into his arms, trusting that he'd be there to catch her and send her off again.

Carlo had created their dance. Captured the optimism of youth and tempered it with the maturity of experience. It dazzled Nicole even more, seeing him embody that spirit in his dancing. It left her breathless. Dizzy. Feeling as though she too floated slightly above the ground. Ready. Almost ready to leap from the earth and find herself in the clouds with him again.

"Okay," he said grinning, when he'd finished, offering her his hand. "Now you try it."

Tentatively, gradually, her courage returned, and with it the dancer who tempted, even defied the laws of gravity. And the choreographer who let Paul Bunyan and his lady love gambol about the stars because it had been natural and right. And the woman who had given herself willingly, joyfully, honestly to the man she was in love with. Nicole's youthful dreams were rekindled.

Carlo was there at her side, at each step, to spark her along the path back. The path forward. Nicole found it easier and easier to dance with him. She no longer needed the boost. The helping hand. The thrust forward. Somehow she'd grown wings on her heels. Springs in her feet. Her bones were light as air.

Her body ached to be ascendant. Her limbs were feathers in the wind. Finding the thermal swells. Soaring with Carlo. Hovering high, as far as his arms could stretch and hold her.

When he held her, it was without constraint. Without tethers. Only to teach her. To show her her own free spirit. To take wing with him.

It was exhilarating and absolutely frightening. Because now she was only going through the motions at night. Because even on stage she was counting the moments till she danced with Carlo. How could she present the flood of emotion, the unrelenting drama of her works, when her heart and soul were in the clouds? How could she return to the anguish? The bounds of the earth? The doom?

How could she? After Carlo set her down from their final lift, she arched backward over the circle of his arms, feeling spent and utterly whole. She arched forward into his embrace, meeting him on equal terms. She met him in a kiss, tender and transcendent, gazing into his dark, shining eyes.

"The dance is you, Nicole," he said softly, reverently. "Since I began choreographing, I've always had you in mind. For me, no dance has been complete . . . until this one. You've made it come real for me, cara. You are the dance."

There was so much in her heart. So many things to say to him. All she wanted was to dance with him. She wanted to love him and be loved by him. She wanted the dancing and the loving to be all mixed up together so that one was no different from the other.

Nicole nestled into Carlo, drawing her arms tightly around him. "We've always belonged together," she whispered.

"Even when we fought?"

"Those weren't fights. They were battles."

"Even then?" he pressed her.

"Especially then."

"And now?" he growled.

Nicole pulled back from Carlo, threatening to pull away completely. Grinning, he held her tightly, not giving an inch.

"Are you trying to teach me a lesson?" she said, glaring at him.

"You're damn right. Are you going to learn it this time?"

"Yes," she said lightly. "Although you might have to remind me from time to time over the next fifty or sixty years."

"That was always my intention."

"Smug bastard."

"Smug maybe. Correct always."

"And the part about being a bastard?" she prompted.

"My parents would be very insulted."

She smiled. "You really haven't changed, have you?"

"Yes. I have changed, cara."

He let his eyes deliberately travel over her revealing leotard, soaked with the sweat of their exertions. "I'm far more patient, for one thing."

His insistent gaze felt like hot sunlight on her skin. She found her own eyes traveling over the oak sinews of his neck. His brawny shoulders. His chest, with its paired sculpted muscles. The dark nipples showing through his tight wet tunic.

"I always thought you had the most perfect body of any man alive," she whispered.

She reached out to run a wondering hand from the hollow of his throat downward. Down the furrow of his breastbone. Down the warm flat slide of his belly. To his groin.

He pressed her hand against him, closing his eyes. He breathed deeply through flared nostrils, as if he wanted this single moment to stretch forever. Until he had savored every eddy, every ripple of feeling her touch brought him. Beneath her hand he pulsed and throbbed, igniting a rhythm deep and hot as blood in her veins, volcanic rivers coursing under the earth.

They opened their eyes at the same moment. There was no need to speak of how long they'd waited. It was naked on both their faces.

"Now," he rasped, sweeping her up in his arms and carrying her up the back stairs to his rooms above the studio.

Nicole lay against his chest, listening to the miraculous sound of Carlo's heart pounding against her ear.

"Wine, my darling," she managed in a trembling voice, as he lowered her onto his fur-covered bed. "Shouldn't there be a wineskin somewhere about?"

They both grinned, recalling the memory of their first night together. The boy and the girl. The innocent urgencies of youth. The wonder and glory of first intimacy. Star magic at the standing stones.

"You have me drunk already . . ." he muttered.

Then his mouth covered hers. Treasuring. Plundering. Finding the most precious wine of all.

He stripped her of her leotard and tights in what seemed like one forceful yank, and she slid her hands inside his tunic to bare his black-furred chest. A deep sigh escaped her as her fingers automatically curled around the crisp hair, winding it in circles as she had done so many times as a young woman. A young woman deeply in love.

He looked down at her, remembering as she remembered how it had been between them. Then he began his voyage. Rediscovering the sweet secrets of her body.

Yes. Yes. This was a man. No boy in grown-up's skin following some scout manual of sex. Carlo's tasting and cupping, clutching and gossamer-light stroking, were all spontaneous outpourings of his heart. His need. His hunger to erase the years and doubts and differences between them. Until they were one body, one soul.

She laughed and cried. She trembled at the unleashed power rearing between them, poised to annihilate their separate selves. It was just as she had imagined in so many unadmitted dreams. The rich music of his voice, all over her body, murmuring incoherencies. Italian love words.

She had made him naked now. All his lush skin. And the panther muscles beneath it. He was hers. Her tongue searched for every beloved taste and texture. Nothing could be this good. This perfect. But it was.

With one impulse, they clasped each other. Bodies pressing and grinding and searching from head to toe. Their arms moved from hold to hold. Desperately. Trying to find the connection that would make them one.

Nicole heard herself repeating, "Please . . . please . . ." mindlessly.

Carlo grinned down at her. His face shiny with sweat. "Since you ask so politely . . ." he gasped.

He was a length of fire, filling her to the core and flaming any resistance, any lack of trust, any final fears. She danced with him then. The ancient choreography of earth and sky. The winged dance. The realm of the air. The kingdom of freedom. They were one at last. At long last.

Later they slept in each other's arms, naked and trusting as the girl and boy they had once been. The night stars gazed down on their love. For just an instant they seemed to pause, shimmer, flashing their approval before continuing their own lordly dance in the heavens.

~~ 59

A sign hung in the window at Trattoria Bari. CLOSED, it read, FOR PRIVATE PARTY. Inside the restaurant, recently expanded for the third time, gaiety abounded. The hum of conversation was punctuated repeatedly by loud bursts of laughter, the good-natured pounding of backs, and the sound of fierce applause.

Waiters scampered about, bustling back and forth between the kitchen and four large tables set in the center of the floor. They poured champagne, red and white burgundies, and, of course, Chianti. They unloaded tray after tray of antipasto and garlic bread, and served veal specialties, calimari, pastas, cacciatores, and tetrazzinis. For dessert they dished up zabaglione, biscuit Tortoni, and spumoni.

"More champagne!" roared Stefano Domenici. "How many times in a man's life does he get to celebrate an event such as this?"

Thunderous approval met his proclamation, especially from the three outer tables at which sat an assorted blend of Nicole's dancers and Carlo's troupe.

"To Carlo and Nicole!" came a shout from one side of a table.

"You mean to Nicole and Carlo," came the report from the opposite side.

"Wait a minute," growled Vanya huffily from the inner table, surrounded by the groups of dancers. "Is duty of father of bride to offer toast."

He stood up, wobbling slightly. Margaret pulled at his arm and hastily brushed the crumbs from his lap.

"There now, Van. Now you look your best," she said brightly.

"To my darling daughter," he began, looking straight at Nicole with his goblet raised in salute. "May she have every happiness."

"All the happiness she deserves," added Margaret, attempting to straighten her hat.

Nicole, resplendent in a slim suit of gold cloth, rose to hug her father first and then kiss Margaret on the cheek.

"And to the man who always owned her heart," continued Vanya, his face reddening, "and was wiser than the rest of us put together. May he prosper, find many patrons . . .

taking none away from British Court Ballet . . . and may he find his happiness in Nicole."

"All the happiness he deserves," echoed Margaret, whose hat now clung to her head at a precarious angle.

It was Carlo's turn to shake hands with his old mentor. To Margaret, he offered a kiss on the hand.

"My son," said Francesca, shaking her head, "the noble corteggiatore."

"You're proud of me, aren't you, Mama?" he teased.

"Proud? *Si, mi figlio.* But prouder still when you make me a grandmother."

"Is that all?" he asked.

He turned toward the small figure seated beside him, plucked her onto his lap and snapped his fingers.

"Alexis," he whispered conspiratorially, all the time looking at his mother and winking. "Would you do me a big favor? Look straight at this woman, say 'presto chango,' and call her your *nonna.*"

"Presto . . ." she said, pausing, drawing the syllables out dramatically, "chango."

Lexie grinned at Carlo, who gave her a sign of approval. Artlessly, fearlessly, she prattled on to the older woman.

"You know what, Nonna? Carlo's going to be my daddy. Mama says he's a dancer like her. But I think he makes magic."

Francesca took the little girl into her arms and said, "There are some people who think they are one and the same."

Nicole and Carlo beamed at one another and, without hesitation, kissed. Rowdy cheering broke out and increased in volume as the couple's kiss intensified.

"Do something, Van," Margaret said, flustered and giggling at the same time.

Vanya and Stefano exchanged glances and shrugged.

"Would you want it any other way?" prompted Francesca.

Stefano stood up and signaled to his maître d'. The man marched off toward the kitchen and flung open the doors, making way for a band of strolling musicians.

"A tarantella!" demanded Domenici, snatching Lexie out of his wife's arms. "And I will be the one to teach la piccola to dance."

In the blink of an eye the dancers were out of their seats and joining in the fun. Not to be outdone, Vanya got to his feet and bowed low before Signora Domenici.

"This gentleman knows how to treat a lady," he flirted, and, despite the tempo of the song, launched Francesca into a dignified waltz.

Aware of authority when they saw it, the musicians segued into a softer piece, set to three-quarter time. Soon the whole room seemed to sway to the genteel romance of the melody. Only Nicole, Carlo, and Margaret were left at the table.

"What are you two waiting for?" Margaret asked impatiently.

Carlo put his arm around his fiancée and said gallantly, "How could I dance with my future wife and leave my mother-in-law without an escort."

"Nonsense, children," Margaret scoffed. "I make it a policy never to dance. I know what I'm up against in this family. Now shoo."

Margaret motioned the young lovers on as though they were scatterbrained chicks in the wrong part of the hen house. Along with Carlo, Nicole obediently stood up. Then paused by her stepmother's chair.

"Peggy," she began, suddenly unsure, only knowing she must speak. "Peggy, everything is so wonderful . . . I feel so lucky to have Carlo and the Domenicis. And Father . . . and you. It would be perfect if only . . ."

Her voice failed her, but Margaret took up her thought.

"I know, dear. If only the others were here to share in all this bliss. Nick would've looked quite elegant, I think, in a dinner jacket. And Alexandra would somehow have kept herself from stealing the show . . . out of love for you."

Impulsively, the two women threw their arms around each other.

"There," sniffed Margaret, dabbing at her eyes, "now you go on with your young man."

Carlo was at Nicole's side, taking her hand and bowing low before her.

"May I have this dance, cara?" he inquired.

"You may have all of them," she answered.

Arm in arm they melted into the swirling waltz amidst family and friends in an endless pattern of interlocking circles. To turn and turn again.